From The Ashes

ALINA MARTYN

To everyone out there that's gone through some bad shit and clawed their way back to center.
Just know that it gets better, I see you, and that you're loved.

Trigger Warning

For a complete list of trigger warnings (be there is a definite **list** with this one, guys. Better hold onto your hats), please check here first!

Make sure that you're okay with what might be in this book before you start. It's so fucking important to take care of yourself and your mental health.

Okay, did you go check?

Good girl.

Are you okay with them?
Enter at your own risk.
Go on, you know you want to.

(But really, do what you need to. Your mental health matters.)

Jade

WHY THE FUCK *am I here?* I ask myself. This is the thing everyone tells you not to do.

Don't go to a party where there is alcohol with people you don't trust. Don't trust someone who has shown you their true colors. Don't put yourself in a situation where you're reliant on someone to get home, especially when you're *hours* from home.

And I've somehow done all of those. In one fell swoop.

Sarah's driving us in her car since my mom doesn't trust me with one. She much prefers Sarah to me anyway, so it's not surprising that she was able to talk Sarah's mother—my mom's fake best friend—into having her drive.

That way, I couldn't come home. I was forced to go along with whatever Sarah decided to do.

The sun has almost set, leaving only a sliver of pink and red in the sky. It felt like the sun was going away so the forgiveness and cover of darkness could shine. I have such a bad feeling about this.

"I really don't want to go," I whisper to Sarah, the girl who has been forced to bring me along with her to a college party.

Sarah rolls her eyes, but paints on a smile that seems genuine. "You'll be fine. I'll be there the whole time."

"I've never actually gone to a house party," I mutter, picking at my thumbnail nervously.

How'd I let Mom force me into this? When will it end?

Sarah whispers something under her breath. I look at her, wanting to ask her to repeat what she said, and find she's saying a small prayer with the most annoyed look on her face.

Why the fuck am I here? I think, not for the first time.

Sarah's mom and my mom had conspired together and basically forced us on this grown-up playdate. My mom is notorious for oversharing with others about how her only daughter is such an 'interesting and reserved introvert that needs help getting out and about.' I have to bite my tongue every single time I hear that. I'm nineteen years old, not seven. I don't need help making friends, and I especially don't need her spreading my business around.

Thus, the current situation I'm in.

She had opened her mouth to her friend, lamenting how she was worried about what I'd be like when I got to college. Worried that I'd be taken advantage of or not know how being drunk felt and something would happen to me. Her friend came up with the 'great' idea of having her daughter take me to one of the college parties she goes to regularly, apparently. Three hours from home.

When my mom brought it up to me last week, I flat-out refused, even knowing what that refusal would cost me. My mother is not a patient woman; she's also not particularly warm. Over the past few years, she's only gotten worse. Harder, harsher, quicker to anger and raising a hand to me. Everything I do, everything I say, every decision I make is the opposite of what she wants me to do or be, and she makes it well known to all just how disappointed she is in me. Again, thus the current situation I'm in.

Sarah and I may be going to the same college, but we *do not* get along. She is a mega bitch; she also got around plenty before dating a guy who lives in the college town we are going to.

I don't know if he even *goes* to college, or if he just hosts parties for college-aged kids. This whole thing screams trouble, but on some small level, I want to see what being away from Mom and out on my own is like.

To my mom, this whole thing seemed like the best way to shove me out of the nest. Aggressively.

She agreed to Sarah's mom's plan, and they set it in stone before either Sarah or I could refuse.

I called Sarah a few days later and I could hear the disdain and reluctance in her voice. She didn't want me to go any more than I did. But here we are. I called to find out what I needed to bring and what I needed to wear, and she just laughed.

"Just bring a change of clothes and whatever drinks you like. Kyle will get us liquor, but in case he's not willing to get you a bottle, you'll want your own," she scoffed before she clicked off the line. That's the exact moment I knew I was fucked.

Sure, I'm a little excited. I haven't been to Carver, a small town in western Arizona, since I visited Kensington University at the beginning of the year. I'm excited to meet some people who live there, and maybe even make some connections so I'll know one or two people before school starts. But it fucking sucks that I have to rely on Sarah freaking McFowell.

The drive has been awful. Filled with awkward silences, music blasting in my ear, and the nauseating feeling of dread. Sarah has dressed to the nines in a shorter than short miniskirt and a tank top that leaves little to the imagination, and her blonde hair is curled tightly and flowing down her back. There's a reason she is so popular; not just for her looks but because she's magnetic to be around. People flocked to her in high school, and I'm reluctantly interested to see how she does in a bigger pond.

Where Sarah is tall and willowy, I'm tall and solid. I'm not a size-two girlie and I won't ever be. But I do fill out the cut-off jean shorts that I'm wearing quite well. I didn't want to stray too far from what I'm typically comfortable wearing, but my mother and her opinions wouldn't let me leave the house unless I passed her inspection. So, a cleavage-showing black blouse that clings to every curve and hangs off my shoulder, and cut-off frayed shorts are what I was able to 'get by' with.

Better than the sequined tank top she was shoving at me.

I push my hair over my shoulder and try not to fuck up the curls I'd brushed out to resemble loose waves. Pulling the visor down to inspect my makeup, I almost don't recognize myself. My makeup is heavy and black, intense to make me look older in case we go clubbing.

I don't like it. I don't like makeup, period. But I have to admit, a cat-eye looks good on me.

"Just another few minutes," Sarah mutters, turning onto a neighborhood street. It's already dark so I can't see anything very distinctive about where we are.

Talk about off-putting.

"Look," Sarah huffs as she parallel parks in front of a one-level brick house. There are already lights flashing from the windows and a heavy bass that I feel in my chest. "I'm here to see Kyle. I haven't seen him in a month and I really like him. I'm not going to hold your hand the whole time."

"Wow, your tune changed really quickly," I mutter.

"No, I'll still be there, just not by your side like a babysitter."

She rolls her eyes and pulls her visor down to inspect her own makeup. "If you really need me, call me, but try not to need me."

"Understood." Rolling my eyes, I slam the passenger door and go to open the trunk to get our overnight bags out, but Sarah stops me.

"What are you doing?"

"Getting my bag?"

"We don't bring that shit inside. Not yet." Sarah closes the trunk. "Just bring your phone and your wallet. The rest we'll figure out." She flips her curls over her shoulder and shoves her hands in her bra, fixing her smaller boobs to make her cleavage more prominent. "Remember what I said," she snaps and walks off, leaving me to either follow her inside or sit out here for the rest of the night.

I don't know which would be worse.

The cool air pricks my skin and makes goosebumps rise, and I concede. Following her cowboy boot stomps inside the house, I swallow my nerves and my reluctant excitement.

What the fuck am I doing here?

THIS PLACE IS THE MOST QUINTESSENTIAL bachelor/frat house I've ever seen. Like, straight out of the movies. It's grubby and dingy; beer cans and red solo cups are strewn across every surface with stray chips and snacks stuck in liquid. People are everywhere. The place is so full, I have to push drunks out of the way just to follow Sarah deeper into the house.

"Delta Gamma forever!" a dark-haired guy drunkenly yells. Everyone around him chants it and holds up their drinks in cheers.

"A fraternity house?" I yell-ask Sarah, grabbing her hand and turning her to face me. "You failed to mention that!"

"Would it have mattered?" She throws her head back and laughs. "You were going to come regardless. Maybe get a drink and finally fucking relax!" With that, she rips her hand from mine and stomps off to find her guy.

What a bitch.

Looking around, I bite the inside of my cheek and take a deep breath. I'm here now, I just have to deal with it. A drink sounds like a damn good place to start.

Pushing through the gyrating bodies, I make my way toward the kitchen. It's an older house, and far too small for the number of people currently partying. The kitchen is slightly less busy. In the dim lighting, it's difficult to really see anyone, but the couple basically having sex in the corner are clear as day. Quickly averting my gaze, I grab a red cup and open a can of generic, lukewarm beer.

"That's not a good call." A guy with dark blonde hair, curled in a perfectly messy way that makes me want to run my fingers through it, leans against the counter and crosses his arms over his chest. His blue plaid button-down stretches with the movement. He's hot, don't get me wrong, but not the type I usually go for. He has this charisma that gives me the ick a little. Like, he's so slick, but it's oil.

"What do you mean?" I ask while making eye contact, refusing to show how out of place I feel.

"That beer has been sitting there for at least four hours. If you want a drink, let me make you one. What liquor do you like?" He takes my cup and tosses the beer down the drain.

"Uh..." I stutter as I try to think of any kind of liquor at all. "Tequila?"

A smile crosses his face slowly and he chuckles darkly. "Tequila, eh? My kind of girl." He moves to one of the dark wooden cabinets and pulls out a bottle of clear liquid.

"Shots or a drink?" he asks, raising an eyebrow.

"Both?" The moment the word leaves my mouth, I wish I could take it back. Warning bells are going off in my head, but I want to be cool. I want to be accepted, to be wanted. By anyone. This seems like the quickest way to achieve that.

This mystery guy bites his lower lip as his eyes rake over me. He's looking at me like he wants to eat me and let me tell you, it's a good feeling. I stand a little straighter and flick my hair over my shoulder.

"I'm Hunter."

"Jade. Jade Henderson."

He smiles wolfishly and winks. "Very nice to meet you, Jade. Jade Henderson." He pulls down two shot glasses and pours tequila into them.

Worry fills my stomach again as I realize I truly have no idea what I'm in for. I've never had any alcohol, yet here I am signing up for tequila. I've never heard great things about tequila, but it was the first liquor I could think of.

Hunter hands me a glass and throws the liquid back without so much as a grimace. My mouth drops slightly, and he raises his eyebrow in challenge.

No going back now.

I drink the shot slowly, letting the liquid pour over my tongue. It's sweet and acidic, and I know right away I hate it. Hunter laughs boisterously at me. I can feel my cheeks heat with a blush. I'm so fucking embarrassed—of course I did this wrong.

Just like I fuck up everything else.

"First shot, huh?" He takes the empty shot glass before

handing me a red Solo cup with some kind of drink he'd made with tequila and some juice. I cough from the burning in my throat.

"No," I lie.

"Yeah, okay." He snorts and opens a beer for himself. "Let's go find something to do." He holds out his arm and offers to tuck me into his side, like he's taking responsibility for me. It's nice—odd, but nice.

"What is there to do here?" I glance up at him, taking in his green eyes that shine with mischief in the dark.

A slow, wolf-like grin stretches across his lips. "Oh, there's always something."

<hr>

"If you've never taken a shot, I'm sure you've never played beer pong." Hunter takes the still-full cup from my hand and sets it down near a six-foot table set up inside the house. There's an array of Solo cups set up in a triangle formation at each end of the table.

"No," I answer meekly.

"It's easy. It's a fun way to get drunk and show your athleticism." He bounces a white ping-pong ball on the table. "Who wants to play us?" Hunter announces to the room.

A flash of blonde curls enters my fuzzy vision as Sarah and Kyle, the guy she was meeting, step up to the other end of the table.

"Always willing to beat you, Hunter," Kyle grins, ignoring Sarah completely while Hunter pulls me to his side. There's a crowd around the table now, and people start to watch as Hunter throws the first ball. It lands in one of the cups with a soft *splash*.

"Drink up, Miller," Hunter orders with pride. He's smug about it, while everyone cheers for Kyle as he chugs. Beer drips from the corners of his mouth before he crushes the cup and throws it to the side.

"My turn." Kyle takes the ball and throws it toward the cups closer to us, but it misses all of them. The crowd collectively says, "Ohhhh," and Hunter throws the ball back to Kyle for another turn.

I don't know this game, but I'm a quick study.

Kyle throws it again and sinks it into a cup at the last moment.

"You earned that one," Hunter smirks cockily.

Kyle winks at Sarah, then Hunter fishes the ball out. "Bottoms up!" Kyle shouts.

Hunter chuckles and drinks. "Ah!" he says proudly before crunching the cup and turning to me. "Your turn, Boobs."

What the fuck? I scoff, "Boobs?"

There are mostly guys around us now, circling the ping-pong table like vultures. One greasy-haired jock laughs so hard, beer shoots out of his nose. Others nod along, eyeing my chest more obviously than they were before.

"Well, yeah. You're Boobs, because *wow*." Hunter looks at my cleavage, gesturing with his hands to my chest, then bobs his head to the side. "And you came here with Boots." He tips his chin over to Sarah, who I just now notice is the only one wearing them. That is definitely weird in this country town. "So, Boobs and Boots. You're up."

I don't know whether to be insulted or flattered. But the tequila is making me feel fuzzy, so flattered is winning.

A guy—no, a *man*—wants me. He's actually showing me attention and seems to be interested in me.

"I'll take it." I shrug as I grab the ping-pong ball from him, making sure to brush our fingers together. "I suppose." Lining myself up so I can throw the ball, he steps in close behind me. So close, I can feel his body heat, and my breathing quickens.

"It's a compliment," he whispers against my ear. I try to brush him off and actually throw well, but his hand comes to my waist.

"I'm sure," I mutter.

"Really. Look, would you rather be called Boots?" Hunter asks.

I chuckle lowly, awkwardly. "I suppose not."

"Exactly."

I throw the ball, and it bounces off the side of the table, making everyone groan. I see Sarah smirking off to the side and she crosses her arms under her boobs in a move I know means she's trying to push up her small chest to look bigger.

"Again." I hold my hand out for another ball and Hunter puts one in my hand.

"Focus, *doll*," he whispers, bringing his other hand to the other hip to steady me. Another weird nickname?

I take a deep breath and throw the ball. It lands in a middle cup and everyone cheers. Hunter smacks my ass and says, "Nice one."

I smirk, feeling more and more confident as the time goes on. The shot makes its way through my system. *Maybe I should drink some more,* I think idly as I watch Sarah chug the flat, nasty-looking beer. She grimaces and narrows her eyes at me in a sneer.

Clearly, she wasn't expecting me to be visible at all.

The crowd starts to chant, "Boots, Boots, Boots, Boots!"

Sarah smiles like she's won something and throws her ball.

Splat. It lands on the first throw. Fuck.

I pick up the cup, scoop out the ball that's been touched by who knows how many people, and see floaties moving about the cup. "Do I *have* to drink this?" I ask nervously.

Hunter and Kyle look at each other, a silent understanding passing between them as the room starts chanting for me to chug. Hunter shakes his head, grabs my cup that I'd sat down on the side, and hands it to me.

"We'll make an exception. But rules are rules, and you'll have to chug the rest of this instead." He hands me the cup that's barely empty with a knowing look on his face.

"Oh, come on," I groan.

"Rules are rules, Boobs. Get to it!" a guy in the crowd calls out, signaling to the rest of them to do the same. I don't want to. I know this is a bad idea, but I'm so far gone already. Hunter is looking at me like he's not going to step in and stop the crowd. Sure enough, he starts chanting with them. I look to Sarah, thinking maybe she'll be chanting too, but her eyes are wide and worried. Her hand goes to her throat as she watches the crowd, watches Hunter, watches me.

I can't figure out what it means, but I feel the pressure to fit in. To be desirable. To be known.

So, I chug the mixed tequila drink and hope I don't throw up.

"That-a girl." Hunter grins as I drink it down, swallow after swallow until the cup is dry and the whole room cheers.

I don't feel so good.

The alcohol mixed with the sweetness of whatever juice Hunter put in my drink makes my stomach turn and the whole room spins. I stumble, turning to set the cup down on any surface and Hunter catches me.

"Whoa, there. Are you okay?" he asks. My vision is off, because it honestly looks like he's smiling. But that can't be right.

Can it?

My vision goes hazy at the edges, making it hard to focus on anything. It feels like everything takes a few seconds to register before I understand what's happening. When I look up at Hunter, I *know* he's smiling.

Sinisterly.

Something's wrong. I feel my legs give out, but Hunter's arms are holding me up as he yells out to everyone that the game is finished. As he ushers me toward the back of the house, I do my best to grab onto anything, anyone.

Something feels... wrong.

"Help me," I whisper, but everyone just laughs. Hunter picks me up and throws me over his shoulder, laughing boisterously and calling loudly enough for everyone to hear, "Can't handle her liquor! I'm putting her to bed, I'll be right back!"

Everyone around us laughs again and I think I start to feel him walk downstairs. I don't really know; it's too dark, too hazy.

I can't focus, can't move. Can't see. But I can *feel*.

I can feel my body thud against Hunter's with every step. I can feel him swatting my ass every so often, like he's trying to reassure me. I can feel the chill on my skin as we descend into the basement of this old house.

"You really are fresh meat, you know that? Too many girls know how to protect themselves these days, but not you. I clocked you the moment you walked in. You look so innocent, so desperate to be seen that you'd do anything. Think of what's about to happen as your first real college experience. Maybe if you're lucky, I'll come back for seconds, but we'll see how you do first." He's monologuing like a fucking villain, and I realize now that's exactly who he is. A villain with the face and charisma of a prince. A wolf in sheep's clothing, luring in the innocent, only to betray and prey on them when they get close.

I have no one to blame except myself. Because he's right. I wanted to be seen.

Terror fills my body as I try to kick, to scream, but nothing happens. I can't move, can't talk, can barely breathe.

I'm completely in his hands. And the person I chose to help me through this whole situation was the fucking villain all along.

"Don't worry, doll." Hunter slides open a door, lays me down roughly on the cold cement floor and starts to undo his jeans. "You'll probably enjoy this," he grunts.

Now it makes sense.

I'm going to become his doll; unable to move, unable to protest, unable to fight. A moveable little doll curated for him to play with how he wants.

"No..." I plead, screaming in my head, but only a whisper comes out.

"It's too late for that, *Boobs*." He sneers at the nickname. "Just let the medicine relax you, or I promise this is going to hurt. Usually, the girls aren't so fucking talkative. You're a fighter. Feisty. I like that."

I can feel whatever he slipped in my drink taking more of an effect and my consciousness starts to fade even more.

"Stop," I whisper, the word coming out no louder than a breath.

"Shush," Hunter commands as he starts to pull off my shorts and shove my shirt up. His hands are everywhere, pushing and gripping. Pulling and prodding. I didn't want my first time to be like this. I wanted to have the choice.

I wanted someone to want me, to maybe even love me.

The agony of it all brings tears to my eyes.

He keeps moving on top of me, and a tear rolls down my face as I realize what a fool I've been.

Black clouds fill my eyes. I almost welcome sleep; at least then I don't have to deal with this. I can't fight him off anyway. I said no.

I *said* no.

I said no.

I said *no*!

His groan is the last thing I hear before I welcome the darkness to take me. Hoping that, however I wake up, I'm still alive to fight another day. Because he has one thing right—I am a fighter.

What am I fucking doing here?

Asher

Earlier that morning...

I ONLY HAVE one client on the docket today and it's some asshole from my brother's fraternity. Kyle.

Ugh. I shake off my disgust at having to interact with him at all. He's such a tool. I mean, he'd have to be to hang out with my brother.

My brother is... well, he's an asshole and I can't stand him. I love him because I have to. Because he's my brother. But I really can't stand him as a person.

Taking a big drink of my black coffee, I get to work opening my shop and cleaning up my station. I like to come in before opening, before anyone else, and make sure the place is as clean and presentable as possible. It's peaceful. No chatter, no small talk; just me with my coffee in the place I've built from the ground up with my best friend. My—our—tattoo shop is, by far, my favorite place.

From The Ashes is a little hole-in-the-wall shop known for quality tattoos, professional artists, and a clean facility. I personally selected two other artists to join me here: Ty, a guy I went to high school with, who's basically my real brother; and Roxie, a girl who stumbled into our lives when she needed help the most. Together, the three of us take care of this place and they're my best friends.

I groan, looking at the outline of what Kyle wants tattooed today. It's going to be an all-day piece. A lion's head, the size of a dinner plate, on his bicep. It's not a bad tattoo by any means; he just wants it as realistic as possible, which will mean hours of shading and stippling. All while Kyle—ugh, *Kyle*—fills my ears with talk about all the new girls he's going to get with tonight and all the new pussy that's coming into the college.

He's always wanted to be on my good side, but how he doesn't realize talking like that will piss me off, I have no idea.

I check my watch, noticing it's close to noon, which is when the shop opens and—speak of the devil and he shall fucking appear. And the devil today is an over-inflated ego in a boy who thinks he's hot shit, standing at the front door and waving at me.

Nodding at him, I take one last sip of coffee—wishing it was whiskey—and pull the keys from the chain attached to my belt. I walk over to the door and usher him in.

"Hey, man! I'm so excited," Kyle greets, pushing past me and into the room like he owns the place.

"Kyle, hey," I say politely, and pull out the forms I have to have him sign. All the normal shit that prevents me from being sued, losing my shop, and people coming after us because they made a stupid choice for a tattoo.

I'm not going to try and talk you out of something when *you* make a dumb decision that's permanently etched into your skin.

Kyle signs all the forms with a flourish and takes his jacket off, plopping down on my chair. The bell above the door rings. In walks Roxie, with her dark sunglasses covering her face and a coffee the size of her head in her hands.

"Rough night?" I chuckle and she sneers at me.

"Shut up, Lee," she snaps and gets to her station, dropping her oversized bag at her feet. It does not escape my attention that her hands are red and chapped. Exactly like how it looked after I'd pull athletic tape off my knuckles.

"She's hot," Kyle whispers and I roll my eyes, but nod. Objectively, Roxie is hot. She's attractive in an alternative kind of way with heavy, dark makeup, black hair, piercings and tattoos galore. Roxie dresses *very* suggestively in leather corsets over her lean torso and miniskirts, showing off her long legs and her ink. She's attractive, but just not my type. Not only that, but I only see her as a kid sister. She agrees—I'm big brother material *only*.

Thank fuck.

I wrap the table I'm using to hold my things and set out all my cups, working in silence. It's nice but temporary; hopefully he brought music or some shit this time to entertain himself instead of trying to talk to me.

"So," Kyle starts, and I catch myself before I let out a groan of annoyance. "What are your plans tonight?"

Pouring the ink into the cups, I organize them so they're closer to the edge for my reach. I grab the tape and start wrapping up my tattoo gun, before turning it on and testing it. *Buzz, buzz.* Music to my ears.

Speaking of music, Roxie turns on the overhead stereo and rock starts playing through the speakers.

After laying the stencil on Kyle's arm and prepping his skin, we're ready to tattoo.

"Nothing," I finally answer. "I'm going to stay here and do the books for the shop."

"Lame!" Kyle boos but jumps like a bitch when the needle

hits his skin for the first time. I pull the gun back quickly so I don't fuck up his arm and do my best not to glare at him.

"No, it's responsible," I reply.

"Come on, man," he scoffs. "You need to live a little. The fraternity is having its first party of the year. A welcome party of sorts. You should come."

I give him a pointed look, clearly saying 'nice try,' and get back to the repetitive nature of outlining the lion, wiping his skin, and outlining again.

God, no. Nothing sounds worse than hanging out with a bunch of underage kids, playing games to get drunk, when I could be doing something productive.

"Free beer," Kyle says in a sing-song tone, and I tip my lips down.

"Keg?" I ask, sitting back.

"On ice."

Sighing loudly, I dip the needle in ink before moving to sit closer to him again. Maybe one night out with free drinks would be okay. I don't need to see my brother. It's just about getting out and relaxing a little; having a few beers and leaving.

"Sure, what time?" I ask, and Kyle's eyes widen in surprise.

That night...

THE HOUSE WAS BUSY. LIKE REALLY FUCKING BUSY. I was worried that I would obviously be the oldest one here. At twenty-five years old, I didn't expect to see some of the people I went to high school with at a frat party. There are definitely underage girls and guys here too, but it isn't my business. The college school year is starting soon, so this isn't abnormal. But again, *none of my business.*

I'm not an asshole that will end their party, but I'll definitely keep an eye out for some of the bullshit I've heard goes on here.

I push my way through the house, sliding past scantily clad college girls and guys that are already so drunk, they're spilling their drinks. Towering above most of them, I can clearly see the kitchen and the promised keg on ice. With my prize clearly in view, I push forward.

"Hey handsome." A girl slides up to me, pushing her whole body against my chest. Her nails are way too long and witchy looking as she scratches my chest above the hem of my V-neck. "Wanna get out of here?"

"Forward, much?" I ask, pulling her hands off me. "Thanks for the compliment, but I'm okay."

"Fuck you," she snaps and stomps off, likely on to her next conquest. She disappears into the crowd of people and I chuckle.

Oh, to be college-aged again, with no responsibilities other than to make it home before you passed out and try to remember to get to class. Or at least, that's what I always thought college would be like. I spent the years I would've been in college working my ass off to help support my mom and little brother.

He gets to go to college and is carefree, but that wasn't my path. It's interesting to see how it could've been.

I grab a cup and fill it with the foamy liquid, happy that it's cold as promised. There's shit everywhere—empty cans and bottles on the counters, opened soda and juice bottles for mixers, shot glasses discarded all over. The bass is thumping so loudly I'm surprised the cops haven't been called yet, since this house looks to be in a residential neighborhood. Then again, we do live in a college town, so maybe they're just used to it.

"Asher, bro! It's been too long, how the hell are you?" I turn to see a guy I knew from school but haven't seen in a long time. Harry and I were acquaintances and played on a rec baseball team together.

I shake his hand and cheers his cup. "I'm good, how are you?"

"Good, good. Just enjoying a Friday night out," he chuckles, gesturing around the room.

"Same." I rub the back of my head, then push back down my brown tresses. I like to keep my hair long enough to run my fingers through, but the waves tend to fall over my forehead and into my eyes. I bring the cup to my lips and drink my beer, doing my best to keep from chuckling as I see Harry's eyes widening while he scans all the tattoos I have. They cover my hand, my fingers, my forearms; there are pieces poking out from under my shirt and climbing up my neck. I definitely don't look like I did in high school. I've put on at least fifty pounds of muscle to boot.

"So, what do you do?" he asks with an easy smile.

"I co-own a tattoo shop, *From The Ashes*, down on 3rd."

"That's incredible," he replies excitedly. "I've always wanted to get a tattoo. Maybe I'll stop by and you can set me up."

"Yeah, man. For sure," I nod, pulling a card out of my back pocket and handing it to him. "I'm always there."

Out of the corner of my eye, I see someone who looks like my brother turning the corner. He has a sick smile on his face that tells me he's up to no good. He hi-fives a guy standing by the wall, and that's when I see it's fucking Kyle.

My brother rolls his eyes and gestures for Kyle to follow him, then I watch as they walk out the front door. A girl in cowboy boots and blonde curly hair follows them reluctantly.

Something's off.

Harry's talking, and I nod along. "Yeah, just call that number and set up an appointment. I'd love to chat with you more about it," I say absently.

"Sweet." He puts the card in his back pocket. "It was good to see you, Asher."

"You too." I smile and raise my cup, turning and walking to where I saw my brother turn the corner.

There is a whole other level downstairs, with people making out on a beat-up couch right as you enter. Averting my eyes, I check the rooms. There are a few couples sleeping on the beds and the floor, and there's also a few solo guests; guys and girls, sleeping or doing other things, in the different rooms. In the main room, there's a game of what looks like poker going on. All the players are beyond drunk, so they're loud and slurring.

My brother could've been fucking around with any of the people down here. He also could very well have just been playing poker. I shake my head and turn back to the stairs when I hear a weak moan.

I pause before heading toward the one room I didn't really check because I saw the laundry machine peeking out.

A second moan sounds. It's definitely coming from the laundry room.

"Hello?" I call out softly. "Is there someone here?"

Another breathy moan.

It's dark and dusty in here, but as I push into the room further, I see someone huddled in the corner. Arms wrapped very loosely around themselves protectively, but completely still.

It's a girl. She can't be more than twenty, and she's naked from the waist down, her shorts around her ankles. Her shirt is dark and pushed up, but her arms block a view of her bare breasts.

"Are you okay?" I ask, walking towards her slowly, hesitantly. The girl moans again but doesn't move. Fuck, this is bad.

Someone obviously raped this poor girl and left her. Rage fills my entire being to the point where I'm sure flames could shoot out of my eyes.

I fucking hate people. I really fucking hate people.

Men who do this kind of shit are *not* men. They're barely people. But even they can be killed.

I shake the anger from my fingers, trying to bring myself back to center and not frighten this girl any more than she already is. If she can even see me. "Miss?" I try again.

Nothing. I press two fingers against her pulse point and find a weak, but there, pulse.

"Can you hear me?" I ask, a little louder this time. She doesn't move, doesn't talk, but her breathing is steady.

I can't leave her here. Pulling up her shorts so she's covered, I tug her shirt down, too. There are only nasty clothes needing to be washed in here, but I spot what looks like a folded sheet on top of the washer. I waste absolutely no time wrapping her up in it and picking her up in my arms. She's light, even dead-weight, and I prop her head against my shoulder so it doesn't flop back and hurt her more.

Making quick work of leaving the basement and getting the fuck out of this house, I push past all the partygoers with an unconscious girl in my arms. Not one of them looks at me with concern. No wonder this girl was taken and hurt—no one fucking watches out for others here.

"Where am I taking you?" I ask, but she doesn't answer.

"That's Jade," a voice calls. Turning to the sound, I find that blonde girl I saw leave with my brother and Kyle. She's sitting on the front lawn, smoking what smells like a joint. My fingers tighten on the girl—around *Jade*—in my arms.

"Who are you?"

"The girl that came with her." She blows a puff of smoke into the air and coughs. "I didn't want her to come. And I don't want to see her again."

"What the fuck is the matter with you?" I snap, exhausted *already* with this fucking bitch that's talking.

"She caught the eye of the guy I was into and slept with him. When she wakes up, tell her to find her own way home." The girl with the boots stands and kicks a bag in my direction. "It's her shit. I took her cash for gas and emotional damages."

"You're a piece of work," I scoff and bend down to pick up the bag.

"Good luck–she's a bitch." She walks off, gets into a car and starts it before flipping me the bird and driving off.

What the hell is going on?

"Okay." Think, Asher, think. "Okay, well I guess you're coming home with me."

I don't know what else to do. I can't leave her here; she's hurt and unconscious, and the person she came with just abandoned her. She must not be from around here if she has an overnight bag packed.

"What else could possibly happen?" I sigh and make my way to my truck.

Jade

MY HEAD FUCKING KILLS.

It's like a million boots stomped on my skull all at the same time, and I somehow lived. The dryness of my mouth makes me cough, and I try opening and closing it repeatedly to get some moisture back. Water—I need water.

What happened last night? I put my hand to my head, hoping to get the room to stop spinning. It doesn't help.

Where am I? Pushing myself to a sitting position feels like I'm pushing the side of a mountain. It takes a million years, but I finally sit upright.

Where am I? Panic sets in as I realize I have absolutely no idea. I can't remember anything about last night. *Why* can't I remember anything about last night?

"Oh god, oh god, oh god," I mutter, trying to push myself out of the plaid-covered bed I'm in, only to find I'm in a huge, unfamiliar T-shirt and black sweatpants that are at least two sizes too big. "What's going on? Oh god." My thighs are sore, my entire body hurts. But especially... between my legs.

No, no, no, no, no.

A hazy memory comes of someone holding me down and not being able to fight them off.

I said no.

Oh, god. I want to cry. I want to scream. But I have no clue where I am, who did this to me, or where Sarah is. How to get home.

A breakdown will happen. It just can't happen right now, Jade.

Stumbling, I use the wall to help me walk to the door. The room itself is illuminated with sunlight that's streaming in from the blinds, and I can tell it's at least mid-morning. The white walls of the room are empty, giving me no information about where I'm at, but at least the room is tidy. The plaid sheets and bedspread seem clean and there's a desk on the side of the room that's covered in drawings. Remarkable, beautiful drawings.

One of a phoenix catches my eye. It's done in charcoal, and seems so real. The feathers are so texturized and lifelike, the beak sharp and dimensional. Don't get me started on the eyes... The artist has given the mythical bird such depth within their eyes. It's astonishing.

I love to create, I love art, and I'd spend every spare second I have with my pencils and my sketchbook if I could. The person that created this picture put all their care into the piece. I can see how they felt with each stroke. It's magnificent.

The wall around the desk has some drawings taped up. There's a pair of boots by the closed door and shoes that look like mine lined up right next to them. I stumble closer and can see my bag at the end of the bed. Thank fuck I didn't lose it. Hopefully my phone and money are still there.

I want to change out of these clothes, but honestly, I don't have the strength for it yet. I need to shower. I want to burn my skin off; burn away every trace of the man who touched me. I want every reminder of him on my body gone.

Falling to the floor, I rifle through my bag, trying to find my phone with the hope it's still charged. The little icon in the top corner glares at me, teasing me with 10%. It should be enough.

It's going to have to be enough.

I dial my mom's number, waiting on pins and needles until she picks up on the very last ring.

"Why are you calling me so early? You're meant to be sleeping off a hangover." Fucking fantastic, she's annoyed already.

"Mom, something... something happened," I whisper.

"What is it?" she asks, not sounding any more awake.

"Well..." Tears line my eyes. I try not to let the sobs flow as freely as I'd like, but they're clear in my voice.

"Oh god," she groans, and I can almost hear the eyeroll. "What happened?"

I don't want to tell her. I don't want to have her hear what I've gone through or what I think happened... but I feel so fucking awful. I need to tell someone. *Someone.*

"There was this guy," I sob. "He, well, he was nice at the beginning, I think. He got me a drink and we played beer pong together. Then I think he took me somewhere and we... I think we..." A broken sob leaves my lips. "I think we had sex."

"That's why you're calling me so early? You had sex? What, were you actually a virgin?" She's fucking laughing at me. God, I'm so stupid to think she might care about me at all.

"I was." I cry harder, careful not to wake up anyone here. I don't know if the guy who raped me is still here, or if I'm somewhere else, but the last thing I want is someone coming in and hurting me more. "But he left, and I don't know who he was really, or any of that."

My mom chuckles condescendingly. "Jade, that's called a one-night stand."

"I don't think—"

I'm cut off by her *mmm*. "It is, and it's okay. It's common. Just find Sarah and come home whenever she's ready."

"That's the other thing, Mom." I wipe my cheeks as humiliation fills my body. "I don't know where I am, and I don't know where Sarah is. She basically left me the moment we got to the house."

"That doesn't sound like her," Mom scoffs. Because of-fucking-course she would take Sarah's side on this. She doesn't even actually know the devil girl except through maybe a passing greeting here or there.

"You don't fucking know her, Mom."

"Jade, don't you speak to me that way."

"I don't think you understand what I'm trying to tell you!" I snap, holding my head in my hands. I'm too hungover, too hurt for this conversation. "I don't know where I am, I don't know where Sarah is, and I don't have enough battery life to go searching. What should I do?"

I hear a scoff across the line and then nothing.

Silence.

"Mom?" I ask, bringing the phone to my face. I find that goddamn annoying blinking light telling me my phone is shutting down.

"Shit!" I hiss in frustration, but then wince because that makes my head hurt more.

I'm on my own.

I don't really have much of a choice, I have to figure out where I am and hope that guy—Hunter? Harry? Hudson?—isn't here.

When I reach the door, I turn the knob as slowly as possible, hoping to keep quiet. Seeing there isn't anyone in the hallway, I step out into the apartment, trying to notice as much as possible while my head feels full of cotton.

There's art everywhere. Where the bedroom only had sketches and hand-drawn work, the walls of the hallway are filled with paintings and framed artwork. There is so much, you can barely see the white walls underneath. Walking into the living room, I hear soft snores coming from a bright purple couch.

Anxiety fills me and my hands start to shake. I tiptoe over to see who is there, whose apartment I'm in, and I'm struck speechless.

It's not the guy from my hazy memory.

This guy is beautiful; dark hair with soft curls that fall across his forehead, black and white tattoos which disappear under the collar of his white T-shirt. His strong cheekbones and jaw are softened with sleep, the five-o'clock shadow darkening his soft-looking skin. His quiet snores are endearing as he sleeps. I'm leery, but I can't help feeling bad that this hulk of a man is smushed on a small couch. He positively fills out the couch as he sleeps propped up on his side, with his arms crossed tightly across his chest so that he doesn't fall. His legs are so long his feet have to hang off the side of the couch for him to fit comfortably.

I wonder what his eyes look like.

I wonder why I'm here with him. I wonder what happened to me... Although, I can guess.

Tears fill my eyes as I try to hold myself together. A soft sob escapes my lips, and I cover my mouth quickly. Shit.

Light blue, a beautiful ocean foam blue, eyes snap open and meet mine.

The mystery guy jumps up into a seated position and looks at me with wide eyes.

"Uh, hi," he stutters, standing quickly. He backs up a few feet and rubs the back of his head before shaking his head to get the sleep out of his eyes. "How are you feeling?"

"I'm... well, I don't know." That's as true of a statement as I can make. I don't really know anything right now.

He nods awkwardly. "Yeah, I understand."

"Who are you?" I ask.

"Oh, yeah, right. I'm so sorry. I told you last night, but I should've guessed you wouldn't remember. I'm sorry." This mystery man moves quickly to stand in front of me, holding out a hand. "I'm Asher Lee. What all do you remember from last night?"

"I know I went to that party with Sarah," I stammer, ignoring his hand. "She ditched me very early on, and I think I played beer pong? And this guy...this guy gave me a drink. Made me chug it when I didn't want to drink the beer." The memories are too much as I try to sort through what's real and what's a nightmare. "He carried me over his shoulder, and I tried... I tried to..." A tear slips down my cheeks and I tighten my grip around myself. I can't lose it now. I don't know this guy. But it's still too raw. Everything is going to shit, and it's like I can't control myself.

"It's okay." Asher comes closer, slowly enough where I'm not surprised when his hand rests on my shoulder. I don't look at him, but can see where his free hand curls into a fist at his side. When he does speak again, his voice is rough, like he's trying desperately to hold back emotions. "It's okay. You don't have to say anything."

"Do you know who did this to me?" I bite my lip to keep the sobs from escaping.

"No, I'm sorry. I wish I did, I'd make them pay." He looks down like he's ashamed. "I found you in the laundry room of that house, naked and alone. I covered you up and carried you out. But I didn't know where to take you, so I brought you here—to my apartment."

"How'd you get my bag?" I point back toward the direction of the bedroom.

His demeanor changes as his eyes narrow, his jaw clenching before he says anything. "I met your friend with the curly hair outside. She's... quite the character." He puts his hands in his jean pockets and shakes his head.

"She's a bitch," I snap. "And she's definitely not my friend."

"I can agree with you there." The way he says that so quickly makes me wonder what happened, what Sarah did to him.

"So, you found me, brought me to your house, and just hoped for the best?" I ask.

Asher chuckles and walks backward toward the small kitchenette in the corner of the room. "That I did. You seemed like a nice girl." He shrugs and gestures to the coffee pot. "Coffee?"

"Sure," I reply hesitantly. I mess with the end of my shirt and pull it down slightly.

Asher smiles, nods, and starts gathering the coffee grounds. "Any specific way? I take my coffee black, but I might have some milk. Maybe I can find a Sweet-n-Low somewhere." He starts rifling through his drawers for sugar, and I have to admit, it's very sweet.

"No, it's fine. Milk is okay." I really only drink coffee with an unhealthy amount of creamer, sugar and flavored syrups, but right now, any warm liquid seems comforting.

I watch him like a fucking hawk. Making sure he's only—*only*—using coffee. After last night, I won't make that mistake again.

He sighs in relief and starts to make a large pot of coffee for us. Taking advantage of the lull in conversation, I start to look around more. The kitchenette is small, functional, and organized. Asher has a butcher block cart in the middle which serves as an island of sorts. The living room is connected, and while it's obviously a bachelor pad, I can see he cares for his place. It's evident by the art on the walls and the way everything is picked up and *clean*. There's a big TV across from the purple couch and a small art-deco armchair next to it.

"I like your place," I offer softly, looking around at all the artwork in the living room. There's no real discernable style to the collection. There's a little bit of everything: paintings, chalk, watercolor, black and white, color, all pastels, neon. It's like he's collecting everything.

"Thanks." Asher brings me a ceramic cup with milky brown coffee.

"Do you have a certain style you prefer, or do you just strive to collect every style?" I gesture to the walls with my cup.

"I collect what I like. That's it." He shrugs. "If it makes me happy, I bring it home."

Nodding, I take a sip of the coffee, doing my best to cover my grimace. I should know by now that saying I like something to be cool will only get me into trouble.

Asher's looking at me, and I meet his gaze head on.

"I'm Jade. Jade Henderson," I whisper.

"Very nice to meet you, Jade." He smiles softly with his reply. It's a smile I can trust, or at least I think I can.

"Very nice to meet you, Asher. Thank you, by the way."

"For what?" His eyebrows furrow together as he sips his black coffee.

"For saving me."

THE FULL FORCE OF EVERYTHING THAT'S HAPPENED hits me all at once, weighing me down until I can't move from Asher's couch. He hasn't pushed me to leave, but I don't know if he has work or something like that. Maybe he has a girlfriend who is going to stomp into the apartment at any minute, freaking the fuck out once she sees me staring blankly at the wall. I'm sure I've overstayed my welcome; I probably should feel guilty about that, but honestly, I really don't care.

"What am I going to do?" I mutter softly. The forgotten coffee mug is still in my hands, well past the point of cooling. "How am I going to get home? How am I going to face people?" The words spill faster as my chest tightens. "How can I face my mother? Fuck, Sarah's going to tell her mom and then she's going to spin a stupid fucking story to make it my fault."

"Your mother would take Sarah's word over yours?" Asher asks, cocking his head in question.

I chuckle darkly. "Without question."

"What a shitty mother," he scoffs and takes a drink of his coffee.

"Sarah was my ride here," I explain. "She was meeting some guy named Kyle who she said she was dating." His lips twitch as he cocks an eyebrow, but he doesn't stop me. "My mom and her mom pushed for this. We hate each other."

As hopeless as I may seem right now, I actually feel calm at Asher's house, in his presence. Calm and safety are two things I need right now, but I know this poor guy probably has other things he needs to do today rather than babysit a nineteen-year-old girl who is, honestly, a fucking mess.

I set the still full mug down on the wooden coffee table and stand.

"Thank you so much, Asher, really. But I better get out of your hair. I'm sure you have better things to do today." I chuckle humorlessly and start to move toward the bedroom to change into whatever clothes I have left.

"Wait," Asher says quickly, standing and reaching out to me. There's an eagerness in his light blue eyes. "How, uh, how are you getting home? Where is home?"

I groan, closing my eyes and letting my head drop forward in frustration. "About three hours from here," I sheepishly admit.

His eyes widen. "Wow. I was not expecting that." He sets his coffee mug down beside mine, putting his hands back in his pockets. He keeps doing that, like he's trying to make sure I know he won't reach out unexpectedly.

While it's a little thing, it *does* make me feel better.

"Yeah. Not my smartest idea," I grumble, even though none of it was my idea.

"You came all the way to Carver for a fraternity party?" Asher's expression shows me just how unimpressed he is with that idea, especially considering the person I came with as 'back-up' immediately stabbed me in the back. "Your ride told me last night that you had to find your own way home. Do you think she left already?"

I have no idea. My phone's dead and apparently Sarah had no problem just letting a random guy take me home last night while I was obviously drugged.

I hate her so fucking much.

My heart starts beating harder and my cheeks redden with anger and embarrassment.

"I don't know. But I'll figure it out." I reply.

"The hell you will," he growls. His voice is deep and

commanding, unintentionally making me freeze up. "I'm sorry, I didn't..." He runs a hand over his hair, shaking his head slightly. I don't know what to do and it looks like neither does he. Asher sighs and tries again. "I just mean, if you're okay with waiting until after my shift at the shop, I'll gladly drive you home."

My mouth drops in shock. "No, Asher, there's no way I'm letting you drive me three hours away just to then drive three hours back home. That's insane." I can't let him do that. He's done far too much for me already. "Thank you, but I can't ask you to do that." I turn back to walk towards the room, but he walks a few steps towards me.

"I'm happy to, really."

"Why?" I ask skeptically, raising an eyebrow. I'm already out on a limb, but I'm not stupid.

"Because it's the right thing to do," Asher replies, shrugging his shoulders. "I know you've been given a shitty hand these last two days, and I can't in good conscience let you 'figure out' some way home. What does that even mean? Hitchhiking? Yeah fucking right! That's not going to happen." He shakes his head, looking angry, but takes a deep breath and lets his hand drop in front of him. "Seriously, if you're okay with it, I'd really like to provide you a safe ride home so that I know you're okay."

"What am I, some charity case to you?" I snap back, my hands curling into fists at my sides.

"No. No, Jade. I just..." He struggles to speak before running his hands through his hair again and sighing deeply. "I feel... I want to—no, I *need*—to take care of you. I can't explain it, I just... I need to." My frustration and humiliation soften a little at how completely desperate he looks. It's confusing.

To both of us.

He takes a step closer to me, stopping right before me.

"Will you let me? I know it's not fair right now to ask, but can you trust me?" The blues of his eyes are icy, clear, and coiled with a clear-sky blue ring. They're so clear, I can almost see what he's thinking.

And he's begging me to trust him.

But can I?

Asher

Last night...

CARRYING Jade upstairs to my second-floor apartment is easier than I thought. She's waking up now, I think, but on the drive here she'd woken up enough to say "drugged" before passing back out. At least I kind of know what I'm dealing with now.

Turning the key to unlock my door with one hand and holding an unconscious woman in the other, I hope none of my neighbors come out and see me like this. That's just what I need; the old lady next door worried about the big, burly man with tattoos and piercings kidnapping women and hurting them, so she calls the cops all because I'm carrying an unconscious girl in my arms. Actually...I would probably call the cops on me, too.

Balancing everything, I start sweating under my shirt. The door unlatches enough so I can kick it open. "Thank fuck," I groan. Jade's not super heavy by any means, but have you tried carrying a whole-ass dead-weight woman from your car, up a flight of stairs, and into an apartment? No?

It's a lot, no matter how built you are.

I carry her to my room, nudge the door open with my toe and set her as gently as I can on my bed. "You're lucky, Jade. I just changed the sheets," I joke with her, feeling silly when I look over and see her eyes are closed. "Aaaand I'm talking to myself."

"Ugghh," she moans.

"Jade?"

Her eyes open and I'm struck by the green of her irises. I could very easily get lost in her eyes forever, and a shiver runs down my back. I clear my throat, pushing her hair back softly.

"My name is Asher. I'm not going to hurt you, I promise. You can sleep now; you're safe." I try to keep my sentences short and voice calm.

I can see her eyes trying to focus on me, but it doesn't seem to happen. She starts to whimper slightly, the sound breaking my heart; worry and fear shine clearly in her lost expression. She scoots back on the bed, trying to get away from me. Fuck, I don't want her to be scared.

I stand quickly and back toward the door with my hands up. Fuck, she's shivering and still in those torn clothes.

"It's okay, Jade. You're safe. I promise," I repeat quietly in what I'm hoping is a soothing tone.

Changing course, I move slowly through my room. Going to my dresser, I pick out a pair of sweats and a shirt before setting them close to her on the bed. Her fight against whatever drug she was given is starting to fade as her eyelids droop.

"Let me help you," I urge softly. "I promise, I won't hurt you. I just want to help."

"Help," she repeats softly before falling back onto the pillows.

"I really hope that was a yes," I mutter, then make quick work of changing her out of the dirty stained shorts and ripped shirt she was wearing. I do my best not to look at her naked body, but it feels nearly impossible when I have to move her head to put the shirt on her.

I didn't look.

Intentionally.

But there's no denying she is fucking gorgeous. Her long dark blonde hair is matted and tangled, but soft and thick. High cheekbones and clear skin, with a few beauty marks here and there, add to her beauty. The makeup she's wearing is smeared and heavy, but it does look very pretty. She's petite and curvy, but just tall enough that her head would come to my shoulder. Sweet, innocent, but so fucking hot.

The girl-next-door kind of beauty queen that has always been out of my reach, out of my league, but I've always wanted.

Finally, after changing Jade successfully without taking any more of her autonomy, I move her under my duvet and rest her head against my pillow.

"Jade," I whisper, shaking her shoulder lightly. I don't want to scare her, though, so I shake a little harder and with more intention. "Jade," I call her name more firmly. Her eyes barely open but when they do, they're still glossed over. How heavily was she drugged?

"I'm going to be on the couch if you need anything. I promise you; I won't let anything happen to you, okay? So, rest easy." I move my trashcan closer to the side of the bed her head is on. "If you feel sick, here's the trashcan."

She sighs, and her eyes close again.

I leave Jade's overnight bag at the end of the bed before I walk out, making sure to close the door tightly behind me.

My mind is racing with everything that's happened. I... I can't believe someone would do something like this. Something so evil and cruel.

Whoever did this drugged her, used her, and fucking left her

—like she was nothing more than trash. Flashbacks fill my mind; I'm thrown back to a time when I had far less power than I do now.

My mom laying there limply, my father scrambling to get out of the house, my brother staring wide-eyed and I'm paralyzed with fear and understanding.

No, fuck. No. I shake my head to focus back on the present. On Jade. It's late, later than I usually stay up; I simply kick my boots off, line them up by my bedroom door, and walk back to the living room to lie on the couch. I'm intent on sleeping in direct sight of my bedroom, in case she comes to.

Fuck has today been a long day, I think as I wipe my hand down my face and nestle into my couch.

The last thought I have before falling asleep is the question; *Why does it seem like there are no more decent people in the world?*

The Next Day...

I need Jade to understand. I *need* her to let me keep her safe.

There's something about her that's pulling me in. Something I can't place or ignore.

"I will stay with you until my phone charges, then I can call my mom or a car service." She raises a finger at me, and I take her concession as a win. I put my hands up in surrender and smirk. I'll take what I can get.

In the back of my mind, I'm already formulating how to get her to agree to me taking her home.

Nodding, I grin and turn back to get my coffee. "I have my shift at the tattoo shop—"

"You tattoo people?" she asks, eyes wide.

"I do." I can't help the way my chest puffs out a little with pride at how impressed she looks. "I own the shop as well."

"That's... really cool." Her eyes rake over me again, this time appearing to mentally catalogue all the tattoos I have. The visible ones at least. "I don't have any. But I'd like to, one day."

"Be careful, they're addictive," I joke, twisting my arms and lifting the hem of my white shirt just enough to show her my fully covered abdomen.

"Wow." Jade's eyes lock on my exposed skin and she bites her lip. Her eyes don't leave my abs until I drop my shirt, then they snap back to my face to find I'm smirking. Jade's cheeks redden deliciously with a blush.

I really, *really* like it.

"I've designed most of them myself," I tell her, shrugging like it's no big deal, but her eyes light up.

"That's... that's really fucking cool." Jade smiles at me, her eye lingering on one of the tattoos on my forearm, before she steps back again, away from me. "Do you have a charger?"

Must have gotten too close, I think. It's sad that she felt the need to move away, but I understand, given how much she's been through. "Sure, let me go grab it."

I have a spare charger in my room, so I set it up for her there. While I'm in my room, I grab a fresh set of clothes and my towel, before leaving so Jade can have the room.

"I'm going to go shower; go ahead and make yourself at home. I have the charger in my room set up for you. I'll change and get ready in the bathroom," I explain.

"I'm sorry," she whispers with her head lowered.

Shocked, I ask her, "Why?"

"I feel like I've kicked you out of a place in your own home, so, I'm sorry."

"Jade," I step closer until I'm right in front of her. With a gentle finger placed under her chin, I lift Jade's face so she'll look at me. Green meets blue, and I can see the myriads of emotions running through them.

This poor girl. Lost, alone, hurt, abandoned. I won't do any of that to her.

"I want to help you. I want to be here," I remind Jade. "I was actually thinking... Maybe you could come to the shop with me and hang out during my shift. That way I could keep an eye on you, and if you need anything, I'm right there."

Jade shakes her head. "I couldn't intrude in your space any more than I already have."

"I insist," I say, leaving no room for discussion. "Please; it would make me feel better, and I know it would make you feel better. If it helps, I'll even put you to work."

She smirks, a soft chuckle leaving her lips, but she relaxes a bit. "Well, I do need some way to pay for lunch. And gas."

"Oh, that's on me. Don't you worry about that." I step back, letting her move toward the bedroom and she pauses before she closes the door.

"Asher," she starts, standing in the door frame. With the light illuminating her silhouette, she looks angelic.

"Yes?" I ask breathlessly.

"There's a part of me that's weary of you. But frankly, I'm out of options other than to trust you're as genuine as you seem. I don't know why you're being so kind to me. So protective and helpful. But I'm thankful."

"Jade," I struggle to find the right words, the words that will encase what I'm feeling and why I feel like this about her when I don't actually fully know. "Because sometimes there are good and decent people in the world, and it's okay to accept their help when you need it."

She looks stunned but nods and closes the door softly. I think about my answer the whole way into the bathroom, wondering if I said the right thing or made her feel more alone. Regardless, it's the truth. And the truth is all that really matters at this moment.

I PLUG my phone into the charger Asher pointed me to and groan when it doesn't immediately light up. Damn, it's really dead.

Worry fills my chest as I wonder what exactly I've just agreed to with Asher: going to his tattoo shop while I wait to find a way to get home. Hope and pray that my mom will actually make the drive to come get me. I can't make Asher do that; it's asking so much, especially after what he's already done for me. Six hours round trip. Who offers to do something like that? What does he want in return? What *will* he want in return?

"Sometimes there are decent people in the world, and it's okay to accept their help when you need it," he'd said.

My hands go to my hair. I want to rip it out. Everything I'm thinking and feeling is a contradiction. I want to trust him, but I can't. My gut says to, but my head screams that I'm being naïve again. I want to believe he'd simply drive me and drop me off at my home, but what if he has some other sinister plan? Last night I was completely out of it, and maybe that was enough to deter him from something more he wanted to do... I don't know. Pushing the heels of my hands into my eyes, hard enough so that the questions stop, I groan loudly.

I'm between a rock and a hard place.

Sighing, I rub my forehead in worry. I have no other choice but to rely on Asher right now. My bag sits basically untouched at the foot of the bed, and I open it to try to remember what I'd packed. Pulling the items out one by one, I thank my past self for being organized. I have a toothbrush, toothpaste, hairbrush, my small makeup bag, clean underwear and a sports bra. I also packed comfy clothes because I thought I would be driving home today.

Flared leggings and an oversized T-shirt, it is.

Changing quickly and shoving my nasty, torn outfit into my bag, I stop. Holding the ruined clothes in my hands, it dawns on me: I'm never going to be able to wear that outfit again without being traumatized. That makes me really sad because I actually felt confident in that outfit. It made me feel attractive and sensual; things I don't usually feel. Biting my lip to keep the tears and frustration at bay, something catches my eye. The sweats and shirt Asher let me borrow, which I'd tossed onto the bed. *He wouldn't mind, would he?* I ponder and quickly make the choice to stuff the gray shirt into my bag as well.

A soft knocking makes me turn, and I quietly open the door to see Asher standing there with wet hair dripping down his face.

"Are you ready?" he asks kindly. "I want to pick us up some food on the way there."

"It's okay," I protest, shrugging my shoulders. I don't have any money to pay for anything, courtesy of Sarah—discovering she had taken my cash from my wallet was the icing on my 'fuck you' cake.

"Oh, stop." Asher rolls his eyes and leans against the door frame. "I'm starving and I ate a snack when we got back here last night—*you* did not. There's no way you're not hungry."

"It's okay," I reiterate.

He sighs and gestures for me to follow him. "I'm going to feed you and you're going to eat. I understand you don't have money right now, and that's okay. I'm good with covering you for a bit."

I grab my bag and phone, making sure to grab the charger, too.

It still hasn't charged at all. *What the fuck?* Maybe it just didn't have enough time. Although I figured by now, it would at least have one or two percent.

"Asher," I start to say, but he just waves me off.

"Seriously, Jade, just leave it. I'm buying, you're eating. You need anything, you let me know." Raising his eyebrows, the look in his eye tells me that he is not going to argue with me.

"But,"

"No, Jade. No! You need something, you tell me." His hand reaches out and grabs the keys on the entry table, before turning and looking at me. "You have everything?"

I put my bag over my shoulder, holding tightly to the straps. Nodding to him, he opens the door and holds out a hand.

"Then your chariot awaits, milady."

<hr>

HIS SHOP IS AMAZING. SMALL AND ARTISANAL, BUT through and through, edgy and welcoming. Asher pushes open the unlocked door and I'm hit with the strong smells of antiseptic, coffee, and vanilla; the latter probably coming from the lit candle at the front desk where a girl with black hair sits, tattooing *herself*.

"Jesus, Roxie!" Asher closes the door, causing the overhead

bell to start ringing again. "You're not supposed to do that at the front desk!"

Roxie rolls her eyes. "Look, your receptionist didn't show up and I don't have anyone on my books until later. So, I volunteered —nay, accepted—the job of keeping this place up and running since you're actually late. For the first time since I've known you, I might add. What would you do without me?" She smirks, leaning back and throwing her arms out dramatically. A patch of skin on her upper thigh is raised and red, standing out sharply against the rest of her pale coloring. My eyes are drawn to it; the beautiful snake she's tattooing weaving through her other existing tattoos. It's really awesome that she can make something so realistic, while also working around what's already there. She's not taking away from the designs, but adding a layer of depth to it. I wish I could do that.

Asher groans loudly. "Thank you for covering. But still, you can't just tattoo yourself at the front of the shop. At the very least, it's not sanitized up here." He runs his hand over his face and shakes his head. "Get back to your station and please, for the love of god, make sure you clean your new ink."

Roxie smiles, showing off how her black lipstick lines her perfectly white teeth. She uncrosses her legs, the short bright-red miniskirt stopping right where the inflamed redness of her new tattoo sits. "And who might you be?" She hops off the table, waving her fingers at me.

I can't tell if she's just super confident or a bitch. Time will tell.

Asher puts his hand tentatively on the small of my back and steps slightly in front of me. "This is Jade. She's a friend of mine."

"She's cute."

I roll my eyes at her condescending tone.

"Hey, lady. I mean that sincerely." Roxie holds her hands up in surrender. "Really have a 'girl-next-door' vibe going on." Waving her fingers at me again, she reaches forward and grabs my hand. "Come with me! I need more girl friends in my life."

Without really meaning to and without knowing *why*, I look back to Asher.

He nods minutely. The gesture is so subtle I probably wouldn't have caught it if I hadn't been looking for any kind of symbol that she's someone safe.

Roxie squeals and drags me to her little work station. "So, tell me everything," she gushes. "Who are you? Where are you from? How do you know Asher? Why is he bringing you to work in the morning?" She asks these in rapid fire, plopping into her chair and crossing her legs. She's got heavy, thick-soled biker boots on and they bob with her movement.

"Um," I start nervously, putting my bag down and quickly clocking the outlet next to the desk, plugging my phone in. In seconds there's a vibration from my phone and it seems to finally fucking charge a bit. Turning to face her, I feel inadequate because of how well she's dressed while I look like I'm in my pajamas. Didn't even have a hairbrush to fucking brush my hair. Roxie has a mirror on her desk, and I groan when I see my reflection.

I look... exhausted. Scared. Rattled. The circles under my eyes are dark and deep. My skin is paler than normal, like I'm sick, and my shoulders are curled in with the weight of the world on them.

"I'm Jade," I finally say. "I met Asher last night at a fucking horror of a frat party and he saved my life. End of story." I shrug and sit down on a chair beside her desk so we're facing each other.

Her mouth drops and she looks stunned. "That does not sound like an 'end-of-fucking-story' statement, Jade," she replies in question.

"That's all I want to say right now." I push my matted hair out of my face wishing for a diversion.

"But—"

Roxie starts to demand more, but Asher walks over and puts his hand on her shoulder aggressively. He looks over at me with a gentle smile, and I can see him tighten his grip on Roxie's shoulder as he speaks. "What would you like from a little diner down the street? I like that it serves breakfast all day. That sounds pretty good right about now. Is that okay with you?" Roxie stays quiet, her eyes jumping between us as we speak, taking it all in like a detective.

"Yeah, that sounds good," I answer with a soft smile. "Are you sure about..."

"I'm very sure. What would you like?" Asher asks, and I watch his hand leave Roxie's shoulder. *Why does that make me feel better?*

"You buying?" Roxie raises an eyebrow at Asher and crosses her arms over her chest.

"Not for you," he scoffs, "just her." Guilt immediately fills my chest, but then he winks at me and crosses his arms over his chest, his fists pushing up his biceps. Not that he needed to—they are already fucking huge. "Just Jade," he repeats pointedly.

My guilt and embarrassment somehow lessen with his words, especially when I see the look he's giving me.

"Whatever you're having is good with me," I answer. "I'm really not picky when it comes to breakfast foods."

"My kind of girl," Asher says with a smirk and walks off, pulling his phone out to place an order.

"I hope you know you're going to end up with at least half of the diner's menu for breakfast. That boy can eat," Roxie jokes, and thankfully she seems to have dropped asking about last night.

Once it's confirmed Asher is out of earshot, Roxie turns back to me with a grin. "So, you met my grump of a boss at a party and spent the night together, huh? Is he as stoic and rugged in the bedroom as he is in real life? I only ask because that particular nugget of information was forced on me without my permission and I'm still healing from the trauma." Roxie rolls her eyes and makes a puking face, and only then do I realize that because he's brought me into work and is buying me breakfast, Roxie thinks we've slept together.

Fuck, I wish I'd slept with Asher instead of... what happened. I bet Asher would've been gentle, kind, but made me feel confident and wanted. I bet he'd have ravaged me, made sure I came and that my legs shook from pleasure. I don't know if we would've done the whole cuddle-after-sex thing, just because I don't really know what Asher likes outside of taking care of people, but I do know that he would've made sure I was cared for. In any way I needed.

"Oh, Asher and I..." I start to say, swallowing the lump in my throat, when Asher himself comes over again.

"Hey, is your phone charged?" he asks, saving me from answering Roxie's question.

"Goddamnit, Asher! Can I not ask your girl two simple fucking questions without you interrupting?" Roxie throws her hands up in the air in exasperation, rolls her eyes and stands. "I'm going to go use your good wrapping for my thigh. When I get back, you will *not* keep eavesdropping on our conversation." She points a finger at him roughly and I giggle. She's a character, someone I can see myself being friends with. Maybe when I move here, I can be.

"You know I'm your boss, right?" he calls after her, but she just flips him off and starts rifling through what I assume are his desk drawers.

"I'm sorry about her." Asher cocks his head to the side,

gesturing at Roxie. "She's an entity of her own and there's no controlling her," he chuckles. I like the sound and pause to drink him in. He's a big guy. Super intimidating when he stares; his eyes hard and closed off, his tattoos making his broad muscles look even bigger, the way he talks is gruff too. But when he laughs, it's magic. I want him to laugh again and again.

"No worries." I push a lock of hair behind my ear nervously as I'm struck with how attractive he is. This older man, who looks like he's a big biker covered with tattoos and a stoic expression, is really my knight in shining armor. Standing taller than I am, I have to tip my head back to look him in the eye, and I'm fairly sure that if I tried to put my hands around his bicep, my fingers wouldn't touch each other.

Asher's demeanor is calm and observant, but I know he wouldn't hesitate to fight for my honor if needed. And do I like that? Do I like that he'd turn to violence to protect me?

Yeah, I really do, my mind whispers.

"If telling her we slept together is easier to say than the truth, I don't mind," he says quietly. The husk and gravel-like tone to his voice while he's whispering makes me shiver.

"Thank you, I really... I really don't want to tell people," I reply softly. But the thought of people thinking that **I** got to sleep with this hunk of a man makes me blush.

"If it keeps you from having to relive what happened, I'll gladly do it."

My heart skips a beat. I'm so fucking... grateful. So touched. Tears line my eyes, and I do my best not to let any drop.

His eyes widen with worry, and his mouth opens, but I put my fingers to his lips.

"Thank you," I say softly. He holds my forearm, keeping my fingers where they are. I swear I feel him press his lips against me, but that's crazy.

"You're welcome," he whispers back before taking a step out of my space. I immediately feel the void of his absence. It's like all the warmth and light leave me as he does.

"Yeah, I can *feel* the sexual tension here," Roxie chuckles, popping her hip and smirking at us both. "I think that's your client, Ashe." She tips her chin forward, gesturing to an older gentleman who is about to open the door to the shop.

As Asher makes his way to the front, Roxie turns to me excitedly. "Come hang out with me while he's busy!" she insists, grabbing my arm and sitting me in the chair at her desk before Asher or myself can object again. "Can I do your hair? It's so long and beautiful, I'd love to do some braids, if that's okay?" she asks, looking at me in the mirror.

"Yeah, okay. Thanks," I answer with a shy smile.

"Hello, Mr. Guzman! Ready to finish up that crest?" Asher smiles politely, holding his hand out to guide the gentleman back to his work station. His area is like his apartment—clean and covered in framed art. He's got a small bookshelf filled with books and what look like scrapbooks as well. His desk is black metal, and he has a very cushy-looking desk chair which glides around easily against the floor.

Mr. Guzman, who I'd estimate is about mid-forties, is already undoing his button-down so that his upper biceps are free. Etched in his skin is a breathtaking design; fine, clean lines and an amazing depiction of a crest with a griffin on one side of the shield and a snake on the other, with vines and flowers curling around the edges.

"He's going to get it in color?" I ask, noticing the three rows of mini cups filled with different colors on a small tray, which is next to the reclining seat that Mr. Guzman's sitting in. Asher puts black gloves on and then begins shaving Guzman's arm.

"It looks like it," Roxie nods, pulling a brush out of her desk along with three or four mini hair-ties.

"Does it hurt?"

"What?"

"Does getting a tattoo hurt really badly?" I ask as she starts brushing my hair, surprisingly gentle for how her personality seems.

"I mean, I think it depends on your pain tolerance," she answers honestly, running her fingers through my hair and lightly massaging my scalp. "My first one shocked me, but I wouldn't say it was painful. Once you get used to it, it's not bad at all."

"How many do you have?"

"Too many," Roxie chuckles, and starts weaving my hair. "I started early, at sixteen. And I get a few new ones every year."

"Is it hard to do?"

"Thinking of entering the business?" Roxie asks with a smirk, pulling back two matching braids on either side of my face and tying them together.

"Maybe," I shrug. "I'm supposed to start school here next month and my major is in business."

"You sound really passionate about it," Roxie quips sarcastically.

I frown and reply, "It's not my plan." *It's my mother's.*

"Girl, life is too short to do things you don't want to do." Roxie steps back and surveys her work. "There, all done!" she announces.

Looking up at the mirror, I gasp at the sight. My hair is twisted and pinned into this Viking-esque style that makes me look powerful, like someone to be feared but who isn't out of place here. "Wow, this is amazing," I exhale. Turning my head to the side, I see that she twisted mini braids within the larger braid.

"Thanks! I wanted to be a hairdresser growing up and even

went to a few years of cosmetology school. Then I found out tattooing is actually what I want to do," Roxie explains.

"Wow," I repeat to myself, unable to stop looking at the intricate design.

"Now the question is," Roxie starts, sitting next to me in her chair and resting her chin on her hand, "what is it that *you* really want to do?"

"Choosing... that's not really an option for me. So, I don't have anything I've ever thought about fully. What I want has *never* been considered," I admit. "It's more disappointing to have dreams and ache for them, than to just do what's expected of you when you have no other choice."

"Ever?" Roxie's hand drops and her mouth opens slightly.

"Ever. Especially recently." It's sad but true. And speaking of my mom, I reluctantly realize I need to check and see if my phone is charged.

"Then we need to change that, girlfriend." Roxie raises her eyebrows, about to say something else, but the front door's bell rings. "I'll be right back," she says and adjusts her boobs in her corset top.

Looking at the door, I see a guy—an attractive, clean-cut, jock of a guy—smile seductively at Roxie as she signs for the three bags he's holding. She murmurs something and he blushes before responding to her. She throws her head back in laughter; it amazes me how positively magnetic she is. She's not like Sarah, where you feel a sense of punishment or cruelty waiting to happen if you choose not to give her attention. Roxie simply exudes lightness, sex, and charm. I wish I was like that.

The buzz of the tattoo gun fades, and I notice Asher stand up, taking off his gloves and pointing Mr. Guzman to what must be the bathroom.

"Oh good, our food's here." Asher comes to stand next to me with an easy smile.

"That's all food? How much do you think I'm going to eat?" I ask incredulously.

"Half of it's for me, sweetheart." He winks at me and pulls out his wallet. The delivery guy immediately pales as he realizes Asher is paying and I can almost see the wheels turning in his head. He thinks Roxie is Asher's girl, and he's worried about getting his ass kicked for flirting. Asher must see the terror too, because he chuckles.

"She's all yours, man. No ties here," Asher tells him, handing him a stack of cash and turning back to me. "I have my eyes somewhere else," he says, so quietly that I almost don't hear him before he looks at the ground. And just like that, my hopes—my stupid hopes—are crushed.

"Time to eat!" Asher says with a smile.

"What about your client?" I point to the bathroom, which Mr. Guzman still hasn't returned from.

"I mean, it's time to eat for you," he teases. "I'm going to grab a breakfast burrito, scarf it down, then wait for our next break in an hour." He guides me to the back room, which is set up simply but homely. There's a card table and a few chairs, a small but seemingly efficient kitchenette with a full fridge, and a very fancy coffee machine tucked in the corner. But what grabs my attention immediately are the photos.

All along the fridge—covering it, actually—are pictures: Asher rolling his eyes at Roxie while she's laughing; Asher with another guy; Asher standing outside holding up keys; Roxie in the arms of the other guy and she's holding his face lovingly; Roxie standing at the front desk with sleek black hair and a bright neon pink stripe framing her face. They all range in age, but the center photo shows a much younger Asher smiling brightly while sitting at his station—which I'm not surprised to discover looks exactly the same, just with more artwork added now—tattoo gun in hand as he leans over someone's arm, about to ink them up.

It's them, the embodiments of the shop, all put together. It's their stories as they live and grow with the shop.

True family, even if it's not by blood.

I want that. I...I don't think I've ever had that.

"That was my first paying client." Asher stands behind me, his hands in his pockets as he tells his story. "I was newly twenty and scared shitless. I had just opened my own business, not knowing if I'd succeed after the shitty upbringing I had. I had absolutely no money; negative balances in every account. But someone walked in off the sidewalk, asking for a Chinese symbol tattoo, and I didn't even care that it was a small little thing. I jumped at the chance to show my skill."

"Your smile," I murmur, tracing his face softly with my finger. "You're so happy."

"The shop has really been the only place I've ever felt at home." Asher sighs, turning back to the bags and rifling through them for his burrito. What he brings out is so big it's like an aluminum covered tree log. He takes an impressively massive bite and I turn back toward the pictures to not stare. It's an odd pause, though not awkward. It feels like there's more to his story with that sentence, but I'm not going to pry.

"That must be nice," I offer and smile back at the Asher smiling in the photo. "I know it's probably not the place you should've found home, but the fact you have one is nice."

"It was hard fought for," he agrees between bites.

"I believe it. But all the worthwhile things are, no?" I ask with a shrug.

"That's been my experience." He takes another huge bite before wrapping up the rest of it and putting it in the fridge. "I have at least another three hours with Guzman, then I can take you home, or whatever you need to do. Have you heard from your mom or that Thundercunt?"

I burst into laughter at his well-deserved nickname for Sarah, laughing so hard my cheeks hurt. "Oh, god," I gasp, wiping my face with my hand as I try to regain control.

Asher's looking at me with... I think with awe? His eyes are wide and sparkling as he watches me laugh.

"You have a really pretty laugh," he compliments with his own growing smile. He takes another step closer to me and the air is suddenly thicker.

"Thanks." My laugh dies down, but the smile remains on my face. "I have to say, though, it's never been my favorite feature."

"I think it should be," he whispers, and I realize just how close we've gotten. How he's suddenly in my space again and I can feel the warmth from his body against mine. Asher's looking right at my lips and, without thinking, I lick them. The movement catches his eye and his crystal blue eyes darken.

"Jade," he whispers huskily, leaning forward. I let him—I want to kiss him, I want Asher to be the last touch I feel, the last kiss on my lips, from this horrible fucking trip to Carver.

"Asher! Bro, your client's waiting—"

Roxie walks into the back room and stops when she finds us standing close together. A knowing smirk appears on her face; she leans her shoulder against the door frame while drumming her fingers together like Cruella de Vil. "Oh, my, my, my. What *have* I interrupted?" she drawls.

I step back, curling my arms around my waist in embarrassment. But Asher doesn't move. Instead he sighs, in what my imagination wants to believe is disappointment.

"Tell Guzman I'll be there in two minutes. And ask him if he wants a drink, please," Asher requests without looking at Roxie.

"Sure thing, boss man." She salutes him, winks at me, then walks out of the room.

Leaving us alone. Again.

"I'm sorry if I made you feel uncomfortable," Asher says softly, rubbing the back of his neck before turning and opening the fridge again. Pulling out a water bottle, he moves towards the door and stops right before he turns the knob. "I *never* want to make you uncomfortable." He walks out, leaving me to overthink things.

Why does he think he makes me that way? I... I know I shouldn't, but I want Asher. And for a moment, it seemed like he wants me, too.

But maybe he just wants us to be friends? Platonic, 'I found her raped and now don't want her romantically' kind of friends.

You know what? I can't even blame him.

Asher

I CAN IMAGINE WALKING AWAY from Jade in general is incredibly hard.

But walking away when she's looking at me like that, with such vulnerability and confusion and trust radiating from her stare? That's a bitch.

Roxie saunters over, raising a pierced eyebrow and instantly sticking her nose where it doesn't belong. "So...what was that?" she asks incredulously.

I take a long drink before setting my water bottle on my desk. "I don't want to talk about it, Roxie," I snap then look to Guzman. "I'm sorry I took so long." As I apologize, I stretch out my drawing hand at my side.

"No problem, Ashe. We've been through this before, I know the drill." He leans his head back and props his arm up.

Sitting down on my chair, I roll back into position, sanitize my hands, and put on new gloves.

"It wasn't nothing, Asher. What is going on with you and that girl?" Roxie, the ever-annoying goth, rattles in my ear. "She's sweet—lost and worried, but very sweet. I like her."

"I like her, too," I admit under my breath. "But that doesn't matter. And I'm working. Go away." Dipping the needle in the navy blue ink, I find comfort in the tool buzzing to life.

"Mr. Guzman doesn't mind, do you?" Roxie looks to the man in the chair, who closes his eyes and shakes his head no. "See! Now spill," she barks. "You totally went all 'overprotective boyfriend' on her earlier."

"Roxie," I snap again. "I will discuss this with you later. Now please—go fuck off."

"Touchy-touchy," she grumbles, crossing her arms and walking off like a wounded puppy just as Jade comes out of the back room. I really hope she ate something. I know she's worried about paying mc back, but I just want her fed.

I glance up every few minutes to look around, and my eyes always gravitate to Jade. The way Roxie did her hair is striking and showcases her natural beauty. Her delicate cheekbones, the light dusting of freckles over her nose. I watch her every movement out of the corner of my eye.

I shake my head, trying to clear it. I need to focus on what I'm doing, otherwise one of my best customers is going to have the wrong shade on his family crest. And he *will* notice. The shop is quiet; the only sound is from the tattoo gun and the soft rock music playing overhead.

Ding, ding. The bell goes off, signaling the door opening and I look up. It's Ty, an artist who rents the other booth and my best friend. He looks rough: a recently received black eye, his brown hair wet and falling in his dark eyes. Ty likes to fight, and he often goes searching for one. Even when I strongly disapprove because more times than not, he finds it easily.

"Need help?" I call out to Ty, but go back to my task.

"No, man. I'm good," he grimaces, and I can see that his lip is split.

"One day you aren't going to be able to walk away from it with just a busted lip and a bruised eye. You know that, right?" I scold.

"I don't need a lecture, Ashe," he snaps, setting his backpack down on his desk and pulling out his overflowing sketchbook. "I have a splitting headache and four clients today. I just want a coffee, an energy drink, pancakes with bacon from Harriet's down the street, and to otherwise be left the hell alone."

"Well, there's pancakes in the back if you want," I reply. "Ask Jade if you can snag those. I did get about three orders of them."

"Who is Jade?" Ty asks, raising an eyebrow involuntarily and wincing.

"You dumbass." I sit up straight, wiping Guzman's skin. "Not you, sir," I clarify.

He chuckles and says, "I understand. Don't worry about me, Asher."

"Again, who's Jade?" Ty asks pointedly, and he's so fucking loud. Louder than anyone I've ever known, except maybe Roxie. How those two haven't been able to get their shit together and actually get together, I don't understand.

"Jade is this kick-ass chick over here. She was Asher's overnight guest who I've decided I'm adopting," Roxie proclaims just as loudly as Ty before wrapping her arm around Jade's shoulders. The blush on Jade's cheeks is cute.

Cute?

"Roxie," I growl through gritted teeth. I'm seriously going to have a talk with her about telling people's fucking business like it's her own to share.

"Jade!" Ty calls with a wink and a finger gun pointed at her. "How are you, doll?"

I see Jade jolt at the nickname and promise to never use it for her. It's obviously a bad thing because her chin starts to quiver, and I notice that she shifts back slightly.

"Back off, Ty." I growl.

"Oooooh, *papi*." Ty rolls his tongue. "We will most definitely be talking about this later," he informs me, but then turns to Jade. Resting his hip against his desk, the look he gives her is one I've seen him give many girls that he wants to take home. "I can see it."

When he says that, Jade's entire demeanor changes. She seems to shake off whatever fear overcame her, because her eyes narrow and she juts out her jaw.

She looks powerful.

And sexy.

Sexy?

"See what?" Jade snaps, crossing her arms over her chest, but not in a way I've seen before. Before it was fearful, scared, protective. Now it's challenging and defiant. She's annoyed.

"What *he* sees." Ty jerks his head to me and answers her with a shrug. "I'm going to eat some of those pancakes and tattoo some cool shit on paying customers," he announces, then walks off toward the back with his muscled shoulders hunched slightly.

"So, uh..." I raise my eyebrows and close my eyes, slightly embarrassed by my best friends. "So, that's Ty. Short for Terecino, but he said he'd knock my lights out if I called him Terry."

"He's hot, but he's a psycho," Roxie stage-whispers to Jade.

Jade quirks an eyebrow and cautiously replies, "He was... nice." I smile because it's obvious she's just trying to be kind. She doesn't have to, though, because Roxie and I look at each other and start laughing.

"He's Ty. He's big, aggressive, and scary, but he'll protect and care for those he deems worthy. Plus, once he's taken pain meds, eaten, and had caffeine, he's a little less... abrupt," I explain, dipping the gun into another color before nodding at Guzman to let him know I'm starting again.

No one says anything else about it. A few minutes later Ty walks out, carrying a takeout box in one hand, an energy drink from his fridge stock in the other, and a fork in his mouth. He stomps right over to his desk and simultaneously starts eating and organizing his work for the day.

It's quiet again; the music playing in the background covers up the girls' soft voices just enough so I can't hear what they're saying.

"You don't need to eavesdrop. I'm sure Roxie will be okay with Jade," Guzman muses quietly. His eyes are closed and his head rests against the seat like a freaking shaman.

"I'm not," I lie through my teeth.

"You are. I'm not even looking at you and I can practically hear *you* straining to hear *them*," he chuckles.

"I don't mean to," I mumble under my breath. My eyes drift to Jade, who's curled up in Roxie's chair while Roxie sketches something and talks incessantly. Her smile is soft and her eyes are bright, like the darkness from last night is fading.

"Son, when you find a girl you can't help but want to protect, want to hold, want to shield against the rest of the world? That's the universe telling you 'This one is *yours*.'" The truth of Guzman's statement hits me like a ton of bricks; so much so that I actually have to sit up.

"After being married for twenty-odd years now, I can tell you: don't fight it. Hold onto her tightly, go at her pace, *be there*. Actions are hard, and words are easy. Remember that." He pats me on the arm with his opposite hand and rests his head back.

I swallow the knot in my throat and shake my head, but my eyes drift right back to her.

Like magnets.

"Way to drop a fucking bomb on me, Guzman," I mumble, wiping his skin and getting back to his design.

"That sucks, girl. I'm sorry," I hear Roxie say, and I stop tattooing. "What are you going to do?"

"I don't know yet. I'll think of something," Jade replies, and I see her phone in her hands.

Pulling my gloves off, I hop off my stool and tell Mr. Guzman, "Let's take a ten-minute break, and then I promise I'll knock out the last little bit within the hour."

Guzman looks up at me with a knowing grin on his face and nods. "Don't even worry."

I march over to Roxie's station and turn the chair so Jade's looking right at me. "What did she say?" My tone is demanding as I lean over her, my arms bracketing her and boxing her in place.

"Which one?" Her eyebrow rises and she bites the inside of her cheek, like she's trying to hold back tears.

"Let me see," I growl, holding my hand out for her to give me the cause of whatever's hurting her right now.

After a moment's hesitation, Jade softly puts her phone face down in my palm. "Don't think less of me," she whispers.

"Why would I..." My voice trails as I see the picture sent from Sarah. My fingers grip the phone tighter and my jaw clenches. Sarah had taken a photo of Jade while she was being raped. What a *bitch*. No, that's too nice. Anger surges in my chest and I have to school my features to remain calm.

"I would never think less of you for this," I tell her softly. "I'm... I'm so incredibly sorry." Maybe I can bust some kneecaps. I personally don't believe in hitting women, but this girl might just be the one that makes me reconsider.

"It gets worse." Jade rests her head against the chair, covering her eyes with her hands. "She sent it to my mother."

My jaw drops. "Your mother?" I go to her messages app and find the multitude of texts her mother has sent her. They are *vile*.

"I didn't take you as a whore, I know I didn't raise one."

"How could you leave Sarah alone like that, what a fucking awful thing to do! To someone that was just trying to be nice to you! How horrible are you?"

"It's like I don't even know you. Don't bother coming home until I've cooled down. Stay with whatever bastard you took from Sarah."

"I can't believe you let someone have sex with you in such a public place. Like a common whore. Like a prostitute. Who have I raised?"

"I can't believe you'd act this way. No, scratch that, I can. You've always wanted attention from men. It's probably your daddy issues."

"I'm so incredibly embarrassed. Of you, of the situation you've put me in. Of how it's going to look to Sarah's mom. You've ruined me, ruined everything."

"Find your own way home and be ready to go to Carver early. I don't want you living in my house."

I resist every urge I have to crush the phone under my fingers and throw it across the room. I grew up in a shitty situation, with a mother who didn't care and made sure I knew it; but fuck, at least I didn't grow up with this bitch. How strong Jade is in my eyes now for enduring such an awful mother in what must have been such trying formative years.

I exhale loudly through my nose, trying to find the right words to say. Ones that will bring her comfort, make her feel safe. The words that will help her overcome this fuckery.

But all I can think of is *murder.*

MURDER.

That's all I can see in Asher's pale eyes as he stares between me and my phone. I watch his fingers grip a little tighter as he reads on, and his chest heaves faster as he becomes more frustrated.

Well, more like enraged.

His eyes flash to mine and he stares me down. It feels like forever that we stare at each other before he exhales roughly.

"Are you safe at home?" He asks this with no finesse, no hesitation. Just straight to the point.

"Yes," I say immediately. The rehearsed half-truth comes naturally, but I subconsciously move to cover myself.

"Jade," he growls, stepping closer into my space. So close, my breathing quickens with a mixture of fear and want. "Do. You. Feel. Safe?"

Standing straighter, our chests touch, but I'm not going to be pushed around. This guy... Asher, he seems like he'd never lay a hand on a woman to harm them.

I have a good radar for that by now.

I don't shy away from him. In fact, I lean closer.

"That's none of your business."

His nostrils flare up with indignation and he looks around quickly. I note both Ty and Roxie are gawking at us, like we're their new favorite soap opera and all they're missing is the popcorn. Mr. Guzman actually looks like he's fallen asleep. Asher grabs my arm, and I panic.

I scramble out of his arms and rush backwards until I hit the front desk. My chest tightens, and my body jerks even though my mind *knows* that Asher won't hurt me.

"Jade, wait," he pleads while trying to follow me.

Roxie is much quicker, standing between us with her hands up in front of her. "Hold it," she barks.

"Roxie, you don't understand." Stuttering, Asher tries to step forward again, but Roxie doesn't budge. "I'd never, I didn't... Jade, I'm sorry," he insists.

His eyes meet mine and regret is clear on his face.

I huff in embarrassment. "It's fine, oh my god, it's nothing." I shake my head and try to dispel this fear. It's misplaced and makes me feel out of control. Like I'm crazy for reacting this way when he's only ever helped me. Tears prick my eyes, but I straighten my shoulders. "God, Asher, I'm sorry," I insist.

Roxie nods at me and I see an understanding flash in her eyes. She steps aside and Asher rushes to me. "Can we please talk in the back?" he begs.

"Sure. Yes," I nod.

"If Guzman wakes up, tell him I need to sort out some things and his last hour is on me," Asher throws out over his shoulder before guiding me to the back, leaving at least a foot of space between us.

Closing the door behind him, Asher turns so we are facing each other, and I have to apologize.

"I don't know why I did that. I'm so sorry! Fuck, I'm so

embarrassed," I mumble as a stray tear falls down my cheek. It's been so fucking exhausting. So hard.

I try to sit down, but the chair scrapes along the floor loudly. I set my head down on the table with all the food on it, still untouched from when Asher bought it.

"No, Jade. No." Asher sits down gently, and I look up at the sound of his voice. His hand snakes out, like he wants to touch me again, but doesn't.

And that's all my fault. *Shit.*

"You have nothing to be sorry for or embarrassed about. *I'm* the one that's sorry. I shouldn't have grabbed your arm out of nowhere—or at all. I just want us to talk about how fucking completely awful your mother is and what I can do to help. I got mad—I *am* mad—but not at you," Asher explained sincerely.

"I don't know what happened," I admit softly. "I... I trust that you're not going to hurt me, but the moment you grabbed me like that, I jolted and ran. *I know* it wasn't like last night, but it's like my body didn't know it." I pull at the roots of my hair. What is wrong with me? Why is this all happening at once? Or at all?

Clutching my hair, I drop my head to the table with a painful *thunk.*

"Jade," Asher says softly, almost a whisper. "There is no right or wrong way to handle what you're feeling. Whatever you're feeling, it's valid."

Lifting my head slowly, our eyes meet, and I can see how much he means it.

"I'm so embarrassed that happened in front of everyone," I lament, covering my face in my hands.

"Oh, you can't be embarrassed in front of those two. They're insane," he chuckles. "Roxie understands. I understand. Ty would too, if he knew." He believes in his found little family so much, I can't help but be jealous.

"Anyway," I sniffle and sit up straighter, trying to change the subject. Fuck, my life is such a mess. "You wanted to say something before?"

"Ah," Asher sighs, sitting back. He rubs the back of his neck and then leans forward on his elbows on the table. "I just got really angry that your mother thinks of you like that. That she said those things to you, about you. It's just disgusting *of her*," he sneers, clenching his jaw as he speaks. "I wanted to talk to you in private so we could make a plan."

"We?" I repeat, cocking my head to the side.

"Yes, we," Asher repeats, as if this is just a conversation about the weather. "Haven't I already said that I'm here to help?"

I drop my hands to the table loudly. "Do you even know what you're suggesting? What you're offering?" I question, my voice sounding foreign.

"To be honest, not exactly." *Well, I can give him credit for being upfront.* Asher runs a hand through his dark hair. "But I do know that I want to help. Let me drive you home, or you can crash at my place again tonight if you need time away from your mom."

"Why are you doing this?" I ask, my voice strained. "I know you told me there are good people in the world, but that's maybe buying a meal, letting someone crash at your place, intervening when necessary. But you're offering to help even though you could easily just wash your hands of me and this bullshit. So why?"

Asher sighs and folds his hands together, looking down at his fingers.

"Look, there are some things in my past that... have hit close to home with your situation. I don't like talking about that shit. Just trust me when I tell you I'm being genuine in my offer to help, in any way I can. There's nothing wrong with having a true friend," he surmises.

Scrutinizing him, looking into his eyes, I'm struck again with how I do believe him.

"You're telling me the truth, aren't you?" I confirm.

"Yes," he says and nods.

Sighing, I know I need to accept his help. My mother has all but kicked me out, and if I'm being brutally honest, I'd rather move as far away from that woman as soon as possible.

"Can you drive me back to my mom's house later? I need to pack and decide where to stay before classes start. If I even go to college at all." I try not to sound like I'm looking for pity, but I'm devastated.

Asher's eyebrows shoot up. "Do you not want to go?"

Shrugging, I say, "I really don't know... but I do know I want out of that house. Away from someone who thinks I'm no better than a chivying bitch out to hurt others."

"You do realize that if you go home today, she might be... worse?" The way he says it sounds like a question. Like he knows just as well as I do that the moment I step through that door, my mother is going to become someone unrecognizable. I know that. If she was able to *send* me those things, there's no doubt in my mind that she is more than willing to spit them at me violently as I actively ignore her.

"I know," I agree solemnly. "But what choice do I really have?"

Asher shakes his head in frustration but relents. "Fine, I'll drive you tonight after I'm finished with Guzman." He stands up, huffing in annoyance. I don't know him well, but even I can tell his annoyance is due to the fact that his hands are basically tied. There's nothing for him to do.

"Thank you again." I grab his hand as he turns to leave, bringing his attention back to me. "For your kindness."

Asher turns to face me, and slowly, softly, cups my cheek with his free hand. His rough, tattooed palm is astonishingly gentle against my skin as he caresses my cheekbone.

With a subtle nod, he rips his hand away and turns, leaving the back room before I can say anything else.

Or ask *what the hell that was.*

———

"Is Asher a...good guy?" I ask Roxie, not looking at her but instead keeping my eyes on Asher as he's hunched over Mr. Guzman's arm. He's working intently, trying to finish the tattoo I've so annoyingly interrupted like three times.

Roxie's sitting at her desk, working on her own design for something and god, it's beautiful. A koi fish wrapped around the outline of an arm, with waves curling around and florals interwoven. She's done it in thick lines that look like the other kind of older tattoos I've seen. She's shading the colors when I walk up and lean against her desk.

"The best, actually," she answers without looking up. "Why?"

"So, if he offers something, he's not just *saying* it?" I ask as nonchalantly as possible.

Roxie puts the orange-colored pencil down and glances at me with a raised, pierced eyebrow and a quizzical expression. Crossing her arms over her chest, she cocks her head to the side, looking at me like she's trying to figure me out.

"Let's go get a drink," she suggests, standing abruptly and grabbing her bag.

"Ashe, Ty! Jade and I are heading out for a coffee. We'll be back later. Don't miss us too much," Roxie announces to the room, and both guys barely look her way.

"But do you—" Asher starts to ask something, but Roxie just *tsks* her tongue at him. He sighs, pulling back from Mr. Guzman and wiping his arm before looking up at us. "When will you be back?" he asks instead.

"We'll be back when we're done," Roxie states firmly with a flip of her hair before pulling me along.

Asher looks at me with a question in his eyes, clear as day. *Are you okay with this?* I nod and give him what I hope is a reassuring smile.

"Okay," he says reluctantly with a nod. Those blue eyes make me feel protected and strong once again. "Call me if you need me."

I know he's talking to me, but Roxie answers him. "Will do, big bro!" she chimes, then rolls her eyes and pulls me out the front door. The bell dings above us and she takes a deep breath of the warm early-summer air.

"Is Asher actually your brother?" I ask, gesturing to him with my thumb through the painted glass of the front window. It's a gorgeous phoenix, rising from smoke with its wings spread. Its colors are magnificent. It looks like someone took paint and literally created the design *on* the window, but I saw some merch inside with the same logo. Either way, it's amazing. I follow Roxie down the street as she laughs boisterously, throwing her head back and letting the sound out joyfully into the world.

"No! No. He acts like it enough, though." She smiles and continues, "You know the whole story; he took me in and helped me become the kick-ass tattoo artist I am today. And now he thinks he has to protect me all the time. Just like a stray he's adopted. Proudly, I might add."

"Oh," I say softly. My eyebrows inch together as I process the new information. Is that what he's doing with me?

Downtown Carver is quaint. It's a small town whose only real traffic comes from the college. The downtown area is older and more antique, with shops and restaurants to try and entice tourists. The tattoo shop is actually in the perfect spot along the long strip of West 3rd Street—Carver's 'Main Street.' It's right in the middle with dedicated parking spots, instead of making patrons park two blocks down in a public parking lot.

I can imagine this place at Christmas. All the shop windows would be frosted over and adorned with lights. Wreathes on the lamp posts. I bet it's beautiful.

Roxie stops and opens a door for me, ushering me inside. This must be the diner. It's busy, filled with people in almost every booth and even some sitting at the bar, chatting with the cook at the grill. It's loud, and it smells heavenly. Just like the meal I ate way too much of earlier today.

"Roxanne!" a musically deep voice rings out, cutting through the other conversations.

"Harriet, you know I hate it when you call me that," Roxie groans, but reluctantly hugs the sweet Black woman who demands one from her wordlessly.

"Oh shush, I've known you since you were a baby, and you lived with me for a year! I'm going to call you what I'm going to call you." Harriet smirks proudly at Roxie before turning to me. "And who might you be?"

"Harriet, this is Jade. Another *From The Ashes* recruit." Roxie smiles widely at me.

"Oh, no, I'm just... Jade," I finish lamely, not actually knowing what else I was going to say.

"Well, 'just Jade,'" Harriet smiles at me welcomingly, "you're always welcome here. And if you're hanging out with those kids down the street, you'll be just fine. I know it. Hell, I've seen it." She chuckles, taking two menus and handing them to Roxie, then pointing us to the open back booth.

"Go on, now." Harriet waves us along, and I can't help but feel seen. She has this aura, this energy, that you can't quite ignore—nor do you want to.

"We better do as she says, or she'll get cranky." Roxie walks away, waving to people left and right before sliding into one side of the booth.

"You know everyone," I muse.

"When you've lived here your whole life, move from place to place as a foster kiddo and wind up raised a little bit by everyone, there's one or two good people you gain in your life." Roxie explains.

Nodding, I curl my lips together, not knowing how to respond. My upbringing was comfortable, plush and filled with necessary, albeit materialistic, things. But my dad wasn't in the picture, and my mom continues to blame me for it. So, my moving away is a dream come true for her. I doubt I'll hear much from her once I leave.

"Good riddance," Roxie retorts, scoffing at what I must have said out loud. My cheeks burn with a blush. I didn't mean to get that deep with someone I barely know, no matter how well we already seem to get on. "Seriously, life is much too short to be surrounded by people who drain your peace."

"Even if they're blood?"

"Especially if they're blood." Roxie nods, waving over a college-aged girl with an apron on, and orders coffee for us. "Wait," she paused, halfway through ordering, "do you drink coffee?"

Normally, I'd say it's fine and choke down the liquid, but

Roxie's given me confidence and a hell of a lot to think about in the few hours I've known her.

"I really don't, actually. Can I just have a Coke?" I order, sitting up straighter with a cautious grin.

Roxie smirks and nods at the waitress, waiting for her to leave before turning to face me. I can tell she is dying to ask the burning questions I know she has.

"Look..." Roxie clears her throat and lowers her voice. "I know we just met, so I don't expect you to tell me every little thing about your life or what you've gone through. I'm an open book, and I totally get that not everyone is like that. But... I can see you're struggling a little, and your energy..." She waves both hands in my face. "Your whole aura is muted."

I shake my head and feel myself deflate. "I don't know what you mean," I try to persuade her.

"Ah, but you do." Roxie narrows an eye at me accusingly. "And like I said, you don't have to tell me. But I did notice something before; something I've been through myself and want to offer some help if you want."

I swallow, looking at her suspiciously. "What do you mean?"

Roxie holds my gaze and says, "You jumped and ran from Asher when he moved toward you too quickly." I drop my gaze to the table, wanting to ignore all of this already. "That was a very specific type of jump; one that only someone who has gone through it too knows what it is from." My eyes flash up to her as she speaks, and I nod. Roxie looks at me with concern. "Was it Asher?"

My face blanches and I jump to his defense. "No, no! Absolutely not. Asher... he found me... after." I can barely get the words out.

"Oh god." Roxie covers her mouth with her hand. "Well, thank fucking god."

What?

My face must speak for me because Roxie immediately backtracks. "I just meant thank god it wasn't Asher. I'd have to castrate him myself." She shakes her head. "I'm not going to push for more information but just know I'm here if you need someone to talk to. Especially someone who knows what you're going through and how hard it is. Asher is great, but he's fully in protector mode."

"Thank you," I reply meekly. Our waitress comes over with our drinks, giving me a moment to think about what to do. Should I confide in her and hope she won't fuck me over like every other person I've tried to trust?

"Thanks, Leslie," Roxie says, taking a sip of the coffee. I unwrap my straw and take a sip of my drink, enjoying the small sugar rush. "If you don't mind, I'd like to tell you about what happened to me. Maybe that will help you be a little more at peace, knowing you're not completely alone. I wish I'd had someone there for me," she admits quietly. Her normal confidence and charm is suddenly gone as she gets lost in the past.

I shake my head vehemently. "I don't... I can't... Please, no details," I urge. I get what she's saying. I understand why she's offering. But I just don't know if I can hear 'exacts.' Not after what I went through.

"Of course," Roxie agrees kindly, patting my hand. "I don't want to make things harder for you, so if it's too much, just let me know. I won't be offended." She wraps both hands around her coffee mug, as if to absorb the warmth. "I was young, probably a little younger than you are, and I was on my own for the first time. He was someone I met in a bar I'd gotten into with my fake ID, and we'd been flirting all night. At the end of the night when I decided I'd had enough and wanted to go home, I said goodbye and paid my tab, but this guy... he didn't like that. He said I 'owed him' for taking up his evening. That I was asking for it all night and he was *deserving*." She scoffs and my jaw drops. "I thought I could fight him off, but he was so much stronger than I was. The drinks didn't help, and as I was trying to get out of the bar, he followed me and grabbed my arm. No one helped, no one cared—they just watched this guy manhandle me. No one did a goddamned thing." Roxie's eyes mist over at the memory, and I nod, biting my lip to keep from saying anything.

"After it happened, I sobered up and ran off. I felt disgusting, used, gross. I just wanted out of my skin. Everyone who looked at me posed a threat; everyone who offered me kindness wanted something else. It took me a long time not to jump like you did any time someone rushed towards me."

"I couldn't help it," I whisper.

"Neither could I. It still happens every once in a while, and it's out of my control. It's a self-defense thing; your body and mind trying to protect themselves. Nothing to be ashamed of." Roxie puts a warm hand on my forearm before tipping her lips up in a sad smile. "Trust and decency are hard to come by, but even harder after you've been violated like that."

"Yeah," I mutter frustratedly.

"Is that why you were asking if Asher is a good guy?"

I nod, taking another sip.

"Like I said, Asher is a protector. It's all he's ever known really. That's not to say the guy is a saint. He fights and has beaten the shit out of people, but they've always deserved it. He drinks and fucks around when he feels the urge, but he'd never lay a hand on a woman if they were unwilling. The biggest thing I've learned about Asher in all the years I've known him is that if he says something, he means it."

A sigh of relief that I didn't know I was holding leaves my body and tears line my eyes.

"I'm just so tired," I sigh, the tears and watery emotion clear in my voice.

"Oh honey, I know." Roxie takes my hand in hers. "I *know*."

I can't hold back my thoughts anymore. "I don't know who to trust. My mother is horrible. The girl I went to the party with is telling lies and I'm sure my whole town knows it. Asher is here, offering me help and I don't want to inconvenience him, but I also don't know what else to do. I have two weeks before the dorms open and I don't even think I want to go to college. My mom just pushed me towards it, and I thought it was the next logical step."

"Okay, okay." Roxie waves both hands in front of her in a 'this-is-too-much' motion. "Those are all things in the future. You need to focus smaller—one thing at a time. First things first, getting your shit and getting to the dorms. I assume you want to move there because it's paid for already?" she asks.

I nod, feeling a pang of anxiety starting to form in my chest.

"Then that's your first step. Go home, pack your shit, ignore *everything*, and get here. Once you're in Carver, Asher, Ty and I can help you with anything you need."

"Why?" I ask, yet again. "Why do you guys' care? Why are you putting yourselves out on a limb to help someone you barely know? *Why?*"

Roxie smiles warmly. "I'm helping you because you seem like a cool person who just needs a little support. I don't have many friends, especially not girlfriends, but I think you and I could become besties. It's a win-win." She shrugs.

"You... want to be friends with me?" I ask incredulously. No one wants to be friends with me. This whole situation came from being forced into creating a friendship with someone.

"I do." She smiles brightly.

"I don't really know how to be friends with people." What a fucking embarrassing thing to admit to someone.

"That's okay. Me either. But I think the first step is getting a drink and talking about our troubles." Roxie raises her coffee cup to me in cheers. I lift my cup and clink against hers.

"So, what are you going to school for?" she asks, taking a sip and relaxing back into the booth, like we're two *friends* just catching up.

"What do I *want* to go for or what am I *enrolled* for?"

"Oh, there's a story." Her eyebrows raise as she continues, "But I want to know what you *want* to do. Fuck whatever anyone else wants you to do."

A true smile crosses my face. "Art, actually," I share honestly.

"What a coincidence that you've met some people who happen to be really badass at all things artistic!" Roxie smirks and winks at me, and I know then that I can trust these people.

THEY HAVE BEEN GONE a long time.

Too long, really.

I don't want to storm into the diner, crashing whatever little coffee date they're having just because I feel like I need to have Jade in my sights at all times. It doesn't make any sense. And unfortunately, I'm well aware that I have no claim on Jade.

There was one near-kiss, but that doesn't mean anything.

Does it? Fuck.

I feel like a teenager instead of my seasoned twenty-five years. Like I'm starting to develop a crush that won't leave my mind.

I shake my head and count the stack of cash Guzman left. He's been coming to me for years, so I know he won't have screwed me over, and he always leaves a hefty tip. I made sure to dock his last hour since I kept him longer than needed, but the old man just smirked and patted my shoulder, saying, "Don't be an idiot about things. You're a smart kid who grew up too fast, but you've done well for yourself. Be sure to make some impulsive decisions every now and then, too."

Sage, old wiseman.

"What do you think is taking them so long?" I grumble, not for the first time since the girls left two hours ago.

"*Oh dios.* I don't know, Ashe," Ty sighs, wiping away the ink and blood from his client. "If you're going to get your panties in a twist, why don't you just go talk to her?"

"No, no. That'd be weird." I wipe down my chair for the third time. "Wouldn't it?"

"For fuck's sake. *Estúpido,*" Ty groans. "They're girls. You know how Roxie is, she doesn't shut up. And apparently," Ty widens his eyes and circles his hand in an overly dramatic gesture I don't appreciate, "your girl is going through some stuff. Let them work through it."

He's right. Damn it, I hate it when he's right.

"Also, stop being so fucking pussy whipped," Ty drawls, dipping his needle in ink and getting back to work.

"You're fucking lucky you're inking someone up right now or you and I would be in the street," I snap, disgusted that he'd even say something like that. "Be a decent human being."

"Oh, relax, *papi.*" He shakes his head, never looking away from his work.

"Read the fucking room." My voice booms as I yell at him, and his second client, who is waiting in the lobby, jumps.

Just as he makes eye contact with me, I hear the bell over the door jingle, and I hope for Ty's sake it's Jade and Roxie.

"Uh, oh. Did you guys watch porn together or something? Why is there so much tension?" Roxie rolls her eyes and makes the whole room uncomfortable but keeps me from wanting to kill my best friend.

"*Hermosa mujer loca.* Why do you always have to make it so weird?" Ty asks, never looking up.

"You wouldn't have me any other way," she boasts, blowing a kiss to him—one that I know he'll hold close to his heart like the pining bastard he is—and skips over to her station, while Jade just shakes her head at Roxie's antics and giggles.

She looks lighter. Like she's not as burdened as she was when she left, and for that, I'll need to thank Roxie.

She might be the pseudo-little sister who is a constant pain in my ass, but she's a good person to have in your corner. She's a good person, period.

"Hey," Jade greets me softly, stepping over to my station and taking a closer look at all my things. She's observant, with a keen eye for art. I've noticed this as I've watched her today, and I like it. "Did you do all these?" she asks, pointing to the framed work.

"I wish I could say I did, but no. Some, yes." I move to the side of my corkboard hanging over my desk, the side I save for the really intriguing ideas and sketches I can't perfect. "The sketches here... these are mine."

"Wow," she breathes, and I feel my chest puff with pride. "You are able to do so many different styles." She steps closer, leaning over the desk so her back arches slightly and her ass sticks out. I do my best not to ogle, but I'm only human.

She's not wrong. I've spent years perfecting as many different tattooing styles as I can; traditional, fine line, watercolor, Japanese, new school, tribal—the list goes on. I wanted to be able to say yes to whatever a client wanted when they came in with an idea and a wish, so I got to learning.

"It took a long time, a lot of practice," I offer, shrugging my shoulders like it's not a big deal.

"What's your favorite?" Her green eyes sparkle at me with intrigue.

"Traditional, probably. Or maybe that's just the style I do most often. It was the first style I learned." I point to a framed sketch on the wall by the corkboard. "That was the first piece I ever designed; it's probably still my favorite to this day." It was a labor of love. The client wanted a piece to celebrate recording his first demo album. He came in with a specific idea and trusted me to bring it to life. He wanted a guitar, an old school microphone, the lyrics 'It's only going to get better from here,' wrapped around the instruments, all while being surrounded by roses and music notes. It came out beautiful. And the client was happy, so I was happy.

"It's amazing," Jade compliments with a smile, leaning in closer to look at the drawing that's faded over years of exposure to light.

"Thanks," I reply. I can tell she's interested, looking at each piece with a new hunger. She had the same look at my apartment, but it was softer. More awe. "So, what did you decide?"

Jade sighs deeply, stepping back from my desk much to my inner dismay, and crosses her arms over her chest. "Couldn't let me stay in a good mood?" she groans.

I chuckle. "Sorry, darlin', I just wanted to know what the plan was. I'm a planner."

"Honestly, me too." She grins and it makes me happy to see. She's been through too much, relying on people she doesn't know and hoping that shit doesn't get worse for her. And that's just been the last twenty-four hours.

Jade sighs, dropping her head in reluctance before turning to me. I'm not one to have girls hang around past breakfast the next morning—I *am* a gentleman, after all—any longer than that usually makes my skin crawl. With Jade, though, I find myself not wanting to see her leave. My protective instincts are screaming at me, but I don't want to seem like a creeper.

"I should go home," she admits. "Face my mom and the bullshit Sarah's been spewing, then in two weeks I'll be back here. Alone and independent. Officially on my own." Jade stands straighter, like she's facing a battle head-on. With her hair done in the Viking braids, she looks like she could very well ride into a battle and *win*.

"I don't want to. I know it's going to be hard as fuck. But I think... I think it's something I need to do." Her eyes sparkle with determination and I nod. I get it. I really do.

"Let's go," I suggest, closing up my drawer and picking up my phone. Jade takes a steadying breath and moves to pick up her bag and her phone. That fucking thing took forever to charge, but at least I know she actually has her phone on her and it won't die soon. The messages from her mom and Sarah kept coming in while she was gone. I almost turned the damned thing off. Okay, okay; if I'm being honest, I *actually* almost read each and every one of them to know what I'm literally driving her back to.

I didn't, I didn't. But my self-control was being held by a fucking thread.

Jade goes to Roxie and gives her a hug; a tight whole-body hug that makes me seethe with jealousy. Roxie leans back, gives her a piece of paper and speaks in a low tone, which of course ensures I can't hear them over the music and Ty's tattoo gun buzzing. Roxie cups Jade's cheek and my fists clench. I have to turn my head when I see Jade hug her again.

Why do I care so fucking much?

Because this girl, who I only just met, has me wrapped around her finger. I know it.

I turn back just in time to find Ty looking at me with a knowing, annoying smirk before he goes back to work.

"Ready?" Jade asks, to which I nod.

"Let's go." I gesture with my head to the front door where I've parked off to the side.

"Don't forget what I said! I'm expecting to see your ass in this building in fourteen days, Henderson!" Roxie yells from her station.

Jade turns around with a laugh and an easy smile. "I promised, didn't I?" she calls, then Jade waves and walks out.

I stop at the door and look at Roxie with a 'what was that' glare and she rolls her eyes. "Be a good *friend*, Lee. She needs one," she warns.

"You don't need to tell him that. He wants to be more," Ty shouts in his gravelly tone. Dropping a mic without even trying, like the fucker always seems to do.

"Shut up, Ty," I mumble under my breath and let the door close behind me.

Jade leans on the passenger door of my dark blue, beat-up Honda. It's nothing fancy, but it's reliable; honestly, most of the time I use my bike, so it doesn't make sense to get anything newer. Even though I could kick myself for it now.

Unlocking the door, we both climb in and get situated. She said it was a three-hour drive and so we settle in for the long trip. I turn the ignition and look at Jade, taking in her sweet face.

"Know any good car games?" I ask.

***

THREE HOURS GOES BY INSANELY FAST.

After stopping at a rest stop to fill up the car with gas—and our arms with goodies—we get on the highway and talk. Jade is easy to talk to. She's open and curious; she asked interesting questions and offered information. I was almost expecting her to clam up and for the drive to be awkward, but it seems like she's finally starting to trust me.

I learn so much about her; she loves art, she's going to school for business at her mother's demand, but dreams about drawing all day long without any interruptions. Jade graduated high school with honors and got a free ride to Kensington, which she took even though she wasn't completely sure she wanted to go. She doesn't have a boyfriend, and she blushes a beautiful bright red when I ask if she has ever had one. My knuckles grip the steering wheel a little tighter when she asks me the same question and I have to figure out a way to describe my 'dating' situation. And by that, I mean one-night stands I pick up every once in a while, but never anything serious. I've never found someone I want *more* with than just the physical side.

She gives me a tight grin and a jolty nod before changing the subject to how I got into tattooing.

We talk and talk and talk. And what's more, I actually enjoy it.

She smiles, she laughs, and her whole being lights up. I find myself smiling and laughing along with her.

But the closer we get to her town, the more her light dims. I don't know if she was checking or had checked her messages while we talked, but as I exit the highway, she starts to subconsciously curl into herself, wrapping her arms around her stomach, crossing her legs and hunching over slightly.

The mood shifts and I can't blame her for it. I'm also incredibly concerned about leaving her here. I've been thinking about it the whole fucking drive—about how I'm going to have to watch her physically leave my presence and go into a place I know harms her.

A little voice in the back of my mind whispers at me to just turn around, take her back to my house and keep her safe.

But I know I can't do that.

And that'd be fucking weird if I asked her to stay with me... right?

The GPS goes off, telling me we have five minutes left before we pull up to Jade's house, and we both are silent.

"Look, Jade," I swallow nervously. "Can I get your number?"

Her head snaps to the side, looking at me with shock. "Wait, really?"

"Yeah," I reply. I reposition myself, scooting down in my seat to hold onto the shifter. The GPS signals for me to turn and I follow it, turning into a residential area. I try to slow down without her realizing it. We have less than two minutes now, and I'm not ready for it to end.

"Yeah, okay." The smile Jade gives me is shy and true. It's adorable. "And before we get there and my evil mother comes to collect me, I want to tell you how thankful I am. I don't know what would've happened to me if someone else found me last night..." I grit my teeth at the memory of her drugged, naked, and alone in that room. "You've been so kind, so generous. I truly am indebted to you, Asher. If you don't call or message me, I won't blame you. But...I really hope you do," she admits hopefully. "Thank you, for everything."

I pull up next to the house number she gave me. It's a white house with blue shutters and two big open windows on either side of a red front door. I park, and before I can even turn to her in my seat, a slender woman with dark hair and dark eyes comes storming down the front steps.

"Told you," Jade groans and takes a deep breath. "Trust me, get away from here as fast as you can. It's not going to be pretty." There's a joking tone to her voice; I can tell she's trying to be funny about the whole thing, but I'm pretty certain her words are true.

It won't be a nice sight.

"I'm going to text you," I promise. I grab her hand and shove a pen into it before pulling my flannel sleeve up so she can write her number on my arm. Based on how her mother looks, I don't have enough time to get my phone out and actually save her information. Jade neatly scrawls her number on a small patch of untattooed skin on my wrist.

"Thank you." She smiles sadly, almost like she doesn't think I'm going to.

"I am," I say again, stronger. "Fourteen days, Jade. Fourteen and you'll be out of here. Stay strong." *I'll help.*

She nods and gathers her duffle bag before taking a deep breath and climbing out of my car.

"What the hell do you think you're doing here?" I hear her mother hiss from where she's standing with her arms crossed.

Jade looks at me with kindness, whispering, "Bye, Asher," and I hope the desperation to keep her with me and safe isn't as overwhelmingly splattered across my face like I feel it in my body.

"Bye, Jade. I'll talk to you soon," I stress, not breaking her gaze. She shuts the door, and it feels like there's a finality in it; like she knows she's not going to hear from me.

Oh darlin', how wrong you are.

Asher

Nine Days Later...

I'M SITTING at my desk at work, waiting for my next client, when a meme of Michael Scott yelling *"Noooooooooo!"* pops up from Jade. Chuckling, I text her back, telling her that it's fine.

My client was given the wrong time by the receptionist. Again. Now my whole day is fucked because this girl doesn't take her job seriously. I messaged Jade to tell her how I'm so annoyed because now my night is going to go even later. I was really hoping to be able to go home early, watch a show that Jade demanded I watch—which, secretly, I'm now obsessed with, but refuse to tell her that because I'll never hear the end of it—eat my dumb meal prep of chicken and rice, and pass the fuck out. But now, because of freaking Holly, I'm going to have to be here for at least three extra hours.

Don't get me wrong, I love my shop and the people here, but I want to go home.

"Something needs to be done about Holly, man. *Esa chica tonta, lo juro por Dios, Asher. Arreglarlo,*" Ty snaps, coming over to my station and throwing down a receipt. I know he's really annoyed when Spanish flows from his lips this freely.

Sighing, I put my phone down and pick up the receipt. "What happened now?" I ask.

"She doesn't know how to run the fucking machine and overcharged my client by $600!" he shouts. Thankfully Holly ran to lunch, so I don't have to make Ty control his volume. I groan, dropping the receipt and running both hands over my face. "They were understanding about it, and luckily it's one of my repeat customers," he continues. "What if it wasn't, and they blasted it all over that a tattoo by someone at *From The Ashes* is insanely priced and no one knows what the fuck they're doing? *Si pierdo clientes por esto, voy a perder la cabeza. También es malo para tu negocio, ¡así que haz algo al respecto!*"

He's right to be so mad. Tattooing, especially in a small town with other shops close by, thrives on word of mouth and recommendations *a lot*. One bad review and all the hard work we've done to make sure our reviews are immaculate goes out the window.

Holly could've lost us a lot of clients, which would mess with our livelihood. To mis-schedule a client is one thing, but a charging mistake of this magnitude...

"I'll talk to her," I promise, groaning at the inevitable awful conversation that's just been penciled into my future.

"Seriously, Ash. This isn't rocket science and she's messing with my clients. Fix it, or I will." Ty points a finger on the table roughly and I roll my eyes. *"Eres mi hermano y no dejaré que esto siga así."*

"Calm down, brother. I said I'll handle it," I snap.

"You know who would be a great receptionist?" Roxie drawls from across the room, sanitizing her station and her utensils seriously before looking up at me. "Jade."

"*Ooooh!*" Ty nods and raises his eyebrows, looking at me with a teasing smirk. "I can see that."

"She's not here, though," I shrug. I couldn't agree with her outwardly, but I would hire Jade in a heartbeat. I didn't waste any time messaging her after I left nine days ago, sending a simple text as soon as I got home: *"I told you I would."* Since then, we've basically talked nonstop.

Jade's the first person I talk to every morning, and the last one I talk to every night. More than that, she is the first thought I have when I wake up and the last thought I have before I go to sleep.

I can't wait to have her here. I offered to help move her into her dorm and she gladly agreed... after I talked her into it a little.

She was reluctant to let me help; her mother told Jade she would be driving the rest of her stuff so that Jade wouldn't bother her every other day for something. Her mother is a real piece of work. All the shit Jade's told me over the last nine days has not helped my rage. Or my guilt for leaving Jade with her.

Only five days left until she is out of that house.

"No, but she will be," Roxie smirks. "Maybe sooner than later."

My eyes snap to hers. "What?"

Roxie shrugs. "She was telling me that her mom is forcing her out a few days early, so I offered for her to crash on my couch until the dorms open up. She'll be here tomorrow."

"What?!" I say louder than I mean to. Ty smirks, raising an eyebrow and crossing his arms over his chest.

Embarrassment floods my chest, but I force myself past it, clear my throat, and try again. "I mean, what? She didn't say anything to me."

"She probably didn't want to bother you. You know how she is." Roxie shrugs again and goes back to organizing her ink bottles.

"But we talk all the time…" I'm so confused.

"Yeah? So do we," Roxie replies like it's not a big deal.

"Damn, do I need to get this chick's number and start chatting her up, too? Should we make a group chat?" Ty laughs, but it's not fucking funny. Jade isn't up for grabs.

"Don't even think about it."

"Relax, relax, *papi*. I know she's yours." He holds his hands up before checking his watch and jumping to the reception area.

"Seriously, Roxie," I turn back towards the offender I *thought* was one of my closest friends. "She's coming to town early? I was supposed to move her into the dorms. When is she coming in tomorrow?" *Wait a damned minute.* "Is this why you took tomorrow off?" I snap as realization kicks in.

Roxie sighs deeply and mutters, "I told her this would happen." She turns to me with a frustrated look on her face. "Don't make this a big deal, Ashe."

I shrug, trying not to make it obvious that I'm feeling some kind of way about the situation. "I'm not."

"Oh my god. You're just as gone for her, aren't you?" Her mouth drops open, like she's surprised I'm showing this amount of emotion.

That's not the part that stops me. "Just *as*?" I stammer.

Consider my interest *very* peaked.

Her eyes roll so far back the whites are all I see. "Really?" she groans.

"What?"

"Just be at my house tomorrow morning at nine," Roxie tells me. "You can help me figure out where to store all her shit until she can get into the dorms."

"Okay, I can do that." I nod, going back to my phone and typing out a quick message to Jade before I notice my next appointment walk in. "Should I tell her?" I ask Roxie, trying to appear nonchalant.

"That you like her?" She pauses, thinking of the best approach. "Maybe give it a little time; build more of an in-person relationship before you drop that on her. But yes, you should—soon. Until then, keep being her friend," Roxie answers before going back to organizing..

"No—that I know she's coming? Maybe I could bring coffee?" I ponder.

Roxie turns to me slowly with an awed look on her face. "You know what, Asher, I think you surprising her would be sweet."

I wave at my customer, motioning for him to come back past the reception desk.

"Don't bring coffee, though," she suddenly adds. "Your girl isn't a coffee drinker. She likes full-sugar Coca-Cola to wake up."

"Really?" I ask, my eyebrows knitting together as I groan. "Fuck."

"What?"

"I made her coffee the day she stayed at my house. I wondered why she didn't drink it."

Roxie chuckles. "Don't worry. You definitely didn't lose any brownie points with her over that, bro."

THE NEXT MORNING, I'M AWKWARDLY HOLDING A TO-go carrier of soft drinks for us all as I knock on Roxie's apartment door. I made sure to show up a few minutes early, but damn, nine in the morning came really fucking quickly. The perks to owning your own business—especially a tattoo shop—is that I usually get to sleep in until ten every morning.

I yawn, waiting for Roxie to open the door, and check my watch. I'm five minutes early, but she should be awake.

"I wanted to do something nice to welcome you to town, and after hearing that, I'm glad I did. Surprise!" I hear Roxie say cheerfully, and there's a *woosh* as the door opens.

Revealing Jade, standing in the middle of Roxie's living room.

With a fucking black eye and busted lip.

"Jade," I whisper and rush forward, shoving the drinks into Roxie's hands. Being very, *painfully* aware that she might recoil, I step into Jade's space, but she doesn't flinch away from me. Her green eyes are lined with tears, but I don't know if they're happy or if she's in pain. "Who did this to you?" I growl, my fingers ghosting over her hurt skin.

"It's okay," she whispers back and wraps her hands around my forearms. She's holding onto me like I'm a lifeline—or am I projecting that? *Maybe she's mine.* "It doesn't matter anymore. I'm out of there." A tear drops from her bruised eye, and I gently wipe it with my thumb.

"Your mother did this to you?" Rage swirls in my chest; tension forms throughout my body with the effort to keep from scooping Jade into my arms or going to her mother and making her pay.

"It's okay," she whispers, covering my hand with hers.

"It's not. It's really fucking not, Jade. Why didn't you say anything?" I press.

"Yeah, Jade," Roxie snaps, putting the drinks on her small coffee table. "Why didn't you say anything?"

"Shut up, Roxanne," Jade snaps back with one eyebrow raised.

Roxie cocks her head to the side and raises her eyebrows; it's a well-known look that says if it were anyone other than Jade, she'd be full-on fighting.

"I'm going to let that slide, but don't let it happen again." Roxie points a finger at Jade but in the same moment blows her a kiss and walks off towards her room. "I'll let you two talk. Don't do anything I wouldn't do!" The door closes and I turn back to Jade.

"What happened? You've lost weight, Jade," I comment offhandedly, knowing it's not the smartest thing to do, but it's astonishing. It's only been ten days but she wasn't a big girl to begin with. She had curves in all the right places; now, her face is gaunt, her eyes sunken in and her skin is paler than it was, drawing all the attention to the dark purple and navy blue of her eye.

"Thanks... I think."

I shake my head, stepping closer to her. "What happened to you?"

How do I save you from the darkness?

"My, uh, my mom... ." Jade sighs, stepping back toward the couch and perching on the edge. "I went to my doctor. I wanted... no, I *needed* to make sure that nothing ... 'stuck' with me after what happened. My mom found out and she got mad because I got an implant."

I sit beside her, putting an arm around her hesitantly. I know we've gotten closer over text these past few days, but I don't want her to get scared. My fist clenches on my knee and I put all my energy into not reacting.

"I'm not sure how she found out. I thought I was careful, but it was probably Sarah's mom. The whole fucking town is a gossipy hellhole and she was over one night. She and my mom were drunk and talking shit like they normally do. Sarah's mom was saying how she couldn't believe my mom let me get an STD test–thank fuck that was clean–and birth control. How she couldn't believe I was planning on being so 'easy' at college... That the party was just a taste of what *I wanted*. Like I *wanted it to happen again and again.* My mom... my mom told her that I called the next morning and that I was a virgin-turned-slut who gave it up to the first person that looked at me." Jade doesn't cry, doesn't look hurt, but looks *angry.* I'm fucking angry and my plan to hit my first woman solidifies a little more.

She was a virgin?

My jaw clenches as I breathe deeply to control my pounding heart. She was a virgin before that night. And someone took that from her. Unwillingly.

I swear to fucking god if I ever find out who it is that did that to her, I'm beating him within an inch of his life with my bare fucking hands.

"I walked in and snapped that I was raped," Jade continues, "and I didn't take Sarah's man from her. That what happened to me wasn't consensual, and they should be disgusted with themselves for being such catty bitches."

My eyebrows jump up and I grin without meaning to. "I wasn't expecting that," I admit.

"It's true!" she insists.

"Oh, I know, I know. I just wasn't expecting you to call them that." I chuckle. "I'm proud of you for sticking up for yourself. I bet that wasn't an easy thing to do."

"It really wasn't, and obviously they didn't take it well." Jade gestures to her face and scoots back to rest against the couch. Her head falls back and her eyes close.

She looks exhausted. So tired.

"What can I do?" I ask. I'm desperate to do anything, to somehow help like I promised I would. I scoot closer so our shoulders are touching, and I rest my arm next to hers.

"Nothing. It's done. She told me to grab my shit and get out. I didn't have anywhere else to go." Jade's eyes open and I see the fight in them still, but there's a weariness that is troublesome to me.

"Jade," I shake my head and sit back up. "Jade, I would've driven there and gotten you. I would have... I would have done everything in my power to get you out of there. Anything. I would have done anything." *For you.*

"I didn't want to bother you."

My jaw drops. "Are you fucking serious?"

Jade stands up and walks over to the duffel bag on top of a small suitcase, pulling out her phone. "I am! There's a limit to kindness I can accept from people. I can't be a burden."

"We seriously need to talk about this *'I'm doing too much and you're taking advantage of me'* mentality you have." I turn her to face me. Her hips are smaller than I remember as I put my hands on them, pulling her as close as she's comfortable. I feel her give and fall into my body. My eyes drop to her lips, and there's the same unstoppable draw from last week. "I promise you, darlin', I will do anything for you. Don't you know that?" I insist.

Her emerald eyes shine as her gaze drops down to my lips. "Kiss me," Jade whispers.

"Are you sure?" I murmur but move closer. Her fingers twist in the fabric of my shirt and I let Jade drag my mouth to hers. Not that she had to try that hard—I'm powerless against her. Willfully and rightfully hers. And I have been completely hers since the moment I found her. It's magnetic and explosive, but tender at the same time. I'm careful of her split lip, but that makes the kiss no less alluring. She's shy and innocent, but I find that so fucking sexy.

My fingers tangle in her hair as our lips fuse together perfectly.

I deepen the kiss, licking the seam of her lips and she yields, giving me entrance. She tastes fucking addictive, and I already know I'm going to crave her for the rest of my days. Jade's sweet and minty, tinged with something metallic.

Blood.

Fuck.

I pull back quickly to see our kisses have caused her lip to open again.

"Oh god, Jade. I'm sorry, does it hurt?" I ask hurriedly.

"Worth it," she smiles brightly, and I have to agree.

It was most definitely worth it.

***

"WHAT IS THE PLAN, DARLIN'?" I ASK. MY SLIGHT country accent slips out as I hand Jade the fountain drink I'd gotten for her. "I thought I'd show up before you got here, so I could help move all your stuff in."

"The plan is I'm staying here with Roxie until I can move into the dorms and get out of her hair. I know I'm cramping her style and don't want to overstay my welcome. Once I get into the dorms, I'll find some kind of job and hopefully be able to make enough to get my own place," Jade explains with confidence.

"Are you still going for engineering?"

"Well, that's my declared major, but since I'm not trying to keep the peace with my mom as much anymore, I might talk with the art department. Maybe start making life choices for myself rather than others." She takes a long sip of the drink and closes her eyes with pleasure. "Ahh, so good."

"You could've told me, you know," I mutter, taking a sip of the Coke Zero I got myself.

Jade quirks an eyebrow at me. "Told you what?"

"That you didn't like coffee. I think I offered it to you twice and made it for you once. Hell, I watched you choke it down," I say with a half-hearted smile.

A short laugh slips from her lips. "I was in a stranger's home after he had just saved me from hell. I was completely at your mercy and kindness and was not going to look a gift horse in the mouth." She rolls her eyes just as I roll mine.

Knowing how she is, I understand where she's coming from. She's scared to take up too much space, to ask too much. But she shouldn't.

She... She deserves the world.

And now that I understand how she feels, I'm going to make sure I give it to her.

"I'll make sure to have your preferred caffeine hit of choice next time." I smile, dipping down to kiss her forehead.

"It's really not—"

"Don't even say it," I growl, shaking my head.

"It's not though." Her eyes flick down to inspect her cup before she looks back at me. "Thank you, Asher."

"Any time." I kiss her forehead. I can't stop kissing her now that she's here. In my arms. I'm so far gone for this girl it's not even funny. Ty's been teasing me relentlessly and now I realize it's for good reason. "Can I help you bring in the rest of your stuff?"

"Oh, that's it." She points to the duffel bag on top of the suitcase.

"All your stuff fit in those two bags?" I question incredulously. That can't be right.

Jade shrugs. "It's all I could grab. It's enough. I got my laptop and all my big, important stuff. I'll make money for more clothes and the little things later."

I shake my head. "What do you need?"

"I don't need anything. I have enough." She looks at me

pleadingly. "Roxie's letting me borrow some stuff and I have enough to get by."

"You *will* tell me this time if you need anything. Or if anything happens." The tone of my voice leaves no room for argument. "I'm still pissed off that you didn't tell me someone laid their fucking hands on you, or that you needed help."

"Asher—"

"I get why you didn't. You didn't want to inconvenience me. But darlin', are we clear now that I want you to inconvenience me at every possible turn? I want you to tell me everything. I want to take care of you in any way you need. Do. You. Understand?" I crowd her space, looking down at her while she stands her ground.

Placing her Styrofoam cup on Roxie's table, Jade crosses her arms over her chest like she's gearing up to fight me. "Asher, I didn't want to worry you or cause you grief. You've already helped me so much. I couldn't ask for more."

"Ask for more! I'll gladly give it to you!" I snap, throwing my hands up and caging her against the living room wall. "Do I make myself clear?" I say quieter, raspier, in her ear as I push her back. She has nowhere else to go.

"Asher," she whispers breathlessly. Fuck me. I can die a happy man; the way she said my name will be what my mind plays as I stroke my cock for the rest of time.

"Yes, baby?"

"Asher," she whispers again, adding a little whine to the end. *Goddamn it that's hot.*

"Tell me what you need, Jade."

"I need you..."

"I'm right here, baby. I've got you." I go to kiss her lips, and this time, I know I won't be able to stop. She's breathing heavily and her tits rub against my chest with every movement. She's squirming and I see her thighs clenching together.

I groan deeply. She wants me.

Just as much as I want her.

As I go to kiss her, though, a loud and obnoxious cough interrupts us. The haze of lust is instantly gone.

Fucking *Roxie*.

"Roxie..." I growl through a clenched jaw, my annoyance at her interruption *very* clear.

"What?! You're about to have sex in *my* living room!" she shouts. "Or were you too wrapped up in each other to remember that?"

"I'm so sorry, Roxie." Jade all but tries to push me away, but I hold onto her tighter. I'm not willing to let her go.

"She's fine," I grumble, rolling my eyes.

"I could've walked out here and saw your bare ass! I'm not fine at all!" Roxie cries.

"Don't be dramatic or anything." I turn to face her, finally getting the chub that was starting to form under control.

"Look, I'm all for this relationship. But I just don't want to see any more than necessary of someone I view as my big brother. Jade, though, you're hot A. F. So if I sneak a peek, who can blame me?" Roxie pops her hip out and crosses her arms, while making a show of looking Jade up and down.

"Don't even." I drop my head back, cursing Roxie for being bisexual and hot and amazing enough to turn anyone to the other team.

"I'm just saying!" Roxie throws her arms out indignantly.

"Well, don't! She's my girl, okay?" I raise an eyebrow at her and the room falls silent.

Shit...did I just say that out loud?

"I'm your girl?" Jade asks in a soft, musical tone. My attention falls to her as she rests a hand on my chest. "Really?"

I sigh exasperatedly, "Did you not listen to anything I said before? 'I'd do anything for you' and 'I want to give you everything.' Any of that ring a bell?" I ask with a soft smirk, letting Jade know I'm teasing. "That means you're mine, darlin'. And I take care of what's mine."

Her eyes shine as she nods, and her mouth curls slightly into a lip-biting grin. It's a look I haven't seen before, and her confidence... Well, her confidence does something to me. Fuck.

Jade tosses her dark blonde hair over her shoulder and my eyes get caught on her long pale neck, free from any marks.

I'm not a vampire, but the way my entire focus locks onto that one spot above her collarbone... I might as well be. I need to taste her. To leave a mark—a sign that someone cares for her, adores her. A mark that tells everyone else to fuck off. Any imprint I make will be born of pleasure, not pain. Jade must feel the heat of my gaze on her skin because we're drawn together, slow and inevitable, until the tension shatters.

Roxie coughs obnoxiously again, and my fists clench as I look up at the ceiling. "Why are you still here?" I snap.

"It's my place!" she snaps back.

Jade stands between us and puts her hands out, like we're two toddlers fighting over a toy. "Now, now, let's not fight over me," she teases.

"If you don't have any more stuff to move in, I'm going to go take a long bubble bath and a nap. I was preparing for at least three or four trips up and down the stairs," Roxie announces. Honestly, I was too. I wore shorts that show off my very tattooed legs to try to beat the Arizona heat. Roxie walks over to the table we're standing by and picks up a keyring with one lone key on it. "Here is your copy."

Jade frowns slightly. "You didn't have to do that." I'm getting better at reading Jade's tones because she definitely sounds like she's feeling guilty that Roxie went through the trouble of making her a key.

This girl. Somehow I'm going to get her to understand just how amazing and *worth it* she is.

"I already had it made and lying around. No problem, girl." Roxie waves off her worry, but I clock the too-relaxed look on her face. She knows her as well as I do, it seems. "Come and go as you please. *Mi casa es su casa* and all that."

"Are you sure?" Jade holds the key to her chest.

"Very." Roxie nods. "I'm going to go relax on one of my extremely rare days off. You two have fun. Do *not* have sex in my living room." She walks backward, pointing at us aggressively. "Asher Lee, I'm talking to you."

"Don't worry, Roxie." I wave her off, pulling Jade so her back is against my front. I hold her close and croon, "I'll behave..."

Roxie rolls her eyes but walks off. I take the chance to whisper darkly in Jade's ear, "Here. I'll behave *here*."

Jade's sharp intake of breath sets me off. "Let's go to my place," I suggest.

"God, yes."

Jade

ASHER'S HAND holds mine roughly as he leads me down the stairs. Roxie lives on the third floor of a nice apartment building, so we race down the stairs, stumbling like two fools over the steps.

We reach the bottom and I see a black, sleek motorcycle sitting in the first parking spot. It's a Harley, with the logo painted on the gas tank. Asher drops my hand to walk to the side of it, and I'm struck.

"This is yours?" I ask dumbly as I watch him unlock a saddle bag and pull out a black helmet.

"It is." He smirks, holding the helmet out for me to take. "For you." I hesitantly take the helmet from him. Asher kicks his leg over and straddles the bike before it roars to life.

My mouth drops open at the utterly panty-ruining image in front of me. Asher's arms are lit up by the sun as he revs the engine, twisting the handle. His arms are bare; the thin white T-shirt he's wearing is clinging to him in the horrible summer heat that's suffocating us already.

"Come here, baby," Asher calls over the roar of the engine,

curling his finger at me in a come-hither motion. Stumbling forward until I'm standing right in front of him, I'm awestruck at the gorgeous man in front of me. He puts the helmet on my head, tightening the chin strap before kissing my chin. "There. All nice and safe," he says softly. Our eyes meet and I get lost in the adoration I find in those big blue eyes. He kisses my lips gently and flips the visor down. "Hop on."

Thankful I'm wearing shorts, I throw a leg over the bike and hold onto his waist.

"Oh no, baby," Asher chuckles. He yanks my arms, and I fall forward. My thighs bracket his hips, my pussy pressed against his waist and my chest against his back. "That's better." He yells and holds my bent knees against him.

Asher revs the engine again and walks us backward to get out of the parking spot. Then he looks at me over his shoulder with a devilish grin and says, "Hold on tight, Jade. I want to feel you against me."

My jaw drops behind my helmet and he winks before we take off with a jolt. I grip onto Asher so tightly I feel like I'm a backpack.

With every bump, I'm jostled impossibly closer to him. With every turn, my chest presses against him tighter.

I don't know Carver super well, but I certainly didn't know it still had cobblestone streets in some neighborhoods. When Asher turns onto a street lined with stones, we bump along. It's then that I'm reminded just how spread I am around him.

The first few minutes are a shock, but then things start feeling... good. *Really good.* With Asher's scent filling my nose, his torso free for me to explore, the constant bump, bump, bump, rub, rub, rub, against my clit... I'm starting to feel intense. Asher arches his back slightly so there's more constant pressure, and his arm curls around my leg that's squeezing him to keep me from moving.

Moaning, I hope he doesn't hear me as I start to surrender to the sensations taking over me. I know I'm not that quiet, even over the engine and the wind. My panties are drenched to the point where I'm a little worried he can feel it through my shorts.

Just as I'm about to explode from pleasure, Asher turns one more time, and I groan when the cobblestone streets turn to smooth asphalt. I open my eyes—I don't know when I closed them—and recognize where we are.

We're almost at his place.

Asher takes my hand in his and slides it from where I had it resting on his pec, slowly down his abs and lower to the soft fabric of his shorts.

He's hard. Really fucking hard.

He squeezes my hand around his cock and beneath my other hand, which is still on his stomach, I can feel him shiver.

I'll be honest, I didn't think I'd ever want sex after what happened to me. I was worried I'd always be fearful, but with Asher... With Asher, I want him. I want him to show me how good it can be.

I want him to use this big, hard cock on me and show me what sex is supposed to be like.

Asher turns into a parking spot and cuts the engine, putting down the kickstand abruptly. He pulls the keys out and gets off in one smooth motion. Without missing a beat, he turns to me and unbuckles the helmet, slipping it off my head. The way he's looking at me... it's desperate and possessive, predatory and needy. Apparently that ride was just as fucking arousing for him as it was for me.

His tongue slips out, wetting his lower lip before he bites it. I can feel the heat of his gaze as it roams my body, stopping where my thighs are still spread over the back of the bike.

Asher leans in closer, pinning me within his bulging arms.

"Did you like the ride?" he whispers before barely kissing my lips. "I know I did."

"It ended too soon," I whisper breathlessly.

"That was just a teaser, darlin'." His slight accent that only really comes out when he's turned on... it gets me. I gasp as his hand slips between my legs and trails higher and higher. "I want you hot and ready, but I want to be there for the main event," Asher husks.

"Main event?" My mind is swimming in arousal; nothing makes any sense except for his hand on my leg. That, and the very needy question of how to get him to touch me. To spread me and take me right here.

Asher smirks and picks me up, crushing me to his chest. His arm goes under my ass to hold me up and the other presses against my back. Wrapping my arms around his broad shoulders, I look down at him.

"Let me show you."

ASHER CARRIES ME UP TO HIS APARTMENT, OUR LIPS locked together the whole time. I'm pulling at his hair, desperate for more of his touch. He's deepening the kisses and I let him, content and excited to follow him.

The whole time I was home, we talked every day. We messaged, sent funny pictures, memes;, whatever we could to keep the conversation going. But the one thing we never talked about was sex. I know without a doubt if we had discussed sex, that would have led to a conversation about that night, and it takes all of my energy to not think about that night at any given moment. I don't want to give it any power over me, or any more than it's already taken.

I felt so out of control that night. So... taken advantage of. So used.

I never want to feel like that again.

Asher backs us up to his door, only setting me down when he has to. My body slides against his in a slow, torturous drag. The space between us feels unbearable, but he needs to unlock the door. His fingers fumble with the keys, his breathing uneven; cheeks tinged with a soft pink which only makes the heat in his glossy eyes more devastating. He wants this, wants *me,* and the way his hands shake just slightly tells me he's barely holding himself together. Sneaking a peek down at his shorts, it's *very* obvious he wants more.

I slip between him and the door and lift up on my tiptoes to kiss his neck. I bite, lick, and suck at his pulse point, absolutely fucking *relishing* the noises he makes. Asher groans and wraps an arm around my waist, drawing me closer as he tries to unlock his door with the other.

"Baby, baby. I need to open the door," he whispers-groans.

"So, open the door," I whine, nipping his collarbone. Asher grunts and I can feel the struggle it is for him to open his eyes and actually focus on getting us inside. The lock clicks and he all but kicks the door in.

"Fucking finally." He ushers me inside, kissing my lips roughly before turning around and locking the door behind us.

"Asher," I moan. I'm dripping, both from sweat and from my pussy, desperate for him. For some relief.

When I say that night was my first time, it was my first *everything.* I've kissed a guy before, but that's it. Any sort of physical pleasure has come from my own hand. As Asher turns to look at me, a predatory look crossing his face that promises to eat me alive, it hits me that I have no real idea what I'm doing.

And he's going to know it.

"I've got you, darlin'." Asher brushes my cheek tenderly, as if he's reading my mind. "I want to know something before we go any further, though."

I swallow harshly. "Yeah?"

"I need you to understand that if you get uncomfortable in any, any way, you will tell me." His other hand cups my cheek, cradling my face in his hands. "You're too important to me. I don't want to cause you any kind of pain. I need you to promise me that if you get uncomfortable in *any* way, or if something hurts, you will tell me immediately." His other hand comes up so that he's now holding my face gently. "No second guessing yourself. No questioning if you're going to hurt my feelings or upset me. No thinking you're asking too much." His words are stern, but I sense nothing but sincerity. "You're too important to me. I don't want to cause you *any* kind of pain," he insists.

My heart swells at his words and I put my hands on his kind heart. "I will," I whisper.

"You promise?"

"Promise." I bite my lip. "But I do have something I want to clarify before we..."

Asher drops his hands to my shoulders, his thumb grazing my pulse point. "Okay."

I clear my throat before revealing, "I haven't done this before... like *any* of it. Unless you count that night." Biting the inside of my cheek, I look down in a mix of shame and hesitation. I know I shouldn't feel guilty, but I do.

Asher shakes his head and insists, "I don't." He tips my chin up with a crooked finger. "That should have been your choice. It should have been something you gave to someone, not something that was taken. I am so sorry that it was." He kisses my lips softly, sweetly, lovingly. "I am not pressuring you at all. If all you want to do is make out on the couch, I'm totally more than happy with that. We go at your pace, Jade. *Yours.*"

I surge forward, taking his lips in mine in a dominating kiss with a ferocity I didn't know I had. I want him. Asher Lee. My knight in shining armor, my protector. I want *him*. I jump up, trusting him to catch me—which of course he does—and I thread my fingers through his hair, pulling his head back slightly to deepen our kiss.

His hands grab the globes of my ass to keep me up and walks us back toward his room. A place I'm familiar with. A bed wrapped in his scent that I've missed.

Asher pulls away abruptly, looking me in the eye to make sure he's not misreading my cues. "Are you sure?" he asks hesitantly.

"So fucking sure," I reply breathlessly, grinding myself against his stomach to prove it.

"But—" he starts to say, but I cut him off with a devouring kiss.

"I want you, Asher. I choose you."

At my words, his eyes widen, and he nods before that feral smirk crawls back onto his face. Anticipation licks up my spine as he drops me onto his bed. I resist the urge to climb under his covers and breathe his scent in. It's comforting and addicting. I wore his stolen shirt every day until it lost its manly smell, replaced with my own.

He reaches behind his neck and yanks his shirt over his head, showing me his bare chest for the first time. Fuck, he's gorgeous. He's not shredded, but it's definitely obvious he takes care of himself. Asher's skin is, unsurprisingly, completely covered in tattoos. There are small blank spots here and there, but there's a piece of art covering the majority. He's like a walking gallery; the pieces are etched into his skin, making him even more eye-catching.

My eyes slide down his body until they get to his Adonis belt, the V-cut going down into his shorts and I feel my cheeks go red. My eyes snap back to his face, blushing because I know that he *knows* I was looking. Looking is too nice of a word. I am ogling; openly checking him out like a piece of fine meat and I'm a hungry animal.

But Asher's smiling and, if I'm not wrong, puffing out his chest a little; like he's proud I'm reacting so openly to his body.

"Like what you see, darlin'?"

I gulp, nodding. I don't trust my voice to answer. It'll crack or squeak or something equally embarrassing.

"Don't worry," he drawls as he leans over me, overwhelming my senses with all things *Asher*. "I'll be gentle."

His confident look is suddenly replaced with one that shows me he is just as nervous as I am. Why, I'm not sure. I cup his jaw, looking deep into his blue eyes.

"I trust you," I whisper against his lips, and he sighs in relief. Pushing forward, he takes my lips in a heated, deep kiss that makes me see stars. Asher is... Well, he is unlike anyone I've kissed before. Not that there is a big pool of people to pull knowledge from. I seriously doubt, though, that anyone could compare to him.

No one could compare to him.

Asher slips his hands up my sides underneath the loose material of my shirt. The sensation makes me jump slightly.

And he freezes.

"No, no, keep going," I beg.

"Are you sure?" he whispers against my lips. I'm going to

fucking die from embarrassment. Or from the frustration of not being able to control my own body.

"So sure." I wrap my arms around Asher's neck and pull him to me, fusing our lips together. Hopefully he gets the hint. "Please," I whisper.

His hands move higher, slower this time; more intentional and softer somehow. His fingers trace along the underside of my sports bra and he pushes up slightly, giving me time to stop him.

I raise my arms.

Asher bites his lip and pulls my shirt and bra off together, so we're both shirtless. Instead of laying further onto me like I thought he would, he moves back, rising from the bed fully to look at me. Asher looks long enough for me to start fidgeting and want to cover up, but his hands snake out to hold mine down. Lacing our fingers together over my head, he kisses me roughly before standing back up.

"You're beautiful. Fucking *stunning*. Don't cover up an inch, baby, I want to see it all."

My cheeks heat at his words yet I melt into his hold. His eyes darken to a navy-blue as he notices and grins. Ducking his head, he hovers over my breast and makes sure to keep eye contact with me as he licks my nipple sensually and blows on it. He actually *blows* on my wet nipple, making it instantly pebble.

When my body responds to him, he chuckles darkly, and I groan. That sound. Fuck, his voice. My eyes close and I clench my thighs together as much as I can with Asher between them.

"Need some help down there too, baby?"

I nod and a little whine escapes my throat.

"I can help you, darlin'. Just lay back." Asher moves to stand up straight again but drags his hands this time until they both cover my breasts, squeezing as he moves over them. I close my eyes, basking in the lust and desire blooming between us. I just want to *feel*. I don't want to get caught up in thinking and worrying, comparing or feeling insecure. I want Asher to have sex with me because he wants me, and I want him. I want him to make me feel good. I want him to erase the feeling of that other man's hands on me.

I want him to be *my first*.

His fingers slide over my soft stomach and dip below my athletic shorts. I can hear Asher's quick, quiet breaths as he tugs them down. As my thong and shorts slip down in one smooth motion, I squeeze my eyes closed.

I'm completely naked in front of this hunk of a man. I'm willingly naked in front of a man for the first time and I'm desperate for him to like the view.

"Fuck, Jade," Asher growls. I hear his shorts being tossed aside before I feel his hands very quickly return to my skin. He softly massages me, starting at my calves. Bringing up my legs so my ankles rest on his shoulders, he rubs my tight muscles. When he's satisfied that my calves have been shown enough attention, he slips up higher to my thighs and gives them the same love.

My thighs slowly relax and open when Asher sets them down on either side of his hips.

"Are you sure?" he whispers. The way he asks doesn't take me out of the moment at all. His voice is husky and deep, and when I crack an eye open, I see how affected he is by me. I can see what I do to him.

His hands move over my skin with slow, deliberate pressure; fingers flexing, gripping, soothing—though the heat rolling off him tells me he's anything but calm. Every stroke sends a shiver through me; a silent battle between control and need *plays* out in the way his forearms tense, muscles shifting beneath his skin. His stomach tightens with his fight to keep from thrusting forwards. And his shorts... Well, they're very tight on him now.

"Yes. Just... so much yes." The words sound breathless as they leave my lips and I'm not the least bit embarrassed about it.

"Good." Asher nods, stepping back and pulling his shorts off. "Condom?"

My head tilts to the side, in confusion. And he catches it. He always does.

"I've always worn condoms, but it's your call, darlin'."

"Always?" I ask, tipping my head to the side.

"Always." He steps back and goes to his side table to pull one out. Holding it up, the black and gold of the packaging catches the light.

"Put it back," I demand, surprised by the strength in my tone.

His eyes snap to mine and his expression reflects how shocked he is. "What?"

"Fuck me bare, Asher," I beg, sitting up and holding his biceps tightly. "I have the implant, so we don't have to worry about that. I'm clean... are you?" I'd made sure to go to the doctor when I got home. I wanted absolutely no surprises after the worst night of my life.

"Yes." He looks torn, holding the condom in his hand with confusion. Like he desperately wants what I'm offering but doesn't know if he should take it.

"Only if you want to." I slide my hands down to his and kiss his chest. "But I want to give that to you. Just like you're giving my first time to me."

Asher nods, throwing the package to the side and cradling my face in between his hands.

"Fuck, yes," he groans against my lips. "It made me nearly come right here, just thinking about entering you without a glove." His hips stutter forward and his cock bobs. "But first..." He bites his lip and gently pushes me back until I'm flat against his bed again. "First, I want to feel you on my fingers."

With little warning, Asher pushes his index finger into my mouth and growls, "Get it wet."

I swirl my tongue around his digit, sucking and pulling at it while I watch him. Asher shudders and with his other hand, he reaches down to hold onto the base of his cock tightly.

"Damn, Jade." He's breathless, and my skin blazes with desire. "I didn't think you'd suck it like it was my cock. I'm going to need your mouth on me later, okay?" He nods at me, breathing heavily like I am, and pulls his finger out of my mouth. I nod back to him, staring at him through my eyelashes.

"Good girl."

Good girl. That phrase sends me off. I can feel myself get wetter at his words. Fuck me.

Asher smirks, clearly seeing the impact of his words. "You like that, do you? You want to be my good girl?"

"Yes," I whine. I don't moan or sigh. It's a full-fledged whine that comes out of my mouth and I'm surprised, myself.

"I like that sound, baby." Asher slides the finger I just had in my mouth down my body, sliding over my belly and my mound until he effortlessly finds my clit. The first touch is a shock, but then... then it's euphoric. He's gentle but firm as he circles my bundle of nerves a few times. My eyes roll back, and I surrender just as Asher dips his finger into my center.

"You're so wet, darlin'. So fucking wet." The way he's speaking... *Fucking hell.* There's a rough edge to his voice, desperate and hoarse, making every syllable feel heavier, more intimate. It doesn't matter what he says—it's the way he says it, the way his tone curls around the words, dripping with restraint and something far more dangerous.

Something I can't wait to discover.

Pumping his finger in and out a few times, I can hear my wetness and almost move so that sound isn't filling my ears. But just as I'm about to, Asher groans and pulls his finger out roughly before plunging it into his mouth.

My gaze is locked on him as my eyes widen. I watch with rapture as his eyes roll back in pleasure. "You're so sweet, baby," Asher moans. "So sweet and so tight. We're going to have to stretch you out before I can fuck you."

"Please fuck me," I moan. I want to feel him completely inside me. I want to know what his beautiful cock feels like inside my cunt. His dick is thick, veiny, and curves slightly—like it would hit all those secret spots inside me I don't even know I have yet. "I can take it," I insist.

"I know you can. And you will." He presses his finger into me again without warning and I jump, but this time, it's from pleasure. Asher adds a second finger, and I feel the stretch. He pumps into me a few times before twisting and curling them, making me gush.

"Oh god," I cry out.

"That's it, baby. Just relax. I've got you," he croons deeply.

"Daddy," I whisper, breathing deeply as my orgasm quickly approaches. The word slips from my lips so easily, so quietly, that I do my best to forget it happened. My heart beats faster as a flush of embarrassment makes my cheeks and chest burn. Fuck, maybe if I don't bring attention to it, he won't say anything about it. The way his fingers are playing me leaves me with no choice *but* to come. Even embarrassment can't deter my body from trying desperately to reach its peak.

"That's it, baby girl. Come for me," he whispers, moving his fingers in the same exact curling motion but faster. "Another one," he growls, and I feel a stretch just before my orgasm explodes through me.

"Fuck, fuck, fuck, Asher!" I moan loudly.

"No, baby girl, call me that again." He moves his hand faster, wringing every last moment of pleasure from my body. "Call me Daddy."

"Daddy! Daddy! Please!" I scream as I come hard, and I feel a wet spot forming under my ass.

"Jade, oh, baby..." Asher pulls his fingers out quickly, dipping his head down and licking me from clit to ass, cleaning my cum up and making me wet all over again. He sits up, pulling me to him by my head and kissing me deeply. I can taste myself on his tongue and, strangely, it doesn't bother me.

I find it really fucking hot, actually.

He leans away, looking as needy and desperate as I feel. Pulling my hair, Asher turns my face up to his and holds it in one hand. I was expecting him to not be into it, to not like being called Daddy, but his expression tells me he is *very* into it.

"I'm going to be as gentle as I can. Tell me to stop and I will. But fuck, you've gotten me so riled up I have to feel you. Daddy has to feel you, baby, okay?"

Hearing him talk this way... I feel the intense heat in my cunt again, and it's only getting warmer. Almost painful with need.

"Okay,"

"Say 'okay Daddy,'" he demands.

"Okay, Daddy," I parrot and his head tips back with a moan.

"You're fucking perfect. Goddamn made for me." Laying me back, he helps me slide up higher so my legs are on the bed. Wasting no time, I let them fall apart to show him how wet I am, and I'm rewarded with a growl.

Asher slides between my legs, letting me feel every inch of him against me. His hardness is trapped against my slit.

I'm nervous, but so ready.

With one hand, Asher reaches between us and notches his head against my entrance. With the other, he holds my hands above my head.

"Ready?"

I nod.

Asher slides in slowly, so slowly. At first the sting wasn't bad. It's just like it felt with his fingers... and then he keeps sliding in. It's never ending. The pressure is intense, and the sting worsens, but it's manageable. I bite my lip and squeeze my eyes closed, trying not to whimper with discomfort.

"You're unbelievable, baby. So tight for Daddy. So good. Fuck, I don't know how long I'm going to be able to last in your sweet cunt," Asher groans, nibbling my earlobe as his words make me even wetter and keep me open for him. "Almost there, baby girl. You almost have all of it."

"Ugh," I whine, groaning just a bit from the pressure.

Asher keeps pushing in until I feel him pause. "There you go, darlin'. You did it." The way he says it makes me proud. I like the praise.

Correction: I like *his* praise.

"Daddy," I whine again, unable to control my tone anymore. Not when I'm this far gone.

"Give me a minute," he growls. "I need to... You feel so good... I can't..."

He sounds tortured, so I let him do what he needs to. Slipping both of my hands up his back, I drag them back down, scratching slightly with my nails. He moans.

"Are you okay?" he asks.

"Move," I insist.

"Bossy, baby girl." He bites my lip in punishment but does what I ask and finally moves.

Holy fucking hell. I thought his fingers felt good. His cock... his cock is even better.

"Asher," I groan, but he *tsk tsk tsk*'s with his tongue.

"Call me Daddy, do it. Call me Daddy." His motions speed

up as he grabs my hair and pushes my head to the side so he can suck on my neck. Goddamn it, he feels so good.

"Daddy..."

"Yes, baby girl. That's it," he moans darkly in my ear, making my toes curl. I've always kind of fantasized about calling someone Daddy, but I'm amazed at how effortlessly it left my lips with him.

Because he takes care of me; he has since the moment he met me.

Asher bites my neck, hard enough to send a zing of pain down my body, but not enough to truly hurt. His hands are all over me, and his touch is heavy. I feel his fingers gripping my skin in such a way that it leaves me breathless. His cock drags out of my pussy, and I immediately try to chase after it. I want more. I want him, all of him.

"You're going to come for me again, baby girl," he growls, kissing from my ear along my jaw, before he takes my lips in a passionate kiss.

"I don't know, I can't," I whimper, my words laced with the whining I know he likes.

"You can," he challenges, changing his motion from thrusting to grinding. And oh my god, I'm breathless. I'm desperate. I need to come. I *need to come.* The way his pubic bone rubs against my clit with each thrust is forcing me higher and higher.

"Daddy, fuck, Daddy!" I cry out, wrapping my arms around his head. I hold him to me tightly as I'm fucking thrown off the ledge into an ocean of pleasure.

"Oh FUCK!" Asher growls roughly, his hips pistoning into me as I come. I'm lost as my body turns to jelly while he fucks me senseless until he finds his own peak. I hope he comes in me, I really fucking hope he does.

I drag my fingernails down his shoulders and his hips stutter. He pumps into me one more time before his whole body goes rigid, and he pulls out of me so fast I don't realize it until his cum hits my belly.

"Jade, fuuuuck. Baby girl, goddamn it," he mutters as he jerks off over me until the ropes of cum stop and his head drops back in relief.

"Oh my god," I sigh. My eyes flutter closed and, breathing deeply, I feel truly relaxed for the first time in... I don't even know. It's like I'm floating, like I'm truly weightless and able to just be.

Asher's breathing is as heavy as mine and he climbs off me. Feeling the bed shift, I know I should get up, but I'm just too comfortable. I don't care that his jizz is drying on me; in fact, I kind of like it.

Sighing contentedly, I hear the toilet flush before the bed dips again. When I crack open an eye to see where he is, I'm met with the softest smile on his handsome face. A warm washcloth covers my stomach while he cleans me up. His touch is so different as he moves me back and forth to make sure I'm clean.

"Jade?" he asks softly and I nod. "Are you okay? Was I... Was it..."

"Perfect? Everything I'd imagined?" I reply, unable to keep myself from beaming at him. "Yes. Yes to both."

He sighs in relief and his head drops down. "Thank god. I was worried when you didn't move..."

"I was just enjoying the afterglow, that's all. You should come join me," I smile, moving up to cup his cheek lovingly.

"You won't hog the covers while we take a quick nap?" Asher teases, already climbing into bed naked.

"No promises." Cuddling into his chest, I breathe him in. Content and safe for the first time since I was in his arms last.

Asher

JADE FALLS ASLEEP SO QUICKLY, I can't help but wonder when the last time she actually got decent sleep was.

Probably not in a long time. Too long.

Her blonde hair tickles my nose as I breathe in her scent. What just happened between us plays on repeat in my mind.

She called me Daddy. Fuck, even just remembering it makes a shiver go down my spine and my dick bob. She'd said it so softly that at first, I didn't think I'd heard her correctly. But when her cheeks blushed, I knew I had. I tried to reply quickly without giving her any time to second-guess if I was okay with it.

Because I was. Really fucking okay with it. So unbelievably okay with it.

My dream girl calling me Daddy as I fuck her? Only a fool would pull away from that.

Jade's soft snores fill my ears, and I sigh comfortably, knowing she's safe.

That black eye makes me cringe in pain for her. It's deeply bruised. The kind of bruise I've seen Ty walk into work with many times. The kind I've had more times than I want to remember. It means a fist hit the orbital arch, or the bone under the eyebrow, in just the right way and it hurts like a fucking bitch. I've watched grown men fall down and cry from that kind of hit.

Shit. Did she cry? Was she sitting there all alone, hurting, forcing herself to push through the pain just so I wouldn't worry? Was she sending me those funny little jokes, hiding behind them, trying to convince me that she was fine? The thought slams into me; a tight, twisting knot of guilt forming in my gut. I should have known. I should have seen past the words, past the forced lightness. The image of Jade suffering in silence, putting on a brave face for my sake, makes my chest ache with something raw and unbearable.

She's safe now. Safe in my arms, and I'm not going to let anyone or anything hurt her again.

"Daddy" plays in my mind, and I let myself fall asleep knowing that she's right here.

⚬━⚬━⚬━⚬━⚬━⚬━⚬

A SNORE AS LOUD AS A FREIGHT TRAIN WAKES ME UP with a jolt.

Jade, where's Jade? My sleep-ladened brain immediately asks.

I look over to see Jade with her back toward me and feel her foot between mine. She's fucking exhausted—hence the snoring—and I don't plan on waking her up anytime soon. Slipping out of bed as quietly as I can, I check my phone to see I got in a good two-hour nap before she woke me up and it's almost lunchtime.

If I couldn't provide breakfast in bed today, then lunch in bed it shall be.

I pull on my boxers and head into the kitchen to see what food I have. Hopefully I have stuff to pull together into something recognizable as a meal. I'd normally wait and go out to eat, but I want her to be able to sleep as much as possible. I could run to the store quickly, but I don't want to take the chance that she wakes up before I get back and thinks I've left her.

No, I'll make do with whatever I have here.

Sunlight pours through the windows, catching the glass of the artwork on my walls and scattering prisms in every direction. The room glows with color, and my breath hitches at the sight of a rainbow resting on Jade's shoes beside mine—both pairs kicked off carelessly at the door. It's a simple sight, but something about it feels right. I could get used to seeing our shoes side by side like this.

Hope. Rainbows mean hope, and I take this as a sign.

Smiling to myself, I run a hand through my hair—is it getting too long already?—and head to the fridge. I already know its contents are going to be awful. I haven't had the time or mental energy to actually cook, so I'm pretty sure all I have is meal-prepped food from a few days ago; chicken, rice, and broccoli. The boring shit that makes me look good and fuels me... but it doesn't necessarily taste good. I have eggs and bacon, though; a rarity that I usually only order somewhere.

When I order out, I usually get a lot of food and I'm not as strict then. But if I'm going to cook, I'm going to be good.

Pulling open my cupboards, I find old pancake mix and hope it hasn't expired yet.

Breakfast for lunch it is.

Trying to be as quiet as I can, I pull out all the stuff needed and get to work. While I cook, my thoughts wander.

'What are we?' floats through my mind. The dreaded question. It doesn't really matter what she might *think* we are, because I *know* what we are. She is mine and I am hers. End of story.

Jade's mom kicked her out, taking the word of a catty bitch over her own daughter. How could a mother do that? My mom... Well, my mom did what she had to do to protect and provide for us. In her own way. But my mom never raised her hand to me or let anyone else hit me. It helped that I was over five foot ten by the time I was in middle school and already corded with muscle. I took my job of protecting my little brother very seriously and he didn't always hang out with the best of people.

Cracking some of the eggs into the dry pancake batter, I start mixing it quickly.

Did Jade have anyone to protect her? Or has she always had to protect herself?

I'll have to ask her, though it doesn't really matter anymore. I'm here now. She'll never have to worry again.

I lean over and get a cup of coffee brewing for myself, and curse when I realize I don't have a can of pop for her. There's a little pad of paper I keep on the kitchen island for when inspiration strikes—I have one in every room—but I rip a piece off and start a grocery list.

Buy:
Diet Coke/ Regular Coke
Any other drink preferences?
Actual Food
Ask her what she likes to eat
Ask her what I can cook for her to eat
Breakfast foods? Snacks?

Putting the pen down, I pull out a pan and get it warm before pouring in a good-sized pancake to cook.

"I woke up and you weren't there."

I jump when Jade's soft, sleepy voice fills the air. I look behind me to see a fucking vision. I'm struck with the intense desire to see it for the rest of my life.

Jade is standing in the doorway, her messy blonde hair pulled over her shoulder as her pretty pink lips part with a yawn. Her legs are bare as she's wearing only my shirt that comes down to her upper thigh. My shirt is big on her, and it's the one I slept in last night, so it's all stretched out and slips off her shoulder.

"You're beautiful," I say breathlessly.

Her cheeks redden as she looks down and crosses her arms. "Thank you."

"I'm sorry I wasn't there when you woke up." I cross the room in three strides, enveloping her in my arms and breathing her in. "I wanted you to sleep as long as you could. You were so tired."

"Yeah, I haven't really slept since..."

Nodding, I cut her off gently, "I figured. You snore like a bear though."

She gasps loudly, smacking my chest playfully. "I do not!"

"You do!" I laugh. "Woke me up from a dead sleep."

"Oh god," she groans, burying her face in my chest.

"Very cute."

"Yeah right," she protests, but the words are muffled against my chest.

"Everything about you is cute, Jade," I admit seriously, pulling back to have her look at me. "I mean it."

"I'm a mess," she sighs.

I shrug. "So am I."

"I've got these issues."

"So do I."

Jade frowns, like she doesn't believe me. "I'm needy and will want constant reassurance. That's just shit from my past coming to haunt me."

"Baby girl, I will tell you how much I want you every single day if you let me. How much I want this. I know we haven't known each other long, but this thing between us... it's strong and powerful." I cup her cheeks and keep her eyes on mine. "Stay with me. Please. I want to hear from you every day, I want to see you every day. I want us to be together. I want to be the one by your side, to care for you, to protect you. Will you let me?" My heart is pounding so hard in my chest. I wasn't planning on asking her this, but I just have to know.

So many emotions swim in Jade's eyes as she bites her lip to keep from smiling. "You want to be exclusive?" she clarifies.

"So fucking exclusive, darlin'. I don't share. If we're together, you're *mine* and only *mine*," I growl, slipping my hands down her body. "Will you? Be mine?"

Bending down, I grab her thighs as she jumps effortlessly into my hold, wrapping her arms around my shoulders.

"Will you be mine in return?" Jade asks. There's no self-consciousness or worry in her tone and she's looking at me straight on.

I see what's happening here. Her hard look makes my lips turn up in a smirk. My girl doesn't share either.

"Completely yours. Only yours," I vow.

"Then yes. I'm yours." She breathes the words, her eyes entranced by my lips and before I even know what's happening, our mouths are crashing together. My heart pounds, slamming against my ribs in happiness.

She's mine—officially.

Jade grinds against me, making her want clear and I'm all too happy to oblige. Stumbling forward until her ass hits the kitchen island, I roughly set her down, our lips never parting. Her thighs tighten around my hips and I run my hands down to her shapely thighs. Squeezing the bare skin, I really fucking hope she didn't put on panties.

I'll make us breakfast and eat her out, too.

I'm completely obsessed with Jade. With her scent, her movements, with the little noises she makes as I move from her lips to her neck and suck on that spot I found earlier. I thrust against her core, pleased to find she's warm and grinding against me. Ready to go. My fingers inch higher up her thighs and I'm going to find out if her cunt is covered or if I can eat right now.

Beep, beep, beep, beep, beep!

Fuck!

Jolting apart, I rush to the stove and see smoke billowing from the frying pan. The fucking pancakes are burned to a char.

Well worth it, though.

"You were cooking for me?" Jade asks with an awed smile, and I'm reminded again how shitty people have been to her.

"I was. But not very well, it seems. I still have eggs and bacon, though. Or we can go out? That's probably a better idea. I'm an okay cook, but not that great. I mean, eggs and bacon are kinda hard to mess up. I thought that way about pancakes but look what I did." I'm rambling. I know I am. I take a deep breath and run a hand through my hair, pushing out the air audibly. "I didn't want to wake you up."

She's got a look that says she knows exactly how frazzled I'm feeling, and she thinks it's cute. Her smile is quirked to the side, and she fiddles with the hem of my shirt.

"So you've said."

"I also don't know what you like to eat. Do you even like eggs?" I turn toward the counter. If she doesn't like anything I have, I can run to the diner. It's not that far at all. They're speedy too, so I'll be in and out in ten minutes.

Plans start forming in my mind to make sure she's fed, but I feel her small, warm hands wrap around my waist.

"I'm not picky. I like eggs and bacon, who doesn't?" Jade chuckles, and the knot in my chest loosens in relief. Putting my hand over hers, I smile at the domesticity of the moment. "But what I really like is you standing here, cooking for me after you fucked my brains out so nicely."

"So 'nicely?'" I ask, turning in her grip. "So...nicely?" I crook an eyebrow at her and bite my lip.

"I meant..." Jade starts to explain, but I want to see her squirm.

"I know what you meant, darlin'." I turn back and shut off the burners. Food can wait. "We'll get food later. I need to make sure that you remain 'nicely' fucked and satisfied." My words reverberate between us and her mouth drops open. Kissing her roughly, I turn her around and force her over to the island.

"You remember your promise?" I growl in her ear. I want to take her and fuck her senseless, but I also want to make sure she tells me if it's too much.

Jade nods. Her body is relaxed, and she lets me move her into the position I want.

"Good girl," I whisper in her ear and kiss her neck. "Now, I've been dying to see if you put on panties before you came out. Let's find out." One hand pushes Jade's torso over the island so my shirt rises higher, and the other hand finds the hem to lift it up.

I groan immediately. "Oh, baby girl," I mutter. "Trying to entice me?"

"My panties were all wet from earlier, so I—"

I cut her off with a bite to her neck and she groans. Her panties were destroyed because of *me*. I like that a little too much. My dick, already half-hard, starts to bob with want.

I run a lone finger through her folds, and she shivers, shaking her hips from side to side involuntarily. My fingertip slips inside her already soaked cunt, and I move her wetness around before sliding my fingers up to rub her clit.

Jade's head falls back, her blonde tresses falling over her shoulders. I watch with rapture as her mouth parts on the sigh she lets out. Without thinking, I wrap my hand around her exposed throat and bring our lips together.

Jade pushes her ass back against me. I take that as a sign she's okay with what I'm doing and push a finger into her heat. She's tight, still so fucking tight, but my finger enters her a little easier now. My cock is at full attention now, fully ready to be buried in Jade as deeply as I can.

"Daddy," she whines, and all my self-control is gone.

"I'm right here, baby, I've got you," I moan, taking my hand from her throat to pull my dick out of my boxers, just enough to notch the head at her entrance. "I've got you." I can hear how fucking desperate I sound, even though it's only been a few hours since I had her last.

"Please, Daddy, *please*," she whimpers, leaning her head down on the cool counter, pushing her hips back so my tip slips inside. We both moan and my fingers clench her hips to hold her in place. I'm going to come far too quickly if she keeps this shit up.

"Don't move, baby girl. Let me," I order. I push forward slowly, teasingly, achingly into her cunt, and we both groan. She's so fucking tight. So. Fucking. Tight.

I feel like she's choking my cock with her pussy. It's perfect.

"Daddy, please." An impatient whimper. I like how vocal Jade's becoming. How she's welcoming her desire and letting herself be open with me.

I can't wait to explore this side of her further. And I can't lie —knowing I'm the only one who has had her this completely? It does something primal to me.

Pushing in with minimal resistance because of how dripping wet she is, we both sigh. It's a relief. Like I'm finally home.

"Hold on, baby girl," I order huskily and watch with delight as she grips the countertop. "Such a good little girl." Moaning at my words, Jade drops her forehead and surrenders.

"Yes," she drags out the word as I start to pump in and out of her. Finding a rhythm she likes—I *know* she likes it when she stands on her toes and throws her ass back against my hips with each movement—I know this won't last long. She feels too good; she's working my body just the right way to make me see stars and I'm too worked up already. My hand slips up her back to clasp her shoulder tightly, holding onto her for leverage.

"That's it, fuck. That's it, right there!" She arches back against me and I fuck into her shallowly, but roughly. My movements are so small that my cock never leaves her body. I slide my other hand to her front and start to circle her clit. I need to see Jade fall apart. I know I won't be able to come until she does.

"Come on, baby. Come for me. I can't come until you do," I whisper hotly in her ear, resting my naked chest on her shirt-covered back. "I want to watch my cum paint your back. I bet your pretty little asshole will look so hot with my cum covering it."

"Oh my god," she cries, her head falling back, causing her ear to rest closer to my mouth.

"I want to feel you fall apart on my cock, Jade. Do as I say and be a good girl for Daddy."

"Oh fuck!" Her eyes screw shut, and she shakes just as I feel her pussy clamp down on my cock. I groan loudly. Her hot, wet walls are milking me dry and when she cries out for me, I lose it. *"Daddy!"*

Pulling out of her abruptly, I do what I promised and jerk off aggressively, wishing it was still her cunt around me. I cry out her name and spurts of cum shoot out, covering her back and ass with white milky ropes. I watch with rapt attention as it drips down her.

"Oh, baby girl, oh god," I groan loudly with total pleasure taking over. My hips thrust into my hand as I ride my orgasm out.

"That was..." I say, or try to say, as I catch my breath and recover from that amazing orgasm.

"You've ruined me, haven't you?" Jade asks, standing and letting the shirt drop over my cum on her back. I reach over and grab the kitchen towel before turning her back around to clean her up.

"What do you mean?" I ask when I'm done. Throwing the towel toward the corner where my laundry machine is, I focus back on her.

She smirks, her lips reddened and a satisfied fucking look glinting in her eyes.

"You've ruined me for all other men. There's no way sex will ever be better."

My chest puffs up a bit, unintentionally, but most definitely noticeable.

"My pussy is molded to you now. I think I like it."

I wrap Jade in my arms and kiss her deeply. Sliding my hand into her hair, I lightly pull on the tresses at the base of her neck.

"You better like it, because I'm your Daddy now and you are mine. Forever." I growl, knowing that I am so fucking far gone for this girl, there's no way out for me.

SPENDING a few nights on Roxie's couch has been like having a quintessential sleepover in a '90s movie.

We drink too much wine, dance to good songs, eat takeout because Roxie does not agree with cooking, and laugh so hard my cheeks hurt.

Underneath all that bravado, Roxie is just such a fucking star. When I got back from that first night at Asher's, she was sitting at the table, scrolling on her phone and waiting with a glass of wine. As soon as she saw me, Roxie popped up from her chair and screeched, "Tell me everything."

Having this time with a girl friend who is genuine is... priceless to me.

Asher has stopped by every single morning and offered to take me anywhere, for me to come to work with him, for us to drive around town. We spent the first two days just tangled up in bed together, learning about each other. He has helped me learn a lot about myself. What I like and what I don't, what I can do, what I absolutely love that he does to me, how fucking amazing he can make me feel... how I can make him cry out my name as he comes.

It was an amazing two days that did absolutely nothing to satiate either of us.

Asher is so caring and attentive. It's surprising, really. In every movie I've ever watched with badass tattooed hotties like Asher, they're portrayed as these playboy womanizers who let the girls run to him... Thank god I found a man who doesn't like those games. I hate them, I'm bad at them, and all they ever do is make people feel like they have to 'win.' A relationship, a healthy relationship, shouldn't be about winning against each other.

He's upfront and honest with me, always valuing my opinion and feelings. Asher's really great at messaging me and making sure I'm alright. In between those nice texts are naughty ones that would make a sinner blush.

I guess that's what I am now: a heathen. A rebel. Independent.

I really like it.

Roxie convinced me to come into the shop one day and pierce my nose with a small, thin hoop. I'm so glad I did it. It gives me a lot of confidence. Asher didn't stop staring at me for the rest of his shift before taking me back to his place and fucking me from behind on the bathroom countertop so I could watch us in the mirror.

I've discovered I really like to watch.

And so does he.

Grabbing the last shirt I'd unpacked, I put it back in my duffel bag before zipping it up and sighing.

"Do you really have to go?" Roxie asks, watching me pack my meager belongings from the kitchen table. It's early for her, though it's nine in the morning, and her black hair is sticking up all over from sleep as she cradles her coffee cup.

"I can't mooch off of you forever," I chuckle. It does warm my heart that she's upset I'm leaving. I'd rather she wish for me to stay than hope I'd leave. "We're still going to see each other, right?"

"Fuck yeah." Roxie nods, sitting taller in the chair. "You're going to come to *Ashes* tonight, right?"

"Sure! I think you all have a late client, so I'll just hang out at the front desk, and you can come chat during breaks."

A knock on her door tells me that Asher's here to help me move. Roxie sighs and stalks over to the door, opening it with a pout on her face.

"Fine, come take my best friend away," she grumbles and walks back to the kitchen to refill her caffeine fix. "I'm going to go back to sleep," she announces, then envelopes me in a hug with one arm around my waist while the other holding her coffee. "Text me when you meet your new roomie. They aren't going to be as kick-ass as me, though. You know that, right?" Roxie pulls back and her eyes narrow.

Like she's actually worried I'm going to not be her friend anymore. That's never going to happen.

"If I didn't know better, I'd say you're scared to be replaced," I tease, which earns me a horrified, unimpressed look from her. I giggle and continue, "Trust me, Roxie. No one is as kick-ass as you." I hug her back as tears line my eyes. This bitch took me in when no one else would; she cared for me when I needed a friend and gave me a reality check when I needed one.

She's a good friend. Someone you don't just drop.

She's a ride or die, for sure.

"Hey!" Asher scoffs, holding his arms out in offense. Fuck, does he look good. He's in the same basketball shorts from last time, but he's paired them with a cut-off T-shirt so when he turns to the side, I get a flash of his abs. And oh my god, his tattooed arms are on display. I'm obsessed.

"You already knew it, so don't act surprised, Lee," Roxie tosses in his direction before looking back at me with a soft smile.

"You need anything, anything *at all,* you call me." She's looking at me like a big sister would, like someone who wants to protect me from the world.

And a tear drops down my face.

"I will, thank you, Roxie." I nod, holding her hand and trying my best not to sob.

"Take good care of her, Asher, and make sure her roommate isn't a fucking asshole. I don't need to be murdering anyone this early in the day." I laugh, a watery chuckle that lets the room know I'm trying hard not to cry. Roxie looks at me and scrunches her nose at me. "Don't you make me cry. I'm going to see you in a few hours." She groans and pulls me in for another hug.

"Thank you, Roxie. For everything." I bite my lip to try and keep from crying.

"You got it, bitch. You're part of the crew now." She nudges my elbow and walks back towards her room.

Roxie might be a badass bitch, but she's also a sensitive one.

Asher stands at the door with my suitcase in hand and my duffel slung over his shoulder.

"Are you ready?" he asks, holding out his hand for me to take.

"Sure am."

***

THE UNIVERSITY IS LIKE A LITTLE CITY ITSELF, WITH restaurants, bars, a few bookstores, plus all the different academic buildings on the edges. Looking around with the windows down in Asher's car, I take it all in. Trying to read all the signs and figure out where everything is, I start to worry that I might get turned around.

"Oh, Troydon Hall, over there." Pointing to the left.

Asher smiles knowingly. "Yes, I know."

"Did you..." I start to ask, but stop, worried I might offend him or make him feel bad with the question on the tip of my tongue.

"Go to college?" Asher looks at me with a raised eyebrow and a knowing smirk. I nod. "No, I didn't. Well, not in this setting. I went to a few semesters of art school and took some night classes on business to help start the shop, but no, I didn't traditionally go to college. My brother is currently going, though," he shares.

"Your brother?" Interesting. He's never mentioned having a brother. Or any family for that reason. I guess I've never asked.

I turn to face him a little more, guilt swirling in my stomach about it.

He nods. "Yes, I have a younger brother. He's a sophomore this year—he actually goes here. He should be moving back into the dorms in the next few days." Asher pulls up in front of an old limestone four-story building on the small campus. "We're here. Your home for next year."

"Home," I repeat, looking out the window and seeing an empty shell of a building. Soon, maybe, it will be bustling with people, students, and potential friends. Sighing, I unbuckle my seatbelt but don't make a move to actually get out.

I don't know why I'm more nervous about moving into the dorms than I was moving in with Roxie.

Asher puts his warm hand over mine. It's strange how quickly my anxiety lowers when he touches me. Turning to face him, all I see are empathy and understanding on his face.

"It's okay." He threads our fingers together.

"Is it?"

"It will be."

⸺◦◦⸺

WALKING INTO THE BUILDING WITH MY DUFFLE ON MY shoulder and my purse across my chest, Asher carries my suitcase in one hand and holds my hand tightly in the other, which helps me feel a little better.

He walks in front of me with his head held high, looking intimidating as fuck with his tattoos and burly manliness. I feel safe with him; like he's my own personal bodyguard, intent on punishing anyone who dares to hurt me. Squeezing his hand in mine, I smile up at him and he winks at me.

"Well, hello there!" A very cheery older woman holding a clipboard steps in front of us, stopping us from going any further. "I'm Pam. I'm the residential advisor in charge of everyone here at Troydon Hall. And who might you be?"

"I'm Asher," he replies warmly, "and this is Jade."

"Jade Henderson?" Pam asks, checking her list.

"Yes, that's me," I say, giving her a tight-lipped smile.

"Oh good! I have your room all ready, if you'll follow me this way." Pam turns on her heel and her blonde curly ponytail whips around.

"Well then," Asher says, turning stiffly to me.

I crack a shocked grin, shrug and pull him forward. "Come on," I tease.

"If you want to follow me, you're on the fourth floor," Pam calls out, standing by the elevator. She's holding the door open and eyeing us, as if she is trying to figure us out.

Asher lets me enter the elevator first, then holds the door

open for Pam. Once he is sure we are safely inside, he walks in and stands close beside me. My man is ever the gentleman.

There's absolutely no music or anything to lessen the awkward tension; only the creaks and groans of the old elevator pulling us up. Pam starts flipping the keys in her hand and looking at us. Actually, she's looking quite pointedly at our clasped hands, then at Asher, then finally at me before opening her mouth.

I can't wait to see what this question is.

"So, are you her brother?" Pam asks Asher, fishing for information.

"Me?" Asher chuckles, lifting our hands and kissing the back of mine. "Yes, I'm her brother," he says sarcastically, causing me to laugh softly.

"That's so kind of you to move her in," Pam awes, not catching the sarcasm in Asher's voice. My jaw drops, as does Asher's, and I can't help but wonder what kind of fucked up relationships she sees while moving people in. How close are some of these brothers and sisters?

Asher shakes his head again; I can tell he wants to say something really biting, but the moment his mouth opens, so does the door.

Thank god.

"Here we are!" Pam steps out first to lead the way. Mutely, I follow and drag Asher along by the hand. Thankfully my dorm room seems to be right off the elevator, so we won't be subjected to a full-blown tour by Pam. She unlocks the door, and an unsettling feeling falls over me.

The hallway is dimly lit, with only one window at the very far end. There's one door after another, seeming to stretch on forever. I look behind me, making sure that Asher's still there, but also to see the common room which joins the two wings of the building. The way the website laid out this dorm, it appeared to be one long rectangle with a larger circular room in the middle of each floor. Either side of the circle extended into wings that held the actual rooms and bathrooms. The floor I've been assigned to is a co-ed floor, meaning boys on one side and girls on the other. At the time I'd gotten the email, it didn't seem to be that big of a deal, but now…

I can't think about that right now.

"So, here's the room." Pam holds her hand out to let us in, and I glance over what is to be my home. At least until I can earn enough money to get my own apartment.

It's not stellar, but it'll do. There are two very typical thick vinyl-covered college twin-sized beds pushed up against the wall, two desks built into the wall, two chairs pushed in at the desks, and two closets built in on either side of the desks so it's just one big wall of storage.

It's dingy and definitely old, but it's livable.

It's mine.

Well, mine to share with some unknown roomie.

"The girl's bathroom is in the middle of this hallway. Going into the guy's bathroom is off-limits for obvious reasons. The cafeteria that accepts your food card is on the first floor toward the back of the building, you can't miss it. There are really only five people checking in as early as you are, so you should have the place to yourself for a few days." Pam is rattling off information like she's done this a million times, and I bet she has. She has a very 'residential college for life' air about her. "I have my own apartment opposite the cafeteria, so if you need anything, just give me a knock. Your floor RA will be here in a few days, and then they'll be your first point of contact. Here is your key," she says, holding out two keys on a ring. "And also, your mail key for your mailbox. I need you to sign a few things and then I'll be out of your hair!" I take the keys from her, giving her a tight-lipped smile, and nod.

Asher walks over to the bed closest to the window and sets my duffel bag down on the mattress, effectively claiming that bed for me.

"Do I have a roommate?" I ask, signing the first and second page of the contract.

"You do, but they won't be here until the official move-in day," Pam explains, then puts the contract back into her little folder. "I think that's it! You're officially a Dragon!" she says cheerfully and backs up. "You know where to find me if you need anything! When you leave, big brother, just please make sure to latch the locking door on your way out." She points to Asher with a *click* of her tongue and a wink before flurrying out the door.

"I can't tell if she's actually fucking serious," Asher mutters, eyes stuck on the door before looking back at me with a shocked expression.

Shrugging, I walk into his arms, which immediately wrap me up, and look at him. "Nah, let her be oblivious. But if that bitch tries to get at you, I'll kill her," I reply nonchalantly.

That breaks his staring contest with the door as his shocked expression turns to me. I smile at him sweetly before reaching up and kissing his chin.

"Oh, that's how it is now?" Asher raises an eyebrow and slaps my ass with one hand.

"That's how it is," I nod, scrunching my nose as I try to pull off an innocent smile. "You said you don't share; well, neither do I."

"Very understood," Asher says softly, leaning down and whispering against my lips. "To be honest, I really like this side of you."

"Oh yeah?" His arms wrap around my waist. He pulls me in

tighter before one hand slides slowly up my side and caresses my breast, then moves up to my neck to hold me in place.

"I told you I'll always take care of you, baby girl," he growls. Swiftly lifting me up, Asher places me on the mattress and bites down softly on my neck, making me moan. "I will never make you second-guess my fidelity. I swear."

The way he *vows* this makes me weak in the fucking knees.

"Asher," I sigh, but he *tsks* his tongue and I immediately know where I went wrong. "Sorry...*Daddy,*" I correct myself.

Asher groans into my neck. "You don't know what that does to me," he mutters gruffly, almost like he's being tortured. "You don't know how much that affects every single part of me. It calls to my protective side, but it also calls to my fucking *filthy* side. I can't control myself when you call me that." He nips my neck, right under my ear, the place that he knows I love. "And I think you like it."

"I do, Daddy. I really, *really* do." I drop my head back, giving him more access to my throat. His hands wander from my waist down to the top of my shorts and slip underneath. Pushing him back, I look at the door. "Go close it," I whisper.

A feral smile crosses his face.

And I know I'm in for it. In the best fucking way.

"Absolutely not."

"What? Why?" I don't want anyone to see us having sex. I know the building is nearly empty right now, but there's a possibility Pam comes back or someone else that's moving in early walks by. I can't.

"Because I want everyone on this fucking campus to know who takes care of you. *Me.*"

"Asher..." I don't know about this, but I trust him.

"Baby girl, I won't let anything happen to you," he whispers assuredly.

"What if someone sees?"

"Let them see." He kisses me roughly, but I can feel the adoration in it. "You're mine and I'm yours."

He's right. And really, the chances of someone walking by are so small... right?

Asher smiles and slips my shorts down, turning me slightly so I can lay on the slick material. Looking down I see the huge, now-familiar bulge in his shorts and smile when I notice just how perfect the height of the bed is. He can fuck me into tomorrow against the mattress while he stands and I lay comfortably.

"Do you like hearing that, baby girl?" Asher leans over me and slips one of his long, thick fingers into me. Moaning, my eyes close without permission, and I fully surrender to him. To the moment.

To let Daddy take care of me.

"That I want everyone to know you're mine? That you're taken? Do you like being claimed by me?" He whispers darkly against my lips as his finger slips all the way out, to then thrust back in and curl.

"Yes," I moan.

"Yes..."

"Yes, Daddy. I do," I whimper, opening my eyes and staring at him as I say the words I know he wants to hear. I'm rewarded when he sits up straight and shivers before the feral look comes back.

"Fuck yes you do." He fingers me quicker, rubbing his fingers against the spot he's found that makes me gush; the spot I never knew existed before Asher.

"Now listen to me, sweetness," he commands softly, "I'm going to come inside you. Understood?"

What a fucking *prince*.

"Please," I nod.

"Where do you want it – your mouth or your pussy?" he asks, slipping another finger into my heat, stretching me out and bringing me that much closer to coming. "Where do you want my cum?"

"My mouth," is the first thing that pops out. I don't think I even rationally thought about my answer before I just blurted it out. I haven't done that before… but that's not really saying anything, I hadn't done anything remotely sexual before him.

Asher groans and his forehead drops to mine, like he's dizzy with desperation. Like just me saying that pushed him too far.

"Fuck, that mouth, huh, baby girl?" he rasps in my ear; the excitement I can hear makes me want it even more. Nodding, I thrust upward while clenching down on his fingers which are still rubbing on that perfect spot inside.

"Come here," he growls, pulling his fingers from my cunt and licking them clean quickly. Before I know it, he yanks me to the side and spreads my thighs open, just enough that his hips and erect cock sit flush against mine. He's so hard and I'm so wet that he slides in perfectly, without any assistance. He didn't have to guide the head in or anything; just lined up and pushed forward until he was fully seated inside me.

"This isn't going to take long," he grunts, wrapping his hands around my thighs.

"Good, because I'm not going to last." Slipping a hand down, I start playing with my clit, but I know if I do too much I'll come too quickly. "Fuck me, Daddy."

"Good girl, baby. Good girl," he praises me heavily. "Now let me show you how fucking crazy I am about you." He holds my ass tightly against himself and fucks me so deeply, so quickly, that my eyes roll back and I gasp. Circling my clit, I push myself closer to climax. His fingers slip to where we're joined, and my eyes open quickly as I wait. What is he doing?

I already feel fucking *stretched* with his cock in me. I don't know if he's going to try to fit his fingers inside me as well.

"What do you think I'm going to do, baby?" he whispers. My gaze meets his; he's staring at me intensely, smirking like he knew what I was thinking. "Maybe more will fit one day, but today, I want to feed you my cum."

"Yes, Daddy," I whisper breathlessly.

His fingers slide around my stretched lips and gather the wetness before replacing my own fingers at my clit.

Groaning, my eyes roll back in my head at the perfect fucking way he plays my body. Like I'm a fine instrument he's become an expert at playing.

"That's it, baby girl. Just let go and come around my cock," he whispers in my ear before nosing his way down my neck and bites down. The cord in my lower belly gets tighter and tighter as my cunt gets warmer and wetter. I'm so fucking close that I start thrusting and grinding against him.

"Yes, fuck. That's it. I love it when you do that, fuck!" Asher whispers loudly in my ear. His words, along with his breathy, gravelly, desperate tone, set me off. I come around his cock, gripping him tightly as I ride the waves of pleasure while my body relents. Asher holds me together and fucks me deeper, faster, harder, to prolong my orgasm as long as possible.

I start to scream his name, but his hand covers my mouth quickly to muffle the noise.

"No, no, baby. Only I get to hear what you sound like when you come."

My eyes close again, allowing me to focus on my other senses. Asher is panting heavily, his breaths stuttering like he's trying to hold back. The bed is starting to squeak under the force of his thrusts, the vinyl of the mattress protector scratching against my back. Our bodies are hot, so fucking hot, as we work together to make each other feel good. To claim the other as our own.

Asher pulls away from me, pulling out of me so quickly that I fucking *mourn* the loss of him.

"On your knees," he orders, standing tall and stroking his wet, shiny, hard-as-fuck cock. He's stroking it so hard, so furiously, I'm mesmerized, but he adds, "Now, baby girl." I slip to my knees, so I'm face to face with his dick.

"Open wide, I'm coming. Fuck, open up." His voice is... I could come again just from hearing him talk to me while on the brink of orgasm. It's dark, desperate, low, needy. I love it.

I'm nervous—who wouldn't be? I don't know what to expect really, but I know I want to try.

I open my mouth and take him in, sealing my lips around his cock and suck, lick, bob my head. And fuck me, the noises he makes are so erotic, I feel myself get turned on again. He holds my head, but never forces me to move or to stay; just wraps his fingers in my tresses and thrusts shallowly.

I like it. I like blowing him. I like this *a lot*.

"Fuck, baby, I'm coming. I'm coming, you're so fucking gorgeous on your knees for me. Such a good girl. Oh god, this is better than I ever dreamed. Goddamn, you're beautiful," Asher babbles, and twists his fingers as his hips stutter. His cum lands on my tongue; it's salty and viscous but not altogether unpleasant. It's well worth it for the look of reverence on his face as he stares at me.

"Show me," he says breathlessly when he stops coming. "Open and show me. Please." He looks so awestruck, and that's even before I open my mouth. I caught it all on my tongue and held it, before opening my mouth and showing it to him. Asher cups my chin; his breathing slows down but his dark eyes take me in.

"You're perfect. You're perfect and *you're mine*." He nods, before tucking his softening cock back into his shorts and helps me up. "Here," he says, holding out a few napkins for me to spit into.

But I simply swallow everything he gave me.

His jaw drops.

"If I didn't just come so hard, I'd flip you over and fuck you from behind against the desk so you could look at yourself as I made you squirt," Asher says darkly before grabbing my face and pulling me in for a deep kiss.

"There's still time," I tease with a weak laugh when he pulls away.

Asher walks over and closes the door finally, before unzipping my duffel bag and pulling out my big blanket to make a cocoon for us on the bed.

Safe, sated, and warm, I take comfort in his arms as we both rest. His heart beats strongly against my back.

"I hope you like it here," Asher says after a few moments of silence. "I hope you like it here, but I also really hope you like my place, too."

"I do," I answer quickly. "I really like your place. I feel so safe and at home there."

"Good. Because it feels so much more like a *home* when you're there." My breath catches at his words and my heart swells. He kisses the back of my head and sighs deeply.

As long as I'm with you, I feel at home.

THREE WEEKS LATER

HOW MUCH THINGS can change in three weeks.

I went from seeing Jade daily—getting to hold her, talk to her in person, wake up to her smiling, gorgeous face—to seeing her maybe every other day during the day. But more often than not, I'm woken up from my slumber late at night by a soft knock at my door and Jade standing there. She always looks exhausted, like the only time she sleeps is with me. She's usually gone before I wake up though.

Tonight is no different.

I've started sleeping on my couch to make sure I don't miss the knock. She doesn't call me beforehand, not wanting to 'burden' me. Ridiculous.

It's 11:30 at night and my TV is flickering with reruns of a ball game I've seen a few times with the volume down low. My eyes flutter with the effort to stay awake. The knock hits the door, barely audible but just in time, like she doesn't really want to wake me up.

This stupid, wonderful, considerate girl.

I practically leap to the door and pull it open. My girl is

standing there; her backpack slung over her shoulder, her head resting painfully against the door frame and her eyes so sunken in.

"Jade," I breathe her name. What do I need to do to take care of her? Because I'm obviously doing a shitty job. "What's wrong?" I ask, noticing her eyes are lined with tears and her cheeks are red. She's been crying.

Someone made my girl cry. Every instinct I have yells at me to go beat the motherfucker that made her feel this way, but to avoid jail, I need to find out what happened first.

"I hate my roommate. She's... She's just awful," Jade sniffles. I pull her into my arms, hugging her tightly. I close the door behind us, threading our fingers together as I pull her toward my room so I can make sure she sleeps well.

"What'd she do?" I question, trying to keep my tone even.

Jade sighs and I can hear the tears in her voice. "If I'm not available at her beck and call, she says I'm not actually trying to form a friendship. If I don't stay in the room at every available opportunity, then she complains I'm never there. She's just... controlling my every move. I feel like I can't even breathe when I'm in my own freaking room! I can't do homework when I decide to because she wants to go do something. I can't sleep there most nights because she fucks any guy that looks at her and she kicks me out. I tried talking to her about it and she laughed, saying it was part of the experience. I just..." She sighs heavily and says, "I just want to be able to live how I want. I don't want to feel trapped anymore and... she's got all these fucking expectations that when I don't meet them, she's pissed off at me."

I get why she's so upset. She's finally free from her mother in this regard, but now someone has already tried to occupy that controlling-bitch role in her life. Jade should be able to be free. She fought for it. She deserves it.

Your home is supposed to be the place where you can truly

relax and just be. Not another place you have to put on a front. Typically, we already have to put on a mask everywhere else in life; your home should be the place where you can set the mask down.

I wrap my arms around her shoulders, pulling her in for a hug and wishing I had more to offer her. "What can I do?"

Jade sobs and her forehead drops to my chest. "Nothing. This. All I need is you."

"Well, that's easy then," I say softly. "You'll always have me."

"I'm sorry to bother you, but can I crash here tonight?" She looks up at me with a sad, hopeful smile.

"You can stay here as much as you want. I'll never tell you no."

"What if you get really annoyed with me?" She chuckles through tears, but her grip on my waist tightens. "What if—"

"I'm not playing the 'what-if' game, darlin'." I cut her off with a kiss on the forehead. "Believe me when I tell you that you are always welcome in my home. It makes me feel better when you're here. In my arms." Cupping her face, I kiss her lips, salty with her tears.

"I'm always happy here," she whispers and my heart beats harder for her.

"I'm always happy when you're here, too."

***

PULLING UP TO THE BUILDING WHERE JADE'S FIRST class is, I prop the kickstand of my bike up and let the engine idle. Jade climbs off the back of my bike and I immediately feel the loss of her body heat against my back. That's sad.

But I get to watch as she lets her blonde hair fall, like we're in a freaking action movie, and it makes me feel better. The tresses drop and she shakes them out. The sunlight catches her hair, glinting beautifully. I'm mesmerized.

And so are a few other fuckers walking by.

I grab her hand and pull her to me, kissing her deeply. Probably a bit too deeply for a public setting, but I want to make sure everyone knows that *she's mine.*

Pulling back, I kiss her softly. Once, twice, three times.

"Wow," she says breathlessly and I just nod. If I say anything at all, I know I'll embarrass myself because I'm toeing the line of getting lost in her.

"I've got to go," she laments, nodding absentmindedly, but doesn't make a move to leave.

"I know you do." I slip my hands down to her thighs and hold her. She's wearing these denim cut-off shorts that drive me crazy. Her legs are long and lean and so freaking soft. Always so soft.

My eyes look over her shoulder, making sure those guys won't mess with her. That they know she's got someone who will protect her.

I see looks of envy from all the fuckers around. I can't help but smirk like an asshole; but I know what a gem I have. I won't let anyone take her from me.

"Will you text me later?" I look up at her, smiling brightly at the same gone-for-each-other smile she has on her face. "I have a client that's going to run long, they always do, but I'd love to take you out for a late dinner and maybe convince you to come stay at my place tonight."

Jade tries to cover a smile, but I see it. It's there in its sweet, excited glory.

She wraps her arms around my shoulders and looks up like she's trying to decide.

"Hmm," she taps her chin a few times. "That's a hard decision. I just don't know." She laughs as I start tickling her sides.

"Oh, come on," I kiss her, "please?"

"Okay, okay," she nods breathlessly. "Kind of a no-brainer."

"I thought so," I say and kiss her softly again.

"I get done for the day at four, but I'll stay on campus until you tell me you're done."

"Okay, it's a plan." She steps backward and I try not to let it show but I'm already saddened by her leaving.

"I'll see you later," she says, then mouths, "*Daddy.*" I bite my lip and shake my head. Jade smiles even brighter, holding her backpack straps tighter before turning away from me.

"You'll pay for that, baby girl," I call after her. All I hear is her twinkling laugh before I rev my engine and head to *From The Ashes,* only thinking about that sweet sound and how long today is going to feel.

⚬⚬⚬⚬⚬⚬⚬⚬

I SLIP MY BACKPACK OVER MY CHAIR, PLOPPING DOWN at my desk, already in a bad mood. It's probably not the healthiest thing that I'm this fucking addicted to her, but I'll deal with that if it becomes a true issue.

Sighing loudly, I rub my hands over my face and shake it out. I have to get my head together. Someone is entrusting me with permanently tattooing their body, and I don't take that lightly.

I pull my sketchbook out and also my notebook where I keep my client notes so that I can get to work making their next piece. The ding of the bell sounds a few times, but I know I have a few hours to kill before my client comes in.

"Hello, you fuckers. How are you today?" Roxie's voice

booms across the shop, cutting through Ty's gun buzzing and the music overhead.

"Wow, Roxie," I shake my head. "Were you raised in a barn?"

She sets her bag down at her desk and pulls the goggle-looking pitch-black sunglasses off her face to stare right at me. "A zoo, actually."

I scoff and turn back to my work. "Ain't that the truth."

"Rude," she calls out before stomping over to my desk. "Why are you such a mopey dick today?"

Groaning, I drop my pen. "I'm not a mopey dick."

"Are too."

"Roxie," I drag her name in warning.

"You are!" Her eyebrows piece together as she turns to rest against the edge of my desk. "What's wrong?"

"Nothing is wrong. I'm just trying to get my work done before my client comes in. She's wanted every change and alteration on this side piece, so I want to have a solid foundation before she gets here."

"It's not because Jade's classes have started and she's being a good student and paying attention instead of messaging you 24/7?"

"Oh, shut it, Roxie." I throw her a dirty look. "We're two separate people and can survive independently of each other," is what comes out of my mouth. But what I really want to say is, *'I really just wish she wasn't so... unhappy with the aspects of school and her life here. I wish she didn't feel so trapped in her dorm. I wish she got along with her roommate. I love that she comes to my bed every night, fuck do I love that, but I hate that she has tears in her eyes. I just desperately want to protect her and make sure she's happy at all times.'*

"You're not the only one that went from talking to her

everyday to barely hearing from her. Only this time, you see her every night, not me," Roxie pouts.

"You sound jealous, Roxie."

She chuckles, crossing her arms over her chest. "I miss her. I know we kind of became fast friends, but I felt a good vibe with her. She was a good roommate, too."

"I'm sure she'd rather be living with you still than in the dorms, to be honest," I say with a sigh. Sitting back in my chair, I stretch my arms over my head before holding my hands behind my neck.

"I've heard a few things from her about the roommate. She sounds controlling as hell." Roxie makes a disgusted look.

"Yeah, she really is," I sigh. "I have to get ready. I'm hoping I can actually take her out tonight."

"Good for you, boss man. I have a good feeling about you two." Roxie shakes her finger in my face and walks off towards her own desk.

Sighing, I turn my attention back to my artwork, tweaking it here and there to reflect what Sharon, my client, asked for. She's younger than my other clients, but she's older than me and going through a bit of a mid-life crisis, so she's getting this huge tattoo that spans her hip to her upper ribcage.

It's a good tattoo, though, I made sure of that. Not too busy, not too many details that will make it age poorly. It's a sunset on a beach, with a dog running through the shallows, water splashing around their paws.

It's huge and colorful, specifically done in the watercolor technique, which is challenging to say the least. Hopefully we'll get a good foundation done today and then finish in the second session. She's going to be hurting after the four hours we have scheduled today.

"Asher!" I hear my name through the shop, a nails-on-the-chalkboard kind of yell, signaling that Sharon has arrived.

Taking a deep breath, I put my professional face on and vow to try to get through this day as fast as possible to see Jade.

"Sharon, hi." I give her a polite nod. "Let me sanitize and get ready and I'll call you back."

"Okay," she says worriedly, looking at her watch. "The timer doesn't start until you start tattooing right?"

"Yes, not a problem." I've tried telling her that the "hour" I'm charging her for doesn't start until we start, but she asks me every time.

This is going to be a long day.

FIFTEEN MINUTES LEFT. I CAN ENDURE FIFTEEN MORE minutes.

My hand is starting to cramp as I'm taking more and more moments to shake out my dominant hand to keep it steady. Sharon's lying on her side, a bikini suit top on and a blanket covering her upper body to help keep her warm. Luckily, as frustrating as Sharon has been as a client, she doesn't like to chit-chat while I'm working, which I appreciate.

Buzz, buzz.

Buzz, buzz.

My phone is buzzing on my desk. Eh, I'll ignore it. I only have a few minutes left.

Buzz, buzz. Buzz, buzz. Buzz, buzz. Buzz, buzz.

Fuck, now someone's calling me.

"Ty!" I call out, thankful his client is taking a break. "Can you come check my phone please?"

He jumps off his desk, striding over, and picks up my phone quickly. Usually, he just reads the name of whomever is calling me so I can determine if I need to pick up, but this time, he just answers.

"Are you okay?" Ty asks and I pull the needle from Sharon's skin. "Calm down, *chica*. Calm down. Where are you now?"

"Ty?" I turn abruptly.

"Okay, go back to your room and I'll send Asher now. Yes, yes, don't argue with me. Do you think he'll... No, okay. Go lock the door. He'll be there in a few minutes." Ty walks over to me, pointing to Sharon's side and gesturing with his finger to tell me to start wrapping her up.

"What the fuck is happening?" I snap. Fear grips me as I start cleaning up Sharon, wiping her skin and putting saran wrap over top.

"It's going to be okay, I promise." Ty hangs up the phone then grabs my backpack and bike keys.

"I'll clean your station and get payment from her. Your standard fee, right? Minus the fifteen minutes." He pushes the objects into my hands. He's calm and tactical, the way I've seen him be in fights, but I'm about to punch his fucking eye in if he won't tell me what happened.

"Ty, what the fuck is going on?" I shout at him.

"She's in a co-ed dorm?" Ty asks, shaking his head. "*Sólo un maldito tipo malvado.* The guys... *The* guy... he came into the common room, or passed through, and she's terrified."

That's all he had to say.

All the blood rushes from my face and I grip my keys tighter.

"Where is she?" I snarl.

"She said she was going to the café. She wanted to be in a public setting so nothing could happen. Toward the back," he says, handing me my bag.

"Make sure Sharon's not mad, explain that there is a family emergency, she'll get fifteen minutes off today and fifteen minutes off the next session for the delay," I rush, giving Ty orders to take care of my client. I stride out of the door angrily, not giving two fucks about the disgruntled noises from Sharon as Ty tries to calm her down and Roxie steps in to help. I might have lost a client, but I couldn't care less.

"Hold on, Jade. I'm on my way,"

Jade

I LUG my heavy-ass backpack off the elevator when it reaches my floor, hoping to get to my room and dump this load of books off before getting ready for my little date with Asher.

This elevator is too freaking old, and it smells like someone has already thrown up in it today. *Joy.*

I knew living in the dorms would be an experience, but I didn't think it would suck quite so much. It's nothing like the movies, and I haven't met anyone who has wanted more than to get in my pants or to get a tampon.

Pulling my key out, I start to unlock the door but stop. A rhythmic thumping and very clearly fake moans come from inside.

My head drops. *Fucking great.* "You better not be fucking on my bed!" I yell through the door. I don't get a response back, nor am I expecting one.

Ugh, this is annoying. My roommate has a new lover every other day, which wouldn't be a bad thing except she always seems to bring them to our room. Can't she ever go to their place? For once? When she's not parading her sex companions, she's demanding I be available to her at all times to "try to bond" and "be better roommates, maybe even friends."

Yeah, I don't see that happening anytime soon. Her need to make sure I'm always available to her, even when she doesn't act the same for me, is quickly getting old. It's already started with the shitty, guilt-trip texts about how we never hang out, or the passive aggressive tone when I tell her I can't go get food besides at the café. It's fucking embarrassing to say I just simply don't have the money to go on a late-night Micky D's run. I guess I should be happy she wants to bond at all? But it doesn't really feel that way.

It feels forced. And to be frank, I'm not exactly sure I actually want to be friends with this person anyway.

I haven't heard from Asher yet, so I don't know how much longer he has with his client and therefore, how much time I have to kill. The common area is just a blank, bare room that separates the two wings of the building. There are some nasty, beat-up couches and a few tables with chairs to entice people to sit and hang out, but I've rarely seen the commons be used.

Except when roommates have been kicked out due to their room being...occupied.

Like I have been, at least three times this last week alone.

Dropping my backpack into the chair, I plop myself in one and groan. This is not how I wanted today to go. But there's no sense in wasting time.

I pull my Macro Economics textbook out and start studying. Since the fallout with my mom, I really, *really*, have to be careful to keep my scholarship. At least until I figure out what I want to do.

I know business is smart, but I just can't wrap my brain around it. My brain has never worked that way; numbers and equations, strategy and moves, deals and trades. I don't like that.

But knowing business, knowing how to successfully *build and run* a business, might be invaluable one day.

I catch a glimpse of my sketchbook in my bag, and I desperately want to open it and sketch something out, but I need to do some homework and focus.

Art is... it's beauty. It's simple. It's the best way I know of that shows others exactly how you see something, how you feel something, how something resonates with you. You can tell someone how you feel about them with a portrait. It's magical when you think about it.

Shaking my head, I sigh.

I need to focus. Opening the textbook to the second chapter, I start reading the words the professor went over today to try and understand it even a fraction more. Honestly, it was like listening to Charlie Brown's teacher. *Whomp, whomp, whomp-whomp, whomp.* Nothing.

"No, dude! It'll be fucking epic! You remember, like this summer." A guy's voice rings out as the doors bang open with the force of their push. A whole group of guys walk through, talking and joking, and the room gets exponentially louder.

But that doesn't matter.

Because the voice that spoke belonged to the friend of the guy that hurt me.

And next to him, smirking and nodding like a fucking prince, is the guy who raped me.

Seeing him in the light and in the flesh—not just through my hazy memories—is scarier than I ever thought it could be.

Ever since that night, I've tried not to think about things too hard. To not put blame on him or myself... but that's bullshit.

He should be blamed. I should be angry—not scared. I should stride right up to him and smack him in the face so hard his eye bleeds.

But instead, I'm stuck in place, trying to remind myself to breathe. It feels exactly like I've peeked under my bed and the monster jumped out.

Only it's not a nightmare.

It's real.

The friend smirks at me, probably thinking I'm checking them out, and then *he* smiles brightly at me, winking as they continue to pass. I feel sick.

My eyes track them, keeping them in my sight from the moment they enter the room to the moment they step onto that elevator.

The figment of my nightmares stride towards the door and my rapist stares me down, a look of distant confusion on his face. Like he doesn't remember me.

I hope to god he doesn't.

I shrink down into the chair and try to move my textbook higher to cover my face, but I'm too late. The doors start to close and his eyebrows knit together, his eyes narrowing, and I scrunch down further. But right before the door closes, his eyes widen and a predatory smile, so disgusting I will need a shower, spreads across his filthy lips and I know.

He knows who I am.

He knows where I live.

And I run to the trashcan making it just in time to throw up everything in my system.

My hands are shaking.

I'm frozen.

What do I do?

My fingers inch towards my phone. To call the one person I feel safe with.

"Asher," I whisper brokenly. I find his contact shakily in my phone and call him. After a few rings, it goes to voicemail.

Fuck. I need him. I need someone. I can't... this... what do I...

I'm going to have a panic attack, damn it.

What if he comes back and I'm alone? What if he finds me when I'm coming back from classes? What if...

I re-dial Asher. "Please pick up, please, please, please," I whisper.

After a few rings, Ty answers the phone. "Are you okay?"

"Ty," I sob, "He was here. He... he was right here. He winked at me, and he knows where I am now. Ty," I cry, trying to muffle my sobs but I can feel myself start to be hysterical.

"Where are you now?" he asks. I can hear in his voice that he knows exactly what happened and how I'm feeling. I need to get out—now.

"I'm in the common area, Hannah's fucking someone in our room. I can't, I can't... What if he's on his way back? Oh god." I start to spiral and load up my book quickly. "I have to get out of here."

Ty snaps me out of it and says, "Okay, go back to your room and I'm sending Asher now."

"No, no you can't. He's got that big client, I can't be—"

"Yes, yes, *chica*, don't argue with me."

"I'll be fine, maybe I'm making too big a deal about this. I just... I don't feel safe at all. He knew. He knew who I was, what he had done and now he knows where to find me," I say softly, the fear clear in my voice as it shakes.

"Go lock the door. He'll be there in a few minutes," Ty orders me, but I can't. I can't because I refuse to deal with Hannah and her bullshit.

"Tell him I'll be in the café, toward the back. Nothing can happen if I'm in public, right?" My voice stutters, and I don't think I believe what I'm saying, but... it's all I've got. I hear Asher snapping at Ty in the background and it's fucking amazing how just his voice calms me down.

The café is downstairs, I just need to get there.

IGNORING ALL TRAFFIC RULES, I speed as fast as humanly possible on my bike to get to the campus. It's not far from the shop—ten minutes if I'm walking—but this drive seems to stretch on for hours.

All I can think of is how scared she has to be. How I'm not there by her side.

I promised I would take care of her and that means protecting her. By any means necessary.

Finally, her building comes into view. I push my bike a little more, adding a few RPMs and cutting through the lawn. Fuck their landscaping. People jump out of my way, dodging to either side, but I don't give one shit. I just want to get to Jade as fast as possible.

Dirt and grass fly around me as I skid to a stop by the front door. People scream at me, cuss me out, but I don't hear them as I kick off the bike, cutting the engine and pulling the keys out.

"Man, you can't park there!" A security guard comes yelling at me, running as fast as he can with his beer belly. Honestly, I could walk faster than he's running.

"Try to stop me," I growl, throwing the words over my shoulder, not even pausing to make sure he hears the vitriol I'm spewing.

The security guard screams at me, telling me to stop and that I can't go in, but if he wants to stop me he's going to have to catch me. And from the way I can hear his panting followed by the jingling of tools and keys on his utility belt fading, it means he's already so far behind me that I don't need to worry.

I pass through the lobby; my age, tattoos and fuming anger attracting a lot of attention from onlookers. I see fucking Pamela clock me and start making her way towards me, but I can't deal with her right now.

"Excuse me?" she asks in her overly friendly way.

"Fuck off, Pam," I snap, pointing my finger at her and continuing my way to the café.

"You can't just barge in here; you have to check in!" she cries, figuratively clutching her pearls.

"Do I look like I give a shit?" I snap loudly the words echoing throughout the room. I quicken my steps and push both doors open to the café, resounding *bangs* drawing everyone's attention to me as I scan the room, looking for Jade.

Everyone is looking at me—some with interest, some with fear, some with confusion—but there is only one gaze looking at me with relief and adoration.

Jade.

She picks up her backpack and pushes through the tables, past the people around us, and I do the same. We meet in the middle, and she collapses in my arms, sobbing against my chest.

"I've got you," I whisper against her hair, holding her tightly to me. "I've got you. Let's get out of here."

"Asher," she cries against my chest softly.

I shush her softly and push us towards the door. Where

fucking Pam is standing. Fuming. She goes to say something, but I throw her a dirty look and shake my head.

"Not the time."

"We'll be talking about this later, Jade. Jade's brother," she snaps, almost like it's a threat, but I could care less. Let her throw Jade out; I'll take care of her. Rushing towards the front door, people are no longer trying to hide that they're watching us.

Fucking assholes, just staring at us.

I cover Jade as much as I can. The last thing I want is for others to feel they can talk to her about this later.

The security guard is standing by my bike, writing down the license plate number in his little notebook, and talking into his radio when we get there.

"Your helmet is in the saddle bag," I say to Jade and nudge her towards the back seat. Her eyes widen slightly when I mention that it's *her* helmet. Hell yes, I got her a helmet. I'm not taking any chances with her safety. Not even one.

I don't let her out of sight as she stumbles towards my bike, and I go to handle the rent-a-cop.

I rip the little notebook out of his hand, pull off the page he's written on, and hand the book back to him. "I get that I fucked up, but I promise you, it's for a good reason," I explain.

"If you had stopped and we had talked—"

"That girl over there," I step closer to him and speak quieter. "That girl on my bike is my life. And she felt threatened by one of the fuckers who lives here. I wasn't going to stop and have a conversation while she could've been in danger."

"I understand, but—"

"No, I don't think you do." I glare at him pointedly, and actual understanding dawns in his eyes.

"Ah."

"Yeah. So, if you could kindly not report my license number and get me banned from campus, I'd appreciate it."

Rent-A-Cop looks from me to Jade, sees her blank expression and the slight shake to her hands, and he nods. "I have a daughter that goes here. If you hear any specific names or descriptions, you let me know." He hands me a card with his name and info on it.

I nod curtly and pocket the card. "I'll keep that in mind. Thank you."

"Get her out of here. She looks like she's been through enough," he says softly and walks inside the building.

So maybe there *are* good people here.

"Come on, baby girl." I buckle the helmet under Jade's chin and close the visor before kissing her masked forehead. "Let's go home."

⸻⸻⸻

"Jade, please talk to me," I whisper. Since we arrived back at my place, she's been silent. I pull a Coke from the fridge, something I'd picked up for her on my last grocery run, and open it for her, placing it in her hand. "Do you want this, or maybe some tea? I know you don't like coffee, but hot chocolate? Baby, tell me how I can help you." I'm speaking to her as calmly and as gently as I can.

But she doesn't say anything. Just looks dead ahead.

"Jade?" I try again, putting my hand on her knee, but she jolts. I pull my hands back abruptly, raising them both to show that I don't mean any harm. "I'm sorry, I'm sorry."

"Don't... I... I can't right now," she stammers and her tone breaks my heart. Her eyes fill with unshed tears and I slowly move to sit beside her on the couch. Jade brings both of her legs up and wraps her arms around her knees, tucking herself in.

"It's okay," I say softly.

"It's not!" she cries, breaking in such a vulnerable way. "It's not okay. I'm freaking out. I'm alone. I'm terrified to go back to the dorms. Even if I could break the contract and move out, I'd never get the rest of the money that I've already spent for the year back *or* have enough money to rent somewhere. I feel so bad that I had to call and pull you away from a client, but you're my person, Asher. You're the only one I feel safe with. But you can't even touch me, I can't even ask you to hold me, because I saw someone across the room and now I feel like my skin is on fire. How is any of that okay?"

Her beautiful eyes sparkle with tears as she pulls her knees tighter to her chest, and I slowly move my hand to hold hers.

"Jade," I murmur softly, "You're not alone. You're not. I'm so glad you called me. So fucking glad. I wish I had been there to keep you from feeling this way. I wish you never had to see his face again. I wish I had been there to punch the fucker's lights out." Not a word of this is a lie. I wish I had been there to take away her fear, to keep her space safe.

To go back to that night and kill the asshole that did this to her.

Jade shakes her head against her knees and sighs another sob. Watching the woman I'm quickly falling in love with break down like this, especially when I can't do anything to help, breaks my heart. I want to wrap her up in my arms, whisper in her ear that I'm here and that I won't let anything happen to her. But all I can do right now is tell her. Tell her everything.

"Whatever you want, Jade, I'll make it happen. You want to break your contract? We'll do it. You want to move to an apartment? We'll find one. I'll lay the world at your feet." I move in slightly closer, wanting to make sure she's comfortable, so I look for any sign that she needs me to back off. Finding none, I hold my hand out, giving her the choice. She can take it or not, no hard feelings. But the choice is hers.

Jade sniffles, turning her face to look at me. Her eyes are shining so desperately with hope from my words. Her cheeks are wet and shiny from her tears, and her normally creamy skin is red from crying and frustration. My heart lurches. I just want to take all the pain, fear, and sadness from her. I'd do it gladly if that meant she didn't feel it.

She doesn't say anything, but she softly places her hand in mind and threads our fingers together.

"Will you stay with me tonight?" I ask. "I'll order pizza and we can just cuddle on the couch while we watch something. Does that sound okay?" Jade nods, trying to smile but it doesn't reach her eyes. "You take as long as you need," I stress, "and remember—you owe no one anything."

Jade sits up, looking me straight in the eye, searching for something. I don't know what she's looking for, but I do everything in my power to keep from changing my expression in any way.

If she needs to make sure I'm telling the truth, I'll do whatever she needs to show her I'm being honest.

She nods again, looking slightly more comfortable.

"But I'm not watching The Office one more time, baby," I scoff. "You've already made me watch it like three times. There's only so many times you can make me watch Dwight and Michael fuck around," I tease, nudging her knee with my fist.

Jade chuckles with a watery voice and launches into my arms. Wrapping her arms around my shoulders and her legs around my waist, she clings to me tightly like a koala bear.

"Asher," she breathes into my neck, saying my name like I'm a tether holding her together.

"I'm right here, baby girl. Nothing can hurt you now."

Jade

TWO WEEKS HAVE GONE by since I saw… him.

Two weeks since I've stayed at the dorms. I'm just… I don't know what I want to do yet. Every night I say I'm going to make a plan, and every day I get swept up in other things.

I've been sleeping at Asher's. It's close enough to campus that it's a brisk twenty-minute walk back to the apartment or ten minutes to the shop. Not that Asher has ever let me walk alone; he is always driving me or walking with me. He's been overprotective these days, but I'm very grateful.

Asher's amazing, and he has done nothing to suggest he feels like I've overstayed my welcome. I feel like I am, though; like I'm taking advantage of my boyfriend's generosity. But he hasn't asked me to leave or even hinted at it. Every afternoon when I'm done with classes, I walk to the shop and get the apartment keys from him, and every time he smiles brightly and gladly hands them over.

It's very domestic, and I'm quickly getting addicted to it.

Sometimes I take the keys and head back to the apartment so I can study in silence, and sometimes I hang out at the shop.

Roxie's always asking my opinion on her designs and chats with me about everything and anything. Ty is still warming up to me, but I've learned that being standoffish to anyone but Roxie is part of his personality.

I'm seated at the front desk, my sketchbook under my fingers for the first time in a long time, and I'm letting my feelings dictate my artwork. My pictures always have floral undertones, depth beneath the flowers. Pain under the beauty.

Each stroke of my pencil feels like another string of stress being released and burned from my system.

Why did I ever stop this?

I'm so focused, so lost in my piece, I hardly register that there's someone standing in front of me until a hand comes down, smacking the counter.

"Hello?" a guy snaps rudely. "I've been standing here for five minutes and you haven't even had the decency to look up. What the hell is wrong with you?"

"Oh, I'm sorry. I didn't even realize..." I apologize, but I should've known this kind of guy wouldn't let it go. He's probably a few years older than me, but younger than Asher. A real wannabe-looking guy who's trying too hard to look effortless. He's got a gold hoop in one ear and a toothpick hanging from the corner of his mouth like he's some kind of knock-off mafia gangster. And his attitude matches. Unfortunately.

"You're damn right you didn't realize. I've been coming here for years and you just ignore me? How dare you." He looks past me and points at someone. "Ty, man. Help me out over here."

A grunt tells me that Ty's already not okay with the interruption, and the whole situation makes me nervous. "Ty, I didn't see him, I'm sorry," I stutter.

"It's not your fault, Jade," he says flatly, putting a hand on my shoulder before turning to look at the customer. "Yes, Sean?"

"I want her dealt with. She's obviously not very good at her job." The mafia-wannabe leans forward and grabs my arm roughly. I freeze.

Ty *immediately* grabs Sean's hand and twists his wrist—hard —in a way that looks painful. Sean's head hits the counter as he tries to lessen the angle that's causing the pain.

Ty looks down on him, his eyebrows raised, and he growls more fiercely than I've ever heard him speak. "You piece of shit, you think you can touch her?"

I cover my mouth to stifle my whimpers as Sean cries out in pain while Ty twists his arm more. But Sean sticks to his guns.

"You heard me!" He hollers. "She ignored a customer and she should be dealt with. Where's the owner?"

"I'm a *co-owner* and I say get the fuck out!" Ty snaps angrily. Sean's eyes widen and his mouth opens in shock as he realizes what he's done.

Asher comes up behind me, crosses his arms over his chest and sounds very professional to meet Ty's aggressiveness. "I'm the other owner. What the fuck is going on?"

Ty releases Sean's arm and I'm still frozen in fear.

Why do men keep aggressively grabbing me? Why do men think they can do this shit to me? How do I make it so they never think it's okay again?

"Throw him out, Ashe," Ty growls and cusses at him in Spanish.

"What the fuck, Ty? We have a session in twenty-five minutes, I've already paid my deposit!" Sean snaps angrily, which makes me step backward, hitting Asher's chest.

"I'm going to ask one more time. What *the fuck* is going on?" Asher's voice booms as he notices my reaction, and I shrink. His hands go to my hips, moving me gently behind him so I'm not at the forefront of this conversation.

"I've been standing here, waiting for that bitch to notice, so I can check in and sign the paperwork. But she was too involved with her stupid little sketches. She ignored me. I want her to be talked to," Sean sneers and looks between Asher and Ty, then looks me in the eye with all the hate in the world. How does someone hate another person they don't even know?

"Ah," Asher says, nodding. "I see."

"Yeah, you have some dumbass employee who can't even do the bare minimum. You should drop the dead weight." Sean keeps talking, like it's common knowledge I'm an idiot.

Maybe I am.

"Although, I can see why you both would want to keep her around." His eyes snake down over my body and I step closer into Asher's back. "She's easy on the eyes. Especially in that shirt of hers."

I look down and fiddle with the end of Asher's oversized shirt I'd borrowed, realizing it's so long it's covering the shorts I'm wearing. Sean's eyes linger at the hemline and he bites his lower lip, like he's considering changing his mind and hitting on me instead of complaining.

And people think *women* are ruled by their emotions. Jesus Christ.

"If you don't do something about him, I will," Ty hisses darkly. His chest heaves with anger, and it's obvious he wants to handle this. With his fists. I don't think Sean would survive.

Asher takes a moment. His back tenses and his hand curls into a fist at his side. I can feel the struggle within him on how he wants to react versus how he should.

"Don't," I whisper.

"As co-owner of *From The Ashes*, I want to say I've heard your complaint and I apologize for any dissatisfaction in service. However, Ms. Henderson is not an employee and was simply sitting at the front desk, minding her own business. Something I suggest you do in the future." Asher takes a step closer to the counter. "That being said, you are barred from coming to this shop ever again. I will refund 50% of the paid deposit, as per the contract you signed. We will keep the other 50% for the lost time in our schedule due to your cancellation."

"I'm not fucking cancelling! I already said that!" Sean shouts, his fist hitting the counter and causing me to cry out in fear and jump. Asher puts his hand out to shield me, almost unconsciously, because once he realized I was okay, all the professionalism dropped from his face, his tone, and his energy.

"I believe that's the most polite way of saying what is about to happen, though." Asher's voice is calm—eerily so. And Ty has a big, knowing smile on his face. "Now, like I said, *as the owner*, I'm asking you only one more time to leave."

"This is fucking ridiculous. I'm not leaving, damn it. I paid for this tattoo, motherfucker, I'm getting it," Sean grumbles and complains, trying to talk over Asher, but Asher simply raises his voice.

"Now, *as her boyfriend*," Asher's words linger. Sean's face pales and his jaw drops slightly as he realizes the mistake he made. "I'm going to do this," Asher finishes. Reaching over the counter quickly, he grabs a handful of Sean's shirt and punches him once. My hands fly to my mouth in shock and I hear yelling all around me.

Asher jumps over the counter and holds Sean to the ground, punching him again.

"Don't you ever touch my girl again, do you understand me?" Asher snarls. "You piece of shit, motherfucker!" Another punch. Sean's eyes are wide with fear as he tries to defend himself. He manages to get a punch in himself, but Asher's too strong. Too angry.

"Stop!" I cry out, but it's like no one can hear me. Roxie grabs my arms and helps me stay upright, but I can feel myself hyperventilating.

Asher must look back and see me close to breaking because he drops Sean's shirt and wipes his bloody knuckles on his own shirt. "Don't you even *think* about coming back here or you'll be met with the same." Asher spits at Sean and stands up.

"Ty, get him out of here."

"You got it, Ashe." Ty leans over and pulls Sean up, sneering at him the whole time. "You're lucky it was him that popped you first. If it was me, I'd hit you so fucking hard you wouldn't get back up."

"Hey, hey, are you okay?" Asher comes over and holds my face in his hands gently. The same hands that were so angry and violent are now sweet and soft with me.

"You're going to be in so much trouble," I say, but my voice stutters. The air is starting to become harder to take in.

That guy could sue; could ruin the shop's reputation. That would affect everyone's lives and livelihood. All because Asher felt he needed to stand up for me.

Shit. I've got to fix this somehow. My anxiety is racing.

I've got to fix this.

"I'm going to apologize," I say, walking out of Roxie and Asher's hold.

Asher steps in front of me, growling, "The fuck you are." I can tell he wants to grab me to stop me from going, but he's aware of how it might affect me after what just happened. "He said unspeakable things about you. He *grabbed* you. If anything, he should be crawling on his hands and knees back in here to apologize *to you*."

"Asher, if he sues—"

"He'll be hit with a lawsuit from me, saying he was sexually harassing someone in my shop. I was defending my girlfriend from the hands of some unknown creep who got too aggressive. I have cameras and all the footage. He has no case, so don't worry about that." Asher takes my hands in his. "Not only that, but that fucker knows now that if he comes after me or mine, I'll beat him up again. But he won't be walking this time when he leaves."

That shouldn't be as hot as it is.

"But your reputation..." I protest weakly, guilt gnawing at my throat.

Asher nods in understanding. "It might be affected. It might not. I really couldn't care less, Jade." He looks so genuine, so sincere. But how can he feel that way when, because of me, this shop that he's worked so hard for might be in danger? His finger curls under my chin and he lifts my face to look at his.

"I care about you. I care about how you feel. How you're treated. Fuck everyone else." His light eyes shine with his truth.

"Are you sure?" I whisper shakily.

"I'm more than sure." He kisses me quickly, pulling me in for a tight hug before leaning back and holding my arm gently. "Did he hurt you?"

"No, I don't think so." I twist my arm to show him, and low-and-below, there's a few bruises starting to form from that asshole's fingertips. "Or maybe he held on tighter than I thought," I admit meekly.

Asher's jaw juts to the side and his eyes narrow in regret. "I should've taken him outside and killed him."

"You can't say that," I scold quietly.

"I should've. But I'm sure Ty's getting his anger out as well," Asher says with a reserved look, and pulls me towards the backroom. He looks over his shoulder, and I see Ty walking in with an avenged look on his face as he tries to discreetly wipe red off his hand.

Asher nods to him and Ty nods back. Asher walks over to his station where there's a male client lying on his table, his pant leg rolled up to show off where half a Captain America's shield is tattooed on his calf. The guy pulls out one of his headphones, looking at Asher.

"Andrew, my man, I'll be right back. I just have to get some ice for her arm," Asher tells him and points to the backroom, all while keeping a tight grip on my hand.

"No problem, man. I saw the whole thing." He looks at me and frowns. "I'm really sorry that happened to you."

I give him a small nod but don't say anything.

"I'll be right back," Asher tells him and we walk to the backroom. My anxiety and embarrassment are so loud that it feels like the whole shop is whispering and chatting about what happened, and my cheeks only grow redder, the guilt gnawing at me a little more.

"Sit here," Asher says, pulling out one of the chairs for me before going to the freezer. This all feels very déjà vu from when he saved me all those weeks ago. I place my head in my hands, embarrassed and hurt *again* from a man who felt it was okay to touch me without my permission.

"Is it me?" I snap, my anger with how this continues to happen to me bubbling to the surface. My hands bang on the table in frustration. "Is there something about me that men can fucking pick up on that makes me an easy target? Do I need to have you tattoo 'fuck off' on my forehead for guys to get the picture?" Pushing away from the table, the chair under me knocks over. "Is this shit always going to happen? Seriously, Asher, what is it about me that men look at and say 'She looks like a fucking weakling and I'd like to *hurt her*'?"

"Jade," Asher says softly, walking over to where I'm pacing

with an ice pack in hand. "Stop," he tells me gently, touching my shoulder kindly and turning me to face him.

"What's wrong with me?" I brokenly ask him.

"There is absolutely nothing wrong with you, darlin'. Not a single thing." He puts the ice pack on the spot where the bruises mark my skin. "I can tell you right now that those guys, they're not *real* men. Real men will stand up for those who need it. Real men protect others. Real men are respectful and fucking kind. This stuff, it has nothing to do with *you* and it's more about their character. I'm just sorry that they've taken it out on you." Asher cups my chin and tips my face up to his. "I'm so sorry, Jade."

"What do you have to be sorry for? You're the only, *the only*, good man I've ever met in my life," I whisper. He smiles, but it doesn't reach his eyes.

"I'm sorry I didn't stop him before he ever got close to you. He should never have had the time to." Asher looks down, guilt clear to see.

"That is *not* your fault."

"I promised you this kind of shit wouldn't ever happen again. And here it happened, in my own shop, with me not ten feet from you. Fuck, I'm so sorry." His head hangs heavily and his voice cracks. Putting the ice pack down, I cup his face with my hands this time.

"Asher, do you even realize what you did for me?" I say breathlessly. "You... You punched a guy out for me. You threw him out of your shop without a second thought. You put your shop's, and your own, reputation at stake. For me. That... You chose me first. You put me first." I rise on my tiptoes and kiss his lips softly, chastely. But full of the love I'm feeling for him. "No one has ever put me first like that. No one. And you've done it since day one." I tip my mouth up in a shy grin. I know right then that I love him. I'm *in* love with him.

Asher nods, the guilt still present in his eyes and I know it's going to take a while for him to forgive himself, even if I don't think there's anything to forgive.

"I'll always choose you. I'll always put you first. I swear it."

The way he says those words, it's like a vow and I gasp under my breath.

"I know," I say, because I do. I trust him. He's my person, my safe place, my new home. I take a deep breath and move my hands from his face to his hands, threading our fingers together. "It's one of the reasons why I love you."

Asher's eyes widen almost comically, his mouth opening with shock. When he doesn't immediately say anything, I cringe.

Fuck. Fuck. Fuck. Fuck. Fuck.

Fuck. Fuck, fuckity-fuck fuck. Goddamn it!

I said it too soon. He doesn't feel the same way. I fucked this all up.

How quickly can I get out of here?

Where's the door?

<h1 style="text-align:center">Asher</h1>

SHE LOVES ME.

She **loves** me.

She loves **me.**

My chest explodes with happiness. I knew we were going somewhere; that she and I were special. I'm just surprised that she said it first. I thought I was going to. I already had a plan laid out to make it a significant moment, but here we are.

For me, it's monumental that she said it first and it makes me happier than I ever thought possible.

I *know* I love this girl more than anything. I know that she's it for me. She's the one.

And she loves me.

Holy fuck.

When I finally crash back to reality, I see the damage my silence has done.

Jade's hazel-green eyes shimmer with unshed tears, their brightness only magnifying the storm of fear, embarrassment, and sadness swirling within them. Her lip trembles before she bites down. Then, as if the weight of my silence is too much, she squeezes her eyes shut as her face twists in pain. My heart lurches —I understand too late.

Just as I open my mouth to speak, she takes a step back.

I know if I let her leave this room without telling her just how madly in love with her I am, our relationship won't be the same.

"Jade." I reach out and grab her hands before she can move any further from me. Pulling her tightly into my chest, I kiss her soundly. Deeply. I put as much passion and love as I can into the kiss, hoping that she can feel it all. Hoping she can feel just how crazy in love with her I am.

"God, Jade. Hearing you say that to me... it sent me into orbit for a minute. You love me? I *love you*. I'm so in love with you, it's not even funny," I say with a smile, pulling back and resting our foreheads together.

She lets out a sigh of relief before her body falls into mine. "Asher," she whispers.

"I love you, Jade," I whisper against her lips and wrap my arms around her waist. "Never doubt that."

"I love you," she repeats against my lips and I shiver. Our mouths meet again in an eager clash of teeth and lips, we're both smiling brightly. "You have a client waiting for you."

I groan. I just want to hold her. To stay in this little bubble with her, warm with the knowledge that we *love* each other.

"You're right," I say. The last thing I want to do is go hold a guy's leg for another two hours, but I need to go do my job. "Do you want to stay and hang out? Or head to my place and relax?"

"If it's okay with you, I think I'll go to your place and try to chill." She looks shy, like she hasn't been asking for my house key for weeks. I just need to get her a key of her own.

Fishing into my back pocket, I pull out my keys and slip the house key off. I place it in her palm, wrapping her fingers around it. "Make yourself at home. I just got groceries so please help yourself to anything."

Jade smiles at me from under her lashes. "How late are you going to be?"

I run a hand through my hair, looking at the clock to check the time. But then I understand Jade's expression. Her eyes seem darker, yearning with a want I know all too well myself. She bites her lip as we stare at each other. I reach out and slide my fingertips underneath her soft shirt to feel the warmth of her supple skin. Slipping up further, I start lining a slow trail up her side and around to her back. She shivers under my touch and I feel the small goosebumps arise.

"Why do you want to know?" I smirk, breathing softly in her ear. It would be the best fucking day if I get to hear her say she loves me *and* how explicitly she wants me.

"Well..." She picks at a little string on my shirt, not looking at me. I lean my head to the side to try and entice her to meet my eyes. Hers are so telling. So clear. Just looking into her eyes tells me how she's feeling. "I think we have something big to celebrate, no?" Her eyes flash to mine.

And I'm blown away. Shining brightly, the happiness she's feeling is palpable. She's happy, and it's because of me. Behind that happiness is a desperate want that I'm feeling as well.

Fuck, I want her so much.

"We definitely do, baby girl," I say deeply. "How do you want to celebrate?"

"I have a few ideas," she muses softly, with a mischievous smile on her face. One that I answer with my own.

"I do, too."

Jade lifts up on her tiptoes to reach my ear and whispers, "I think you'll like what I have planned, *Daddy*."

My fingers grip her skin tighter beneath her shirt at those words and I have to keep myself from moaning.

Jade nips my earlobe and pulls back, leaving me leaning into the space she vacated to keep trying to feel her in my arms.

"Baby girl..." I open my eyes and the corner of my mouth tips up. "You're playing with fire."

Jade bites her thumbnail and smiles back at me. A confident, gorgeous, full of love smile on her face which leaves me breathless and *wanting*.

She looks at the key in her hand then back at me, and winks.

"I'm okay with getting burned."

⦿

GOD, OR WHATEVER IS LOOKING AFTER ALL OF US, MUST be fucking playing around with me. The three hours after Jade left me—with a semi, which was not at all helpful—*inched* by.

Andrew was understanding with the little break in between, but the moment he popped his headphones back in and Jade left the shop, it was like time stopped. Every time I looked at the clock, thinking an hour had passed, it had only been ten minutes. I did my best to get lost in my work; the rhythmic buzzing of the machine in my hand, the spark of joy I have as I see the art emerge on the skin. All things that usually suck me into my work... but nothing's working this time. Then an hour passed, then the next hour.

Finally, I have forty-five minutes left. I can do this.

All I can think of is Jade. In my house, on my bed, touching herself and getting her slick and her scent all over my sheets.

*Do not get fucking hard right now while you're holding some dude's leg. Do **not** get fucking hard right now while you're holding* *some dude's leg.* I repeat this over and over as images of Jade keep floating through my mind.

I pull the needle back from Andrew's skin and roll my neck, shake my arm out. Trying to get my head back in the game, I pop a headphone in my ear. I change my settings so any messages get read to me and put on AC/DC. As the first few notes ring out, I can feel the tension start to melt away from my shoulders.

"You okay?" Andrew asks, pulling an earbud out and cocking a questioning eyebrow in my direction.

"Yeah, man. Sorry," I tell him quickly, putting on a fresh pair of gloves.

"You're good. I know what happened earlier probably shook you both. I don't know what I would've done if a guy grabbed my girl like that. I'm glad you fucked him up." Andrew lays his head back down.

"Yeah," I say, letting the word hang between us. "I should've knocked him out."

"I'm pretty sure your friend did. I watched him drag that guy out and give him a few punches of his own before he came back inside. I didn't see the other dude stand up. I don't even know if he's gone from your front door, if I'm honest."

I look at Ty and suddenly I'm scared that, for the last two and a half hours, we've had an unconscious fucker just slumped outside our door.

"Ty!" I call, motioning him to come over. When the big guy lumbers over, not giving a care in the world that people are waiting on him, he crosses his arms.

"Yeah?"

I raise an eyebrow. "Did you knock him out?"

"*Si,*" he repeats, and crooks an eyebrow towards the front window. Fuck.

"Has he gotten up yet?" I hold the bridge of my nose and sigh in frustration.

"Yeah, about an hour ago. He's fine, man," Ty grumbles and walks off. Some people might think Ty's being an asshole with how he just ended the conversation regardless if I was done talking to him, and if I didn't know him, I'd probably be pissed too, but that is just Ty. He doesn't say anything if he doesn't need to.

"Fuck," I sigh. "Well, that's that, then." I pick up the tattoo gun and clean Andrew's skin again. "Only a little longer, okay, man?"

Andrew nods, popping his headphone back in and getting comfortable. I dip the needle into ink and get back to work. A few minutes pass and my music stops. The text message *ding ding* plays before the automated voice starts reading out the message.

"Daddy, I don't know if I can wait for you much longer." The voice reads and my whole-body freezes.

AC/DC starts playing again, and I do my absolute best to resume tattooing after hearing that gift of a message.

Five minutes go by and I hear the *ding ding* of another incoming message.

"Your bed smells so good. Like you. I'm touching myself with my nose in your pillow, imagining it was your hand on me."

Oh fuck. This girl is going to kill me.

Do not get hard holding this guy's leg. Do not get hard holding this guy's leg. **Do not get hard holding this guy's leg, Asher.**

I can't message her back right now, but I feel like she knows that. She knows I'll read these messages and it'll make me rush home, ready to ravage her exactly as I intend to.

My eyes dart to the clock, and I'm relieved to find I only have fifteen minutes left. I can do it. I can make sure I'm not fantasizing about my sexy-as-fuck girlfriend in my bed, rubbing her clit as she moans for her Daddy...

I can do it.

Right?

Taking a deep breath, I wipe Andrew's skin and dip my needle in the ink again. AC/DC starts back up and I lose myself in the music for the length of a song.

One song is all she gave me before I get hit with message after message.

"Daddy, you've gotta help me."

"I'm so wet."

"You've ruined me, I can't come unless you're here now. Now that I know how it feels to come by your hand, I can't be satisfied with just my own."

"Daddy, please,"

Holy *fucking* shit.

I scoot closer to the table to hide my quickly growing erection which gets a little bigger with each message. Even the automated voice isn't deterring my cock.

Wiping Andrew's leg one more time, I decide I can't take it anymore. Staying seated, I take my gloves off and throw them in the trash by the table, then roll over to the compartment where I keep my aftercare stuff in. Cleaning his leg and wrapping it up takes up a lot of time, so our appointment ends early, but not *so* early that I feel bad.

"All right, man. You're good to go." I put the last piece of tape over the saran wrap and pull off my gloves.

"Wow, that was quick!" Andrew sits up, stretches and pulls both headphones from his ears. "Damn," he exclaims, marveling at his leg. I like wrapping the tattoos in clear plastic so people can see what they look like. "Perfect, as always. Thanks, man." Andrew hops off the table and goes to the full-length mirror beside my desk. "Sick," he says, smiling brightly at the reflection in the mirror, and it makes me so happy that he likes my work. That I've made someone this happy with my art.

Normally, I'd sit and ask him to take a picture, then chat with him a bit about what our next session is going to look like.

Not today.

Andrew walks over to his bag, pulls out a stack of cash, and hands it to me. "Your standard three-hour fee, plus a little extra," he offers.

"Thank you," I reply with a nod and put the cash in my back pocket. "And thank you for understanding earlier."

"No problem." Andrew slings his bag over his shoulder and slips his shoes on. "I know how much you want to get back to your girl," he teases, cocking an eyebrow with a smirk. "I'm pretty sure anyone with eyes knows how much."

Chuckling, I run a hand down the back of my head and cup my neck nervously.

"Sorry," I groan. "I tried."

"I know you did," Andrew laughs loudly. "I didn't say anything because if what happened to your girl had happened to mine, I would've left when she did. So, I get it. I'm also very glad that you knocked that guy on his ass."

Andrew's a good guy; a long-time client, so I know he's on my side in this.

"I appreciate it." I shake his hand. "Jade... she's been through a lot. More than anyone should, really. She and I... we've both had to grow up way too fast. But with each other..." I try to think of a way to explain how fucking easy it is with Jade. How right it feels. "With each other, it's like I can breathe easy for the first time."

Andrew just nods, crossing his arms over his chest with a knowing smile.

"Congratulations, Asher." He slaps me on the shoulder and I

finally stand. "A word of advice, from someone who's probably not qualified to give you advice?" Andrew smirks and points at me before saying, "If she's your world, make sure she knows it."

"Solid advice." I nod and take his hand, shaking it again as we walk towards the exit. "I'll remember that."

"Do! And I'll email you when I'm ready to finish my leg."

"Yes, I'll be waiting!" I say as he walks out, waving.

My customer service smile drops and I basically run back to my station, cursing myself for making it a rule that all stations need to be sanitized, organized and spotless at the end of your day. I rip through the chores I have to do. Wiping, bleaching and cleaning every surface I touched and everything that touched Andrew.

"Whoa, *hermano*," Ty urges, "slow down, you're going to run into someone!"

"Sorry," I mumble, moving around him to throw my trash out.

"I'm sorry," Ty blurts out suddenly, stopping me in my tracks.

"What?" I turn around, my eyebrows scrunching together. Why would Ty need to apologize?

"I'm sorry I didn't stop him before he touched her."

"Ty, how could you have known he was going to be an asshole like that?" I set the trash bag down and put my hand on his shoulder. "Thank you for stepping up for Jade when you saw it happen. Don't stress."

"She was hurt before, wasn't she? I thought so, after what happened when I answered the phone... but I didn't ask right out. But how she skirted back today... She was hurt before, wasn't she?" Ty asks gruffly, not beating around the bush or sugarcoating it.

I sigh, leaning down and picking the bag back up.

"Ty... I can't. Just... don't worry about it." I'm not going to answer him because it's not my story to tell. I don't know if Jade wants me to tell anyone. The only reason Roxie knows is because Jade told me that she guessed it. Roxie has been through something similar, and she was able to see the signs. I'm not going to betray Jade's trust like that.

Turning, I walk through the break room and toward the back door where the dumpster sits right outside.

Ty follows me.

Fuck.

"You forget that I was there when everything went down with Roxie. You forget that I *know how it feels* to be in your shoes. It's no one you know, right?" he asks gruffly.

"Ty," I warn sharply.

"Just tell me it's no one we'll have to see. Tell me this is a safe place for her to hang out."

"Of fucking course, it is!" I throw the bag into the dumpster with a bit more force than necessary. "You think if I knew who it was, I would let them within ten feet of her?" I snap at Ty. He's posturing, ready to receive a punch if I decide to throw one.

I know that if I did, he'd simply let me get my aggression out and not retaliate. He knows me well enough to know that I fucking hate men like that; men who hurt innocent women. Now that Jade and I are so close, it hurts me even more to not be able to harm those who hurt the woman I love.

I wouldn't hit Ty, though, not unless he really deserved it.

"She doesn't know exactly who it was," I say softly. "He lives on campus, though, and he apparently lives on Jade's floor. So, I'm trying to keep her at my place for as many nights as she'll let me."

"What if she works here? Like legitimately works here?" Ty asks.

"You think she'd go for that?" I'd be lying if I said I hadn't thought about it myself. She's already at the shop a lot; she knows the repeat customers, the rules, the duties; hell—she's cleaned and mopped before just because she was bored. She knows the systems, and most importantly, she knows us and we know her. She won't fuck up like the last receptionist.

Ty nodded. "I think if you present it in an... inviting way, she would."

"So, I shouldn't say that I'm giving her a job so I'll be able to keep an eye on her?" We chuckle and I put my hands in my pockets, thinking it over.

"Yeah, don't do that. I'd probably offer it casually, saying we need a new receptionist and we all like her, so why not get paid to sit around and hang out with us?" Ty shrugs. "But I don't blame you. If that *cabron* is hanging around her, I wouldn't let her out of my sight. Having her here whenever she's not in class means we can all have eyes on her. She's a good person, and I like her for you. And I don't think any man who hurts a woman should feel safe."

"Agreed." I nod, and we bump fists. "I'm heading home now to make sure she's okay and I'll talk to her about the job."

"Go get your girl," he says with a knowing smirk and walks back inside.

I NEED ASHER. I *need* him desperately.

I knew he wouldn't respond to my messages while he was working, but knowing they were there and he would read them when he was done makes me happy. And unbelievably horny.

Not having sexted before, my anxiety is sky-high, but not enough to deter me from trying to get myself off.

Fantasies of Asher and I play in my head. Memories start mixing in, but I know that no matter how wet I get, how close I bring myself, I won't be able to tip over the edge until Asher's hands are on me.

Groaning in frustration, I look around for the time, and see that maybe—just maybe—Asher will be home soon and I can show him just how much I love him. Pushing myself out of our bed—*our bed? Damn, Jade*—I head to the bathroom and jump in the shower to relax. Today, despite how wonderful it ended, was also scary.

I look in the mirror, surveying the woman staring back at me. Her blonde hair is tangled slightly and falling around her shoulders, the light green tint of her eyes shines with happiness, her skin is clear and flushed rosy pink from earlier activities. But for the first time in a long time, I feel like I not only look sexy, but strong, too.

My eyes drop to my arm in the reflection, and I deflate at the sight. Five ugly, purple blotches wrap around my forearm, throbbing like a beacon of weakness and male idiocy.

I'm tired of being weak. I'm tired of men thinking they can touch me without my permission. It won't happen again.

I *won't* let it happen again.

I'm done being naïve and small.

Reaching back, I turn the shower on and wait for the water to warm before stepping under the spray. I'm going to become stronger. Mentally and physically.

I'm going to stop being afraid.

"It starts today," I promise myself. "I know who my real friends are. Who my real family is. I know who *I am*. No one else matters."

The water runs over my body, and with each wave, I let my perceptions of myself flow right down the drain with the water.

It's a new Jade. One that's done taking shit from others.

⌒⌒⌒⌒⌒∞⌒⌒⌒⌒⌒

STEPPING OUT OF THE BATHROOM, CLEAN AND WITH A new determination, I'm toweling my hair dry when I hear something at the door.

Asher rips the door open and slams it shut, staring at me like a bull that's been flashed red.

"Asher," I greet softly, clutching the top of the towel wrapped around my body.

Instead of answering, he drops his bag at the door and kicks his shoes off roughly before charging towards me.

"Are you okay?" I ask worriedly, but the moment he's closer, I can see the heavy need and desire on his face. His arms wrap around me tightly and he lifts me up, spreading my thighs around his hips. Without saying a thing, he starts walking me towards the bedroom.

His eyes...

They're dark and hooded, hungry and happy. He's staring at me with such need and desire, there's no doubt in my mind that this man loves me. It's like the thing of movies, of great romances that make your heart skip a beat. Something I've always wanted, but never thought I'd get to experience myself.

Leaning down, I press my lips to Asher's. My kiss is soft and gentle as I run my hands through his hair. I know I've riled him up, and that some *very* satisfying sex is in my immediate future. But first, I want to show him how much I love him—for more than just sex. More than just his protection.

I love him so fucking much for all that is *him*.

His lips push against mine roughly. Hungrily. Demandingly.

I slip my tongue into his mouth, moaning at the taste of him, and he responds in kind. Wrapping my arms around his shoulders, one hand threads into his hair and I pull on the locks slightly.

Asher groans, pulling back with his eyes still closed and a euphoric look on his face.

"Do that again, I like it," he growls and gives me an incredibly hot feral grin.

"Oh, do you?" I smirk.

"I like anything you do." He looks at my lips and we meet in the middle for a harder, deeper kiss. We move together, like we need the other to breathe. His grip on my thighs is tight, but I welcome his touch. I *hope* he leaves marks on me.

My towel slips, but I don't move an inch to cover up. Instead, I let the fabric fall from around me. My breasts jiggle with every step he takes. Asher sets me gently on his bed and pushes me back. I'm laying down, and he can look at me in all my naked glory.

His normally light blue eyes are darkened, like a stormy day at sea, and gazing over every inch of my skin. It's fucking arousing to see just how hot I make him, just how attractive he finds me. His dick is hardening in his jeans, and I see a slight twitch in his hands before he pulls his shirt up by the front of the collar.

In one motion, his shirt flies off and Asher throws it to the floor as my eyes take in the vision in front of me. I know I've seen him shirtless many times now, but it's still a glorious sight to see. Broad shoulders, defined arms, a strong core, all covered with dark tattoos that compliment his physique instead of taking away from it.

"Your messages made me hard as a fucking rock, baby girl. *I was working*," he growls.

Breathing hard at his words, his gaze, his show of masculinity, I pout, "I know, Daddy. But I wanted you to know how much I want you."

Asher hums, nodding as he unbuttons his jeans with an audible pop.

"Do you know how hard I was just imagining you fingering yourself in my bed? And then to hear you say it to me... I did everything I could to keep my professionalism when all I wanted to do was race home and fuck you senseless."

"Yes," I whisper, breathlessly.

"The last forty minutes were torture. But I'm here now."

"You're here now," I repeat softly as Asher leans over me so his chest is touching mine.

"And I'm going to show you exactly how much I love you," he rumbles with a kiss that leaves me dizzy. Pulling back, he trails kisses down my neck, over my collarbone and down to the swell of my breasts. Without a moment's hesitation, Asher takes my nipple into his mouth and swirls the bud around, sucking it further into his mouth with a wet tug.

My head falls back with a moan and I lay flat against the mattress, letting him do with me what he may.

"Baby girl," Asher growls, and our eyes meet. He's looking at me through his incredibly dark, long, jealousy-inducing eyelashes.

"Yes, Daddy?" I ask breathlessly.

"Did you come without me?" he asks through the kisses trails down my abdomen.

"No..."

"Are you sure? Should I check?" His voice is that low, gravely, almost-a-rough-whisper sound that I am addicted to. Raising an eyebrow, he grins wickedly, like he knows exactly how wet I'll be when he reaches down to my pussy.

I've been painfully turned on since I got here. Since Asher said he loves me. Since our kiss in the backroom that felt like it was going to go further.

"Yes, Asher," I whisper, sighing his name in desperation at the feeling of his rough hands on my thighs.

"You've had a hard day, so I won't get upset that you didn't call me 'Daddy.' But remember it for the future, okay, baby?" Asher warns quietly, his warm breath tickling the bit of hair at my mound.

"Okay, Daddy."

Asher slowly glides his tongue between my lower lips, as if he's savoring the taste he finds there. I gasp, bracing myself as I anchor my hands into the sheets.

He pauses, glaring up at me. "You showered," he growls accusingly.

I frown. "I wanted to be clean for you."

Asher shakes his head. "I want you any way you'll let me have you. Hair, sweat, whatever… It doesn't bother me. It's about how you feel best." His hands slide under my thighs, and he pushes my legs back so I'm spread before him. "You are fucking amazing, baby girl. Your pussy is so pink, puffy and wet, pulsing with need. Need for *me*. You need some relief, don't you, baby?"

I need his touch so fucking badly. I'm shaking with desire at this point. Nothing but Asher's hands on me—or his cock in me —will tame this desire.

"Please, Daddy," I groan. My breathing is shallow; I look down the length of my body to watch him as best I can.

"I've got you, Jade. Daddy will take care of you," he hums deeply. His fingers push inside me, curling in the best way possible before he pulls them out and plunges back into my wetness. My body curls involuntarily as he continues to fuck me with his fingers. I'm so close already; I've been on edge for so long that it doesn't take much. Asher twists his fingers once more, and his free hand reaches up to my tit. When he rubs my clit with his thumb, right as his middle finger rubs against the wettest spot inside me, *and* he pinches my nipple—all at the same time—I combust.

Sparks erupt all over my skin as I writhe with pleasure and scream, "Daddy!" over and over.

Asher keeps working me through the orgasm. As I come down, he pulls his fingers from my pussy, spreads my legs that I'd unintentionally clamped closed, and licks me. His tongue cleans up every drop of my cum. He keeps going, and going, and going, until I'm too sensitive and have to push him away.

"Daddy, Daddy, stop!" I grab his hair and yank him up. Reaching as far down as I can, I grip his pants and push them down, using my feet when my hands couldn't reach any further. "Fuck me, please."

"Fuck you?" he asks, his mouth and chin shiny with my juices as he steps out of his jeans. He walks back, his shoulder dropping while he stares at me, standing there biting his lip. "Nah, baby girl. I'm not going to fuck you," he utters passively.

Suddenly, Asher surges forward and cages me under him. He smells so fucking good and he growls in my ear, "I'm going to make love to you, baby."

I moan, wrapping my arms around his shoulders and crushing our lips together. He pushes up and enters me with one delicious thrust.

"Fuck!" I cry out, my fingernails digging into his shoulders. I'm sure I'm leaving marks on his skin, but he doesn't seem to mind. In fact, he seems to really fucking like it, if his masculine groans in my ear mean anything.

"You're so fucking tight, so warm, *so wet*." His back muscles tense under my hands as he rocks into me over and over. He's thrusting quickly, setting an amazing pace, one that promises I'll come again far too quickly.

"Yes, yes, yes, right there, *Daddy, yes*," I whine, my eyes closing as my head falls back. Asher grips my cheeks in his hand and pulls my face down to look at him roughly.

"I told you I was going to show you how much I love you, and I am." His quick thrusts change abruptly into a slower, deeper pace. One where every movement fuses our bodies closer together. Asher shifts so he's grinding up and it makes his cock hit the front wall of my pussy. I shiver.

"Look at me, baby," he demands, and I immediately follow his direction.

My belly tightens as I move against him, as much as I can from underneath him. He doesn't say anything, and neither do I. The complete and total look of obsession in his eyes as he stares into mine says it all.

His movements stay steady, but deepen so that each brush of his cock against my G-spot brings me closer and closer to my next orgasm. His arm moves overhead so he can hold onto the headboard.

And what a *panty-ruining* sight it is. Asher hovering over me on his elbows, his body weight pressing down on me perfectly, his tattooed arm holding onto the headboard, and with each movement, his muscles flex.

I can't help what happens next.

Reaching up, I bite his bicep. Hard.

Hissing, Asher's eyes darken even more and his jaw sets to the side. I release his skin, looking up at him through my eyelashes, portraying innocence.

"Do it harder next time, okay baby?" he growls, fucking into me harder. My tits bounce with his thrusts. Asher grips my cheeks tightly, pulling my lips closer to his. Our breaths mingle as he teases me with a near kiss. Our lips hovering over one another, I can taste his breath, and I so fucking desperately want him to lean down and properly kiss me.

"Do you believe me now? Can you see how crazy I am for you? How much I crave you? How no matter what, I'm always in your corner? I love you so fucking much, Jade," Asher proclaims against my mouth.

"I love you so much," I moan breathlessly, slipping my hand up to the back of his neck and pulling him down roughly to get the kiss I've been dying for.

It's like he loses all self-control at my words and my kiss, because his hips snap against mine quicker. We meet together kiss for kiss, thrust for thrust, moan for moan. With one last groan in his ear, I come violently.

"Fuck, oh fuck! Daddy! Please!" I cry out, probably hurting his ear from screaming so loudly, but Asher doesn't flinch. My walls clench tightly around him, squeezing and milking him as his hips stutter. He falls against me, breathing brokenly and moaning just as loudly.

"Oh god, Jade." He sounds like everything he had was taken from him. And I have to say, I feel the same way.

<hr>

LAYING IN ASHER'S ARMS AFTER TWO POWERFUL orgasms, having him gently play with my hair as his strong heartbeat thrums under my ear, might possibly be the most relaxing thing I've ever experienced. My eyes flutter as I fight against sleep. I don't want this moment to end.

A tattoo on his bicep catches my eye. Running my fingers over it, I lean up on my elbow to get a better look.

"What does this mean?" I ask softly. Running vertically on his inner bicep, there's a saying in another language tattooed in beautiful script. I can't quite make it out—the ink is somewhat blown out—but I can see from a few of the words that it's Spanish. He's kept quite a bit of free space around the words, and my teeth have left indentions right beside it. Blushing, I run my finger over those marks too.

"*De las cienzas,*" Asher says fluidly, the words slipping off his tongue like he's fluent in Spanish. My eyebrows raise in surprise, and he chuckles.

And oh my god, the way he smirks—with his eyes and the five

o'clock shadow on his strong jaw, his bare chest and genuine laugh —I nearly combust with happiness myself from making him look so content.

"It means *from the ashes*." He gently traces the words on his skin and I wait patiently, hoping he'll tell me the story.

"It's actually my first tattoo from someone else," he reveals softly, with no fondness or excitement. Just softness. I don't know if it's a good story. Scooching down to tuck into his side again, I raise my chin to look at him as he continues. "I got it when I was nineteen, I think. I was young. Ty did it for me. He'd started saying he wanted to get into tattooing with me, and I offered to be his first test canvas."

"You guys have been friends a long time."

"Oh yeah. Ty and I have been friends since freshman year of high school. I told him I wanted to open a tattoo shop and he jumped right on board. Said if I opened it and got it going, he'd be one of my artists. And he's helped me every step of the way. A few years ago, I told him that he was now a co-owner, as he's put in just as much time and effort as I have."

"Did you name the shop after the tattoo, or get the tattoo after the shop opened?" I ask and immediately wish I hadn't.

Asher's eyes drop and the lightheartedness in his expression vanishes. "A little bit of both, actually," he admits. "I've had some bad things happen in my life, especially growing up."

I say silent, letting him choose to share, but only if he wants.

"My mom... My mom struggled," Asher began. "She had her own demons, her own traumas, and unfortunately, she put a lot of it on me. She wasn't there when I was growing up, choosing instead to go get high or drunk and bring home belligerent assholes to fuck. All while she had me and my younger brother at home, barely making it by. I would do odd jobs for neighbors to earn some cash to feed us when she forgot to go shopping, or for when my brother needed something for school. I was the one who kept us from going to foster care. I did whatever I could to keep us together." He breathes deeply, pushing the air out quickly. Asher's not making eye contact with me, instead looking straight ahead, but his eyes are glazed over like he's unseeing. He runs a hand through his hair frustratedly.

"One night..." he starts saying, but his voice wavers and I instinctively hold him tighter. Asher pauses to collect his thoughts before clearing his throat. "One night, she brought this guy to our apartment. I immediately ushered my brother into our room so we could barricade ourselves in. I tried to not listen—what teenager wants *that* soundtrack in their mind?" He makes a disgusted expression, pursing his lips and shivering with ick. "But I had to make sure the guy wouldn't get any ideas about coming after me or my brother. So that night, I heard my mom start to fight back, screaming for him to stop and that she didn't want it anymore. He didn't stop. He pushed and pushed, and I... I was stuck. I didn't know what to do. I remember being fifteen, trying to figure out if I should go try to protect my mom and leave my brother unprotected? Or should I stay with my brother and let my mom keep being hurt? It was brutal. I... I still have fucking nightmares about it."

"Oh god, Asher," I console breathlessly and climb on top of him, holding him completely in my arms. I nestle his face into my neck and he wraps his arms around me. "I'm so sorry."

"It's been a long time. But my mom... she changed after it happened. She didn't go out; she didn't leave the house. She just drank, got high and watched her shows at all hours. She wasn't ever there before, but after... after she was a shell, and I had one more person I had to take care of. Two years later, she left. Just up and left. One day she was gone. *And I was relieved.*" Asher's voice wavers as he admits it. He keeps his face pressed to my neck, refusing to look at me.

He doesn't want to look at me.

"Asher," I say softly, tipping his chin gently to face me. "That's okay."

"How fucking awful am I?"

"You are the best person I know," I insist strongly. "You were a fifteen-year-old *kid*."

He huffs sharply. "I was only four years younger than you are now."

"Does that really matter? You and I are different people, in different situations, and have gone through different things. You're a good person. And you were put in a really shitty situation that no kid should ever have to go through. Growing up, I never had to worry about food or shelter. Or protecting a sibling. I don't know how I would've coped if I'd had to do that. I definitely wouldn't have done as well as you," I stress.

"Jade," he begins and I know he's going to try that self-sacrificing shit, insisting he should've done more, been more, given more.

"No, Asher." I sit up and put both of my hands on his chest. "You cannot take responsibility for this. You were fifteen years old —younger than that, even—when your mother started expecting you to parent and provide. You had to make an impossible decision and I understand. Boy do I understand the guilt and the regret and the what-ifs, but I'm telling you now: you. were. too. young." I emphasize those words with alternating kisses to his cheeks. It breaks my heart when he looks up at me with those big, beautiful eyes, and bites the inside of his cheek like he doesn't know what to believe. But he wants to believe what I'm saying. To feel some relief from the guilt he's carrying around unjustly.

"Well, I leaned heavily on Ty and his family after my mom

vanished. I was going to school full-time, and I got a night job as a security guard so I could pay the rent in our shitty one-bedroom apartment. That left just enough for some ramen and a gallon of milk after all the bills were paid. Something had to give—we weren't going to survive like that. I didn't let his mom know what was happening, but Ty saw that I had started dropping weight quickly. I had to make sure my brother had all the food he needed, so I went without. After I told him, Ty started sneaking food to my brother and I, and his mom caught him. Once she knew the situation, we started getting baskets of meals and whatever necessities they could spare every few days. I truly don't know how I would've been able to do it all without their help. That, and..." He pauses briefly, like he's hesitant to finish his sentence, but finally adds, "I also got into bare-knuckle fighting in underground rings a few nights a week. It was the only way to let go of my anger without destroying stuff."

My eyebrows shoot up in shock. *We definitely will be circling back to that.*

He brings one of my hands from his chest to his lips and kisses my palm softly.

"I told Ty, when he first found out, that it felt like my whole life was on fire. Every single thing. And he told me that phoenixes rise from the ashes of tragedy and hardship. Something beautiful and strong is formed from something else burning to the ground. And I took that to heart."

"That's beautiful."

"And heavy. After that, things got better. Slowly, bit by bit. My brother was old enough to get a part-time job. Ty's family started helping us. My night-shift job gave me a raise. Little things like that, but all in a row, and I was able to get my footing. I started being able to save money and the moment I graduated, I applied to different tattoo internships to learn the craft. Still working nights, fighting for cash with Ty, doing everything and anything I could to earn money, six days a week. I was determined. Then Hunter turned eighteen and he was off to college, with the clear understanding that I could not help him financially at all. Again, I still feel like the shittiest human alive, but having him out of the house freed up a lot of my resources. That's what helped me be able to open the shop and take a breather. Which I did, with his blessing."

"You are not a shitty person," I repeat myself, trying to push that to the forefront of his mind. I don't like him thinking that about himself... but I understand.

Hunter... why does that... where have I heard that name before? My unconscious whispers, but I push it away. I can tell it's going to become a nagging itch. Like I've forgotten something but don't know what it is.

"You say that, and I appreciate it. But since the shop started taking off and I've gotten more stable, I've been able to give him some cash every here and there. He also knows that if he were ever really in trouble, I'd help him out."

I raise an eyebrow. "Like the good guy you are," I tease. He just proved my point.

He smiles and rolls his eyes, sighing heavily. "I guess."

"Am I ever going to meet this brother of yours? Assuming you would want me to." I tack the second part on at the end, and steel my resolve. No matter what, I will not let my feelings be hurt about this.

"Hunter is... well, I don't know how to explain him without sounding like the biggest asshole brother on the planet." Asher runs his hand down his face and I cock my head in confusion. "He's not a good person," Asher admits with a false laugh. "He's not the kind of person I want to surround myself with. I don't know if it was the trauma from my mom's issues, my fucked-up parenting, or being left alone so much because I had to work—I don't know. I tried to correct his behavior calmly a few times, and then once I heard him talking about some shit I won't repeat while snorting the same shit my mother used to, and I knocked him out. Since then, we've kept contact to a minimum."

My eyebrows shoot to my hairline. *What the fuck?*

"Yeah," Asher groans. "Yeah. So, that's my family. Drugged-out alcoholic, deserter mother, and a piece-of-shit, probably an alcoholic brother who can't stand the sight of me. Good times." Asher looks away, turning his head toward the wall that has his sketches pinned up and tucks a hand behind his head, moving his bicep near his face.

De las cienzas.

We stay silent for a moment because I honestly don't know what to say. He's upset and hurt; this hurt, I now realize, isn't just going to go away. It's decades old, deep and festering, and he's miraculously pulled himself from such a destructive family cycle.

"You're amazing," I whisper, cupping his cheeks.

Surprise flashes across his features. "What?"

"You're amazing," I repeat. "You got yourself out of that shit. You stood up, stayed strong, and did everything possible—against all odds, I might add—to get to where you are today. Fuck, Asher," I marvel with a smile, "can't you see how amazing you are for overcoming all of that?"

I can almost see how my words aren't computing in his brain. He's looking at me as if he's heard what I said but doesn't understand it. Slowly, I trace his cheekbone with my thumb and lean down to kiss his lips.

"I've always wanted a tattoo, you know," I change the subject with a coy smirk.

"You've said," he replies. "Are you going to let me do the honors?"

"I don't even know what I'd get."

Asher's hand slides up my back gently before his fingers tangle into my hair, and he flashes a knowing smile.

"Don't worry, baby girl. I'll think of something beautiful. Something worthy of you."

WE LAY in bed for hours, wrapped in each other's arms.

"What's your favorite color?" I ask, twirling a piece of Jade's hair around my finger.

"Yellow. Yours?"

"Black."

Jade laughs under her breath. "That's not surprising."

I turn on my side, pulling her into my chest and tickling her waist. "What's that supposed to mean?" I ask over her giggles, while she squirms around trying to avoid my tickles.

"Stop!" She cries breathlessly. She looks up to try and move away, all with a big smile on her face. "Asher!"

"What's that supposed to mean, huh?" I tickle her more, and she wraps her legs around my hips. The soft skin of her thighs meets mine and she pulls us together.

Oh fuck. I try not to groan. Her warm pussy pushes against my soft cock and it twitches with the contact. Like it automatically wants to be inside her. I already knew how attracted I was to Jade, but seriously, just a hint of her cunt near my cock and it flares to life with the possibility.

I'd fucking live inside her if I could. I'd bring her pleasure every waking moment.

"It's just that every tattoo you have is black and white, and I think I've seen you in one shirt that's not black. You obviously have an aesthetic." Jade laughs, and I stop tickling her, wrapping my arms around her waist and sliding my hands up both sides of her back to bring us closer together.

"I like being mysterious."

"It's definitely a choice," she teases as she traces my jaw with her finger slowly. Like she's trying to memorize this moment.

"You like it." I peck her nose, resting my head back on the pillow.

"No," she says, completely deadpanned. The happy-go-lucky smile on my face drops and I'm already wracking my brain to figure out what went so wrong. She doesn't like my style? Okay, so what do I change? I'll wear a fucking potato sack if that means that she's happy.

Her cheeky voice breaks my mental spiral. "I love it."

She smiles innocently. I jut out my jaw and narrow my eyes playfully at her. She absolutely knows what she just did to me.

"You little..." I start to say as she squeals with mirth. I jump on her, holding her down and attacking her with kisses.

Her laughter fills the air along with the smooching sounds of my kisses as I plant them all over her face and neck.

I'm genuinely happy for the first time in my life. Maybe a close second would be when I finally opened the shop, but this is different. So different.

Having Jade love me, and getting to be so *domestic* like this, is what I've always dreamt of. I never thought I'd get to have it, though.

"I love you," I say softly. Looking at her closely, I'm struck with how naturally fucking gorgeous she is. I have nothing against girls who like makeup or prefer to spend their days making their hair and faces perfect. But I've always gravitated toward the natural girls. The ones who prefer not to wear a stroke of anything on their skin.

Jade is one of those girls. She wears mascara sometimes, maybe Chapstick here and there, and aside from the night we met, I don't think I've ever seen her with makeup on. The constellation of freckles across the bridge of her nose and the natural blush she has from my kisses and from laughing draw me in. Her eyes are magnetic, the golden flecks shining brightly in the warm abyss. I move a hand over her head slowly, and my fingers thread themselves through her silken, gold strands.

I'm the luckiest motherfucker.

"I love you, too." Sealing her words with a kiss, I smile.

I have a feeling I'm going to be doing that a lot more often.

<hr>

"I need to find a job." Jade barges into the bathroom while I'm rinsing the shampoo out of my hair, and her abruptness makes me jump.

"Jesus!" I shout, pushing my hair back to get the rest of the bubbles from my face.

"Sorry," she apologizes meekly, but pulls the curtain open a bit so she can see me. "I was just thinking. I need to find a job. You've been so kind, too kind, letting me stay here this long for free. I can't impose on you forever."

"False," I interject.

"And I can't keep relying on you to feed me. I need to make my own money or toughen up and get back to the dorms."

"Again, very wrong." Turning around, I face her while also

giving her an eyeful. I open my eyes just in time to see her ogling my body.

I may not be someone who is built like I live at the gym, but I like my look, and I like that she likes it too. Seeing her appreciate my body makes the tasteless healthy diet and the few days a week I work out worth it. Her pink lips are parted and she's looking at my cock like she wants to suck me dry.

I'd fucking love that. I'd pick her up and set her on her knees against the porcelain of my claw-foot tub; make her take every inch of me until she gagged. I wonder if she's deep-throated anyone before. I mentally shake my head. She told me she's not tried much of anything, and my caveman side likes that. *A lot.* I fucking love that I'm the lucky bastard who gets to teach her all about sex, oral, foreplay and pleasure. I fucking love that I'm the only one who has gotten to hear the noises she makes when comes, the only one who has touched her like that because *she wants me to.*

She **chose** me and I intend to never take that for granted.

"My eyes are up here, darlin'," I croon with a wink. Jade quickly closes her mouth and gives me an unimpressed look, but I don't care—I love that I turn her on. I feel my cock start to swell just from imagining her on her knees for me.

"I'm being serious, Asher." She crosses her arms over her chest, making the fabric of my T-shirt that she's wearing bunch over her breasts.

I love her in my clothes. Just another way I'm claiming her for the world to see.

"I am too, Jade," I reply with finality and turn off the shower, pulling the shower curtain open all the way.

"I need a job."

"And I can help you with that." I reach around her to grab my towel, kissing her cheek as I lean into her space, before drying off.

"How?" she asks hesitantly.

"Well, we need a receptionist. I had to fire the last girl, and you'd be perfect for it. Ty and Roxie have already asked if you would, but I didn't want to overstep. Only now, you're looking for a job and I'm looking for an employee. It's a win-win." I take the towel and dry my hair to give her a moment to think. Flipping my hair back, I wrap the towel around my waist and secure it. "What do you think?"

"Isn't there, like, an ethical issue there?" She scrunches her nose in an insanely cute way and I chuckle.

"An ethical issue?" I repeat, looking at her in the mirror. I pull my toothbrush from the holder and start to brush my teeth.

"Well yeah. I mean, if you're my... boyfriend?" Jade says the last word like it's something secret, something that she's nervous about, and I could kick myself. I don't think we've actually had the full on 'label' conversation. I jumped straight to loving her, and will for the rest of my life.

I spit out my toothpaste, watching her nerves take over in the mirror. I can practically see her thoughts as she silently freaks out, but then I crack her a toothpaste-y grin. Boyfriend and girlfriend doesn't seem like a strong enough title for what I feel we are, but I guess I'll have to accept it for now.

"Boyfriend, huh? I like that. But I think I'd like hearing you say that you're my girlfriend even better."

"I'm your girlfriend," Jade repeats, like she can't believe I just said that.

Nodding, I pretend to think about it. "Yeah, I like that. A lot."

I twist so I can see her and give her a wolfish grin. She responds in kind, stepping forward to wrap her arms around my naked torso before kissing my shoulder.

"I do, too."

"You were talking about an ethical issue?" I prompt her to continue down that line of thought. Getting back to the topic at hand because I know that, in my heart, she was mine already.

I fucking beat up a fucker for touching her so I've basically proposed already.

Jade ponders for a moment before asking, "Well, if we're together-together, isn't that a problem?"

"No," I laugh, "No, not at all. We didn't start dating while you were working for me. There aren't any power dynamics at play here. Plus, if you work at the shop, we can see each other every day. I can check on you, make sure none of the assholes at your school come around." I nod to try and convince her. "Please, say yes."

She's hesitant. "Won't it be weird?"

"Weird? Not at all. Getting to see you all day, every day? Getting to make sure you're fed for breakfast, lunch and dinner? Getting to make out in the breakroom when it's slow? Sounds like a dream, really."

Jade laughs softly and rests her forehead against mine. She wraps her arms around my shoulders and leans back to look at me with a teasing glint in her eye.

"Is there a possibility of advancement, though? Of holiday pay? What's the shop's position on PDA?" She cracks a grin and I tickle her sides. Jade squeals, bowing in my arms with laughter. "Asher! Asher, stop!" she cries.

"I'll make sure you're taken care of, baby girl. Don't you worry," I tell her, and already start planning finances in my mind.

"Then I accept."

Jade's holding onto my waist as we speed down the road, trying to make it to the college as fast as possible. Our morning quickie may have pushed us too close to her first class' start time.

Getting to fuck her against the bathroom counter and see how her back arched as I held her neck, my tattooed fingers gripping her blank skin... I don't regret it. That sight will live in my memories and play in my fantasies at night when she isn't with me.

I can still taste her on my tongue.

I push the machine harder, trying to go faster, and lean us slightly to pass a car. Jade's thighs tighten against my hips and her fingers grip my chest where she's holding me. I know she's not quite comfortable on the bike yet, so when I take tight turns or lean, she holds me tight enough that it feels like she wants to crawl into my skin.

I love it. If it would make her feel better, I'd fucking figure out a way to unzip my skin and let her live there.

That's kind of morbid and gross, but that's the level of obsession I'm at.

She taps my chest three times, a sign for 'I love you', and I smile brightly. Reaching back, I hold her bare leg and squeeze her calf three times. I'll never miss a time to tell her how much I love her.

Signaling I'm going to turn, I put my hand back on the handlebar and slow down enough to turn and pull up in front of the now-familiar building. I glide into a handicap parking spot and wait. Jade, unfortunately, pulls back from me and starts taking off her helmet.

Why did I have to make that drive so quick again? Who cares if she's late?

"Fuck, I've got three minutes to get up there," Jade curses, looking at her watch and handing me the helmet.

That's right—she cares.

Putting her helmet in the saddle bag, I'm intent on giving her a toe-curling kiss before I leave her for the day. But when I look back at Jade, she's frozen.

"Babe?" I ask softly. I'm immediately worried; she's so still, I wonder if she's even breathing. My eyes scan the area, trying to see what she is, but there are only a few people walking towards us. A pair of girls, talking excitedly about something. They're still far off, so I don't even know if they're the reason she's gone mute.

"Jade?" I ask, pulling at her arm to get her to turn and face me.

And that's when I feel her shaking.

Kicking the kickstand in place, I push off the bike as quickly as I can and stand in front of her. Between her and the unknown danger that's got her so scared.

"Baby, tell me what's wrong," I plead softly, trying to curl my broad shoulders around her so she's as hidden as possible. I still can't see anything concerning.

Narrowing my eyes, I even look around the trees and in windows, trying to see anything immediate. Jade steps into my chest, hiding her face while her whole body shakes. I try to control the shaking as much as possible by wrapping my arms around her. Is she having a seizure? No, she's still upright and breathing correctly.

What has her so scared she's frozen like this?

"Jade, tell me what's going on," I whisper, looking around us to make sure there isn't a guy with a gun staring us down. Aside from those two girls, the campus is fairly still, as all the one o'clock classes have started.

"It's okay," she whispers against my chest. "It's okay. I'm okay. I'm okay."

I don't know if she's trying to tell *me* that, or *herself*, but it doesn't make me feel any better.

Cupping her cheeks in my hands, I tilt her chin so I can see her beautiful face. Her eyes are shiny, sparkling from unshed tears, and she's biting her lip so hard she may draw blood.

"You're okay." I nod with her, trying to put as much conviction into those words as I can. "What happened?"

"I, uh..." She starts to say with a stutter, but catches herself. "I saw someone... from that night."

My hackles rise and my blood boils. I immediately whip my head back and forth, craning my neck as far to the side as I can so that I can see.

"Where?" I snarl.

"They're gone. I'm sorry, I just... froze." Jade wipes her eyes free of the tears. My strong girl refused to let them fall.

"It's okay. You scared the hell out of me, though. I didn't know what was wrong." I let out a sigh of relief that she's okay, but I feel increasingly off the longer she stays here. "No one is in any of your classes, right?"

"No, no." Jade shakes her head. "Just the fuck-up of the dorm, but we're working on that. I'll be able to get my own place or get a roommate soon, thanks to you."

I don't answer, but I don't like this. I don't like that, at any moment, one of those fuckers could find her and...

Breathing angrily through my nose, I clench my jaw and tighten my grip on her.

"Asher, I'll be okay," Jade insists. "I probably won't see her again."

Her. So it was that bitch, Sarah. The one who basically fed her to a rapist and turned her mother against her.

"I'll get through classes and come right to the shop. Promise," she says with a very fake smile. I can tell she's trying to make me feel comfortable about leaving her.

"I don't like this," I admit under my breath, surveying around us again. "Maybe you should skip today."

"Absolutely not." Jade stands back, firm and determined. All her fear vanishes as she tells me off. "I will not let those assholes take more from me. I'm sorry that was my knee-jerk reaction. I'll get better at it, but I'm not going to go and hide... I can't."

She's such a fucking rockstar and I totally understand where she's coming from. But that doesn't mean, especially in this instance, I'm not worried for her.

"Jade," I groan.

"No, Asher. I'm not going to skip class because I saw someone from my fucked-up past," she argues. "She didn't even stop or notice me, so I'm going to put on my badass lady panties and go get the schooling that I may or may not need." She glares at me, the flame of determination shining in her irises.

I'm not her keeper or her warden. I'm her boyfriend, who loves her so much it hurts, and underneath the determination she's showing me right now, I know she's scared. I want Jade to feel supported, to know I always have her back, and I think I'll need some help. Maybe I can enlist some of my buddies to shadow her, just to make sure she's safe. I've got some favors I could call in, or I could offer a few free tattoos...

Not a bad idea.

My eyebrow cocks up at the thought. I like it, but I don't think she'll appreciate it very much.

"Your phone stays on loud, and vibrate, and *on* your person at all times," I bark in negotiation.

"No," she protests. "I'm going to three lectures today. I'm not taking the chance that my phone starts ringing and drawing everyone's attention."

I narrow my eyes. "Fine. On vibrate, on your desk."

"Deal."

"And you message me as often as you can. Even if it's just 'I'm fine.'" I pull her back in. "I need to know you're okay." After taking a hug I needed more than she did, I reluctantly let her go.

Jade sighs like she's annoyed, but secretly she loves it. She fiddles nervously with her backpack strap. I can't help but smile softly; she's trying to decide whether or not to push back because she doesn't want to inconvenience me.

This silly, sweet girl.

"I will. But you're also super busy today, Asher. Don't worry about me."

Shaking my head, I playfully roll my eyes. Reaching out again, I grab her quickly by the waist and pull her into me. Jade gasps, her hands catching her fall on my chest. I smirk and look down at her as she glances at me through her eyelashes. I love the anticipation; the way she's waiting to see what I'll do. If I'll kiss her, if I'll leave her hanging, or if I'll pick her up and fuck her on my bike.

I lean in close, until our breaths are mingling together, and whisper against her lips, "It's my privilege to worry about you. I'll gladly do it for the rest of my days." Kissing her, I know that we could both let this go further. But an alarm goes off on my phone, letting me know I need to get to work.

"I'll be late at the shop tonight. But if anything happens, anything at all, you call me and I'll send Roxie, Ty or I'll come myself. Understood?" I present it as a question, but it's not.

She knows it. I know it.

Breathless, Jade nods. Silencing the alarm, I make sure she's secure on her feet before I step backward, maintaining eye contact while I climb back onto my bike and rev the engine.

"After your last class, call me and I'll come get you between clients. Okay?"

"Okay." She says so softly I almost can't hear it over the motor.

"I love you, darlin'." I reach forward, grabbing her shirt which looks suspiciously like one of my own, and kiss her again.

"I love you, too," she replies so sweetly, it makes my heart flutter.

"Bye, babes." I sit back and take off.

Worry and anxiety are my constant companions today. Leaving my girl after she's had a panic attack doesn't feel like the right thing to do, but I know I have to. The wind flows through my hair and I already know that for the next few hours, I'm going to be glued to my fucking phone.

Jade

I WASN'T GOING to let fucking Sarah tear me down. Fuck that **bitch**.

After watching Asher drive off—that man is too sexy for words, especially on his motorcycle, *fuck me*—I steel my nerves and force myself to walk into the econ building. I still don't want to have this major, but right now, I can't do anything about it.

The old limestone building has seen better days, it's obvious that the college has tried to keep it clean, repaired and pristine. Opening the door, I'm so fucking thankful the A/C is blasting. This heat wave hasn't left us yet. Plus, I have three flights of stairs to run up.

I start my ascent, thinking about tonight. Ever since we talked about tattoos, I've been stuck on getting one. I don't think Asher would charge me for it, especially if he's the one that gets to do it. But I want to do something for him in return.

Maybe I could entice him with sexual favors. I do need to perfect my blowjobs.

I turn the corner in the stairwell and keep climbing. I think I'd

218

want a butterfly. Maybe right in the valley of my breasts, that way I could hide it if I wanted. I think that's an incredibly tempting spot. Perfect for my emerging sensuality.

Shit, I'm out of breath. I need to run more, or do any kind of cardio. Only two more flights. I'm already so late—does it really matter if I run?

Slowing down, I keep climbing the never-ending hellscape, but walk this time.

I'll ask Asher tonight to do it. And I'll ask about the receptionist job so I can get more information. I'm very cautiously excited. Not only will I get to work on my art, but I'll get to spend time with the crew. It's going to be great.

Spending the rest of my involuntary cardio session planning and designing the tattoo in my head, I finally push open the third-floor door and try not to wheeze too much while I catch my breath.

I'm late enough that the noon classes are being let out and the hallway is starting to flood with people. Fuck, it's going to be so embarrassing when I push open the lecture hall door and everyone stares at me. Hopefully, I'm not *so* late that my professor will automatically count it as an absence. If that's the case, I would've stayed with Asher.

The hallway starts to fill with chatter and that static noise where you can hear everything and nothing at the same time. Keeping my eye out for the right room—it's only like the fourth time I've been on this floor—I look ahead a ways, and one person stands out.

Him.

The blood leaves my face and I feel nauseous as I stop walking, acutely aware that he's walking toward me. He's talking with the same guy I saw him with last time, the same guy that was there that night. His light hair reflects the shine of the fluorescent lights above us and he's deep in conversation with his friend. They aren't really looking where they're walking, so I put my head down and hope to the universe they don't suddenly pay attention.

I have to keep going. I have to make sure he has no reason to stop. I force my feet to move as bile turns my stomach and makes saliva pool in my mouth. My fingernails slice into my palm as I squeeze my hands into fists.

One text. One text to Asher and he'd come get me.

But I won't let *him*, the drugging-girls-fucking-rapist, take this from me. I won't live in fear. I won't stay in that laundry room. Not when I have so much going for me.

Not when I'm determined to be strong.

I can be strong.

I will be strong.

When we pass each other in the hallway, memories of that night—or what I can remember of it—threaten to pull me under. But they don't. *"Boobs, it's a compliment…"*

He's at my back without any sort of glance or expression of knowing and I breathe a little easier.

There's my door to the right, but my stomach starts to turn. Maybe I should just…

No. **No.**

I have a choice here. A choice to let those fuckers win and take more from me, or push forward and become who I've always wanted to be. That's not saying the trauma I've endured will magically go away, but it does mean that I can choose not to let him—*them*—hold any power over me.

And with that thought, I open the door and take charge of my life with my head held high.

ASHER IS NOT KIDDING ABOUT HIS REQUEST FOR ME TO check in often throughout the day. The funny thing is that he has done most of the texting. I did what he said and left my phone on my desk so I could see when he messaged. I started to wonder if he even had a client today because he was texting me so much.

I sat through the lecture without an embarrassing conversation about my attendance since I was only about fifteen minutes late. The professor only looked at me with an annoyed expression, but kept going as I sat quietly in the seat closest to the door.

Thank my lucky stars.

One lecture turned to two, and finally around six in the evening, I had my last one. It was only an hour and a half but time flew by, between trying to actually pay attention and Asher's non-stop messaging. He even got Roxie to message me too, checking in and shooting the shit to pass the time.

After making plans for the weekend with Roxie while hearing how she's ready to pass out from exhaustion over text, the professor ends his lecture on college algebra. My freaking brain and ears are full.

"You're all dismissed. I'll see you in two days. Don't forget to upload the assignment to the student portal by midnight tomorrow," My professor announces and shuts his computer roughly. "You're dismissed." Everyone stands up and starts talking all at once.

I'm so ready to jump into Asher's arms. It's been a long fucking day.

Checking the time on my phone, I see that Asher hasn't

messaged me back—he's probably busy with his last client. It's only seven thirty at night, so if I walk, I should get there when he's cleaning up. A quick glance out the window tells me that the sun is just starting to set, so I should be okay.

My bravery about walking in the dark only extends so far. I usually get an Uber from my dorm to Asher's apartment building so I never have to walk on campus alone.

In the dark.

But I'm feeling good, despite my freakouts earlier. What are the chances that *he* or Sarah are walking around right now? Besides, the shop isn't that far...

I text Asher that I'm walking to the shop, then put my phone in the back pocket of the shorts I'm wearing. Straightening my spine and rolling my shoulders back, I emulate the badass I'm trying to be.

I can do this.

Getting to the ground floor is much quicker than going up, taking me just a few minutes from the lecture hall. All the other students scatter once we step outside. The sun setting means it's finally a tiny bit cooler and the fresh air is so nice. I try to distract myself with the beauty around me: the way the wind makes the leaves move in the trees, the soft hum of the street lights turning on overhead, the way the clouds mix in the sky. It's going to be a nice night to walk. But in the back of my mind, I'm extra observant about what's around me. My eyes don't stop darting around, making sure there isn't anyone lurking or following me.

I try not to think about it too much as my pace quickens. I walk across the street and pass the residential area so that I'm able to walk closer to downtown where *From The Ashes* is located.

My phone vibrates in my pocket, but I ignore it. I don't want to take the chance that when I look down, someone could come up behind me.

Breathing deeply, I try to slow my heart rate and my mind, just focus on the present and on what's around me. I can do this.

Quicker than I thought, I arrive on the sidewalk of Main Street and pass all the shops and little restaurants until I see the warm window of Asher's shop. The phoenix under the masculine writing of *From The Ashes* shining brightly in the window.

I smile when I see it, because that means Asher—my person—is almost within my reach. I almost feel like I'm *home* again.

Looking inside, I can see Asher hunched over the table as he's tattooing someone at his station. It looks like it's the last moments, too; Asher sits up, rolls his shoulders back and wipes down the guy's leg. I can't see who it is yet, but they exchange words and Asher smiles politely, nodding and wrapping up the fresh tattoo before helping the guy sit up.

It's... Kyle.

It's... the guy who Sarah was meeting.

The guy who basically gave me the drug himself.

The one that lives on my dorm floor.

The one who is best friends with a rapist.

And from the looks of it, is pretty buddy-buddy with Asher, too.

Asher laughs at something Kyle says, and helps him up before returning a hug.

I can't believe this.

The door opens as another customer leaves, and I hear Asher say, "Anything for a...friend," as he slaps Kyle on the shoulder.

I'm frozen in front of the window. Like my mind physically can't understand what it's hearing or seeing.

Ty makes eye contact with me through the window as he's cleaning his station, and cocks his head to the side in confusion. I'm sure I look creepy, staring in the window with my mouth wide open as my world crashes down around me.

Is Asher *friends* with these people? Have they been playing me? Making me fall in love with him, just for what? Fucking sport?

The door opens again with a *ding* and I hear Kyle say, "Your brother is my roommate! It all worked out like we wanted after all."

And there goes all the oxygen from my lungs. My hand goes to my throat. What the fuck is happening? I can't... I don't... The world starts to slant as I panic.

"Jade?" Ty's accented voice hits my ears, cutting through the static.

Asher had to know... He *had* to. There's no way he didn't know. His brother? Kyle... the only guy I've seen him around campus with is Hunter...

Asher's brother.

"Jade? Are you okay?" Ty asks, reaching out to hold my elbow. "What's wrong?"

"That guy," I croak out, a finger shakily pointing at Kyle. "Is Asher good friends with that guy?"

"Kyle? I mean, I guess?" Ty answers with a wishy-washy shake of his head. "Kyle's good friends with Asher's younger brother, Hunter. They've always been attached at the hip, and Kyle likes to try and get on Asher's good side. I'd say they're friendly."

"Oh god," I gulp, and dry heave onto the pavement.

"Fuck," Ty curses, "what's wrong?"

"Kyle... Hunter... Hunter's the one..." I can't even say the fucking words right now. So fucking much for being strong. I spit out the bile that refuses to leave and wipe my mouth on the back of my hand.

"What?" Ty's eyes widen and he looks inside quickly before turning back to me. "Jade, come inside, let's talk this out." He's holding a hand out to me like he's going to grab at me, but I can't.

Was Asher just trying to get on my good side so I wouldn't do anything against his brother? Or what if... what if... what...if.

"No," I refuse, pulling my arm out of his reach. "No."

I turn and I run.

I run away from the pain.

Away from the betrayal.

Away from the complete breaking of my heart and my trust.

KYLE IS my brother's roommate? That's not surprising at all. Hunter and Kyle have been thick as thieves since they were in high school.

As much as I don't like my brother, I like Kyle even less. They feed off of each other.

Kyle wants to break the rules? Hunter shows him how.

Hunter wants to steal something? Kyle's scoping out the place.

I'm sure they're getting up to no-fucking-good in college. I would expect nothing less from my degenerate brother and his half-brained bestie.

I have not one fucking clue why Kyle likes me so much, but at least I can still scare him. When he came in for his first tattoo and paid handsomely, I told him I'd be good with being his artist. Now his sleeve is almost done and the thigh piece we started tonight will be at least another grand. I don't have to like the guy, but his money, on the other hand, I need.

It's a shitty way to end the night, but he insisted on the last appointment slot so he 'could go to a rager right after.'

What a dumbass.

Kyle's being the little kiss ass—that hug about made me nauseous—he always is, when Ty walks outside randomly. I don't pay much attention to it because Ty's gonna be Ty.

"It's so sick!" Kyle exclaims, looking at his new tattoo in the mirror before pulling the bottom of his shorts down and walking to his bag for the payment.

"I'm glad you like it. Next time, we'll add in the stippling and some shading to add dimension." I let my customer service face drop and write up the receipt that Kyle always requests. "It'll be $580 this time."

"Money well spent," Kyle says excitedly, handing over a stack of cash. "Keep the extra one twenty for yourself."

"Thanks, man. I appreciate it." I nod and start immediately counting the bills. I trust Kyle about as far as I throw both him and my brother.

The bell dings and I ignore it. Ty's coming back to his spot and I need to finish counting.

"Hey, Ty," Kyle greets him, monotoned. His tone is so different from when he was talking to me that I want to laugh. Kyle and Ty have never seen eye-to-eye. Thank fuck for that. It tells me that Ty is actually a good person with morals.

I don't hear Ty respond; not that I would, normally, but instead of words, I hear the crunching of a nose and Kyle crying.

Spinning around, I see Ty holding Kyle by the shirt collar. What the fuck is going on?

Ty rears his fist back and lets it fly again, the second punch well-placed over Kyle's eye. The skin splits, and blood immediately pours down his face.

"What the fuck?!" Kyle screeches, trying to hit back, but Ty's too strong of a fighter for him to even touch.

Moving to stand closer to Ty, I know better than to touch

him right now, but I have to at least say something. "Ty, man, what's going on?" I ask, keeping my tone even. He may be a hothead, but he would never do something to jeopardize our business. He would never hurt someone that wasn't deserving, or hadn't already agreed to fight. I know all the unspoken rules of his underground fights, especially because Ty follows them in his daily life, too.

Kyle must have done something really fucked up for Ty to use these tactics to get justice.

"Tell him," Ty growls at Kyle. "Tell him, *or I will.*"

"I don't know what the fuck you're talking about, you crazy motherfucker!" Kyle screams in his face, spewing blood that's dripped from his nose into his mouth.

Ty looks like he might actually murder him. "You rapist piece of shit!" Ty screams and punches Kyle in the mouth, making his teeth look like they're coated in blood.

"What?" It feels like the word is knocked out of me with the punch, and my eyes go wide.

"Tell him, Kyle," Ty spits his name mockingly. "Tell Asher how you and Hunter worked together so Hunter could rape Jade. *Tell him.*"

Fury.

Anger.

Rage.

Murder.

My entire body shifts from confusion to pure destruction the moment Ty says her name. My gaze moves carefully from Ty to Kyle, who no longer looks confused, but instead, scared for his life.

As he should be.

"You did what?" I ask, my fists clenching tighter and tighter with each word. I'm so fucking angry that I sound calm. Kyle's squirming, trying to get out of Ty's hold, his eyes wide with fear.

"Look, I don't know who Jade is. I've never raped anyone," Kyle stammers nervously, his eyes shifting between Ty and I. A bruise is already forming over his eye where Ty hit him.

"You sound awfully nervous for someone who's innocent, Kyle. You also chose your words carefully just now. *You* might not have raped anyone, but did you help Hunter?" I snarl, my lip curling like I'm a fucking wolf about to pounce on my prey.

"I..." He gulps.

"Hunter. My sad sack of shit for a brother, who I've always known is a horrific human. But I never thought he'd become this terrible, this goddamn awful. Not after how we grew up." My breaths are coming in rougher as my anger starts to become unbearable.

I need to fix this.

Now.

"Asher, man..." Kyle tries to rip himself from Ty's grip, but Ty's holding onto him like a python ready to cut off its prey's oxygen.

"Don't you fucking 'Asher' me." I grip his face in my hand and force him to look at me. "Tell me that you and my brother, with the help of a bitch named Sarah, didn't drug and rape Jade Henderson at a house party this summer, before leaving her alone in a fucking dingy laundry room. Tell me I'm making this up."

I see Kyle's eyes widen before he schools his features and shakes his head.

He knows.

He knows exactly who I'm fucking talking about.

"I don't know who Jade Henderson is!" He screams, like he's trying to give me the least amount of information possible.

"Okay." I pull Kyle from Ty's grasp and hold him by the throat, pushing him toward the bathroom. "We're going to take a little break now. And when you're ready, you're going to tell me the fucking truth!" I throw his ass into the bathroom, hard enough that his head hits the wall and dents the sheetrock.

Quickly glancing around, I see that Ty has left my side; for a second, I think he's gone. But I should've known better. Ty's locking the front door, switching the neon sign off and pulling the rolled-up curtain down, effectively closing us for the night.

Also making it so no one walks in as we fuck this guy up.

"Asher, come on, you know me. You know Hunter. Do you really think either of us would do something like that?" Kyle stands up, his hands stretched out in front of him like he's talking to a wild animal. I *feel* like a wild animal right now. And someone's hurt one of my pack. That just won't fucking do.

They'll pay with broken bones and spilt blood.

"I absolutely fucking do," I growl and lunge forward. Kyle screams as I open the toilet seat with one hand and shove his head in the water with the other. He's fighting against me, his shoulders and arms pushing up against the porcelain, but I just put more of my body weight on him. I've got at least fifty pounds on this fucker.

"Asher!" Ty yells at me from the threshold. "Stop—we can't do that."

"Watch me," I snap, pulling Kyle's head from the water. "Are you ready to talk now?" I hiss close to his ear. His lip is trembling like a little bitch, and I smirk. "Good. I'll ask you again. Did you and my brother set Jade up to be raped?"

"You crazy ass motherfuckers!" He gasps, but nods his head over and over.

"Did you?!" I scream at him, pushing his head toward the water again, but he fights back.

"YES! Yes, okay, we did!" Kyle says shakily, fearfully. "I didn't touch her, but I gave Hunter the roofie. Sarah pointed her out, said she needed to let loose and would be a good target. Hunter said he needed a fuck, and she was desperate, man! It just lined up." Tears are running down his battered face as I hold the back of his head, pulling his hair painfully tight.

"Where's Hunter now?" I snarl, my face inches from his.

"Probably at the party!" Kyle snaps. I let his head go and he falls forward.

"Call him," I snap. "Have him come here now."

"What?" Kyle asks worriedly.

"Yeah, what?" Ty pushes my shoulder so I'm facing him. His eyes are wide, concern racing across his features as he searches for any ounce of humanity in my eyes.

I cross my arms over my chest. "Did I fucking stutter?" I snarl, turning my attention back to a shaking Kyle, kneeling by my legs. "Call Hunter *now*." I won't let this stand. Jade's pain and torment came from my brother? No, no, I won't let this go. I won't let him get away with this.

He was my responsibility, but not anymore. Now, **she's** the priority and it's my responsibility to fuck up the person who hurt her.

Kyle gets his phone out and his fingers shake as he dials Hunter's number.

"What's your thought process right now, Ash?" Ty asks quietly.

"I'm going to have a little talk with my brother." I roll my head, cracking my neck. "It seems I failed as a parental figure, but I won't fail as a boyfriend." Ty looks at me with a nod and understanding, which I appreciate, but I don't need his approval. "You should get out of here," I suggest. "Actually, you should go wait out front for Jade and make sure she doesn't see either of these pieces of shit near me."

Ty purses his lips and narrows his eyes.

I raise an eyebrow. "What?"

Ty takes a moment to reply. "She was here... earlier."

My heart drops to my stomach and stops. "When?"

"She ran off right before I came in and attacked Kyle. She... She saw you two being friendly and I told her that your brother was Kyle's best friend. She put two and two together."

My ability to breathe vanishes. "I'm going to kill him," I mutter angrily under my breath.

"You can't kill them," Ty says pointedly, trying to bring me back to reason. "But you *can* take care of business."

"Where is she now?" I growl. I want nothing more than to run after Jade, explain all the shit that's going on. It physically hurts me to know she's walking around, thinking that I am in any way working with these fucking assholes. Fuck, does she think...

Goddamn it.

"I don't–" Ty starts to say, but he's interrupted by his phone ringing. "One minute, it's Roxie," he says to me before answering. "Hey *amor*, I can't talk right now."

"YOU TELL THAT MOTHERFUCKER I WARNED HIM NOT TO HURT HER! I VOUCHED FOR HIM, AND WHAT DID HE DO? HE'S COLUDING WITH FUCKING RAPISTS?! WHO THE **FUCK**-"

I hear Roxie's screams burst through the phone, loud enough that Ty's phone speaker cracks from the volume. Ty cuts her off, speaking softly in Spanish, his explanation laced with *hermosa chica, calmate, amante.* I know enough Spanish to recognize he's calling her beautiful and saying sweet nothings to calm her down.

"Roxie, you have it wrong," Ty insists when Roxie stops screaming. "I know what it looked like, I was here when she saw him. No, I know. Roxie, Asher beat the hell out of Kyle when he found out. I only got like two hits in and this dude looks like he's gone through a full five rounds." Ty nods and makes affirmative noises. "No, he didn't know... Yes, he's handling Hunter, too. I'm going to stay here and make sure Asher doesn't go to jail. Yes... Yes... Make sure she's okay. Make sure she knows that Asher didn't know and it isn't what it looked like. Okay. Okay I will."

He hangs up the phone. "You're in a big shitstorm, brother." Ty's eyes widen and he takes a deep breath. "With both girls."

"How fucking far is he?" I yell at Kyle.

And just as Kyle goes to answer, there's a knock at the front door.

"Open the door, Ty," I say in a scarily calm voice.

My brother—my *brother*, who I've raised and who I loved— drugged, raped, and hurt my girl. He *hurt* her.

She's still recovering, but I don't know if she will ever truly heal.

I feel like I'm dissociating because as Ty unlocks the door, my anger simmers to a controllable level.

And that should scare us all.

"Asher! How are you, bro?" Hunter walks in, arms spread wide and a big smile on his stupid face. "Where's Kyle?"

Just then, Kyle crashes out of the bathroom, intent on making a run for it. His eyes dart around, looking for the next sign of danger, and he holds his hand to his head. I see fresh blood trickling down his face from an open wound hidden beneath his hairline. Probably from when he hit the wall.

"What the fuck..." Hunter's eyes widen and he looks to me with alarm. "Did you do that?"

Kyle takes that moment to try and run out the front door, abandoning his stuff and Hunter. *Chickenshit.* The front bell dings and I jerk my head to Ty, letting him know he's got Kyle. I know Ty will make sure he doesn't open his fucking mouth.

The doorbell goes off a final time, signaling that it's just Hunter and I in the building. Hunter shifts his weight back and forth on the balls of his feet while his eyes scan the room, as if he thinks someone else is going to jump out at him.

"What am I doing here, Ashe?" Hunter asks, throwing his hands out to the side.

My nostrils flare as I noisily suck in a deep breath.

"What have you done?" I ask through gritted teeth.

"Nothing as of late." Hunter shrugs and rolls his eyes, putting his hands into his pockets like he's bored.

"How about this summer?"

Hunter narrows his eyes. "Just spit it out, Asher. You obviously have an agenda. What are you getting at?"

My hands curl into fists so tightly, I can feel my knuckles pop.

"Did you drug and rape someone?" I say it clearly but my voice is so low. I didn't know I could make myself unintentionally sound like Batman.

"What?" He scoffs, pushing a breath out and rolling his eyes. "Seriously, Asher? You think I'd do something like that?"

I stare at him roughly, looking for any sign of deception. I obviously can't trust him; never have been able to, really. But I didn't think he was this far gone.

"I'm going to ask you again. And don't insult my intelligence by giving me some bullshit answer," I snap while pointing at him aggressively. "Did you drug and rape a girl this summer?"

Hunter laughs and shakes his head.

But he doesn't say no.

"Did you?!" I push, moving closer to him. The way his eyes dart to where I stepped tell me that he's scared.

As he should be.

"Look, brother," he says with a nervous tilt to his voice, putting his hands up in front of him. It doesn't escape my attention that he's trying to use that word to remind me of our relation. Not that it means jack shit to me anymore. "I don't know what you've heard, but you know me."

"You're right, Hunter. I do know you," I reply calmly with a nod. There's a ghost of a pause between us as he waits for me to continue. When I don't react or continue, Hunter smiles in relief.

"Unfortunately," I snarl at him, my eyes narrowing in rage, and I punch him square in the face.

Blood squirts from his nose as his eyes scrunch in pain. My knuckles sting with the force of my punch, but I welcome it. Hunter's hands immediately cover his face as he screams in pain, his body recoiling from the force of my punch as he looks at me with disbelief.

"You are the scum of the fucking earth. I cannot believe you're my brother. I could fucking kill you," I growl before gripping his innocent looking blonde hair, holding him steady while punching him again and again.

"What the fuck, Asher?!" He screams at me, putting his hands out and throwing back a few ill-aimed punches. He's so fucking weak that he's easy to dodge. I get one more in before he falls to the ground and I climb on top of him, holding his shirt and punching him back down.

"You drugged and raped a girl this summer. A sweet, innocent blonde who came with a chick named Sarah. Her name is Jade Henderson. Ring any bells?" I snap, pulling him up by his shirt. Hunter's face is covered in bright red blood, his hair completely disheveled from my grip, and his eyes are wild with pain and fear. But underneath it all, I can see recognition.

He knows.

He remembers.

"What does that bitch have to do with this?" He snaps, spitting blood in my face as he speaks.

"What does she have to do with this?" I repeat, getting closer to him. His jaw ticks and I can practically smell his fear. and I growl, "*Everything.*"

Standing rapidly, I drag him to my station and throw him into the wall. Hunter clobbers to his feet and jumps to attack me, but I'm ready. I hit him in the face, and while his head is flung to the side, I jab him in the kidney. Hunter grunts in pain and throws a punch of his own that catches me by surprise. Pain blossoms over my eye; the point of impact feels like it's fracturing and I grunt with the sting. Great, I'm going to have a black eye.

"How the fuck do you even know her? What, you want to know if her pussy was good?" Hunter says cockily, spitting a wad of blood to the side as he smiles like a fucking psycho. We start to circle one another, his hands halfway up in a fight stance. I happen to know he's never been in an actual fight, though. He just gets others to do his dirty work.

I, however, have been fighting since I was seventeen and know how to take a punch.

And how to knock someone out.

"Shut the fuck up." I snarl.

"Oh, does my brother have a crush on my sloppy seconds? You do, don't you?" He laughs like he's an evil villain in a horror movie. "She wasn't even worth it, but she was *begging* for it. So fucking desperate. 'Pick me, pick me,'" he mocks in a girly tone, "I should've thrown her outside when I was done and let someone else have a go at her. Maybe she'd be half decent for them. I still got mine, though—I was even the first fuck of her life. Maybe it took. Is that why you're so pissed? Is the bitch pregnant with my bastard?"

I growl but try to keep my eye on the prize. He's trying to rile me up now. And he'll fucking pay for it.

The mental image of Jade pregnant with my brother's child makes me sick. For more than one reason.

I have to shake it.

Clenching my fists again, I go to throw a punch but he jumps out of the way.

"Oh, man, have you got it bad," Hunter says teasingly. "No stupid bitch is worth this, Asher."

"You've got it wrong, asshole. She's worth everything and more." I throw another punch out and he just barely dodges it.

Hunter seems to want to egg me on, leading me in a circle, getting closer to the bench I use to tattoo people. "She's nothing but a used-up cunt. But I will say, I was pleasantly surprised when I found out she's on my dorm floor. I've been watching and waiting to catch her again... She might not have been the best fuck, but I'd be willing to show her a few more things." He raises an eyebrow and winks as he says that filth. I grab his shirt, pulling him closer to me. My hand wraps around his throat, cutting off air to his lungs. Hunter's hands wrap around my arm to try and throw me off, but it's easy to ignore.

"You will never touch her again. You will never look at her again. Tomorrow, you will go to the dorm facility advisor and you will completely move dorms, I want you *nowhere* near her. Do you understand?" I sneer in his face, the rage I'm feeling seething through my voice.

Hunter snorts at me. "That's not going to happen."

"It's going to happen, or I'm going to kill you," I warn.

"You wouldn't," he says like it's a joke, but from the way his eyes shake, I can see he's actually worried.

Without saying a word, I pull my arm back and punch him in the sternum. Hunter immediately starts to wheeze, the small bit of air he had left pushing involuntarily from his lungs. He gasps for a breath. While that's happening, I wrap my hands around his throat again.

"Are you sure about that?" I whisper menacingly.

Hunter kicks his leg out and lands a solid blow to my thigh, but instead of falling back, I grit my teeth and don't let the pain deter me. Punching him one more time, I push all my power into it and aim at his head. I don't want my brother to die, but I want him to remember this moment every time he even *thinks* of repeating what he did. He fucking deserves it after hurting Jade.

My punch lands on the side of his head and Hunter collapses on the ground, unconscious.

I feel nothing. No sense of empathy or brotherly comradery when I look at him. Only disgust. Only the need for revenge.

Touching my eyebrow, I wince and pull my fingers back to see that I'm bleeding.

I'll live.

Out of the corner of my eye, my tattoo gun catches the glint of the overhead light. I hadn't had time to put everything away yet, and now, that might have been a good thing.

There's one way to make sure everyone knows who Hunter is. What he likes to do.

Permanently.

Mind made up, I grab the tattoo gun and a container of ink. I kick Hunter so he's lying on his back and pull his shirt up. His jeans are stupidly, ridiculously low and tight. Normally, I'd make fun of him, but right now it's going to work in my favor. I don't even shave the area, I just click the machine on, dip the needle in the ink and get to fucking work.

In thick block letters, the word 'RAPIST' is tattooed on Hunter's lower stomach, right over his dick. From now until the end of time, whenever he tries to get with someone, they'll know the kind of person he is.

There's no forgiveness. There's no mercy.

Just like he didn't give any to Jade. Or any of the others I'm sure he's hurt.

He'll carry this reminder of what he did for the rest of his life. Just like she will.

The bell goes off overhead, and I hear Ty come in.

"He's taken care of," Ty says ominously, his footsteps letting me know he's getting closer to my station.

"So is Hunter," I reply. My voice is still that oddly calm and flat tone as I answer him, sitting back and tossing my tattoo gun on the metal tray.

"What did you do?" Ty asks, looking over my shoulder. "You didn't kill him, did you? Otherwise, we have a shit-ton of loose ends we need to tie up. I have some people we can call."

My head whips to Ty quickly in surprise. "You have 'people you can call'? Are you a part of the mob or some shit?"

"No, no. Don't worry about it." He grabs a towel from my desk and wipes his hands.

"Alright, we'll be talking about that later." I put my fingers on Hunter's pulse point to make sure he's okay. I don't ever want to see him again, so I have to make sure he's alive to get the fuck out of my life. "He's fine. That ugly, coal heart is beating strong. I just knocked him out and gave him a new tattoo. On the house."

His face matches the worst tattoo I've ever done. Both of his eyes are already bruising, puffing his face out grossly, I'm sure his nose is broken from the slightly skewed way it's sitting on his face now. All of the skin on Hunter's face is red and painful looking. Same as the skin around his tattoo. It's probably going to get infected, but I don't care. Serves him fucking right.

"That's... deserved," Ty compliments, tipping his head downward and nodding.

"Let's get him out of here."

Ty helps me pick Hunter up and stuff him into the backseat of the car he used to get to the shop.

"We're going to need to drop him off at a hospital," Ty says, scratching the back of his head. "Not that the asshole deserves to have someone take care of him, but we don't want this shit to fall back on us."

"Fine," I grumble and pull the keys from Hunter's pocket. His jeans are rubbing right on the tattoo and I chuckle darkly. When he wakes up, it's going to bother the fuck out of him as it heals.

"I'll drop him off and say we found him in an alleyway. You need to go get Jade." Ty pulls the keys from my hands. "She needs to hear it from you that you had nothing to do with this. You should've seen her face, Ashe. She felt betrayed."

Fuck.

"Goddamn it."

"She also needs to know these fuckers won't be a problem anymore. They **won't** be a problem anymore, right?"

"If me knocking Hunter out and threatening him to move didn't send the picture, I'm not sure what will."

"Good for you." Ty nods in surprise and appreciation.

"I'll make sure he gets the fuck out of her dorm. But I also think Jade wants to move out on her own. After this, I'll be pushing for her to move in with me so I can make sure neither Kyle or Hunter fuck with her."

"Good idea." Ty holds his hand out to shake mine. I shake it and pull him in for a hug.

"Thank you. For having my back. For having Jade's back. We owe you," I tell him, clapping him on the back.

Ty returns it and chuckles. "You owe me nothing. We're family."

I smile at my true brother and run back toward the shop to gather my stuff, clean up any blood, and delete the video footage before going to my girl.

"HE... He isn't like that. Ty told me that he didn't know." Roxie tries again to calm me down and to convince me that Asher is one of the good ones.

Logically, I know he is. I know he's worked hard to prove that. But seeing him hug Kyle... hearing him say that the demon I've been running from is Asher's brother... Is there any way Asher might become like his brother? He might end up agreeing with what Hunter did. Would that mean he would start... A fresh round of tears fills my eyes as I bury my face in shame and despair.

I feel like I've lost my home. Lost my support system. It sounds stupid, but I feel like I've lost my family.

Roxie's amazing. She took one look at my face as I stood at her door and immediately pulled me in. I told her through tears what happened, and she tried to bring me back to life. I was numb.

And I kind of miss the numbness because right now, all I can feel is heartache. My heart is breaking... no, actually—it's broken.

It's like Asher pulled my heart straight from my chest and now I just have an open, gaping wound killing me slowly. My cheeks haven't been dry since before I walked into Roxie's apartment.

"Jade," Roxie plops on the couch next to me. Drawing my feet up, I hug my knees to my chest and rest my forehead on them. "The guy that you've known, that you love, **that's** the real Asher. I'm sure he told you about his upbringing." I nod and she continues, "Then you know why he'd never turn on you. He'd never be that evil."

"How can you know that? Hunter is his brother. What if Hunter tells him I asked for it? That I wanted it? Would he believe him? And who am I? Just some girl. How can my word compete with Hunter's?" I cry into my knees, sobbing uncontrollably. I feel an arm wrap around me and Roxie's crying with me, softer than I am, but with no less feeling.

"I know it's hard. I know it's scary. But he's a good guy, Jade. I promise. You're just going to have to let him show you that he can be trusted," she says against my shoulder. "Take tonight. Think it through, and then see what happens tomorrow."

I nod, never pulling my head up, just letting the tears stream down my face.

A knock sounds at the door and we both jump. Sometimes I forget that Roxie has a past like I do. That she has the same fears, the same reservations, the same feeling of being constantly on guard. She's so strong and outspoken, it's easy to think she'd murder anyone who dare look at her sideways. And then in these little moments, I remember.

She's scared, but never willing to let anyone except her close family see it.

I'm going to be like her. I have to be.

"I'll get it," she says, giving me a kind smile and nodding before patting my arm and standing to open the door. The way she's standing blocks my view so I can't see who it is. I have a pretty good idea, though.

There are only two people I know who would think to come here this late at night. Especially after what went down earlier.

"Tell me she's here," Asher bellows. He sounds desperate, worried out of his mind and hopeful all at the same time.

"She's here." Roxie pops a hip and shifts slightly so I can see him, and he can see me, but she doesn't drop her arm. Her message is crystal clear.

"Jade, thank god," Asher breathes the words out in a sigh of relief. I can see his clothes are askew, as if he's been in a fight. There's a deep purple bruise forming around his eye that makes it look like he might have broken his nose. Asher rests his arms on the door frame, not trying to push inside, just resting like he was terrified that I went somewhere else. "I was so worried. Ty told me what you heard and saw and—" Asher tries to explain, but I just know I can't hear it right now.

Standing, I turn my back on him and high-tail it to Roxie's office. It's basically a junk drawer if a junk drawer was a room. She throws everything that she doesn't know what to do with into that room.

Luckily for me, she also keeps an old futon in there that I can lay on and hide under a blanket until I'm ready to face the world.

"You've gotta give her time, Asher. I honestly don't know how I would've reacted if it had happened to me," I hear Roxie tell him. I don't know if she's intentionally speaking louder so I can hear what they're saying, or the walls really are that ridiculously thin. I appreciate it either way.

"Fuck," he sighs nosily. I can imagine that he's running his hands through his hair. "I really fucked up... I didn't know, Roxie. I swear, I didn't know."

"So, you're saying it's just a coincidence that her fucking

rapist—the fucking snake who haunts her dreams—is your brother? And you met her that same night?" Roxie sounds like she's holding back a scoff. "There's no such thing as coincidences."

"Normally I'd agree with you, but I swear on everything I fucking own, this is *exactly that*. I was thinking about it on the way over here. Kyle invited me to that party over the summer. He had just finished his tattoo and told me there'd be free drinks, so I went. I knew that if Kyle was going, there was a good chance Hunter would go too, but I never saw him until the end. As he was leaving." He's speaking quickly, making sure that the dots connect. "I saw Kyle and Hunter walking away, looking like they did some shady shit. That's when I went downstairs to make sure there wasn't a fucking dead body or a pile of drugs, but it was worse—I found Jade. I should've put two-and-two together right then. I should've known, but I never thought Hunter would cross that line. I never thought to even ask him. There's a silence as Roxie takes in what he said.

"Fuck, Asher! What happened to your knuckles?" Roxie cries and I hear him scuffle inside the apartment. She's banging around the kitchen looking for the first aid kit she never keeps in the same place.

"I beat them up. Basically water-boarded Kyle and hit Hunter so badly that Ty dropped him at the ER." Asher's voice reveals he is wincing and Roxie growls. She must be cleaning his knuckles.

He did that for me?

Why?

"Fuck. That must have felt good, though. I know how you feel about shitty people like that," Roxie stresses but I can hear in her voice she's distracted. "What did you do?"

Asher shuts her down. "I don't want to talk about it."

"Damn," she curses. "There, all wrapped up."

"Thanks." He sighs. "Is she okay?" Asher asks, quieter, but it's kind of amazing how noises travel in this apartment. No wonder Roxie didn't want us to have sex here while she was home. You can hear everything.

"She's shaken. It's a lot, Ashe. Borderline too much." Roxie sighs. "I think she's struggling with both the fear that you might agree with Hunter at some point—"

Roxie's cut off by Asher. "Never. I'll never agree with him," he snarls.

"I know," Roxie insists with a tilt to her voice like she's annoyed. "But I can't say that if I was in her shoes, I wouldn't have the same fear."

Asher starts to chime in again, but Roxie cuts him off.

"She's also feeling betrayed. I think she knows you didn't hide it intentionally, but watching you hug the guy that drugged her, acting all buddy-buddy... Yeah, I could see why she's feeling that way."

Asher sighs loudly. They're both quiet for a moment before there's a loud bang accompanied by a cry of outrage by Roxie.

"The fuck, Asher?! That was my drywall!" she yells.

"I'm sorry, I'll fix it." Asher sounds a mix of overly apologetic, exhausted, and frustrated. "Okay, I'll give her some space." He sighs heavily before pleading with Roxie, "Please, don't let her go back to the dorms. I don't want her near them *at all* until I can make sure they keep their word."

"She's going to stay with me. I'm actually going to ask if she wants to move in. The office is empty," she shares and I peak my head out of the blanket, looking around at the mountains of piles. This room is anything but empty. "And it would be nice to have some help with the rent on the slower months at the shop. Plus, I like Jade. She's a good one and a bad bitch. I think we'd do well living together."

"I think that's a good idea," Asher replied, but then says, "until she starts living with me."

Roxie laughs abruptly. "You're pushing for that?"

"I will be. As soon as all this Hunter shit is over. She's it for me, Roxie."

My breath catches under the blanket when I hear that. He sounds so resolute. Like there is absolutely no room for discussion or second thoughts. I guess that makes sense; he always seemed to make decisions and stick to them. No matter what happens.

I guess this time, the choice he's sticking to is me.

"Well," Roxie sighs and I can hear the smile in her voice. "I think she'll be very glad to hear that. Just... give her some time to sort through all the stuff going through her head. You better fucking step up to the plate though, Asher. You've got some groveling and trust-earning to do."

"I know."

They chat about when Asher can come over to fix the hole he apparently made in her wall and then he leaves. The front door closes and I burrow deeper into the fuzzy blanket, intent on blocking out the world so I can rest. I just... want to sleep.

"Jade? Are you in there?" Roxie's voice sounds far away, and I don't have the energy to answer her. "It's okay, just sleep," she tells me and her permission to sleep makes me fall deep into the dark abyss.

***

Three Days Later

"Jade, you have to get out of that room. Even just for a moment so I can clean it out more. It's a shithole in there!" Roxie bangs on the door, her words loud but not pushing me like she thinks they will.

It's been at least three days since I ventured out of the room for anything except to use the bathroom. My stomach has long since stopped growling. I'm sure I smell fucking horrible, but I just can't find it in myself to care.

"Jade, come on. Talk to me," Roxie pleads through the door. There's about two minutes of silence before she knocks again and shouts, "That's it. I'm counting to three and I'm coming in." Anxiety spikes through my system, but there isn't really anything I can do. I plan to just stay curled under the blanket and hope she leaves.

"One!" Roxie starts counting, "Two, Three!" Then the door opens quickly.

"Jade," she says softly, walking over to me before I hear her kneel by the futon. "Jade, this isn't healthy. I tried to let you do your thing, but I'm worried."

Silence. I can't answer her.

"Have you eaten? Showered?"

I don't answer her. I can't find my voice or my will.

"Maybe I should call Asher," she says softly to herself and my chest tightens in anxiety. "He'll know what to do."

"I..." I croak out, my voice hoarse after days of no use.

"There's a water bottle over there, let me get it." Roxie steps to the side before coming back to my side and gently pulling the blanket away. "Here."

I take a small sip and hand it back to her.

"I think it's time I call Asher."

"No," I whisper. He can't see me like this. So defeated and broken.

"Okay." She nods, then stands and grabs a couple boxes before walking to the door. "I have a shift at the shop. I'll be back later, okay? Please try to eat something at the very least."

She leaves the door open, I'm sure in hopes that I leave to find food.

I lay back down and close my eyes. I'll figure it out later.

✦◇◇◇◇◇◇◇✦

"Jade, baby," a soft voice whispers. A warm hand rests against my head, pushing my hair back. "Oh god, baby. This is my fault, I'm so sorry."

"Asher?" My voice is still shaky and hoarse, and my vision isn't completely stable as my eyes open. Is he really here? Or am I just hallucinating?

"I'm here, darlin'. I'm here." He pulls the blanket back farther, letting a cool draft of fresh air wash over me. "I know I said I'd give you some time, and I did my best, but when Roxie said you hadn't left the room in days, I got worried. With good reason, it seems like."

He looks so fucking handsome. His stubble is perfect, his hair is shiny and glossy. He's let it air dry and that makes his natural curls look luscious. Makes me want to run my fingers through it. It's not fair that he looks so good while I'm sure I look like a greasy, nasty mole rat.

I smell and I look atrocious, so I do the very mature thing and try to pull the blanket back over my head. If I can't see him, then maybe he can't see me and he'll leave.

"Oh no, no, no," he argues and pulls the blanket back. "We're getting you in the bath right now. While you're taking a bath, I'm going to make you something to eat."

"Don't want to." All that sounds like so much work. So much work and so much effort when I can't even lift my head.

"I know," he says softly. And before I know it, he's lifting me into his arms and carrying me to the bathroom.

"Please, no," I whine, but can't find it in myself to push his arms away.

"Jade, let me take care of you. I know I messed up. I know that what you've gone through is overwhelming and more than anyone should ever have to, and I'm so fucking sorry for the part I played in it. Let me take care of you, like I've always wanted and tried to do." He sounds so sincere as he whispers the words while we walk towards Roxie's bathroom. My gaze falls over his shoulder and I see some boxes from the office in the hallway, like Roxie's been sneaking in and pulling them out one by one to give me space.

Oddly, I feel very appreciative of that.

He pushes the bathroom door open with his foot and moves me sideways inside the small room. Without any help from me, he somehow holds me *and* turns the hot water on. He's so strong; if I was in my right mind I would've fucking swooned.

Hopefully I'll get the opportunity later, when I'm not drowning in emotions.

Hot steam starts to fog up the room as Asher sets me on the sink, holding me until he's sure that I'm not going to fall. His arms are like soft guardrails, making sure I'm safe. Always looking out for me when I can't anymore.

"Do you need help getting undressed or can you do it?" he asks me gently. "I don't want to overstep here, baby, but you can't get into the shower with clothes on."

"It's fine," I say numbly.

"You need to say what you want. What you're okay with. I'm never going to cross a line you don't want me to. Ever." He leans his head down so that he's looking me in the eye. "Do you understand?"

I nod.

"Do you believe me?" Asher asks, his voice breaking slightly. Normally, he'd look me clearly in the eyes, making me be the one to back down with his seductive eyes and confidence. Not now, though; now he's looking down and holding his breath.

He's worried that I don't believe him. That I can't trust him anymore.

And that kind of pulls me out of this... void.

Slowly, I move my hand and tip his chin so his eyes meet mine.

"I do." My hand drops, but I make sure that my eyes don't. I know I trust him. At least with this. With me.

Asher takes a deep, steadying breath. It's strong, but shaky. Nodding, his hands touch my arms gently, slipping up with intention. I watch through hooded eyes, still so fucking exhausted. It's obvious he's touching me slowly so I know where he's going to go and where his hands are, giving me plenty of time to move away if I don't feel comfortable.

I'll be honest, I don't know if I could move. I don't think I want to, either.

His hands move up my arms, over my shoulders and start to pull up my well-worn shirt that I think is actually his. It's big and baggie and slips easily over my head, leaving me in only my sports bra.

"You haven't eaten?" he asks gently, though his worry is apparent. His eyes are moving over my body, and he wraps his hand around my wrist. I don't answer, because he already knows. So why should I spend my very finite energy answering him?

"God, baby," he mutters. "I should've taken care of you

better. Roxie said she was, but now I know she wasn't really. Not like I would've."

"Asher," I say with a tilt, dragging his name out.

"No, Jade. I should've been here the next day and demanded that you eat. Sleep. Hydrate. You could've taken all the time you needed, but I should have taken care of you and I failed. I'm so sorry," he apologizes quickly, moving me so that I'm standing with my legs locked out while he pulls my shorts down.

"I'm going to leave your underwear on, and when you get into the bath you can take them off, okay?" he says gently, and puts his hands on my hips to steady me. He looks me right in the eye while moving his hands under the band of my bra. He quickly and clinically pulls my bra off.

Asher keeps his eyes on mine, refusing to let his gaze drop.

"Don't fall, okay?" He raises his eyebrows and nods when I don't move. He turns around and shuts the bath off, checking the temperature before pouring some soap in. "Here," Asher says, holding his hand out for me to take.

He gingerly moves me into the tub and, oh my god, the warm water feels so amazingly good. It's like every ache, every bad thing, seems to just slip away. Leaving my body and being replaced with warmth and care.

"Is it okay? Not too hot?" Asher asks kindly, lowering onto his knees by my head.

"'S perfect," I slur, the warmth making me fuzzy and sleepy again.

"Don't fall asleep, Jade." His voice is so commanding and soothing at the same time. I know he means business, but he also doesn't want to push me too much. "I mean it."

"I won't," I reply, but at the same time my eyes are already slipping closed.

"Jade," he snaps and my eyes jump open, looking at him.

Asher's eyes are wide with concern and it's so adorable. He falls back on his butt, sitting beside my head as I lay back in the tub, and shakes his head. "I guess you're not getting food until you're done in the bath," he mutters.

"You do not need to stay here," I protest softly. I don't want him to feel like he has to babysit me, but I won't lie, I want him here. I want him by my side, no matter what.

"I know." Asher leans his elbows on the edge of the tub, resting his chin on his folded arms. "But I want to be with you. Four days is too long to be without you, darlin'."

I don't say anything. Because while I agree, these past few days have been torture without him—for a multitude of reasons—there's still so much we need to discuss. So much that needs to be said and worked through.

I shift uncomfortably and the water splashes around me, warming me in places that aren't submerged yet. My nipples pebble and I gasp.

"Jade, I'm sorry about what happened," Asher says sincerely, looking at me with those beautiful blue eyes. "I promise you, though, it's not what it looked like. Kyle..." He sighs and sits up straighter. "Kyle has always been a kiss-ass to me for some reason, but he tipped amazingly well. He never acted as fucking crazy as he actually is in front of me. Kyle's always wanted to be on my good side, so that's why he said those things. I could not give one fuck about him and his feelings, though.

I turn my head to face him slowly. "But he's best friends with your..." I swallow loudly, trying not to throw up at the thought. "...brother."

"They've been friends since high school. Same as Ty and I. So, when Ty came in and knocked the fuck out of him, I knew he had a good reason. And when I heard the reason, I almost fucking killed him."

"What?" I whisper. I heard, or *overheard*, that he retaliated but I had no clue what he actually did... And immediately, I'm filled with guilt. He's burning bridges with people who are like family... *for me.*

"When I found out what he and my brother did, I lost my shit. Even when I used to fight, I'd never, ever, been as close to killing someone as I was that night. The only thing holding me back was how you'd feel about it. I didn't know if I could look you in the eye again knowing I'd killed someone. Even if that person deserved it." Asher doesn't mince words and I inspect his facial expression, his eyes, his mannerisms, for any kind of guilt or remorse.

I find nothing.

In fact, the fire in his eyes almost makes him look angry. Angry and revengeful.

"Asher, he's your brother."

"I don't give one single fuck if he's my brother. I did my best to raise him to be a decent person, not a rapist. To not treat women, men—fuck, anyone—like that. The empathy and compassion stick never hit him on the back of the fucking head and it shows. I don't care if I ever see him again. I'll never forgive him for what he did to you. Ever." He sounds like he has thought this through, not like it's a spur of the moment decision.

I *know* how close we are, how much we love each other, but I don't want to cause him any pain just because I'm hurting. My chest feels tight and my eyes sting as I try to hold back the forming tears, but I don't want to let them fall.

"For the rest of his life, everyone will know what he did," Asher explains sternly. "What kind of person he is."

I paused, suspicious of that statement. "What does that mean?"

"After we 'exchanged words'..." His nostrils flare and he

clenches his teeth. Whatever his brother said really, *really* pissed him off. "I knocked his ass out and tattooed what he really is on his stomach. Any time he tries to pick up a girl, she'll see what he's done and hopefully get the hell away from him."

Jolting upright, the water splashes around me. My eyes widen and I grab his hands. What has he done? Fuck, he's going to lose the shop. There's no way Hunter doesn't try to sue or have Asher arrested. There's no way Hunter doesn't try to get revenge.

"What have you done?" I whisper.

"I protected what is mine," he replies plainly, the words loaded with meaning.

"You've jeopardized everything you built."

"I'd do it again."

"You're crazy," I say shakily, holding a wet hand to my head.

"I prefer obsessed." He quirks an eyebrow, smiling cockily before pressing a soft, light kiss to the hand that's holding his. "I told you; I will always take care of you. However you need me to." Asher purses his lips and raises his eyebrows.

He's so unaffected. My guilt gnaws at me tenfold now.

I shake my head vehemently. "I can't let you walk away from your family because of me, Asher."

He sits up, leans over the tub and takes my face in his hands. I have no choice but to look at him. His eyebrows pull down as his lips open. He looks so desperate, so sad.

"Do you really think any family I have would be more important to me than you? You and I, we make our own little family. And some day, we'll have kids of our own and be an even bigger family. You, Jade, are more important to me than anything. My business, my shitty family, whatever else comes our way. I choose you. I choose you every time. You are more important. Your feelings and protection matter more to me. Do you understand?"

I wrap my hands around his wrists, and a tear slips down my cheek.

"I don't think I'll ever be able to see him. There will never be a time that I'll be able to be in the same room as him. As a brother-in-law, as your brother. I don't ever want to see him."

"I don't either," Asher replies, nodding without hesitation. "Seriously, fuck that guy."

"Fuck that guy," I repeat with a watery laugh. It feels good to let some of this emotion out. Asher rests his forehead against mine and he chuckles softly with me.

It feels like we're on the same page.

Finally, I can breathe again.

Asher

JADE WAS thin to begin with, but not eating anything and being comatose for three days has made her look sickly.

Jade is beautiful—she'll always be beautiful in my eyes—but when she laughs, I can see her ribs poke from under her skin in a way that isn't healthy.

I need to get food into her ASAP.

But I don't want to break this up. It's like we are finally in order again. She's letting me in and showing me she trusts me. Hell, she even told me straight out that she does. I don't want to leave this bubble we're in. Not after being without her for that long; not knowing how she was, or if she'd ever let me see her again. I could barely sleep; stress and anxiety ate at me every fucking hour, every minute, every second.

Roxie's check-ins did help, but not much. And when she walked in and said that she was starting to get really worried... I snapped. I decided right then and there that I was going to get Jade and do whatever it took to take care of her. Even if she didn't want me to. I couldn't just let her hurt...

Finding her like this shows me that she hurts far deeper and far stronger than she ever let me know. It was the surprise of the fucking century to learn the horrid pain she's been going through is because of me and my fucked-up family.

I fucking wish I could take every single beat of pain she's had away from her. Every hard moment, every pained thought, every tear, every agonizing breath. I would take everything from her in a moment so that she'd never have to feel a bad thing again.

Her sparkling green eyes look into mine, and there's a flicker of relief that I can fully understand. I'm feeling it myself. I lean forward and wrap my arms around her shoulders, hugging her to me as tightly as I can while leaning over the ledge of the tub.

Jade pulls my shirt tighter, twisting her fingers in the cloth on my back and crushing me to her body. So much so that I lose my balance and fall into the cooling water.

"Fuck, I'm sorry," I sputter as my face hits her naked collarbone and my body crashes onto hers. The water splashes around us and up over the side as we both shift. I'm trying to move so I don't hurt her, and she's moving to keep hold of me.

Once I figure out that she doesn't want to let me go, I stop trying to give her space and hold her close. This tub isn't big enough for both of us, but that doesn't seem to bother her. She doesn't let me go.

My arms wrap around her, flipping us over so she's sitting in my lap and I'm holding her to my chest. Our hearts are beating together, holding each other as we heal.

I love it.

I love her.

"I love you," I say softly in her ear, pushing as much emotion into my words as I can. I never want her to second-guess it again. "You are my world. My life. My future."

Jade keeps her head against my chest but looks up at me through her dark eyelashes with a soft smile.

"I love you, too. More than I ever thought possible."

And my fucking heart soars.

We're going to be together for the rest of time. I know it.

I can see her walking down an aisle towards me in a plain white dress that makes her glow; I can see us sleeping in on Sunday's, spending the whole day sleeping and wrapped together; welcoming a few adorable, chunky babies—more than I'm sure she wants, but fewer than I want—and working through the late nights and baby cries; slow dancing in the kitchen late at night; growing old together and being that quintessential 'old married couple' who argue about everything but I'll continue to flirt with her every chance I get.

I can see it all.

And it's everything I never knew I wanted, and everything I hoped for but never believed I deserved.

The jeans I'm in are heavy and the coolness of the water is becoming too much. For the first time, I let my eyes dip down to her breasts. Her nipples are hard, and goosebumps have broken out over her skin. It's time to get out, get her warm and get her fed.

Without saying anything, I wrap my hands under and around her to step out of the tub. I'm dripping water everywhere, my jeans making the water pool around my feet as it seeps from the fabric. I don't care about the mess—I'll take care of it later—but I do care about the possibility of me slipping and unintentionally hurting Jade. She's shivering from the cool air around us; from the blasting AC coming from the vents and the water left on her skin.

"Here, darlin'," I say, grabbing a towel that's hanging on the wall. I set her on her feet and towel her off.

"Thank you." She smiles softly, looking up at me. Her hands are folded in front of her and the ends of her hair, wet from the bath, are sticking up all over. She'll need to shower to actually get clean, but I'm happy to see the quick bath helped a little. She's smiling again, *smiling*.

"Any time." Returning her smile, I grab the ends of her hair and try to pat them dry. "Let's get you dressed and something to eat."

Jade smirks and her heated gaze locks on me.

"I don't want to do that," she says in a tone that... *does* something to me. She's commanding and confident. Her voice is low, husky and full of want.

But the question is if I should do what she's hinting at—and let's be real, what *I* desperately want—after such a traumatic few days.

But on the other hand, maybe that's what we need to heal from all this.

"Jade, baby..." I start to tell her no, I don't want to take advantage of her, but before I can say anything, she lunges upward and kisses me roughly. All rational thought leaves my mind and I respond naturally, instinctually, without any delay. As she slides her hands around my neck and up into my hair, I moan and sink into her body. She's warming up now, even though her skin is still cool to the touch.

"Let's get you out of those wet clothes," Jade says as she steps back. She pulls my shirt up and over my head, letting it fall on the ground with a wet splat. My hands are too busy feeling every inch of her back and ass to help. I jump slightly at her cold fingertips touching my lower abdomen while she pulls my button open and my zipper down.

Oh, how sexy is this confident woman. The way she's rolling her toned body is suggestive and my cock bobs. She's even sexier because she's so confident in *us* right now.

"Wait, wait," I protest breathlessly. I need to ask her; I need to actually talk to her about having sex before we just jump in. I can't risk hurting or scaring her. "Baby girl, wait," I repeat more firmly, pulling her hands from under my boxers as I take a deep breath to steady myself.

Fuck, I want her so badly.

Jade's big eyes are staring up at me in a daze, cloudy with desire. Despite being cool before, her cheeks are rosy and her lips are swollen from the force of our kisses. Her chest is heaving with breath and want, her subtle skin soft and sweet. She's certainly leaner than she has been, but I'll fix that soon.

I wish I had my pencils with me. I wish I could freeze time to draw this moment so it never gets fuzzy with time in my memory. She's stunning.

"Why?" She says in the whiny voice that pulls at my Daddy side.

"Because, baby girl," I reply, cupping her cheek softly but strongly. "A lot of shit has gone down, and it's important to me that you feel safe and you *want* this."

"I *do* want this," she says with a cute little pout.

"I want to know that if we do this, you won't feel anything but happiness and satisfaction. No guilt, no anger, no sadness; no feeling like you have to push yourself to be intimate with me. Just the two of us, making love and taking care of each other."

Jade lifts her arms and wraps around my neck lovingly.

"I want to do this, Asher, because I want us to celebrate being together. I want to feel your body on mine, knowing that you chose me. I want us to become one, knowing that we're forever. I want us to make love because that's what surrounds us. Love."

I smile gently, my heart beating faster at her words, and nod.

"I love you," I say and kiss her forehead.

"As I love you." She bites her lip, and I can tell I'm in for it. "Now take me to bed, Daddy."

Jade

I NEED HIM.

Now.

Right this fucking minute.

I could tell that the moment I called him Daddy, it snapped him into gear.

"Oh, baby girl," he coos with a smirk before slipping his jeans off and letting them fall to the floor. Leaving him standing there in just his tight black shorts that hug his huge dick, which is already hardening from our kisses and touches. My mouth waters at the thought of getting my lips around his cock. It's been too long.

Now that I'm 'awake' again, so to say, I need him like the air I breathe.

"Please," I whisper hoarsely. My pussy is quivering and clenching around nothing.

Asher looks at me beneath hooded lids and his light eyes have gone dark. He bites his lip and looks at me—*finally fucking looks at me*—with a heated glance. I can feel his gaze like his hand touching me all over my body; lingering over my pebbled breasts and my wet pussy.

He steps closer to me, and a quick glance tells me that he's feeling this needy sexual energy and tension as much as I am. His boxers are tented and when he pulls me in, I can feel the tip press against my stomach unabashedly.

"Next time will be in my bed as I take my time showing you just how much I love you. But right now..." Asher says, pausing in his thought.

I don't hesitate to finish his thought. "Right now, I need you. Against the wall. Dirty and hard. Just show me that you love me and you want me. *Just the way I am.*" I bite my lip and nod. I want this. I want him.

Asher grins and raises his eyebrows. Accepting my challenge.

"I love you and want you for you, baby girl. Physically, mentally and emotionally. Always and forever."

His hands lift me into the air, and I wrap my arms around his broad shoulders to hold on. Gently, he walks us to the small wall by the door and our lips meet in an explosive kiss. Full of spoken and unspoken feelings, love shifting into chasing pleasure as we rub against each other.

"Fuck," Asher says breathily against my lips as he pulls back slightly. "It's been too long, baby. I can't fucking wait to be buried in you." He growls, breathing deeply against my neck before biting down on the spot beneath my ear. He makes me shiver. I fucking love how he speaks so darkly, so hungrily to me. It's possessive and seductive and it makes me feel so damn sexy.

"I want you. Please, Daddy."

My chest heaves with each breath and I scramble to hold onto him tighter.

"What a good girl, asking so nicely," he breathes against my lips with a smile. "Daddy will take care of you, baby." Asher presses me against his chest so he's holding my weight against the wall and I don't feel like I'm going to fall. I always feel like he's got me, and he's working to make sure I know he'll always catch me.

I know now that he always will.

I believe him. I believe *in* him. I believe in us.

With one hand, Asher pulls his hard cock out of his shorts. There, that's what I want. That's what I'm needing right now. What I'm craving, always. I shimmy my hips from side to side, trying to find some of the friction I so desperately need. But he lifts me higher, like I weigh nothing, to keep his dick from touching me.

"What, why?" I whine, sucking on his neck to try and make him as desperate as I feel. Asher groans, but still doesn't let his dick touch my wetness.

His hand slips between my folds, spearing me with his fingers, coating them in my wetness. Oh, fuck, that's why he was waiting.

"I need to make sure you come on my fingers before I feed you my cock. I want to taste you." he growls. I feel myself getting wetter, racing closer and closer to my peak. It's coming on so fucking fast, I don't know if I'll be able to fight to make it last longer. Asher pulls his fingers from my heat and puts them in his mouth, licking them clean before groaning and closing his eyes in ecstasy.

"You taste so *fucking* good. It's my favorite taste, I swear to god. I could eat from you every day and die a happy man," he rumbles before slipping his fingers back into my cunt and scissoring them quickly. My eyes close and my toes curl as I scramble to try and find purchase, something, anything to hold so the force of the oncoming orgasm is more manageable.

But there's nothing.

And he knows it.

Asher smirks, knowing how close I am and there's nothing I can do to stop it.

"Daddy!" I scream, my voice and mewling noises echoing in the tiled room. "Fuck, fuck, fuck, oh my god," I whimper and cry as the pleasure rolls through me.

"That's it, baby girl. That's it," he groans, like he's as on edge as I am. He pulls his fingers from me and uses his hand to guide his cock into me, inch by excruciating inch. "You're so tight, it feels like I'm going to hurt you," he says softly before biting my shoulder as he groans. "Fuck, baby girl, I'm going to blow my load before I'm even fully inside you. You feel so. Fucking. Good."

I wrap my arms around his neck, holding him tightly as I breathe deeply and try to relax my pussy to let him in. I want to feel him fully seated inside me when he comes. I'm addicted to the feeling of his cum splashing my walls and filling me up.

We gasp against each other as he pushes in further. The drag of his cock stretches me further before our hips touch. We're finally one.

My head drops back against the wall as my chest heaves in relief.

"We're one now, baby," Asher moans, his voice husky and low as he looks at me. His dark hair is damp from exertion, his cheeks red from pleasure and need, his eyes trained on my lips. He's... a fantasy. Sex on legs. Or better yet, everything I ever needed, ever *wanted*, all in one delicious, gorgeous package. "And I'm never letting you go."

I kiss him in response, pressing our lips together in a way that's both sweet and begging to go further. He's mine and I'm his; I'm not fighting it anymore.

"You're mine," I whisper against his lips, moving my hips as much as I can above him.

Asher leans forward, kissing me again. Hard. "Just as you're *mine,*" he growls when he lets me take a breath.

I'm about to promise him that I am, but he starts pounding into me at a needy, desperate, hot pace. My legs tighten around him, my thighs gripping his waist as tightly as I can and I feel them start to shake. I press my mouth to his, knowing that kissing will push us both over the edge. Asher forces his tongue inside my mouth, letting me taste myself on him.

So much hotter than I thought it would be.

Fuckkkk me.

Threading my fingers through his hair, I pull at the soft ends and he moans in my mouth.

"You're mine, Jade. Mine. Mine to love," he proclaims with grunts as he continues to fuck me so perfectly. "Mine to protect." He kisses my lips hard and aggressively. "Mine to fuck." He growls and slips a hand between us to start rubbing my clit. With a tight turn, he pulls and pinches it. I didn't think pinching would work for me, but holy fuck, was I wrong.

His touches, mixed with his kisses and added to the never-ending spearing of his cock through my wetness, cause me to utterly explode. My thighs shake around his as my pussy strangles his cock. I cry out against his neck, nearly in tears from the pleasure wracking my body.

"Oh yes, oh fuck, Jade, baby girl," Asher mutters, his thrusts staggering and speeding up as he fights for his own orgasm against my fluttering cunt. My walls clench around him as he fights to pull out and push back inside. His grip on my skin tightens and I know I'm going to have ten little bruises on my thighs.

Well worth it.

"Fuck! Baby girl!" Asher moans loudly against my chest, groaning as his hips thrust up once more.

"Yes," I scream, tightening my muscles around him as his cum fills me. Running my hand over the nape of his neck, I hold him close to me in a shared moment of satisfaction and intimacy.

Of love and belonging.

Of home and happiness.

"I love you," Asher sighs against my chest. After a moment of catching our breath, he carefully slips out and lets my legs fall to the floor. He doesn't let go of me until he's sure I'm stable.

"I love you, too." I smile, raking my fingers through the dark locks at his neck and bringing our lips together sweetly.

"If I didn't think you would say no, I'd beg you to move in with me. We could do this all day, every day," he laments, resting his forehead against mine. My heart beats faster and I can see us living together; moving forward from all this shit, getting married, bringing beauty to our world through art and tattoos, maybe bringing a sweet baby into our lives... but that's way, way, *way* down the road.

Maybe a dog or cat in the near future instead.

"With a promise like that, who says I'd say no?" I smile shyly, looking up as he props himself against the wall with his elbow over my head.

His eyes widen with shock. He starts to trip over his words as he tries to ask me properly.

"I, uh, maybe... do you think... Jade," Asher stutters.

"Don't worry," I giggle, patting his cheek softly. "I want that. I really do, but I don't know if we're quite ready for that." I can see the hope fade from his eyes, as his head drops between us. I cup his chin and move his face up so he's looking at me again.

"I want to live with you, Asher, but I want us to do it after we've been together a little longer. I want us to really know each other. Maybe you won't want to live with me when you find out I snore and you have to deal with it for more than a few nights." I shrug and try to make light of the rejection. I love him and I don't want him to think that I *don't* want him. That I don't want to take this relationship a step forward.

I just want a little bit of time to grow independently.

I want him to have time to decide if this is actually what he wants.

Because once I'm there, I'm not leaving. There's nothing that can keep us apart now.

Asher

I STAYED with Jade for the rest of the day and slept on Roxie's shitty futon. I needed to make sure she didn't burrow back under that fuzzy blanket she's grown fond of. After we cleaned up from the bathroom, I made sure to feed her.

I prepared her an easy, quick sandwich while we waited for a massive order from the local Mexican restaurant. Complete with a huge fountain drink to get some sugar and caffeine into her. After she'd eaten the small snack, Jade said she was going to go shower and wash her hair. Of course, I asked if she felt okay enough to be alone, to which she just rolled her eyes with a small smile.

She might have acted like she was annoyed, but we both know she loves it.

After I pay the delivery guy and take our three-bag order, I hear the shower turn off. Doing my best not to get hard just knowing that she's naked, dripping wet, and not far from me, I get to work setting out the food on Roxie's short coffee table and find something light and funny we can watch. We don't need any more drama than we've had over the last few days. No more bad feelings. Just happiness and light.

After a few minutes of searching, I land on The Office and wait. It's the show she had me watch when I was needing a break, back when we first met. I think she'll appreciate the gesture.

I sneak a few tortilla chips and jump up when I hear the bathroom door open, steam billowing out around Jade.

I swear to god, it's like I'm in a music video. Time slows down as she walks toward me, a smirk crossing on her face while I watch as she flips her blonde hair, darkened from the water. She's borrowing some of Roxie's sleep shorts and a tank top, and fuck, does she wear them well. The fabric clings to her damp skin, showing how her nipples are pebbled from the temperature change. The low neckline absorbs the water dripping from her hair, making the white fabric turn more sheer.

She's a vision. And I'm so fucking lucky.

"What'd you get? I'm still really hungry," Jade says with a smile, no doubt laughing internally at my dumb, love-struck face.

Clearing my throat, I nod, make sure my mouth isn't wide open, and hold my arm out to show her my haul. "Uh, I got us a little bit of everything. Enchiladas, tacos, fajitas, chips and guac, some queso, all the goods," I stammer as I open the different boxes of steaming food. "Good timing too, everything's still hot."

"Thanks for getting this for us," she beams and takes a seat on the couch, pulling the favorite fuzzy blanket over her legs. "Oh my god, it's a Coke!" She picks up the Styrofoam cup that's as big as her head and takes a long sip with a moan. "That's so good."

I can't help but chuckle.

Jade glares at me playfully. "It's been days since I've had a pop, let me enjoy it without your judgement." She takes another long sip.

I put my hands up in surrender and sit next to her on the couch, digging into our feast. I intentionally didn't bring plates out so we could just eat together right from the containers. I did that so I could see what she prefers and gravitates toward for next time. I never want to mess up a food or drink order again. I'll learn her preferences so I can get her meals right every time.

"Oh, The Office, I love it," she says excitedly, picking up a chip and dipping—yes, dipping, not scooping like everyone I've ever met—a chip into the container of guacamole.

"What are you doing?" I ask, picking up a chip myself and showing her the proper way. "Get a good chunk on the chip."

"I like to spread it out," she shrugs and dips a chip in again, barely getting any on the chip.

"You're not getting any!"

"I'm getting the taste though," she counters.

I shake my head. "Jade, you aren't actually eating the guac." She shrugs, does it again, and raises her eyebrow in challenge.

"You crazy woman." I pull her close to me and kiss her. Letting her go, she smiles brightly and shakes her head.

"Turn it on," she orders with a happy, loving, *content* smile.

"Yes, ma'am."

❦

WE GRADUALLY FINISH EATING—SHE DEFINITELY ATE most of the enchiladas, so that's going in my notes app—and sit back, watching Jim prank Dwight and smiling the whole time. She's quicker to smile, to chuckle, as we cuddle up on the couch.

Jade slips further under the blanket and nestles her side into mine.

This right here. This whole moment is what I hope to have for the rest of my life. I know shit is going to happen, as it always does in life; but if the past four days have taught me anything, it's that we can get through anything. I wrap my arm around her, pulling her closer and kiss the side of her head, breathing in her clean hair.

Perfect.

But like all good moments, they must come to an end. Or be annoyingly interrupted by my kid sister.

The door jiggles and opens as Roxie grumbles, muttering as she walks in, locking the door behind her. Her black hair is skewed all over, her red lipstick faded and smeared slightly. She looks... like she just got caught doing the walk of shame. Catching sight of us, Roxie freezes. My eyes narrow at her as my lips purse in question.

"Hey guys, I didn't think you'd still be up." Roxie kicks her shoes off and scuttles to the kitchen, barely making eye contact with us.

"It's eight p.m.," I reply with a questioning tilt to my voice.

"Hmm," she hums, filling up one of her cups with water.

Jade and I look at each other, questioning why Roxie's acting so weird. Jade pushes the blanket off and holds her hand out as if to say, 'I've got this.' She walks over to where Roxie stands at the kitchen sink and puts her hand lightly on the small of her back, mutely asking what's up. I watch with rapt fascination, hoping to overhear, but they are speaking quietly and also in one-word sentences.

"Yes?" Jade asks, furrowing her eyebrows together.

"Maybe."

"Really?"

"Don't." Roxie points a finger at Jade but there's no heat.

"Never." Jade leans her forehead against Roxie's shoulder in comradery.

"I couldn't help it," Roxie whines.

"Girl, I get it."

Roxie sighs noisily, her head dropping back so she can stare at the ceiling. "I'm going to go shower and then pass out." Roxie looks at Jade and takes both of her hands in hers. "Please, please, move in here. I'll clean out the room you've been staying in so you actually have space. I need help on the rent. We know we get along and we're best friends. So please, move out of those shitty dorms and stay here."

I hold my breath and immediately move my focus from where they're whispering to the TV. I force a chuckle at Jim's dead-panned look to the camera, hopefully fooling them into thinking I'm not eavesdropping.

Although it's really hard not to. This freaking apartment carries voices amazingly. That's something to remember for the future. I wonder just *how much* it carries…

I guess we won't be fucking here, especially if Roxie's here. I don't know if Jade could stay quiet enough when we're together. She's quite the screamer, much to my delight.

"Are you sure? I know I have a job at the shop, but I don't have any cash saved up. It'll be at least two paychecks before I can give you a full rent payment." Jade picks at her thumb, looking down like she's embarrassed.

Not that she should be at all.

"Girl, that's fine. More than fine," Roxie whispers, holding her hand excitedly. "Seriously, you don't have to pay for a while. When we get set up and settled, we'll talk."

"Are you sure? I don't want to fuck this up." Jade holds her hand and bites her lip. I know her well enough now, and I'm sure Roxie does too, to recognize she doesn't want to feel like a burden.

"I'm so sure," Roxie nods and smiles. "So fucking sure."

Jade smiles back and nods. "Alright, if you say so. I'd love that, really."

"Yes!" Roxie pumps a fist in the air and I try to hide a knowing smile.

If Jade doesn't think it's time to, or can't, live with me yet, I feel a million times better knowing she will be here. Roxie's like a pit bull; tough and scary when provoked, but the sweetest friend all the other times.

"Tomorrow we'll recruit Asher and Ty to get your stuff from the dorms, and then you can try to get the school to refund the rest of the year for you." Roxie fires off a plan and gives Jade a big hug which she returns.

Roxie runs off toward the bathroom and Jade stands still, watching Roxie walk off. And then the smile falls off her face.

"Baby?" I ask, stretching my arm out over the back of the couch. Jade looks at me and I can see it.

Worry.

"Hey," I say gently, standing to cross the room as quickly as possible. "What's wrong?" I ask, wrapping my arms around her waist, welcoming her into my arms.

"I'm so excited, so happy," Jade starts to ramble. "Everything is going well. Everything is working out. I feel confident and like everything's going to go my—*our*—way." I nod, cupping her cheek and she leans into it for comfort. "That's never really happened for me, Asher. One or two things seem like they're working in my life and then the other shoe drops and tears my life into tatters."

"I get it," I reply softly, kissing her forehead. "I do. But I promise you that nothing, *nothing*, bad is going to happen. I won't let it."

Jade wraps her arms around my waist, accepting my promise. But I can still see some hesitation in her eyes. I hate that it's there from years of hard time and bullshit, from bad people and those who chose to turn their backs on her.

Her happiness is my first priority. My honor to have, along with her love.

It's an honor I won't take for granted.

"Everything is going to be fine," I offer softly, holding her in my arms and kissing her head. She doesn't respond, but hugs me back.

I'll take it...

For now.

THE NEXT MORNING, I wake up to my favorite sight.

Asher, completely naked, one arm bent with his fist under his pillow, his face turned toward the little bit of sunlight streaming through the uncovered blinds in Roxie's office.

Wait, no, **my** room.

I feel like I can breathe again. Asher didn't betray me, he's choosing me. My man, my love, my protector, my future. He's here.

The sun is reflecting off his bare chest, highlighting the beautiful art on his skin. The man is like a walking museum; gorgeous art everywhere you look. My finger traces the smokey phoenix outline on his chest. The design and talent to make it look like he'd captured smoke under his skin is remarkable.

"That tickles," he says gruffly, and I jump in surprise. His voice is thick with sleep, making his already deep timbre even deeper. I chuckle under my breath and look at him, resting my head on his chest.

"Sorry, I was just admiring you."

"Ah, then don't stop on my account." He smiles, stretching

his arms out on either side of him before wrapping me in his arms. "I, too, like to stare at beautiful things," he muses, right before he makes lingering eye contact with me.

"Oh shush," I tut but I know I'm blushing.

Asher smiles playfully and looks around, glancing at the window. "What time is it? I need to head into the shop today," he explains. "And I'd like you to come with me, if you're ready." Single-handedly reaching to a box next to us, he grabs his phone to check his messages. I smile softly at our surroundings. He put his phone right next to mine. Just like there's a neat little pile of his clothes next to mine. His shoes by the door to *my* room.

The domesticity of it makes me giddy.

"It's only nine." Asher yawns before putting his phone down. "Shower, breakfast, shop?" he asks, cuddling back into me, eyes slowly closing. I'm pretty sure if I didn't respond, he'd fall right back asleep. He's not a morning person.

Ding, ding. Ding, ding. My phone starts going off, message after message pouring in.

Asher's eyes open and he groans as I laugh breathily. Leaning over him, I pick up my phone and open the four messages that have come in since the first ding.

Mom: Jade, I'm in town and going to be at your dorm in 45 minutes. I expect you there.

Mom: I've heard some things that concern me, and we need to discuss your future.

Mom: I'm not pleased with your performance this semester and I'm very disappointed with the things I've heard you've been up to since you've been here.

Mom: Being seen out and about with some older, tattooed man? Getting into fights? I've heard he's dangerous and malicious. Riding around on motorcycles and skipping class? I don't know who you are.

"Fuck," I curse, covering my mouth and sitting up.

"What?" Asher asks, trailing his fingers up and down my bare back.

"My mother..." I answer softly, "My mother is coming to town.Now. She's going to be at the dorms soon and wants to discuss my 'behavior' and my future."

"Maybe you'll be able to tell her about wanting to switch majors."

"I doubt it," I grumble and stand up, letting the blanket fall around my feet. With that movement, I take the blanket from Asher, too. Leaving us both naked and... fuck, his morning wood is *glorious*.

I know my mouth drops open slightly as I stare, but can you blame me? He's a thick eight inches and curved in just the right way. Not to mention the thick veins running alongside his shaft as his cock stands more at attention with my gaze.

"If we don't have time to fix this...situation..." He cocks an eyebrow and moves his arm over his head to show off his muscular body, which does not escape my attention, and continues, "Then you have to stop staring at me like that, baby girl."

"Or what?" I ask, feeling bold. I speak without thinking, but I don't regret it. "Are you going to spank me, Daddy?"

What have I done?

Asher's eyes widen then narrow with heat as he processes my words. His gaze travels over my body slowly, and I swear I feel his fingers caressing me with each pass of his eyes over my skin. I feel myself getting wetter, my arousal flaring to a full-blown inferno within.

"Oh, baby girl," Asher taunts in a gravelly tone. "If you keep talking that way, I'm going to think you want a spanking from me."

I fidget in my spot, trying not to show just how much his

deep tone affects me... how I can feel the wetness gather and slip down my folds.

"Is that what you want, Jade? My hand on your bare ass, turning it such a pretty pink while you're over my knee?" Effortlessly, seamlessly, Asher stands like a wraith and towers over me. "I think you'd like it... I think I could make you come just from the bit of pain and the edging I'd provide," he whispers in my ear as a hand swats my ass. There's a slight bite of pain, but the warmth that blooms...

This is interesting.

Do I like it?

Do I want to give him that kind of power?

The thought alone turns me on in a way that I wasn't aware I could feel.

"I know you're thinking about it, and I want you to take your time and *really* consider this. If you want to explore it, we can. But I'm not going to spank you—really spank you—for being naughty without your explicit, informed and thought-out decision." He smirks, dipping his head and biting the juncture point on my neck, the one he knows I love, and squeezes my ass. "You've got the perfect ass for a spanking, baby. Fuck, I'm getting too turned on," Asher says suddenly and steps back. "We have to go see your mom soon and I definitely don't have the time to fix this." He points down to his raging boner, and I smile.

I really, really love that he reacts to me so much. How, with just a look, I can turn him on and get him hard. The same way he can look at me and I start to drip.

"I'd much rather stay here with you," I moan, trying to entice him to forget about my evil mother, but he's not having it. After he kindly untangles himself from my embrace, I whine and want to stomp my foot like a toddler because I know I'm not going to get what I want. He's determined to meet my lifelong tormentor.

Sighing, I admit defeat.

"Oh, come on, love." Asher chuckles and pulls on his underwear before turning back and kissing my forehead. "I want to meet this woman. And tell her how fucking stupid she is for treating you this way."

"What?" Fear flooding my system. He's going to confront her? "You can't," I protest.

"Can't what?"

"You can't say that to her."

"I believe I can. Free speech, part of the wonderful American constitution." He raises one eyebrow and gives me a smooth smirk.

I sigh with exasperation. "I get that you think you're being cute, but seriously Asher, you can't. She'll chew you apart."

He laughs loudly, boisterously, like he thinks I've told him the best joke he's ever heard instead of metaphorically shitting my pants. He must see how fucking *not amused* I am, because he stops laughing. His eyebrows raise in surprise as he holds his T-shirt out between us awkwardly.

"You're serious?"

"Yes!" I screech loudly. "My mother has basically said she wants to discuss things she's heard and my schooling. She gives no fucks about my mental health or my safety. Only that I'm doing what she wants and acting how she wants. Imagine what will happen when she finds out I want to switch majors from business to art? She's going to fucking kill me." Panic and anxiety replace the ice-cold fear in my veins and my heart starts to beat abnormally fast.

"Jade?" I hear Asher ask worriedly, but he sounds so far away.

My breath comes in gasps and my throat starts to close, even though I'm trying to remind myself to breathe. My body's not working. I can't...

"Jade," Asher barks loudly, shaking my shoulders aggressively. My head lobs back and forth as he shakes me but it does the trick and shocks me out of my panic attack. "Fuck, baby, *breathe!*" His voice is so loud that I know Roxie will be able to hear.

"I can't... I can't..." I repeat, not sure how to end that sentence. My mind spirals uncontrollably. I can't face her. I can't change her piss-poor idea of me. I can't change her mind. I can't tell her off. I can't let her tear me down. I can't go forward. I can't go back. I can't let her change my mind. I can't let her wreck the first good thing I have in my life.

"You can." Asher cups my face with his hands, anchoring me. His eyes meet mine and I allow myself to get swept up in the swirls of light blue. "You can do anything. You've survived so much already, Jade. She's nothing. *Nothing.*"

"She's my mother," I say brokenly. I don't know if I'm defending her, or if I'm trying to explain why I won't be free. But he knows.

Nodding slightly, Asher reminds me, "But she's not your family."

He's right.

He's so damn right.

I put my hands over his and nod. "You're my family."

"That's right, baby girl. And you're mine."

Asher

WE MADE quick work of getting presentable and heading over to Jade's dorm. She held on tightly to my waist as I leaned us on the bike to take a turn quickly. She didn't seem panicked about it anymore though, just moving her weight with mine, so I'll take that as a win.

The roar of the engine drowns out my thoughts; the vibration of the machine under me helps blank out my mind so I can truly be calm before meeting Jade's mother.

I could see right off the bat that Jade wasn't keen on us meeting. I quickly clocked that she wasn't embarrassed of me or any of that shit, but she was worried her mother might scare me off.

Nothing will keep me from Jade, now that we've worked past all this shit. She is mine. For life.

I promised myself, and everyone that mattered, that I would protect Jade.

That means from her mother, too.

I wasn't going to let that woman bully her into anything. But

I don't want to make Jade's relationship with her even more strained if she wants her in her life.

I pull into one of the parking spots in the front of the dorms and cut the engine. I can practically *feel* Jade's anxiety. Not to mention, we're here and she hasn't let up on her tight grip on my shirt. She's slightly shaking against my back.

I remind myself that, as much as she needs a protector, she has to fight some dragons on her own. But she'll never be alone. I'll be standing right behind her, letting her slay them and welcoming her with open arms, telling her how fucking amazing she is when she's done.

It's her choice if we go inside.

Putting my hand over hers, I just hold her to me. Letting her gather her strength and courage, hopefully giving her some of mine.

I hear her sigh through the visor of the helmet and she sits up. I know this is going to be hard for Jade, standing up to her mom and also probably getting hit with some out-of-bounds shit that her mom will say.

But it has to happen.

I know it, Jade knows it. It has to happen so Jade can be happy.

Jade *deserves* to be happy.

I'll do whatever it takes to make sure she is.

WE WALK INTO THE DORM HALL, HAND-IN-HAND. EVERY single time I'm here, I attract the eyes of every student we pass.

I get it. I'm tall, big and covered in tattoos. Not to mention, I definitely look too old to be here, but they don't need to fucking stare. I put on a blatant 'don't-fuck-with-us' expression and wrap my arm over Jade's shoulders, claiming her for any stupid little fuckers who might have other ideas.

Especially for any of Hunter or Kyle's little halfwit buddies they might have set on her.

That reminds me—I need to sweet-talk Pam into telling me if Hunter moved out. I guess it doesn't really matter now, since Jade's moving in with Roxie, but I still want to fuck up his life a little bit.

I know I beat his face in, but I'm still feeling a little bloodthirsty.

Jade waves half-heartedly at Pam, who's sitting behind the reception desk. I think we're almost in the clear of not having a big conversation, but then Pam waves us over animatedly. Groaning, I try to keep walking, but Pam fucking starts going *'psssst, psssssst'* louder and louder, before almost yelling it.

"Come on," Jade says quietly, gesturing to the side with her head and veering off to see what Pam wants.

Ugh.

I try to keep myself from rolling my eyes but follow my girl.

"There's a scary-looking woman here looking for you, Jade," Pam says quietly, covering her mouth with a clipboard. It's like there are people watching us and are interested in what we're saying—I swear, Pam is an idiot. "She knew what room you were in and signed in." Pam pushes the sign-in chart—that I had no fucking clue existed, since I just barreled through to Jade's room —and clear as day, I can see it.

Samanatha Henderson, Mother.

Damn, even her handwriting looks sinister.

"Thanks, Pam," Jade mutters and I can tell there's a little wobble to her voice. Jade straightens her shoulders and hands the chart back to Pam with a nod. "Let's go."

"Yes, ma'am." I wink at her and see a faint blush on her cheeks.

I love this woman so much. Fuck.

I walk behind Jade and watch her back. I can see her struggle to put on a strong front as we walk to her doom. She steps into the empty elevator, standing to the side so I can come with her, and her face is cold, expressionless. But the fire in her eyes tells me she's gearing up for war.

She presses the button to her floor and takes a deep breath. Keeping her eyes forward, Jade doesn't look at me. She doesn't say anything or move closer. She's not giving me anything to go on, so I wait.

I wait for her to dictate how this goes. But I want her to know she's not alone in this. I don't know if I should touch her; if I should hold her hand or pull her into me.

"Jade?" I whisper, letting my voice carry through the rickety elevator.

"Yeah?"

"You've got this."

Jade turns to look at me, the emotionless mask on her face breaking as she smiles at me.

"Thank you," she whispers before sighing again. "I hope your opinion of me doesn't change after you meet her... and hear all she's undoubtedly going to say."

"Nothing will change how I feel about you." My heart beats strongly, and solely for her.

The elevator door dings and she surges up to kiss me quickly.

Light fills the small space as the decrepit elevator door opens and Jade steps back, ready to take on the monster down the hall.

I DO *NOT* WANT to do this.

I would be more than happy to never see my mother again, but I'm pretty sure she will start withholding my tuition if I ignore her. It's a double fucking standard; she can ignore me all she wants, call me any and all sorts of names, treat me like scum, but the moment I back off to protect myself, the narcissist in her can't handle it.

And even though I hate it, I *need* her help with tuition.

At least until I decide with one hundred percent certainty what I want to do. I feel like it's all or nothing. Like she helps me and I bend to her will, or she takes it all away and I don't go to school. But at this point in time, do I even *want* to go?

Would it be the worst thing if I took a year off and figured it out?

Maybe it'd be a blessing in disguise. I'd have time to sort out my life. Heal. Work with Ty. Live with Roxie. Love Asher.

"Hello, Helen."

Fuck. Me.

"I TOLD YOU, MOTHER. I PREFER IF YOU CALL ME JADE. You gave me that as a middle name and I much prefer it." Rolling my eyes, I pull the key to my room from my back pocket and open the door, hoping beyond hope that Hannah is out.

I turn and hold the door open for them, my mom pushing through.

"*Helen?*" Asher mouths at me with a goofy look on his surprised face and I smack him.

"Shut up," I grumble. "It's my legal first name and I hate it."

"Good to know." His eyes sparkle with mischief and I can't help but smile. He's going to be a handful.

"Helen," my mom calls from inside the room. I lightly groan before pulling Asher into the room with me. "And who are you?" she spits in his direction, her eyes narrowed in disgust.

"I'm Asher, ma'am. Jade's boyfriend," he replies proudly, like being my boyfriend is a privilege, not a burden. It makes me stand a little straighter.

I look from his smile to my mom's disgusted face, and try not to let her opinion hurt me.

Asher holds out his hand to shake hers, but my mother just stands there. Judging.

Instead of taking his hand like a decent person, she rolls her eyes and looks right at me. "I'm here to talk to Jade, so Adam, you can go wait outside," Mother says dismissively.

I clench my jaw and breathe deeply through my nose. She's... unbelievable.

"Anything you have to say to me, you can say in front of

Asher," I snap, crossing my arms over my chest and standing closer to him. Visually telling her I'm not budging on this.

"Are you sure?" She cocks an eyebrow, like this is a challenge she wants me to accept. I know right then she's about to make it her mission to embarrass me. To get him to leave me.

But I know Asher.

"Very."

"So be it." Mother looks around the dorm room; it's almost laughable at how bare my side is. I have a minimum amount of clothes, keeping the rest in a duffel bag I've been carrying from place to place along with my school stuff and toiletries. My bed is made and looks practically brand new. There aren't any pictures or mementos on my side, while Hannah's area is wrecked. Lived in.

"Either you've become a neat freak or you aren't actually staying here," she observes.

"Does it matter?" I ask bravely.

She rolls her eyes and sets her designer bag on the small desk that isn't covered.

"I want to discuss some unsettling things I've heard about you recently." Mother pulls the chair out and sits down, crossing her legs and sighing like she owns the place.

"And who have you been hearing things from?" I narrow my eyes, pushing my eyebrows forward in a questioning look.

"Does it matter?" She throws my words back at me in a snippy tone. I breathe in deeply through my nose, waiting for her to continue.

"I hear you've been skipping the business classes, riding around on motorcycles, and getting into fights. You've been spending all your time at some tattoo parlor with this heathen and his crew. Do you even care how that reflects on me?" She speaks as if she's been personally affected by this. As if her stupid reputation is at stake.

I'm sure it is. And I couldn't care less.

Asher stays silent behind me, not interjecting to defend himself.

"Watch how you speak about him. I can call security right now and have you taken from the premises. I won't have you speaking about him, or my friends, like that," I snap.

For a millisecond, there's shock on her face. Shock that I dared to speak to her in such a way. And surprisingly, it makes me feel so fucking good to tell her off.

"You couldn't have found Sarah and made nice with her? Apologized for that whoring accident this summer, and followed her around campus?" Mother sneers.

I clench my teeth at her mention of this summer. "I am not, nor will I ever, be friends with someone like Sarah. She's a cunt and it's no surprise to me that you believe her over me."

"You watch your mouth with me, you brat," Mother starts to say.

I cut her off, stepping forward and putting my finger in her face. "No, you don't get to speak to people, especially not to the man I love, like that." Standing my ground, we stare off at each other. Immediately, I know right then that this is going to get messy. Very, very messy.

"The man you love?" Mother scoffs, rising up to stand a few inches taller than me. "Don't make me laugh. Go on, have your fun. But when the time is right, you'll be given to someone **I** deem worthy."

"Do you even hear yourself?" I snap. "You're not a fucking Bond villain. You're an over-inflated, pompous, self-absorbed, megalomaniac narcissist who only cares about keeping up with the Joneses and pushing me down to keep yourself afloat." Every single word is pointed and angry. Am I out of bounds by saying this? Probably. But I don't care. This is decades in the making.

With every word my anger grows, and with every word her anger breaks through her mask.

"You're going to regret that, you little bitch," she says through gritted teeth.

"Maybe, but it's high time you fucking hear it." I'm not backing down from this. She can hit me again, she can do whatever she wants, but she's going to hear my words.

And I'm going to be free of her expectations.

I'm ready to live my life on my terms. Come what fucking may.

Asher is quiet, but I can feel his body heat behind me. It fills me with empowerment to know he's right here, but he's letting me take care of my first and most controlling bully.

Fuck losing her money for tuition.

Fuck worrying about school. I'll figure it out.

And I **will** figure it out.

My mom takes a step back and purses her lips. The way her face shifts from rage-filled to calm has me swallowing my ingrained fear.

"I can see the first month of school has been enlightening. But I think that's enough. You'll be coming home with me." She steps over and picks up her bag, clearing her throat. "Pack your bag and I'll come back for the rest."

It doesn't escape me that she said *she'll* come back for the rest. If I go with her, I'll never come back here.

"No." I stand strong, lifting my head and squaring my shoulders. Asher growls slightly behind me. I know it's probably killing him not to step in and save me, like he always does, but this has to come from me. "I won't be doing that."

"Helen Jade Henderson," my mother says pointedly. I've

always known her extremely-put-together outer shell was just that: a shell. I can see the cracks now. I can see how her eyes strain when she's mad. How her nostrils flare just a little too much when she's trying not to smack me. How her skin has more age spots but she's taken time to cover them with concealer. Her brown hair, so different from my own, is overly volumized and dry-looking when I know she spends an absorbent amount of time trying to get it just right.

Growing up, my mom was always distant but there when I needed her. Then my dad died, and everything changed. I became something to control. To manipulate. To guilt into things.

That changes today.

No more.

Never. Again.

"No. I'm telling you right now," I retort, "your days of controlling me are done."

She just smiles maliciously, her eyes filled with a depraved joy as her skin crinkles more around the edges than I ever remember.

"You'll do what I say, or you're on your own. Forget calling me when this fucker decides he doesn't want naive little play thing anymore. Forget calling me when you need tuition money. Forget asking for any of the things you left at the house. *Forget that I'm your mother.*" She drops that last one, thinking she's sealed the deal. That I'll cave easily. Honestly, before I met Asher, Roxie and Ty, I would have. I would've folded right then and there and packed a bag. Because I didn't want to disappoint her.

But now...

Fuck that.

"Fine with me," I reply, smiling without a bit of warmth.

Her nostrils flare, and in the space of a breath, her hand raises to me. I see it, I know what's about to happen, but all I can do is turn my cheek and brace myself.

I'm waiting for the sting; for the pain to bloom on my cheek where her hand was aimed.

But there's nothing.

My eyes open—when did I close them?—and I find Asher, gripping her forearm with reserved strength.

"Don't you *ever* raise your hand to her again. Do you understand me?" he says in a hoarse, deep, scary-as-fuck tone. It's dark and dangerous, and I'm so glad he's on my side.

"How dare you touch me?" Mother gasps, her eyes are locked in on his tattooed fingers wrapped around her arm.

"How *fucking dare* you try to touch her?" Asher snarls. "I promised Jade I'd let her handle you and your ugliness, but I won't stand for you laying a hand on her. I've sent men to the hospital over her; what makes you think I won't protect her from you?" He pulls her arm up toward his face and throws it back so hard she stumbles back a bit. "You heard her choice, so grab your knock-off bag and get your sad, fucked-up, evil ass out of here."

My jaw drops, but I stay silent. I've never had anyone, *anyone*, stand up for me like this.

It's kind of turning me on.

Daddy said he'd take care of me in every way and here he is, proving it again.

"Last chance, Helen," Mother threatens, but I don't feel anxious anymore.

"You heard him. Get out," I say calmly.

Samantha scoffs and goes to walk out of the room, but stops right before passing me.

"Your father would be so disappointed with the person you've become," she hisses. She's saying it to intentionally pull me down; one last debilitating barb before she leaves. One last attempt to make me turn to her rather than stand on my own.

I won't fall for it. Nor will I let her tarnish Dad's memory.

"I think he'd be proud of me for finally standing up to you after all these years of being your punching bag. You're the one he'd be disappointed in. You'd probably be someone he'd despise," I say simply, but meaning every single word.

Samantha glares at me with so much hate, so much anger, that it nearly takes my breath away. She checks my shoulder hard and leaves.

She leaves my life.

Forever.

And it's like I can *breathe*.

⌒⌒⌒⌒⌒⌒⌒⌒⌒

"Jade, I'm so—"

I cut Asher off by jumping into his big arms and kissing him senselessly. He catches me easily, one arm wrapping around my waist to hold me and the other holding my ass while my thighs grip his hips.

The position is very reminiscent of the other day in the bathroom and it turns me on. He's just the best. The fucking best.

Pulling back, we're both breathless as I lean my forehead against his and cup his cheek.

"I can't believe you did that for me," I whisper, tears pricking at my eyes. "I love you so much."

"I've never wanted to fight a lady, but she is definitely *not* a lady. It took everything in me not to punch her for speaking to you that way. For threatening to marry you off. No one's taking you away from me, least of all your bitch of a mom."

"As much as I wanted her to hurt, I'm glad you didn't. There's no way she wouldn't have retaliated somehow. You're much too important to be caught up in her shit." I give a watery chuckle as a tear falls down my cheek. Asher gives me a tight-lipped smile with compassion swimming in his blue eyes.

Compassion, not pity.

"Well," he says, clearing his throat quietly. I quirk an eyebrow at him as he starts walking us toward the bed. He sets me down but doesn't make any move to take this further. Asher puts his hand on my face gently, and his thumb swipes my tears away. I don't mean to, but my eyes close as I lean into his embrace.

"You won't have to worry about her again. I promise," he says softly, leaning in and kissing my forehead. "I know what just happened was hard," he whispers, holding me tightly to him so my face is nestled into his chest. "And it's okay to feel whatever it is you're feeling. It's okay. I'm here."

He's giving me the chance to fall apart. The chance to literally cry on his shoulder **again**—although, on his chest this time. I don't want to cry; I know it's not worth my tears, but I can't help it. I've spent so long under her thumb, worrying about what she thought of me, trying my best to be the person—the daughter—she wanted me to be. I constantly tried doing things to make her proud, but it was never enough.

After a little while, I just...gave up. Went through the motions. Tried to do what I thought I should.

Then I met Asher. I felt alive again. Like my life was mine again.

Now that it's over, the threat of everything is done, I feel my body shudder as the tension I've felt for years leaves my body through sobs.

Asher doesn't say anything as I cry. He just holds me as I break apart.

But only through breaking apart can I finally begin to truly heal and grow.

Asher

I DON'T THINK I could be any angrier at the fucking universe for the hand it's dealt to Jade. How could anyone treat her so badly?

I lived through my mom's abandonment and her... trauma, but even she never talked to me like that. She would get drunk and become a vegetable; she'd get high and go find someone to fuck, pretending like Hunter and I didn't exist. I thought being neglected was bad... but seeing how that devil woman talked to Jade, what she was willing to do after the first time Jade fought back?

Nothing compares to that.

Her soft snores fill the room as she sleeps, having cried so much that she passed out against my chest. As gently as I can, I lay her down on her new pillow and wrap her in her blanket like a burrito before sitting back and looking at her.

Jade's eyes are red and swollen and her soft lips are slightly open as she snores. I frown at the sight of her cheeks; they're flushed from tears and exertion and her blonde hair is stuck to one.

I have to get her out of here.

I grab the clean trash bag out of the trashcan by her bed and start packing.

***

"Asher... Ashe... Asher, help, please."

I'm nearly done with packing the few things Jade kept here when she starts to whimper. "No... not you too, please."

"Jade, Jade, baby, wake up," I say gently, pushing her hair from her face. "I'm right here."

Tears gather in her lash line as she squeezes her eyes tightly before she wakes up.

"Asher," her voice broke.

"I'm here," I say, kissing her lips gently.

"I dreamt you left me too. Decided I was too much work, too much drama and left." A tear falls from her eye, staining her cheek as she looks at me with reserved fear.

"Never, I'll never leave you," I promise vehemently, threading our fingers together and trapping our hands between our chests.

My vow rests between us, heavy and powerful, and I think she believes it. But moreso, I think she *wants* to believe it fully.

Her mom really did a fucking number on her. Then my brother.

She has every reason in the world not to trust people and I'll spend the rest of my life proving to her that she can trust me. That I'm worthy of it.

***

"Let's go," I tell Jade, getting up from the bed and holding my hand out to her. "It's time to start your new life. The way you want to live it." I smile when she slips her soft hand into mine and I see a flicker of excitement in her eyes.

She jumps off the lofted bed and stands a little straighter, a little lighter. Like the weight of the world is off her shoulders.

"Yes, I just need to grab the rest of my stuff." She looks around and sighs. "Not that there's a lot here." Jade pulls the comforter, sheets and pillow from the bed, bundling them up in her arms.

"I've got it all packed up already." I put one hand in my pocket while the other gestures around the room. "At least, I hope I did. I figured anything that was on this side of the room was yours, so I threw it all in a bag."

Jade looks around and sees my haphazardly packed trash bag and smiles. She wraps her arms around my waist, staring at me with those gorgeous green eyes. So filled with love and gratitude.

"You're amazing, you know that?" she asks softly.

"Right back at you, baby girl." I smile, tucking her hair behind her ear before our lips meet in a kiss. This one feels different.

Like it's the start of something epic.

We walk toward the door and I step into the hallway, waiting for her to join me. Jade stands in the doorway, looking at the half-empty room with her back to me.

I know she has dreams, passions and ambitions that would be so much easier to accomplish if she got a degree, but I also think she's been through enough and deserves a rest. She can always go back to school in the future.

The world is open to her now: no strings, no stipulations, no living for someone else.

She can decide exactly how she wants to live her life and I'll be there supporting her every step of the way.

"Are you okay?" I ask softly, reaching out and placing my hand on the small of her back. Gently giving her my strength if she needs it.

Jade turns and peeks at me over her shoulder, fear and excitement in her eyes. A bright smile crosses her face and she answers, "Never better."

She glances back at the room, tosses the key in her hand up in the air before turning toward me and kissing me.

"Together?" Jade asks, taking my hand and pulling me toward the elevator. She's eager to get out of here and I can understand why.

I want to tell her that there's no way in hell I'll ever let us be apart ever again, but instead I just say, "Together."

Jade

EPILOGUE- PART ONE

Six months later...

"He has some availability on the seventh. He could do a four-hour block from one to five. Does that work?" I ask a new customer over the phone. When they tell me it'll work, I start asking all the relevant paperwork questions, directing them to Asher's work email to send their inspiration photos and any additional questions.

All this is second nature to me now. I've been working at *From The Ashes* since the day after the showdown with my mom. Asher tried to get me to take a few days off of both work and school, but I wanted to jump right in. I stayed at his house that night and we celebrated my new freedom. With vodka and orgasms.

The next day, after classes, he helped move my stuff into Roxie's apartment and make that spare room my own. It's been six months of the most relaxing, laughter-filled, love-filled days. I have a support system around me, willing to help me when I fall. Always ready to hold me and love me and tell me that my inner critic is stupid. Eager to push me to follow my dreams, my wants, my whims.

If I even mention something to Asher in passing, he gets me all set up as quickly as possible. I said I wanted to try my hand at watercolor and attempt to get better, and the next morning I woke up to a stack of watercolor paper, brushes and an artesian set of watercolor paints.

That's just the kind of guy he is. He's all in. He's all in with me.

Speaking of, two burly arms wrap around my waist as he leans down to hug me. Asher breathes deeply into my neck and doesn't loosen his hold.

"We will see you on the seventh. If you need to reschedule or have any questions, please email Asher or give me a call! We look forward to seeing you," I say in my customer service voice before hanging up and writing the guy's name in Asher's calendar. I'll type in the information when he goes back to work.

"Your schedule is getting more and more full by the day," I murmur to him, holding my hand against his. I'm not-so-secretly relieved that it is. I was worried sick that *From The Ashes* was going to be axed after Asher hurt Hunter and Kyle. But as time went on, nothing happened.

I sat in my chair facing the front door day after day, worried that might be the day the cops were coming to take Asher away. I waited week after week for the ratings to drop on Yelp and all the other websites. But nothing happened.

In fact, the shop's ratings were boosted enough that Asher was thinking of adding another station. He was interested in adding another artist so they'd be able to stop turning away walk-in clients. I mentioned in passing a few weeks ago that I potentially wanted to learn how to tattoo. It would combine two things I love: my family and creating art.

So, while I was working, my sweet hunk of a man started bringing me fake skin and stencils ever so often and let me mess around, learning the machine and how it worked with the synthetic skin. I was getting pretty good at it, actually, if the small outline of a rose on my heel counted.

"That's good. I'm glad." Asher smiles, pulling back and turning me around in my swivel chair to face him. "Last call of the day?" he asks.

"Last call. I'm going to go do my closing duties and then we can leave."

"I had an idea, actually." Asher smirks at me with a heated look in his eyes. One I'm *very* familiar with from the bedroom.

"Oh really? Am I going to like this idea?" I raise an eyebrow and lean back, pushing my breasts out and up slightly as I rest my elbows on the desk.

"I think so," he replies with a shrug before he walks away.

My jaw drops. "Where are you going?" I shriek. Instead of answering me, he winks and walks to the front door. With a resounding *click*, the lock slides into place. It's then I realize we're the only ones here. Roxie left at two and Ty must have left through the back door when I was on the phone. It's almost closing time, so it's safe to expect no one else is coming in today.

Asher pulls the blinds down and shuts off the front window lights, signaling to everyone outside that we're closed and gone.

But we're here.

"Come lay on my table," Asher gestures to his station, which happens to be all set up.

"I thought you were cleaning!" I chuckle.

"Setting up for your second tattoo. The chest piece you told me you wanted."

"That was a while ago," I say softly. He remembered? Not

only that, but he drew up the piece for me? "I can't believe you remembered."

"I remember everything you say," he says. My eyes lock onto him. He said it so honestly, so simply, like it wasn't a big deal. But he has no idea just how much it means to me.

"I love you," I reply, just as simply. Like it's the most natural thing in the world—because it is.

"I love you too," Asher says with a smile, and kisses my forehead. "Now get up here, baby girl. Daddy will take care of you."

His words immediately spark my obedient side and I do what he asks.

"Arms up," he commands quietly, watching me with heated eyes as his sure fingers pull the hem of my shirt up slowly.

"Wait, what if someone sees?" I block him from pulling it up any higher and glance around, anxiety creeping in.

"You think I'd take the chance of someone seeing you?" Asher's eyebrows raise and he *tsk, tsk, tsks* at me. "I'd beat someone black and blue before I'd let them see you. Only I get to see you," he growls possessively, lifting my shirt off my head and setting it on his chair. I'm left in a burgundy lace bralette covering my breasts.

"Oh, I like this one," he groans. "This might be harder than I thought." His finger traces the outline of the cups, right over my nipple which immediately tightens in response to his touch. My body reacts to him, no matter what.

A quick glance to his pants and I see that he means that both metaphorically and physically.

"What are you going to do to me?" I whisper. My chest rises and falls quickly with anticipation.

"I'm going to brand you as my own." His eyes flash to mine, waiting for my approval. My gaze darkens, my nipples press against the lace and my pussy starts to clench under my miniskirt. I shouldn't like this as much as I do.

Fuck.

"Really?" I ask.

"Really. Now, I know what *you* want, and I know what *I* want to see on you. But I also want it to be a surprise," he says strongly, and pushes me back on the table. He turns around and snaps on clean black gloves before turning back to me. "Do you trust me?"

His glove-covered hand trails up my leg before settling heavily on my upper thigh, and he holds me tightly before his fingers spread a little wider. The tip of his middle finger is dangerously close to the apex of my thighs, close to my pussy that's already getting wet faster than I thought possible.

How would those fingers feel inside me with the gloves? Would they drag just right to make me come faster? Would his fingers move faster covered in my cum?

Shaking my head, I focus on the question he asked me and try not to clench my thighs together. He'll definitely know just how naughty my thoughts are if he sees that.

Do I trust him?

With my life.

I nod, breathlessly.

"You'll like it, I promise," Asher says softly before kissing my lips. The kiss feels like it's sealing a deal. With a heavy look, he trails his fingers over my mound and up my torso, making me breathless and so turned on. If I'm this hot from only his touch, how am I going to stand him tattooing me between my tits for an hour?

Asher's usually-light eyes are so dark they're stormy, and his breathing shortens. He's panting as if he's trying to hold himself back from jumping on top of me and taking me right now.

I wouldn't be opposed to that.

He slips his fingers underneath my bralette, tracing down my sides so his hands are caressing my rib cage. I think he might just be hugging me, but the moment I go to ask him what's up, he yanks the fabric once and the latch of my bra snaps.

"You couldn't have simply undone the hooks?" I groan in faux annoyance.

"I'll buy you a new one. I need access to your sternum, okay?" he asks, his voice overcome with a deep tone that I hear exclusively when he's horny, or when he first wakes up and I'm staying over.

I love it.

I crave that tone of his voice.

My own voice has left me as I nod my consent.

Asher slips the ruined bra off my body and stands back, towering over me as he stares.

"God, you're beautiful," he croons, like he's staring at the most breathtaking painting. Awe and overwhelming emotion flow through his eyes. He forces himself to turn back and pick up the oil and stencil so he can place it on me.

The air of the shop, which we always keep cool for the customer's comfort, makes goosebumps erupt all over my skin as I wait for the oil.

Wordlessly, Asher warms the liquid before rubbing it all over the valley of my breasts. His latex-covered hands slip over my tits as he massages each one. My eyes close in pleasure as he gropes my globes and twists my nipples slightly. Just enough to make me moan.

"Asher," I pant, and his hand is replaced by his mouth.

"You can't make sounds like that, baby. I have work to do and you whimpering... you sounding so fucking delectable, spread out on my table in that short little skirt... I need to outline the tattoo. Just outline it. We can attempt shading and stippling another day."

There's no fucking way we're making it more than an hour without fucking on this table.

He takes the flimsy piece of paper with the design and flattens it against the underside of my breasts. There's a thin piece that slips between my cleavage. I wonder what it will look like. What the design is. I've seen his work; all of his tattoos are magnificent, so I know it will be a work of art I'll wear proudly.

After he carefully pulls it off, Asher stands back, looking down to make sure it's centered just the way he wants.

"Perfect," he purrs, nodding as he sets the stencil on his desk. It's far enough away that I can't sneak a peek at what it is. He must catch me straining to look because he pinches my face with his hand. "Don't. It's a surprise."

He takes off the slippery gloves, pulls on a new set—always taking care of my health and safety—and picks up his tattoo gun.

"You ready, darlin'?" he asks and clicks on his machine. It hums to life, filling the air with tension and anticipation. My body is humming, singing with need, and I don't exactly know how I'll react to the sting of being tattooed by someone else.

Nodding, I take a deep breath, trying to steady myself.

Asher smirks, sits down on his rolling stool and gets to work. The first drag of the needle is a shock. It's very different from how it felt to tattoo myself. I can see Asher fighting to stay professional, but his free hand is inching toward groping my breast.

A few minutes go by, and the drag of the needle becomes a comfortable sting I'm able to dissociate through. Instead of focusing on the sensation, I focus on Asher.

I've spent hours and hours watching him tattoo other people. He always looks at peace. Calm. In control.

This time, though, he looks like he's struggling for control. He bites his lip and narrows his eyes as he focuses on his work.

His free hand twitches toward my breast, and I want him to touch me. I want to feel him against me even more than he already is. I get a bit of the pressure I crave when he rests his arm across my bare waist.

I'm not going to lie; the slight vibration, the pressure of Asher's body on mine, his gloved fingers so achingly close to my straining nipple, the sexy look of concentration on his handsome face resting so fucking close to mine... all of this combined gets me so hot, my panties are starting to get damp.

He's going to have some work to do later.

The longer we are in this position, the more heated I become. Forty minutes in and the sting is becoming painful, plus I've had to squeeze my thighs together to try and get some pressure on my clit.

My pussy is throbbing, but I don't dare move or say anything to Asher while he's trying to give me this gift.

I'd also take the gift of his cock when he has a moment, I think.

"Five minutes, baby girl. You're doing so good," Asher praises. His words feed my obedient side and I whimper. "Don't do that," he groans, pulling the needle from my skin so he can drop his forehead on my chest. "It's been hard enough having you squirming under my hands, your nipples screaming for my mouth, and I *know* you've been clenching your thighs because you're feeling it as much as I am." He groans and pulls away, leaving me breathless.

"Five minutes... I just need to finish the outline," he grunts, but he sounds like he's reminding himself rather than me.

"Five minutes, Asher, five minutes," he mumbles under his breath. He looks desperate, uncomfortable and heated. His eyes are wild as they shift from where he's working up to my eyes, down to my lips, then back to his work.

At that moment, when he looks at my lips longingly, I decide to make Asher as turned on as I am. I want him to snap; to take me so hard, I'll never be able to look at his table without thinking about him breaking my fucking back.

Objective decided, I get to work. Five minutes to make him *ache*.

Challenge accepted.

Asher readjusts his hand and I move it so his fingers cup around my nipple like a C.

He sits there, still trying to be as professional as he can, even as I'm topless and forcing his hand on me.

"Touch me," I whisper. "I want to see what it feels like to have your gloves pinching me." He stops the machine, his eyes straying from the tattoo to my nipple. I can feel how hard he's trying to hold back. He wants to finish, but I *need* him. I want to push him as far as I can...

I want to see how much I can test him before he snaps.

Wordlessly, I move Asher's free hand, still sporting the latex glove, and use his fingers to pinch my nipple. It's not quite right, not enough, but the intake of breath I hear from him makes it worth it for the moment.

"You're testing me, baby," he growls, licking his lips predatorily.

"You expected me to lay here naked, while you're over me, touching and caressing me while you *brand* me, and not get turned on?" I scoff. "Do you even realize the power you have over me, Daddy?" I whisper meekly, glancing at him through my eyelashes.

Asher clears his throat, dips the needle in the black ink again, and bites his lower lip in a way that drives me crazy. I want to bite it for him, redden it with my teeth. He gets to work and his eyes don't stray.

"I have two more minutes. You're going to be a good girl and lie here quietly, let me finish my work and then I'll give you what we both want. But only if you're good."

"And if I'm bad?" I ask with a raspy whisper.

Asher raises his face slowly, his gaze heated with want and dominance as I brat against his order.

"Then I'll give you a spanking, baby girl. And you won't like it. Not at first, anyway." He cocks a challenging eyebrow and gets back to work.

Leaving me with the choice.

Two minutes doesn't give me a lot of time to think about what I want to do, but I do know I want to be *fucked*. And the thought of being spanked... I'm pretty sure I'm so wet there's a little pool under my ass.

I don't think about it anymore.

I reach down, pull my skirt up, and start rubbing my clit. I'm nearly crying from the relief it brings me. I can tell how slick I am just from touching my clit over my panties. They're going to be ruined.

Asher growls. "Stop that."

I don't answer, just moan louder. The tattoo needle doesn't stop; in fact, it speeds up.

"If you come before I'm done with this, you're going to regret it," he threatens. But the way he threatens it makes me think that's *exactly* what I want.

"Challenge accepted." My voice is full of defiance that isn't usually there.

I kind of like it.

"When did you become such a brat?" He asks me with a faux annoyed smirk.

"When you didn't give me what I wanted," I lie. Saying that is guaranteed to get a reaction, especially since Asher gives me everything I could ever want the moment I ask for it.

"Oh, baby girl," he groans deeply, and I don't know if it's because he's turned on by this or if it's actually pissing him off. "I'm going to enjoy your punishment. Can't have you mouthing off to Daddy, can we? Especially when I'm almost done giving you something."

The low, dark tone of his voice sets me off. I rub my clit faster, trying to get there before he's done. I'm almost there, too. I hear his little grunts; his breathing is labored and loud in my face. His hand on my tit hasn't moved from where I put it, but now he's groping me lightly. So lightly I don't even know if he's aware he's doing it.

"Daddy," I whimper softly. I can feel my orgasm right there. *Right. There.* It's so close I can almost taste it. My legs are locking as the tension fills my body.

But I still can't come.

Asher chuckles, turning off the tattoo gun and setting it on the tray.

"Hmm, I seem to have won," he gloats with a smug grin before getting a paper towel and cleaning my new tattoo with the cleaning liquid. "Not for lack of trying on your part though, you sassy little brat."

"It's not working," I whine, confused and frustrated. I'm also more aroused than I've ever been before. And that's saying something.

Asher slips the gloves off before putting yet another clean pair on. He hums as though he's pleased and turns back around with a patch to cover my new tattoo—without showing me what it is.

"There," he says.

I pout. "Aren't you going to let me see it?"

"Maybe later." It's his turn now and he knows it. "What were you saying about the gloves? Ah, that's right," he says with a smirk, "You wanted to see how they felt on you. How about how they feel inside you as well?"

There's a glint in his eye that tells me he has a plan. He knows what he wants from me, and he's not going to tell me...

He's just going to *make me*.

"Yes, Daddy, please," I gasp, sitting up on my elbows to see him properly. He's... magnificent. Now that he's able to be in control, he's set on giving me my punishment. He seems like he's as desperate as I am, but his face shows no signs anymore. He's in control; he's determined to punish me and take care of me. Like he always does.

Asher doesn't answer, just walks backward so he can keep his eye on me, and sits down in his desk chair. My chest heaves as I breathe, trying to focus while being unbearably turned on. So turned on that my pussy is starting to painfully ache. All I can think about is getting something, anything, into me. I'll take anything he gives me. I just need to come.

"Come here," he demands, spreading his legs and leaning back in the chair like a goddamn king.

My. King.

Sitting up completely, I swing my legs over and hop off the table. My breasts bob heavily with the movement and his eyes snap down to watch them jiggle. I go to take the first step toward him, but he puts a hand up to stop me.

"Crawl."

My jaw drops. There's no way he said that.

"What?"

"I said," he growls, "crawl to me." Asher sets his head in his hand with a predatory glint to his eyes. He raises an eyebrow, dips his chin, and stares at me. If this is his reaction to me bratting at him, I'll have to do it some more. "Come on, my bratty baby girl. Be good for Daddy. *Crawl to me.*"

His voice is so hypnotic, I find myself falling to my hands and knees. *Crawling* to him.

"That's a good girl. Fuck, Jade. You look…" His voice cuts off as he groans. "Come here, darlin'." He crooks his black gloved finger and I go to him.

When I'm right in front of him, I sit up on my knees and I can feel wetness gush from my cunt.

"Come up here and lay across my knees," Asher demands. "You didn't listen. You touched yourself when I told you not to mess with me until I was done. You were bratty and naughty." Each time he spouted off something I had done, anticipation tightens in my stomach. "And you're going to get spanked for it."

I can see Asher liked this. He likes the idea of spanking me, of this kind of thing. But even after saying that, he leans over and holds my arms, resting his forehead against mine.

"Do you understand?" he asks, a little gentler than before. What he's actually asking is if I'm okay with this.

"I understand," I reply, my voice full of strength.

He smiles brightly and pulls back, tucking a lock of hair behind my ear and kissing my forehead.

"Good," he whispers and leans back. When I don't immediately move, he pats his thigh expectantly. So I move quickly, laying my chest and torso over his lap so he has access to my ass.

He flips my skirt up and rips my underwear at the side.

"If you keep ruining my underwear, I'm going to make you buy me more," I snap with no heat to my words.

"I'll buy you whatever you want," he says distractedly. My

attention is brought to my exposed ass when an abnormally smooth hand starts roaming all over. Normally when Asher focuses on my ass, I can feel the calluses across the top of his palm. This time, it's completely different, but it's so fucking good. He rubs my ass and squeezes it, before surprising me by bending down and biting a globe.

"Hey!" I yelp. He literally bit my ass. I'm even more shocked when the slight pain makes my pussy throb.

"Delicious," he mutters as he sits up. "Now," he clears his throat, "I think three swats will be enough. You're to count, out loud, each time. Otherwise, I will start over."

"Okay," I say breathlessly. I fucking love this darker side of him.

His hand comes down, not hard, but definitely not painlessly.

"Okay, what?" he snaps.

"Okay, Daddy." My hair falls over either side of my face as I fully submit to the experience.

To him.

Only ever to him.

His hand swats my ass hard enough that it takes my breath away.

"One," I say with a cry.

Asher doesn't say anything, but he caresses the hot spot where he just spanked me.

Holy shit. Asher spanked me. And I liked it.

His hand leaves my ass and I try to remain relaxed for the next two. His palm comes down on the same spot, the second smack making the already painful spot burn even more. A single drop of my wetness starts to trickle down my leg. Asher rubs the heat on my ass, spreading his fingers widely so his whole hand covers one cheek. His covered fingertips spread and his smallest finger dips low, so low that his fingertip slides into my wetness.

"Oh, you like this," he groans. "Good."

"Two," I moan softly, trying to breathe through the confusing pain and pleasure.

"Good girl," he praises me. I squeeze my thighs together, trying to get some relief, but Asher sees what I'm doing. "You need something to hold, huh, baby?" he says teasingly.

"Please," I whisper nearly in tears.

Asher shushes me and pushes two fingers inside my cunt quickly. My toes curl and I sigh with relief, thinking he'll help me, but instead, he simply put his fingers there without moving.

"Just hold them," he instructs. "I want to feel just how much you like this. How much your tight little pussy is going to clench down as my hand reddens this perfect ass." I feel the absence of his other hand, and I wait. Wait for what he's going to do. Wait for his fingers to move. Wait, wait, wait, wait.

Fuck, fuck, fuck, *fuck.*

I try to grind against his fingers, hoping that I might piss him off into moving again, but he doesn't do anything. The spot on my ass where he's hit me is still burning with pain, but I want him to give me my last spanking. I *need* it. I want to feel the bite of pain when I'm so close, I think it'll push me over the edge and I'm desperate.

The irony is not lost on me that I wanted to make him crazy with need, and now *he's* successfully made it so *I'm* going to lose my fucking mind if he doesn't do something soon.

Just as I'm about to start crying in frustration, Asher brings his hand down for the final time and crooks his fingers at the same time so he's rubbing my G-spot and I erupt.

"Fuck! Daddy, fuck, fuck, fuck, please!" I cry as I'm coming, clenching down around his fingers. The pleasure rolls through my body and I'm powerless to stop it. I hear splashing, like a glass of water fell over, but am too gone to worry about it.

Asher grunts, groans, and fucks me through my orgasm until I stop squeezing his fingers and my body goes limp.

"You..." He swallows as his voice breaks, "you are the sexiest fucking woman I've ever seen in my life."

Then his control breaks.

Asher picks me up, spreads my legs around his waist and walks us to the table. My thighs are soaked, and I wonder how I got *that* wet.

"I can't stop, I can't," he groans as he sets me down and pulls his cock out of his pants. With one motion, he thrusts all the way, stopping only when his shaft is completely stuffed inside me. I moan and my head drops back. Asher's lips attack my neck; the complete fullness stretching my walls while I'm so sensitive starts building towards another orgasm.

"Fuck me, Daddy." I gasp into his ear and he does exactly that. Asher's thrusts are so powerful he moves the table each time, but I don't give a single fuck. I hold on for dear life while he finds his pleasure and feel my own build with each drag of his hardness through my overly wet cunt.

Asher fucks me like he's desperate, like he's ravaging me, and I know I'm going to deliciously sore from this. From the complete and total satisfaction of being used, fucked, and loved all at once.

This is what I wanted and I'm unbelievably thrilled with it.

"Asher, Asher," I whine with each breath. His hand comes up and holds my throat. I don't feel him tightening his hand to control my breathing, but he just holds it. Holds me by my throat while he fucks me quickly.

"Call me Daddy," he demands roughly.

"Daddy," I correct with a moan as his hand tightens just a bit. "*Daddy*," I breathe.

"Fuck, you're perfect," he roars as he looks at me and his thrusts increase. "So fucking perfect. Can you come again?"

I nod and my hand goes to my clit, rubbing fast and in time with his thrusts.

"Goddamn," he cries, watching where his cock disappears into me. "Fuck, baby. Get there or I'm going to come first," he roars.

"Kiss me," I beg, wrapping a hand around the back of his neck and pulling him to me. Our mouths meet in a passionate, hard, frantic kiss. Open-mouthed, rough and hot as we fight against each other to try and get to our peaks.

"Oh god, Daddy," I cry as I break away and feel my orgasm wreck through me. It's softer than the one before, but no less intense.

"Fuck, fuck, Jade. Jade, Jade, baby. Ugh!" Asher mutters and moans as his thrusts get faster, right before he stops and I feel his cum fill me up to the fucking brim. His head falls forward, resting against my collarbone as he barrels over his edge.

It's my favorite thing when we come together. When my cunt milks him as he fills me up.

Our ragged breathing fills the space as we relax against each other.

"Holy shit," he says breathlessly.

"I know," I agree. His warm lips kiss up my neck before reaching my lips and giving me a sweet, thankful, loving kiss.

He carefully pulls out, but stuffs his fingers back inside me, keeping his cum stuffed inside me.

"Keep it in," Asher demands, and a shock of desire races down my spine.

How is he so fucking sexy all the goddamn time?

With his free hand, he tucks his still-hard cock into his pants and grabs a paper towel to clean me up. Gently, Asher wipes my thighs and then reluctantly, after swearing a few times, he withdraws his fingers and watches the river of our cum flowing from me.

"Oh my fucking god," he whispers huskily.

I bit my lip, slightly worried. "What?"

"I'm never going to not want this now," he answers simply. "Our cum mixed together, dripping from your cunt... It's so fucking hot. I don't want to wipe it away." The paper towel crumples in his hand as he watches. I'm on the edge of the table already, so I just bear down and hear a *splat* hit the floor. "Oh god," he moans again. His eyes... he's entranced and completely obsessed, watching the slit between my legs leak. With his hand, he plays with the cum that's there, twirling my reddened hole and teasing my clit with his cum-covered finger.

"If we hadn't just had sex, I'd be fucking you again. I'm going to keep you stuffed full of my cum, I swear to god," he growls before wiping it away almost angrily.

"I don't know if I would survive another round," I say softly.

He winks. "Oh, you would."

"Are you going to let me see my tattoo now?" I laugh.

Asher throws the towel away and flips my skirt down, picking up my shirt and helping me dress. "Come on, love," he says, holding out his hand, helping me jump off the table to go over to the full length mirror he has hanging up.

I lift my shirt, exposing the patch. Asher takes a deep breath and I want to laugh. He's nervous now? After the tattoo is done and he was so fucking confident with all we just did... and *now* he's nervous?

It's cute, him being nervous. I don't get to see it very often.

"Look, before you see it, I want you to know... One, if you don't like it, I'll design you a cover up. A really good one. One that is exactly what you want. That's why I only did the outline. Two, I've been thinking about this tattoo since the moment you said you wanted one. It has a few layers to it. So, if you have any questions, I'll explain everything. And three, I really hope you like it."

I chuckle and take his hand. "Asher, I know it's probably amazing. If you put so much time and effort into it, how could I not like it?" I cup his face to try and calm the anxiety I see in his eyes.

A soft, relieved grin crosses his face and he nods. With one more deep breath, he turns me towards the mirror and stands behind me.

His fingers gently pull back the covering and my eyes move from his nervous expression to the exposed skin between my breasts.

It's gorgeous.

Filigree vines flow underneath the curve of my breasts; it almost looks like feathers morphing to leaves as both arch together over my sternum. Moving up between my breasts is a configuration of butterflies and rosebuds covering the space, one of the butterfly's wings arching out of formation like a beak. In the middle is a beautiful mandala, intricate and eye-catching. Under the mandala, there are more butterflies and rosebuds, but spread out like a fan with chains dangling underneath to look like smoke.

Each part you look at is breathtaking, but when you step back to see the entire piece, it's a phoenix rising from the ashes.

He gave me his phoenix.

"Asher," I say breathlessly. It's magnificent as is, but I know once he's shaded it... it'll be amazing. It's one of a kind, that's for sure.

"Do you hate it?" he asks nervously, biting his thumbnail.

"Hate it?" I repeat in shock and I see his eyes dip down.

He rubs the back of his neck and sighs. "I'm so sorry, Jade. I should've let you see it before I did it... I just thought you'd like it. The butterflies mean change and growth, the rosebuds mean new beginnings, and the mandala means balance. I put it together in a way that you can see each detail, but when you look at it from a distance, it's a—"

"Phoenix," I finish softly.

"Phoenix." He nods. "The symbol I've chosen for my shop—for my life, really. And I thought with everything you've been through, everything you've overcome, everything you've fought so hard to have... I thought it suited you."

Tears line my eyes and I try not to sob, but one breaks from my mouth anyway.

"Oh god, shit. Jade, I'm sorry, I'm so sorry." In the mirror, Asher looks so heartbroken and guilty. I don't mean to make him feel that way, but I'm in awe. He's apologizing, not realizing that I'm crying because this is the biggest compliment anyone's ever given to me before.

"Asher, I love it so much," I praise, turning to face him.

"You do?" His eyebrows raise in surprise. "But you're crying."

"Well, yeah." I wipe under my eyes and give him a watery chuckle. "You gave me a permanent reminder of how amazing you think I am. How strong, how beautiful, how hopeful. Not only that, but you spent all this time thinking of these things for me? God, Asher..." I sigh. "It's so heartfelt, so thoughtful. I can't say thank you enough." I take his hand, squeezing it tightly, and lean up to give him a kiss. His lips are still swollen from our lovemaking, but he doesn't seem to mind making them more so. When his brain realizes I'm *happy*, his arms wrap around my waist and pull me into him. Our kiss deepens but it's sweet, loving, and it feels permanent, like my tattoo.

"Everyone will know you're mine now," he sighs with a cocky grin, as if everyone didn't know that already. "I have an idea on how you can thank me," he murmurs as he pulls away but keeps me in his arms.

"Oh yeah?" I cock an eyebrow, ready for him to say something sexual.

"Move in with me," he reveals.

I gape at him, not sure I heard him correctly. "What?"

"Move in with me. You already stay at my place most nights because you can hear *everything* through Roxie's walls, and she's rather loud with her new guy. I knew I wanted you to live with me months ago, and you wanted some time, which I respect and understand," he adds quickly before I can say anything. "But I feel like it's time now. You're settled and feeling good, right?"

I know what he's really asking. He wants to know if I feel content. If I'm happy like I've—*we've*—been working towards. And I really, truly am.

"What if you don't like living with me and it causes issues?" I can't help getting in just one self-conscious question. I've been working on my self-worth, but I still have my moments. Changing your mental commentary is a hard thing to do.

Asher just laughs; a joyful, happy laugh which makes me smile. Small wrinkles crinkle around his eyes and his bright smile makes him look so carefree and happy.

"Baby girl, you've stayed over at my place for the last week straight. Roxie even commented that she doesn't know why you pay rent anymore, because you're never there."

This is true. But to be fair, Roxie and Ty have been going at it so much, it's impossible to sleep. To relax. To do anything without the sound of moans, grunts, and her bed squeaking.

"That doesn't make my worry of *you* not liking fully living with me go away," I protest.

"Jade..." Asher shakes his head. "I only meant that I *have* been living with you. I know all your little quirks, I know how you like to sleep in arctic temperatures but only with five thick blankets. I know how you snore so softly it's like heavy breathing, but when you're really tired, it ramps up to pulling the curtains from the wall." He laughs and I shake my head, trying to cover my own giggle.

"I know you like to pay everything using your debit card and are willing to go without if your account gets under three figures. I know you like to wake up early to watch the sun rise, which means you go to bed super early. I *know* you, Jade," he repeats. "And I love everything I've discovered about you. I want us to live together. Officially."

"Well..." I clear my throat and smile softly as Asher cups my cheek. "If you're sure."

"I'm very, very sure." He kisses me passionately, excitedly, and I match him as much as I can. He pulls back with a brilliant smile on his face, and twirls me around. "Finally!"

Asher

EPILOGUE- PART TWO

Three Years Later...

A lot can happen in three years.

Here are the main things, the most important events: Jade and I got married a year into living together. Calling her *my wife* brought me pride I didn't know I could ever feel. That was, until ten months later when our pride and joy was born.

Tyler Tristan Lee. My baby boy came into this world as fast as a bullet after contractions started, surprising all of us when he was born in the hallway of the hospital. He was healthy and happy, with strong lungs and a mop of dark hair. Now that he's a little older, life is even busier, but I'm so fucking happy. Even the middle of the night feedings make me happy. Jade decided to go to art school shortly after we started living together. She worked at the shop during the day and attended art school at night, until she got far enough in the program that she needed to go to school during the day.

We made it work, though. She worked doubles on the weekends and a few hours every night. I told her it wasn't necessary, but she insisted on paying me rent. That the space felt like *ours,* not just mine.

I just wanted her to be happy.

The shop has been prospering and Jade started tattooing clients in the extra booth. I added it years ago, hoping she'd be able to start when she was ready. It's an amazing thing that we can work together every day, parent together, and still want to spend all our time together.

I'm very fortunate and I don't take it for granted.

Today is one of those days that Tyler's daycare is closed. Usually we just bring him into the shop with us and he hangs out in his playpen while we're working. It's pretty sweet being the boss. But Tyler's been sick so Jade decided to move her clients since I have three four-hour long sessions on my schedule.

I get to ride my motorcycle today, so that's the only plus. Pulling into the spot next to the building where I always park, I immediately notice something. There's a hooded figure standing by the front door to the shop, and that's enough to raise my alarms.

Who the fuck is that? They're not a customer, otherwise they'd already be inside. I called Roxie to go in and open the shop since Jade had to stay home. So, I know there are people there.

But they're just loitering, looking nervously from side to side.

Fuck.

I cut the engine, pull the keys out and storm to the front.

"Hey man, you can't just stand there," I snap, pulling the guy's shoulder so I can get a good look at him.

Then my jaw clenches. My fingers curl into fists and I feel rage flood my system.

You can't knock him out right here. You can't kill this motherfucker out here.

"What **the fuck** are you doing here?" I sneer.

Hunter stands up straighter, pulling the hood off his head. He does not look good; nothing like how I left him the last time. The bruises and broken skin have healed, but there's a scar under his eye that I vividly remember putting there.

"Is that any way to speak to your baby brother?" He puts his hands in his pockets, shrugging slightly.

"Go away, Hunter. And don't come back." I push past him, ready to ignore him and his evilness for the rest of my life.

"Wait, Ashe," he pleads, grabbing my hand. It feels like he burned me. I rip my arm away quickly.

"Don't you fucking touch me." I point my finger in his face aggressively and his eyes go to my thin silver wedding ring.

I don't like that. I don't want to give him any sort of information about my life. About Jade. About Tyler. Fuck that.

"Asher," he says softly, like he's pained. "Please, I... I need to make amends. You don't know how hard it's been for me."

"How hard it's been for *you*?" I repeat his narcissistic and insensitive words right back.

"I know I messed up, and I'm sorry, but please. Help me make it better."

"You're joking." I want to spit in his face. There's absolutely no way he thinks that what he did is forgivable.

"No, I'm... I'm trying to be better."

"Tell me this, Hunter," I say, rubbing my chin mockingly. "Did you do that to anyone else? Before Jade or after?"

Hunter gulps, taking a step back and breathing sharply. His eyes immediately dropped to the ground.

"There's my answer." Shaking my head, I realize he's never going to change. He's never going to become the brother I thought I raised, the one I used to have. I will never feel safe having him around Jade or our child. Maybe even future children.

So, there's simply no place for him in my life. "I should report you to the cops," I snap.

"Someone already did," Hunter admits. "I spent the last two years in jail."

"Fucking good."

"Asher, I know we left things on a bad note," he starts, but I interrupt him.

"You're damn right. I don't know what your goal is here, but I can tell you that you're wasting your time. Jade and I have spent so fucking long trying to heal and recover from what you did to her, from what her mom did to her, what trauma and undeserved responsibilities I had to endure growing up. I'm not going to let you fuck up all the progress we've made."

Hunter's head drops and he looks miserable, but I just can't find it within myself to feel bad.

I'm protecting my peace and the peace of my family.

There's nothing more important than that.

When he doesn't say anything, I turn to go inside again. Roxie's standing behind the desk, watching us intently. I see Ty put his hand on her waist, pulling her close to him.

The hell is that about?

"Asher," Hunter snaps and grabs my arm again, pulling me around roughly. "You fucked up *my life*. You tattooed that shit on me and left my face marked up."

"You deserved that, and you know it," I bite back.

"But I haven't pressed charges. I haven't gone to the police, and I even kept Kyle from doing it. I let you keep your little shop by doing that. For you. Now... Now, you're going to pay for it. Literally."

His eyes narrow and his fingertips tighten on my arm, like he's trying to scare me. He should know I'm not one to be intimidated. Especially when I have people to protect.

"Oh really?" I scoff. "Hunter, I think you're trying to play with fire. And you should know by now... If you try to light me on fire, I'll make sure you're burned as much as I am. If not more."

"I just need some cash to get myself on my feet," he barters, giving up on the line of threats pretty quickly. He knows as well as I do that he doesn't have a leg to stand on. The moment they ask why he was tattooed or beaten, he'll go to prison. I'm assuming they didn't have significant evidence on whatever happened when he was sentenced to jail, so he got minimal time. Stupid.

He should be in prison. The guys there would definitely make sure he's taken care of once they saw my parting gift.

"No, Hunter," I snarl. "You're very, *very* lucky that I don't call the cops right now. Just get out of my life and stay out."

"Don't you even care that I'm your brother?!" He screams this loud enough that I see Ty push past the front desk to back me up.

"The brother I knew and cared about, the one I sacrificed so much for, the one I loved..." I swallow the lump of emotions in my throat, and try not to let the tears build. He's not worth it. "Well, it turns out he was never truly there."

Hunter looks like he's shattered for a moment, before he quickly turns angry.

"Fuck you, Asher! Fuck. You!" He points at my chest aggressively, spittle spraying from his mouth. "You know what, she wasn't even that good. All this fucking bullshit for a shit lay! You're a dumb ass motherfucker for this!" he yells at me and my fist flies, popping him right in the cheekbone.

Hunter groans in pain and cradles his cheek. I lean over him while he cowers back, tossing my backpack to the side and grabbing his shirt.

"Don't you *ever* talk about my wife like that again!" I scream roughly in his face and shove him back. I pick up my bag just as Ty walks out. "You're not welcome here. Leave us alone and don't ever come back."

"You married her? Goddamnit, Asher." Hunter screams, sitting up. "I didn't think you would betray me like that. Fucking her is one thing, but choosing her over your own flesh and blood? That's not the brother I had."

Ty steps forward, ready to hit Hunter himself, but I stop him.

"Get this through your dumb, narcissistic, evil ass brain." I lean over, speaking slowly and very clearly. "I will choose her every single time. You're *nothing* to me. The next time you come around here, I'll call the cops and make sure they know *the whole story*. Got it?"

Hunter scoffs, but his eyes widen in understanding. We stare at each other for a few loaded heartbeats before he nods.

I straighten out my shirt. "Good. Now, get away from my shop and stay away from my family."

Without saying anything, or waiting for Hunter to say anything, I turn away from him and let this chapter close.

I don't need him. His decisions are his own; I'm not responsible for him or how he lives his life.

But that also means I don't need to have him around me. I don't need his toxicity in my life. I don't *want* him in my life.

In *our* lives.

Ty follows me into the shop and puts his hand on my shoulder.

"Are you okay, brother?" he asks.

Taking a deep breath, I try to push away the lingering feelings of anger, guilt and doubt. I haven't thought about Hunter in years. So, seeing him now, like this... it was alarming.

"I'm okay," I reply with a nod. "I will be."

"Go home, Asher. We'll clean up your station. Go talk to Jade, love on my godson and just relax. Today fucking sucked," Roxie demands as she takes the rag out of my hand. She's not wrong. After Hunter left, glaring at the front window like he was personally offended, the whole day had been messed up.

My first client completely changed their design at the last minute. Nothing I couldn't handle, but it pushed everything back.

My second client started crying twenty minutes into a three-hour session. And she didn't stop, even after I asked multiple times if she wanted to stop or take a break.

The last client just talked non-stop. He talked and talked and *talked*. And he wasn't the kind of person that could just talk and not expect any input from me. Nope—he actively wanted a conversation, and I just didn't have the brain power or mental energy to keep up a banter. I probably offended him multiple times, but it was just such a hard day.

"Thanks, Roxie," I say with an exhausted smile. "I know you opened today and I appreciate it."

"You got it."

"Will Ty wait with you and make sure you get to your car okay?" I ask, nudging the question innocently enough.

And imagine that, Roxie's cheeks blaze. "He doesn't have to do that," she protests. "I'll be fine."

"Ty!" I call out, doing everything in my power not to smirk. Ty's head pops up from the tattoo he's working on and he nods. "Hey man, Roxie offered to let me go home after all the bullshit from today. Would you be okay hanging out until she's ready to go home? It makes me feel uncomfortable having one of the girls walk alone to the parking lot in the dark."

Ty looks from me to Roxie quickly, nervously for a moment, then slips into a 'trying too hard to be cool about it' look.

I've seen that look many times before.

He likes her.

He *really* likes her.

Still.

Good.

"Yeah, Ashe. Of course." He shrugs and gets back to work.

"Thanks, man." I turn back to Roxie, and her cheeks are lobster red.

"That was not necessary," she protests harshly under her breath.

"I think it was," I reply with a knowing smirk.

"Fucker," she mutters half-heartedly and playfully punches me on the shoulder. "Now get out of here. Tell Jade she owes me a girls night."

I give my pseudo-sister a hug before leaning over and picking up my bag. "Will do."

Stepping out into the night air, I take a few deep breaths.

This day.

Fuck this fucking day.

I need to hold it together until I get home. Just a little while longer, and I can try to figure out how to piece together the healing I've fought tooth and nail for.

My bike comes into view and I could cry. I just want to be home with my woman and my son. *My family.*

The family that the love of my life and I created. Kicking my leg over, I start the engine and it roars to life.

Only a few more minutes, baby.

I hear her singing before I even open the front door. We're still living in my first apartment. If we have another baby—which I very much hope we do—then we'll have to look at getting a bigger place.

She's singing the alphabet to Tyler, and he's giggling so loudly, it warms my heart from here.

As fast as I can, I unlock the door and join my family. The moment I step inside, the warm light and energy bathes me and the shitty day melts away.

"Dada!" Tyler calls loudly, clapping and crawling towards me. I drop my bag and pull him into my arms.

"Hey baby!" Jade turns to me with a warm smile and kisses me chastely. She must immediately clock my stress because her eyebrows furrow with worry. Before she can ask anything, I shake my head with a chuckle under my breath. I can't hide anything from this woman.

"What's wrong?" she asks, holding onto my bicep with worry.

"Nothing that can't wait," I reassure her. I shift Tyler in my arms so I can hug her too, breathing her scent in.

My whole world in my arms.

Jade has become...such a radiant beauty. Way, way out of my league.

She has always been beautiful, but honestly? Every single day we're together, she just grows into her naturally good looks. And since she had my baby, she's been positively glowing.

In the last three years, Jade's caught the tattoo bug and now has two full sleeves and is working on her first thigh tattoo. We basically match now, but she still has quite a few to go to catch up with me.

Leaning against the doorway to Tyler's room, I watch the long blonde braid swing slightly as she rocks back and forth with my baby in her arms, marveling at the sight. She gained some weight with the pregnancy, but honestly, I love it. She's curvy and thick, and she looks like I could throw her around in the bedroom.

I do—quite frequently, actually.

"Shhhh," she soothes Tyler and leans over the side of his crib, putting him to bed. "I love you, baby," she whispers and walks away.

"Go, go, go, before he wakes up," she hisses quickly, pushing me out of the nursery and toward the living room.

"Ah," Jade sighs as she stretches, and I watch with heated eyes as a sliver of her stomach shows. She has vertical stretch marks from pregnancy. I know she doesn't like the marks, but I think they're amazing. I'd kiss every single one every night before bed if she'd let me. Anything to show her just how much I love her, how much I love her new body, and how I'm so incredibly thankful for what she's given me.

"So, my love, what happened today?" she asks, not beating around the bush as she plops down on the couch.

Fuck, I really don't want to get into this right now. But I know we need to talk about it. Sliding down to the ground, I start picking up the mess our little one made to keep my hands busy. I don't understand how someone so small and cute can make such a mess.

After debating how to tell her, I end up doing it in the *worst* way possible.

"I saw Hunter today," I blurt out. *Stupid, stupid, stupid.*

"What?" she gasps.

"I saw Hunter. He was waiting outside of the shop when I got there. I'm so happy you decided to stay home. I would've truly killed him if anything had happened to you," I lament.

A quick glance tells me that Jade's not absorbing this information very well. Her face is blank and so pale, like all the blood vanished. Her hands are shaking.

Fuck, I should've been a little gentler about it. I should've known this would hit her so much harder than it hit me.

"Damn it, Jade. I'm sorry," I profess, abandoning the toys and climbing onto the couch next to her.

"What did he want?" she asks. Her voice is shaky and cracks as she speaks. This is... so bad. After years of being together and trying to work through all of this trauma, I've seen all the panic attacks, all the breakdowns. I'm such an idiot for telling her so bluntly.

"He wanted money. Said I ruined his life. Said some choice things that I'm not going to repeat. He got punched in the face and threatened. I told him where my loyalty lies. He left."

"Where your loyalty lies?" she repeats. "I knew this would happen, Asher. I knew one day that you'd have to choose! Fuck, we have a child now, Asher. I can't let *him* into our life, I can't!"

She's starting to hyperventilate, and I react quickly. Grabbing her hand, I place it over my heart, then stack our free hands like a sandwich over the first.Her panic attacks are less common now than they used to be, but I hate being the reason why she's thrown into one now.

"Breathe, baby. Breathe," I plead softly, watching as her breathing levels out and the wildness in her eyes dim. "I think I misspoke. I told him straight out that I will choose you over everyone else. That he and I being related by blood means nothing. That you, and *only* you, are my family. I didn't tell him about or bring up the baby in any way. I don't think he'd try anything, but I don't want to take the chance."

Jade sniffles and looks up at me. "You chose me?"

"I *choose* you, Jade. Every day, every moment, every lifetime. It's you and me, baby. You and me against the world," I whisper, cupping her chin with my hand and kissing her forehead. "I'm so fucking in love with you, and I will be until we're old and gray. Even then, I'll be choosing you and loving you as fiercely and as loudly as I can. That's never going to change."

Jade smiles softly, a quiet gasp leaving her lips as she sees and feels the truth in my words. I chose her back then, when I found her in that laundry room. I chose to take her and keep her safe. And I've been choosing to do that every single day since. It's been my privilege. And no one is going to take our love from us.

Tyler cries out, and both of us go silent. We strain our ears to hear if he needs us or if he's just moving in his sleep. Jade pulls the baby video monitor out of her sweatshirt pocket and props it up on the coffee table. Wrapping my arm around her, I pull her into my side and hold her tight.

The comfortable silence stretches on while we watch our baby boy on the monitor, and I think through the storm raging in my head.

"We're stronger now, aren't we?" Jade asks suddenly.

"What?"

"All the shit I went through, all the shit you went through, and all the terrible things that happened. We went through all of that, hit rock bottom and somehow pulled ourselves out. Now look where we are. We're married, extremely happy, we have our dream jobs... you own your business with your best friend—our son's godfather. We have a beautiful, smart, loving baby, and great friends..." Jade counts off all our blessings, and with each thing, I feel lighter.

Better.

She's right.

"All that shit we went through... it made us stronger, didn't it?" Jade asks, looking at me with those beautiful, soulful green eyes that I love so much.

I kiss the top of her head, thinking about just how lucky I am.

"Like phoenixes rising from the ashes, baby girl."

Other Works by Alina Martyn

Author's Note

I want to cry.

But before I do, I want to say a massive, huge THANK YOU to everyone that's helped me bring Asher and Jade's story to life. I'm in awe of the good friends, family and support system I have around me. They're always pushing me to keep going and tell the stories I have to share.

Thank you so *so* much to my hubby. This life - everything we have, this life we get to live, and all the love we share - wouldn't be possible without you. I love you, always and forever. From the late night breakdowns, to tech help, to helping me find others to help me out too, I'm in awe of you. I really like your face.

Thank you to Kendra Wilson at Curious Minds Editing for spending DAYS working on this with me. Thank you for your reactions - the best - and caring about this book as much as I do. You went above and beyond, and I love you so much. (@cm_authorservices)

And last, but not least, thank you to my wonderful friend, Allie Santos, for formatting the book and being there for me for every question and being so supportive! (She's also a kick-ass paranormal romance author – check her out! @alliesantos on Instagram and Facebook)